SILVER BLOOD

A TALE OF QUITH,
THE LAND OF TEN KINGDOMS

ENDORSEMENTS

Silver Blood is a striking debut from an author who makes writing a tightly-plotted fantasy look as easy as whistling a tune. The characters feel like real people, growing and changing as they battle darkness from both inside and outside their hearts. I look forward to taking another journey to the land of Quith. I wish I could read this book for the first time all over again!

—**Stefanie Lozinski,** author of the *Storm & Spire* series

With action, sacrifice, and great feats of courage, *Silver Blood* draws you into an epic fantasy world reminiscent of *The Lord of the Rings* or *The Chronicles of Narnia*. But beyond all those things, it's the redemptive power of Elyon and the strong relationships that make this a truly great read. I loved the emphasis on honor and righteousness throughout the story. I hope a sequel is in the works for this powerful epic, so we can see how these characters continue to grow and change their world for the better.

—**Claire Kohler**, author of the *Betwixt the Sea and Shore* series

In her book, *Silver Blood*, Grace R. Pringle spins a tale that has all the most compelling elements every story should have. There are mysteries and secret identities, black knights and laughing ladies, legendary swords, dragons of all stripes and colors, and a dangerous quest through tunnels and over mountains. But emerging from the shadows, growing from a whisper into a triumphant bugle call, are the themes of a bigger and older story, the greatest story ever told. As I read, I was captured, along with some very memorable characters, and stayed captivated until the last page!

—**Rebecca Dye Heron**, playwright and author of *U-turn in the Fast Lane*

Silver Blood will win over readers with its clever tale and fantastical world. I thoroughly enjoyed exploring with characters I loved rooting for. There is a realness to these characters that I appreciate. So much adventure to be had in this novel. Happy to have read it and will do so again.

—**Bryan Timothy Mitchell**, author of the *Infernal Fall* series, winner of the Book Fest and Realm Maker awards.

SILVER BLOOD

A TALE OF QUITH,
THE LAND OF TEN KINGDOMS

GRACE R. PRINGLE

ELK LAKE PUBLISHING INC.®

PUBLISHING THE POSITIVE
Plymouth, Massachusetts

A Christian Company
ElkLakePublishingInc.com

COPYRIGHT NOTICE

SILVER BLOOD

Cover and Interior Design: Kelly Artieri, Deb Haggerty

Editor(s): Esther LoPresto, Cristel Phelps, Deb Haggerty

PUBLISHED BY: Elk Lake Publishing, Inc., 35 Dogwood Drive, Plymouth, MA 02360, 2024

Library Cataloging Data

Names: Pringle, Grace R. (Grace R. Pringle)

Silver Blood—A Tale of Quith, the Land of Ten Kingdoms / Grace R. Pringle

432 p. 23cm × 15cm (9in × 6 in.)

ISBN-13: 9798891342132 (paperback) | 9798891342149 (trade paperback) | 9798891342156 (e-book)

Key Words: Seven words or phrases (separated by semicolons)

Library of Congress Control Number: 2024940384 Fiction

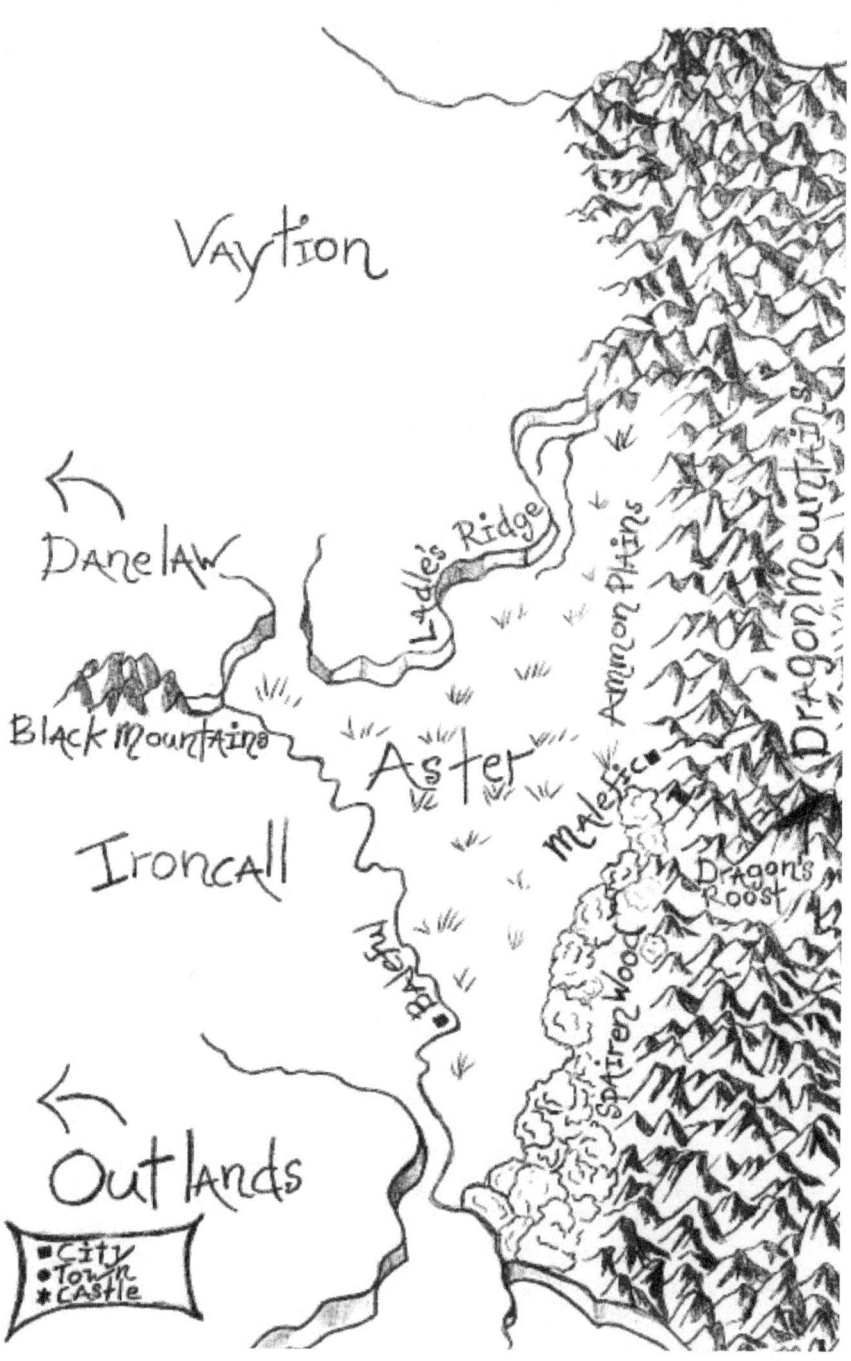

DEDICATION

Dedicated to Johannes Van Nooten. You took a twelve-year-old with a pencil seriously.

&

To the friends I lost and the ones who stayed.

ACKNOWLEDGMENTS

When a story is as long in the writing and editing as *Silver Blood* has been, it's difficult to remember all the people who have had a hand in its finished form. I hope everyone mentioned here knows how they've encouraged me, and those unmentioned remember they're still relevant to the end result.

God: You gifted me my imagination, wrote this story on my heart, and carried me through to its end. You held me as I stumbled and answered every cry of my heart. My prayer will always be "May you be glorified." Thank you for your unconditional love, salvation, grace, and your only Son.

Johannes van Nooten: Your support grew my confidence. You went over every word with me—not an exaggeration— and were the first to take my writing seriously. Thank you, my tutor and friend.

All my friends: Thank you for being so interested and eager to read my book and just being there for me.

Leah Lindeman: Thanks for all the advice.

Stefanie Lozinski: My volunteer marketing coach.

My first readers: Natasha Brodie, Elizabeth Tanguay, Joyce Pringle, Andrew Roth, Reuben and Chrissy Lindeman.

Lia Lindeman: Mom! I owe much of my love of reading to you.

Renee Heron: Your response to *Silver Blood* all those years ago gave me the confidence to keep writing.

My younger siblings: Bethany, Adam, Esther, Victoria, and Isaiah, thank you for being so enthusiastic about my stories and asking me to continue telling them. You were my first audience and helped me articulate my thoughts.

Charity Brandsma: Thanks for all your editing skills.

Esther LoPresto: You took a wordy book and distilled it to its true form. You're a wizard with words!

Stuart: You are the half of my whole and the shoulders on which I stand. God has written us a love story better than any I could ever write.

For what will it profit a man if he gains the whole world and forfeits his soul? —Matthew 16:26

He who loves silver will not be satisfied with silver. —Ecclesiastes 5:10 (NKJV)

CHAPTER ONE

DEATH AND LIFE

Horses' hooves clashed, iron against the cobblestones, thundering into the castle courtyard.

Lady Emerald Shaver tossed her embroidery onto the couch and hurried to the second-story window. Her husband's hunting party had returned. But they had been gone only an hour.

A flurry of shouting men agitated the horses into a din of uneasy whinnying. She watched servants scurrying to take the horses' bridles. Above the noise, Lady Shaver was sure she heard High's voice frantically calling her name.

Emerald gathered her long skirts with one hand and held her large belly protectively with the other. She moved as quickly as she could toward the staircase, stopping only for a quick breath at the top. A kick against her hand told her the baby was energized by the commotion. Emerald had no time to enjoy the moment and, instead, descended the stairs with as much haste as safely possible.

In the courtyard, servants and noblemen surrounded her husband, all trying to help him off his horse despite his insistent refusal. He clutched something protectively in his arms.

"Let me through!" Emerald demanded.

The stablemaster shook his head and blocked her path. "M'lady, you don't want to see this. Please—"

She shoved him.

The others respectfully moved aside.

Lord High's face was buried in the bundle in his arms. His shoulders shook with uncontrollable sobbing.

"My love, what is it?" Emerald's voice quivered with fear. She placed her hand on his knee, and he lifted his head. She glimpsed fair hair, and awareness descended. The limp bundle in his arms was human. The small head fell back and her heart froze in her chest at the sight of a little face, too white and calm.

"No! Rasfell! My boy, my son!" someone was screaming. Was it her? The air became too thick to breathe and her vision darkened. Her legs buckled, but a strong hand gripped her elbow and held her upright.

"Someone help me!" cried the stablemaster.

A shudder rippled through Emerald's entire body and warmth spread down her legs. "No!" she gasped. "Not now, I can't do it right now!"

"My lady?" The stablemaster's face came into focus. "I'm going to help you to your chambers." He and another servant supported her.

Emerald's vision faded in and out. Pressure built in her abdomen, and she cried out, stopping at the bottom of the stairs to cradle her belly. The two men paused with her, worry creasing their faces.

"Is she ..." the younger of the two started to ask.

"I think so. Fetch the midwife." The stablemaster's voice sounded far away, lost in the expanse of Emerald's shattered world.

"No." Emerald panted as the pressure subsided and began to build again. "I don't need—the baby isn't ready—*no!*" Emerald gripped the railing with white knuckles.

"Come, my lady, we'll help you."

The two men practically carried her up the stairs and into her chambers. Then she was alone, stumbling around the room, grasping at chairs, the bed, the curtains, unable to stand on her own and yet incapable of lying down. Alternating pressure and relief consumed her body. In the moments of relief, grief took over and she wailed.

"I'm here, my dear," a familiar voice sounded behind her.

Emerald turned her sweat-soaked face and shaking body to the old woman in the doorway. "Nanilla! I want to see him! I want to see Rasfell! Can someone tell me what's happened?"

"You don't need to worry about that right now, Emerald." The midwife began rolling up her sleeves and emptying her bag of implements on a table by the window.

"Don't"—Emerald pointed a trembling finger at the old woman—"tell me what I need to worry about! Someone needs to tell me how my son is *right* now!"

Nanilla assessed Emerald for a moment, then approached and took her hand. "You must be strong, Emerald, stronger than you've ever had to be. Your son is dead. The hunting party didn't know the boy had followed them. An arrow struck him—no one knows how or whose it was."

A wordless wail poured forth, and she collapsed to her knees.

Nanilla still gripped her hand. "Listen to me, you need to calm yourself. You've had a great shock. This baby is going to be born very soon."

"I can't! I can't! Not now, not like this! Make it stop, Nanilla! I don't want to do it now!"

"Either you have this baby or you're going to bury two children today. Your water broke, so we can't do anything to stop the labor. If you can't calm yourself, both you and the child are in danger."

"I can't do it!" Emerald repeated. Sweat trickled down her face, and she moaned as another wave of pressure rolled through her.

"Yes, you can." Nanilla heaved Emerald to her feet and toward the bed. The woman might have been old but her body was wiry and strong. "You've done this four times already. You can do it again. You *must* do it again."

"I'm dying," Emerald gasped.

"No, you're not. Not if I can help it. The child is just coming very quickly, and your grief is clouding your mind. You're a bit early, but I believe the child will survive." She grasped Emerald's face in her wrinkled hands and forced eye contact. "I want you to take your grief and use it. Give this new child the life your son has lost."

Emerald gripped the bedsheets and cried.

A servant girl entered with cloths, hot and cold water. The girl, features etched with fright, wiped Emerald's face while Nanilla assessed the labor's progression.

"I think you can push whenever you're ready," Nanilla informed Emerald while washing her hands in a pan of soapy water next to the fireplace.

"No, I won't." Emerald shook her head. "I want to see Rasfell. Take me to him now!"

The servant girl turned nervous eyes to the midwife. "If my lady wishes it, perhaps we should—"

"No," Nanilla flatly refused. "Emerald, when you've delivered this child, you may see him. The sooner you push, the sooner you'll see him."

4

"Where's High? I want him, tell him I need him!" Emerald cried out while thrashing on the bed.

Nanilla grasped Emerald's hands and shushed her in a soothing tone.

"He will not come, m'lady," the servant girl explained. "Lord High blames himself. He's locked himself in the young master's chambers and refuses to leave the boy's side."

Emerald wailed again.

"Mother?" a young, worried voice questioned from the doorway.

Emerald propped up on her elbows to see her eldest son, barely ten years old, lingering by the half-open door. His dark eyes were wide with shock and fear.

"What's he doing here? You cannot be here." Nanilla hurried to slam the door in his face.

Emerald sank back to the bed as another wave of pressure overwhelmed her. A touch of sanity and her usual calm returned. When the contraction had passed, she took a shaking breath and said, "All right, I'll do it."

★★★

An hour later, Emerald lay staring up at the canopy of her grand four-poster bed. The luxurious sweeps and folds of red velvet were a mockery. Red, like blood. She hated the color. Emerald took a deep breath and tried to control the waves of anguish crashing into her.

"M'lady?" The servant girl had returned.

Emerald didn't look. "What did his father say when you showed him the baby?" Her voice came out cold and aloof.

Silence responded.

"You can tell me, it's all right," Emerald pressed.

"He says he cannot bear the sight of him. He cannot rejoice on the day Rasfell has died." The girl spoke barely above a whisper.

"Give me my baby." It was more of a plea than a demand.

Nanilla nestled the child into the crook of her arm.

Emerald took a shuddering breath and finally dared to look at the sleeping baby for the first time. "He's perfect." She choked on a sob—an overwhelming mix of sorrow and joy struck her. "He looks just like his father." She fondly stroked the small shock of raven hair.

"His eyes are black too, m'lady." Nanilla smiled.

Emerald gazed at the baby's calm, sleeping face. "He will love you," she promised. "He won't be able to help it." She smiled through her tears. "Your name will be Airith."

"What does it mean?" the servant girl asked.

Emerald gently placed her forehead against the tiny baby's and whispered, "The redeemed."

CHAPTER TWO

NIGHTMARES

Fifteen years later

The flames in the library fireplace flared a mixture of red, orange, yellow, and blue. Lord Jade Stellmear's thoughts wandered through the dancing blaze. He was fire. The flames curled from his breath and burned in his hands. The tiniest loss of control, and the whole room might be consumed. This power—granted to only one man in every generation—threatened to drive Jade mad. Lost ... lost in the black spaces between the flames—in the seeming nothingness.

A floorboard creaked.

Jade jerked from his trance. "Daelay?"

His wife moved through the flickering shadows to stand next to his chair. "I am sorry to interrupt your thoughts. I cannot sleep, so I am going to take a walk."

"Were my thoughts too loud?" Jade murmured. He took his wife's hand, gently stroking it with his thumb.

She smiled and shook her head. "Your thoughts are well known to me, love. They do not make me restless. I think I just need some fresh air."

"Very well. See you soon?" he asked.

She nodded and kissed him before leaving.

Minutes passed before Jade reluctantly stood. The flames still called to him. He swiped his hand through the air with a quick, practiced motion. The fire died like a snuffed candle.

He left the library and traversed the dimly lit corridors. He stopped outside his children's bedchambers. Thoughts drifted from two familiar minds. He smiled as he "saw" his daughter, Meredith, dreaming with her twin brother, Kaydin. Their thoughts mingled in a muddle of dreams, each influenced by the other. As far as he could tell, they were imagining the underground cities in Rackda—a place not many men visited due to the Rackdarian's inhospitality. The twins shared a constant flow of thoughts and knowledge that gave them an advantage over most twelve-year-olds.

Pain exploded in Jade's head, destroying the pleasant childish dreams he had been eavesdropping on. Quick bursts of images assaulted his mind.

Milky white eyes glowed in a black face.

Teeth and pain.

Screams shattered the air: Meredith's, Kaydin's, and ... Daelay's.

Jade ran.

In the main hall, he wrenched open the heavy wooden doors. A blast of cold air struck his face but he hardly noticed—the screaming in his head blinded his thoughts. He felt white-hot pain, but knew it was not his own. He followed Daelay's thoughts across the courtyard, through the stables, and into the gardens beyond.

He saw four panther-like cats. Vagwhar.

Then, part of his mind was ripped from him.

Fire brimmed inside his veins. He threw his arms outward and summoned flames. The black cats ignited.

Their shrieks filled the night air for a few short seconds before three fell dead. The final vagwhar on the outskirts of the circle of flame managed to stumble backward into a pond which extinguished the fire. It scrambled out and fled into the night before Jade's fire could build inside him again.

He knelt beside Daelay and scooped her into his arms. Darkness curled through her veins like cobwebs. Black and boiling, poison from the vicious claw marks quickly spread through her arms, chest, and legs.

"Daelay, Daelay," he whispered over and over.

Her presence was missing. He keenly felt her absence in the gaping wound in his thoughts where her mind should have been.

"Father?"

Jade looked up to find his children barefoot in the grass. Fear marred their innocent faces.

Kaydin said, "We had a horrible dream that Mother died."

"She is not really dead, is she?" Meredith asked, wide-eyed.

"Go back inside," he snapped. "Right now! Tell one of the servants to bring a blanket."

★★★

Meredith grasped her brother's hand and ran across the gardens. *Mother is dead*, Kaydin silently told her. *When I look for her mind, it's gone.*

By the time they reached the castle, there was an uproar. The servants mingled in the main hall, still wearing their nightclothes and murmuring softly among themselves.

Fayhand, the tall, gangly steward of the castle, hurried over. "We heard screaming. What happened? Where are his Lordship and Lady?"

"Mother is dead." Meredith's voice came out barely above a whisper.

"Father is in the garden," her twin said. There were tears in his eyes, but his voice did not falter. "He wants someone to bring him a blanket."

Fayhand ordered a servant to fetch one.

"What is wrong?" Van'N, his long gray beard unkempt at this hour, emerged from his room, struggling to secure his dark blue tutor's habit with its cord. "What is all the fuss about?"

"Did you not hear the screams?" Fayhand asked.

"I am afraid not. My hearing is not what it used to be." Van'N sighed.

"Mother is dead," Kaydin told his teacher.

Van'N blanched. "What happened?"

"There were vagwhar in the garden," Meredith said. She almost added, "And we saw them in our dreams," but caught herself in time. Only Van'N knew about their family's mind-speaking abilities. She exchanged a look of understanding with her twin. Being able to mind-speak opened their minds to things they did not want to experience, like their own mother's death.

"Fetch a healer!" Fayhand shouted to the stable boy who was scurrying past.

"There is no need for one." Everyone turned to the lord of the castle in the doorway, his wife's body wrapped in a blanket and limp in his arms. "A healer would be useless now."

An oppressive silence fell.

Jade slowly crossed the hall and mounted the staircase.

A kitchen maid began to wail, and the others joined in. Sobbing became the prevailing sound.

Van'N put his hands on the twins' shoulders and raised his voice over the lamentations. "Come with me."

Without protest, they followed him upstairs and into the study. He lit a candle on the table in the middle of the room.

"Stay here and wait for me to send someone for you," Van'N instructed, then closed the door behind him.

With the door closed, the wailing from downstairs faded somewhat.

Meredith looked around the familiar room. The square table had three chairs around it, two on one side and one on the other, where she and Kaydin sat for Van'N's lessons. The walls were peppered with charts on astronomy, grammar, and history. Bookshelves covered one wall, while a large chalkboard dominated the other side of the room. The windows displayed the black, moonless night.

Though she had entered this room nearly every day of her life, it seemed different now. She saw mutual realization in her brother's eyes. The thought passed between them silently: *We are different now.*

Kaydin slumped in a chair and rested his head against his folded arms.

Meredith sat next to him. *Are we dreaming?* she whispered into her brother's thoughts.

"No," Kaydin said aloud.

Meredith held her breath and wished herself somewhere else, but when she finally gasped for air, her mother was still dead. Thick mental walls barred her from her father's mind. Meredith tried to hear Kaydin but was met with the same resistance. She was alone with her thoughts, alone with her panic, and alone with her grief. They rarely had anything to hide from each other, and having to face the aching loss on her own scared her. Her mother's mind, a comforting presence in the back of her own, had simply vanished, leaving only an empty space which would never be filled again. Meredith rested her head against her brother's shoulder, and they cried together without a sound.

★★★

Dawn woke them. Its light streamed through the glass and warmed the room. The candle had burned down to drips of melted wax. The castle was quiet.

"Have they forgotten about us?" Meredith wondered aloud. She followed Kaydin out of the study. None of the servants were at work.

"I hear horses," Kaydin told her.

A moment later, their father burst into the main hall, three knights with him.

"I will not rest until it is dead!" Jade growled. He pulled off his riding gloves and hurled them onto a table beside the door.

"My lord, there is no way of catching up to it by now," one knight tried to reason with him. "The beast is long gone."

"We should not have turned back. If we had continued a little farther, I am sure we would have had it."

"Think of your wife, my lord. Will you leave her unburied?"

Jade sat on the stairs and put his head in his hands.

"My lord—"

"Leave me. Go!" Lord Stellmear shouted.

The knights glanced at each other with concern, then quietly left.

The twins stayed at the top of the stairs.

After a minute of silence, Jade turned slowly and looked up at them. "How long have you been standing there?"

"Not very long," Meredith replied.

"Come here." He gestured for them to sit next to him.

They obeyed, and sat on either side of him.

He put his arms around them and said, "There are only three of us now."

"How did the vagwhar find us, Father?" Kaydin asked.

"I can only assume a traitor has betrayed us to the Witch-Queen, Sisinta." Jade's voice carried a bitter edge.

"Are there more vagwhar hunting us?" Meredith tried to keep the fear from her voice.

"I burned all but one of them. The knights and I tracked the vagwhar that escaped, but it eluded us. Regardless of whether we had killed it or not, neither of you are safe here."

"Where will we go?" Meredith frowned.

"With me." The twins turned at Van'N's voice. He descended the stairs behind them. "Your father and I have formed a plan."

"I want you to go with Van'N into hiding," Jade explained. "Do you remember Aunt Seala? We visited her a few months ago. She's your mother's great-aunt through marriage. Very distantly related. No one will think to look for you with her."

"But we barely even know her!" Kaydin cried.

"If anyone is looking for you, they will seek our friends and immediate family."

"You will come with us, right, Father?" Meredith begged.

"Your father's duties must take him elsewhere," Van'N stated, "and his presence will put you in danger. Now that the Witch-Queen knows your family's identity, she will be looking for him. Fayhand is a good steward. He will look after Stellmear castle and its lands in our absence."

"I hate the vagwhar, and I hate Sisinta," Kaydin hissed.

Jade put his hand on his son's shoulder. "Never forget Elyon's promise of justice, no matter what happens. There are times you are called to carry out justice, but vengeance is not your right." He stood and stepped back to look at them with tears in his eyes. "You both look so much like your mother. I will retreat into the mountains. I'll strive to write to you often and visit when I can, but even if you don't hear from me, I have not forgotten or abandoned you."

"How long must we stay with Mother's relative?" Kaydin grumbled.

"I don't know. It could be months or even years. You must look after each other, promise me."

The twins nodded and mind-spoke in unison, *We promise*.

CHAPTER THREE

WILLOW ROAD

Three years later

Meredith sat in the top of the willow tree on the corner of Willow Road, her auburn curls mussed by the wind. She relished the freedom of her bare feet swinging among the swaying branches. She closed her eyes and imagined flying away, clutched in her father's arms, the strong, rhythmic movement of a dragon's wings carrying her home. He had taken her dragon riding only a few times, but the experience was memorable. The late afternoon's chill brought a shiver, and she opened her bright green eyes.

There was no dragon below her, only a dusty road that forked east and west. The east road led to Boldwind, a large merchant city in Tayose, and the west fork, Raven Road, wound its way across farmland and fields until it disappeared toward the Dragon Mountains.

Meredith's heart filled with longing when she looked at the mountains. Was her father there now? It had been six months since his last visit. Whenever her father secretly sent word he was nearby, Van'N brought them to see him in some obscure place—a small roadside inn or a glade off the main road. His one- or two-day visits were never enough.

Dragon's Roost, the mountain range's tallest peak, stood out starkly against the deep blue sky and the reds of the setting sun. The mount seemed to challenge the world to break it down and force it to its knees. The other mountains were dwarfed in comparison, though they were among the highest in the world. Meredith briefly considered running away to those mountains, but they were perilous. If a traveler survived climbing the steep, snow-covered peaks, the mazes of valleys, passes, sheer cliffs, and the numbing cold and frostbite, there were still the colored dragons to fear.

Brown, calloused hands grabbed the branch Meredith sat on. She jumped, then relaxed as a tousled auburn head followed.

Kaydin looked up at her. "Are you going to move over?" She obliged, and he hoisted himself up beside her. "Wow, this is a nice view."

"Nice?" Meredith sighed. "Everything living gives me the impression it is bent on the destruction of my happiness." Her tone betrayed her resentment. She scanned the fields and hid her anger behind mental walls. She bristled at her uncontrollable emotions—one minute she was imagining flying, and the next she wanted to scream.

Even me? Kaydin's voice echoed in her mind.

She darted her eyes at him.

He grinned. *I'm not nice to you at all?*

A small smile reluctantly crept across her face. *Why do you make me feel better when I'm reveling in my misery?* she grumbled in his head.

Kaydin laughed and teased, *Because I'm incredibly funny and witty?*

16

Mind-speaking helped to convey emotions. Meredith knew Kaydin understood her feelings.

All humor aside, I understand, Kaydin thought. *Whenever I have a moment of contentment or find myself thinking of Quire Castle as home, guilt steals my peace. I know thinking that way isn't what Mother would have wanted, and I know Father is doing everything he can to keep us safe, but the truth is, I'm often miserable because I don't allow myself to be happy.*

They'd had this conversation before, but the act of admitting their emotions brought a tiny moment of relief. Since their mother's death, they'd been forced to grow up. Kaydin had cut her off from his grief and attempted to create his own individuality. Their thoughts had become more independent from each other and the mental walls higher. Some thoughts, they'd realized, weren't meant to be shared with anyone. But they could never not be each other's best friends. They easily drifted into mind-speech and shared emotions.

If you work up the gumption and find a direction, I'll run away with you. Kaydin playfully bumped her shoulder with his.

Meredith glanced at her dirty feet peeking under her long green dress. Her doeskin boots lay on the ground where she had kicked them off before climbing the tree.

"Aunt Seala was looking for you," Kaydin told her aloud.

"Is she still angry with me for spilling wine on the carpet?" Meredith asked out loud.

"Furious. What happened?"

Meredith sighed. "I didn't mean to spill it. I accidentally caught it with my elbow on the table. Besides, I don't even like red wine. I wish she wouldn't make us drink it. I don't see how it's good for us." Meredith ruminated on apologies to her aunt, considering what amount of humility would appease the old woman.

Kaydin's back straightened with interest. "Who's that?"

"Who?"

"Over there. Someone is coming down the road from Boldwind on horseback." Kaydin pointed.

Meredith spotted a solitary figure.

"Maybe he's a peasant coming home from market," he suggested.

"No one around here could afford a horse. All the farmers have oxen." Meredith added, "It must be a visitor. Unless he's lost."

"Who would visit us or Aunt Seala?" Kaydin wondered.

They watched the stranger as he reached the fork in the road. He wore hunter's garb with a bow and quiver slung across his back. He turned onto Willow Road toward them. He spotted Meredith's boots lying at the foot of the tree and reined in his horse. Gazing up, he called out, "I thought all the birds had flown south for the season." The rider had jet-black hair and looked to be in his late teens, a few years older than the twins. His eyes were as strikingly black as his hair and a twinkle crept into them as he spoke.

Kaydin laughed easily and replied, "We decided to stay. The travel's not worth it."

The young hunter gave them a lopsided smile. "If you have decided to stay, I would not suggest a tree as a good place to spend the winter."

"I never thought of that. You just might have changed my mind."

"I'm glad you did not take much convincing." The young hunter sounded amused.

"This is my sister, Meredith, and my name is Kaydin."

Meredith realized she'd been gazing at the boy with unabashed admiration and quickly ducked her head in embarrassment. There was a shortage of handsome boys in their small social circle, and she'd forgotten her manners when unexpectedly faced with one.

"Airith of Shaver Castle at your service." Airith managed a slight bow from his place in the saddle.

"Shaver ... are you related to Lord High Shaver?" Kaydin asked.

"I'm his son." Airith glanced back the way he had come and ran his fingers through his hair.

The twins knew not to eavesdrop—an incredibly invasive and rude habit, their parents had said—but occasionally, some emotions were strong enough to leave an impression despite the mental blocks. Airith was distinctly uncomfortable.

Awkward silence lingered as Kaydin searched for something to say. "Then you must know ... how to sword fight?"

"Yes, I do. Why?" Airith appeared relieved at the change of subject.

"My father taught me, but it's been a while since I've been able to practice. Mere knows how to, but—"

"I'm not as good at it as he is," Meredith finished.

"Well, yes," Kaydin admitted, "but that doesn't mean you're bad at it."

"I never said I was bad at it." She grinned at her brother. "I just said that I'm not as good as you are."

"I would gladly fence with you if I had my sword," Airith told Kaydin. "I don't suppose you have a couple of blades with you now?"

"No, though Aunt Seala might. Follow this road to a small village called Juventall just past these trees. Her castle stands beyond it."

"I know the place. Are you related to Lady Quire?"

"Aunt Seala is not really our aunt. She only insists we call her that," Meredith interjected. "Lord Quire was distantly related to our mother. He died some thirty years ago and left Aunt Seala with a rundown castle and some land she rents out to peasants. We're just staying with her while our father makes a trip east. I feel rather sorry for her. Ever since her husband died, she has not been very aware of the world around her." Meredith wanted to kick herself. She was babbling in an attempt to say something—anything—to join the conversation. Van'N had helped them work out the details of their story in case they were ever asked, but Airith hadn't asked.

To her relief, Airith didn't seem annoyed by her outburst. Instead, he laughed knowingly and said, "I have heard of her, and from what I understand, she's quite the character. Who is your father?"

"He is lord of some lands far southwest of here," Kaydin lied.

"What is his name? Perhaps I know him," Airith asked.

"I am sure you do not," Kaydin evaded. "He has not been to court for quite some time."

"I cannot fence with you now, but maybe some other day?" Airith suggested.

"That would be a good idea. We should be heading home now," Kaydin said.

"Perhaps when I pass through here again?"

"I will hold you to it."

"I am very pleased to have made both of your acquaintances. Kaydin, Lady Meredith." Airith nodded to each of them in turn.

Meredith attempted a bob of her head in response, wishing she could think of something clever to say. She didn't want to leave the impression of an awkward girl who rambled about relatives.

He wheeled his horse around and was soon out of sight.

"Come on," Kaydin prompted. "Aunt Seala will want to know why I've taken so long to get you home for supper. You had better put your boots on."

Meredith looked at her bare feet. "I cannot bear to wear them. They slow me down. I feel freer without them."

"All right, but try not to step on anything sharp. I would hate to have to carry you. You weigh as much as a horse!"

Meredith, who was far from heavy, glared at Kaydin, who was grinning again. She took a swing at him, but he managed to duck and scramble down the tree before she could catch him.

He called to her from the ground, "Beat you to the castle!" He ran toward Juventall.

"Hey, that's not fair!" Meredith yelled as she climbed down the tree after him.

CHAPTER FOUR

Boldwind Market

The silence was oppressive. Meredith thought she might go crazy if she had to endure one more minute of it. The only sounds were Kaydin periodically turning pages in his history book and the crackle of the small fire. Meredith's twin perched on a stool across the hearth from Aunt Seala, their great-great-aunt. The small, fiery-eyed lady with white hair sat in a straight-back chair mending a tapestry.

Meredith turned her attention to a more interesting scene: From her window seat, she saw a crow roosting in an evergreen tree. The bird occasionally cawed to another of its kind, an echoing, lonely sound. It reminded Meredith of walking in her family's castle garden just before sunrise. Mist would cling about her ankles, and crows would caw loudly in the trees. How she missed home.

"Meredith, let me see that."

Meredith jerked her gaze from the window.

Aunt Seala reached for the embroidered tablecloth lying forgotten in Meredith's lap.

She handed it to her aunt.

"It is unwise to sit by the window. You could catch your death of cold." She inspected Meredith's half-finished flower. "I remember when I was a girl and had to embroider flowers. I used to think it tiresome. Now, I cannot imagine why." Aunt Seala was bent over the tablecloth and didn't see the face Meredith pulled.

The old woman took a deep breath, no doubt about to launch into a childhood story, when someone knocked on the door. "Come in!" she called as loudly as her crackling voice permitted.

Van'N entered. His keen blue eyes twinkled at the twins. "My lady, I was planning to go to Boldwind market today. I thought perhaps my students could accompany me."

Meredith held her breath and glanced at Kaydin, who tried to hide his excitement.

"Kaydin has not finished his reading—"

"I will finish it later, I promise." Kaydin jumped from his seat, dropping the book. He picked it up, grabbed his sister's arm, and pulled her out of the room.

Van'N followed, promising Aunt Seala he would ensure Kaydin finished his history.

Meredith skipped down the hall singing at the top of her lungs, "I am going to Boldwind market!"

"*We* are going to Boldwind market!" Kaydin corrected.

A servant moved aside to let them run past.

"Kaydin! Meredith!" a sharp voice made them both wince.

Kaydin skidded to a halt in front of the speaker.

Meredith did not stop in time and collided with her brother.

Quaeor barely managed to sidestep before the twins toppled over. The castle steward glared at them from his great height. His shrewd features matched his sharp voice.

He was barefoot under ankle-length dark robes. Meredith thought perhaps he never wore shoes, so he could sneak up on his unsuspecting victims. His sickly pallor evidenced his time spent in his study, a windowless room in the basement of the castle tower. The servants whispered rumors the place was once the castle dungeon. Some said Quaeor could be heard talking to ghosts down there. No one could remember where he had come from or how old he was. He had, it seemed, always been there.

"You two!" Quaeor snapped. "On your feet. What is the meaning of this?" He raged at Meredith, "Meredith, ladies *never* run or raise their voices." Then, at Kaydin, "And Kaydin, as future lord and heir of Quire Castle, you must be worthy of it and not run about shamefully!"

The twins scrambled to their feet. Kaydin looked down and mumbled something about being sorry. Meredith failed to strip the defiant look from her face.

"I do not think you should go out in public if this is the way you will behave." He addressed both of them but glared at Meredith.

They burst into protests.

"I will make sure all goes well, Quaeor." Van'N said as he reached the trio. His calm assurance quieted the twins.

Tension stewed between Van'N and Quaeor over how the twins should be taught. Van'N believed he held authority because their father had put them under his care. However, Quaeor declared that his position as Aunt Seala's steward procured him the right to keep an eye on her only remaining relatives and heirs.

The twins shifted in uncomfortable silence while Quaeor scowled, and Van'N regarded him with quiet confidence.

At last, Quaeor stepped aside.

Meredith and Kaydin felt his angry gaze on them as they filed past.

Aunt Seala had only one horse—an old chestnut mare. A servant hitched her to a cart. As Van'N drove, the cart jerked and lurched along while Meredith breathed in the crisp autumn air.

"Now." Van'N reached into a sack next to him and pulled out the book Kaydin had been reading earlier. "Kaydin, you can catch up on some reading while we travel. Read it aloud so it benefits all of us."

Kaydin reluctantly took the book from his teacher. "I've read *The Records*, penned by Drizzle WeatherWard, twice. We already know all about the Blood Battle and dragons."

"Yes, but review is always important. Start where you left off."

Kaydin sighed and flipped open the book:

Quith, the land of ten kingdoms, was created by the High King Elyon who ruled all, knew all, and was all. When he reigned, peace dwelt in the land.

Yet, it came to pass that a witch called Sisinta rose up and rebelled against the king. Sisinta proclaimed herself Witch-Queen of all Quith. She promised power and riches to some, but for most of her new subjects, sorrow marked her reign. Many foolish nations followed her.

The final battle between Elyon and Sisinta was fought in Aster on the Ammon Plains. It came to be called the Blood Battle because the world was stained crimson that day, and even the very stars in the sky wept. Elyon won the battle and defeated Sisinta, who fled to the west.

Quith split into ten kingdoms: Lower Quith, the five kingdoms claimed by Sisinta's followers, and Higher Quith, the remaining five kingdoms, ruled by those loyal to Elyon. Sisinta persisted in her attempts to rule the entirety of Quith, so Elyon erected the Dragon Mountains as a wall of defense, eventually appointing a dragon in secret to be the first Dragonose, Keeper of Dragons.

Meredith butted into her brother's thoughts, *I'm not sure how accurate an account this is. The first Dragonose was a shape-shifting dragon who married a human.*

That's not common knowledge, and it has to stay that way, Kaydin reminded her. He resumed.

The dragons were a scattered race, divided by their colors and clans. Responsibility fell to the Dragonose to rule and unite them in protecting Quith from Sisinta. The title of Dragonose is, to this day, passed down through the family line. Only Elyon, the Council of Dragons, and the members of the Dragonose clan know the identity of the Dragonose.

Sometime after the Blood Battle, Freesam Tieren, king of Ironcall in Lower Quith, traveled to the Dragon Mountains to meet with the clan of silver dragons. His forefathers had made an alliance with them, each promising to help the other in time of need. King Freesam begged the silver dragons to help him escape Sisinta's rule. His people were starving from the reallocation of all their food to aid her army.

However, the silver dragons mocked the king and turned him away. They told him that losing his kingdom and watching his subjects die was his reward for following Sisinta. Not long after, Sisinta executed King Freesam for suspected treachery. His son took the throne in his stead.

When Elyon heard of this, he went to the Dragon Mountains, where most of the dragons dwelt, and called forth the silver dragons to face him. As was written:

They came forth from the deep of the mountains,
The Cala Drani, the silver dragons,
From the dark places, caverns, and caves.
They heard the High King's voice and trembled in fear.
Fear was in their hearts and dread on their countenance.

For no living thing can refuse the High King and go unpunished.
He cursed them for refusing help to those who needed it most.
He poisoned their blood and shortened their years.
He banished them to the Outlands and shamed their name.

—From *The Chronicles of the First Dragonose, Keeper of Dragons.*

"Stop there," Van'N interrupted. "Meredith, tell me from memory the rest of the story."

She shrugged. "Easy enough, Father told us often. Elyon cursed the clan of silver dragons with a disease called Silver Blood, *cala heem* in the old language. It turned their blood a silver color. The disease remains dormant for the dragon's first twenty years of life until it activates and slowly consumes them. If a silver dragon is wounded, its silver blood will regenerate dead flesh. When all tissues are eventually consumed or replaced, the dragon dies. The process takes seven years. The other dragon clans rejected the Cala Drani and drove them west out of the mountains, leaving them to die in the Outlands. They were in despair until Sisinta offered them a longer life. For every silver dragon who joined her, she offered a Shadow, a demon who would live in them in exchange for lengthening their years. Most of the Cala Drani accepted this exchange and joined Sisinta as enemies of their own brothers. To distance themselves from their rebellious kin, the other dragons named themselves 'colored' and referred to the Cala Drani as 'the cursed.'" Meredith paused for a deep breath.

"Go on." Van'N nodded.

"Elyon has not sat on the throne of Quith for six hundred years. Most assert he's dead, merely the subject of a children's story or someone only sung about in songs and ballads. They have stopped watching for his return and look to the five kings of Higher Quith to protect them from Sisinta's constant onslaught. Though she herself cannot cross into Higher Quith, she always has a hand raised against it. Some in Higher Quith claim Elyon still lives."

"Very good!" Van'N laughed. "I suppose you do know your history."

Meredith smiled, pleased she had impressed him.

Van'N continued having them read and recite from memory the history of Quith until they arrived in Boldwind around noon.

People from all over Higher Quith crowded the port city. There were very few Rackdarians, or Mountain Men as they were more widely known. They never liked the cities of men or open spaces. Meredith remembered a Rackdarian song that claimed non-mountainous cities had "too much sky and not enough earth."

I wonder if there are any Sillians or Paladall here, Meredith mind-spoke to her brother.

I doubt it. The Sillians are farther northwest in Athlon, and the Paladall are rare no matter where you go, Kaydin reminded her.

Meredith knew he was right, yet, she couldn't resist pushing up on her toes to search the crowds for the tall and graceful people.

The streets were interwoven like the threads of a poorly made tapestry—no street was straight for long. The houses along them were tightly packed, some sagging and supported only by their neighbors. Dogs and cats roamed the alleys, surviving on a steady diet of garbage, rats, and mice.

Van'N and the twins followed the main street until it ended in the market square at the city's center. Everywhere, people called to one another, bargaining and arguing over goods, buying, selling, and yelling. A boy chasing a runaway pig streaked past while a merchant seller shouted at him for knocking over a table of pots that rang and clanged as they hit the paving stones. Meredith couldn't help laughing at the antics, though she did feel sorry for the merchant.

In the middle of the square, a fountain depicting a dragon's head spewed water from its mouth into a basin below. Next to it, a performer with an audience of children did handstands on a stone pillar. Chickens ran between the stalls and people. A plethora of pens corralled pigs, horses, oxen, cows, goats, and sheep. The noise was deafening, and they had to yell to hear each other over the din.

Van'N tied the horse and cart to a hitching rail near the edge of the square. He gave a copper to a boy in shabby clothes and told him to keep watch, promising three more when he returned. He informed the twins he had some business to attend to, then slipped two silvers into Meredith's hand. "Buy yourselves some lunch," he instructed. "When you get tired of looking around, go to the tower at the edge of the square. It is the tallest building in the city, you cannot miss it. I will meet you there in three hours when I am done with my business."

They both thanked him, then he disappeared into the crowd.

Meredith picked out three apples, a loaf of bread with butter, and a jug of watered-down ale, letting Kaydin do all the haggling and buying.

"Let's get away from all the noise," Kaydin said.

They followed a side street around its bend, thankful the sounds of the market faded even a small measure.

"Is that Airith Shaver?" Meredith gestured toward a well at the street corner.

Airith seemed to be arguing with a young man while a servant looked on. The young man aggressively poked Airith in the chest, and Airith angrily knocked his hand away. The man shouted something unintelligible and left toward the marketplace. Airith roughly tied two horses to a ring in the wall by the well. He instructed the servant to watch them, then stalked across the street toward the Merchant's House.

"Come on." Kaydin started across the street.

"Where are you going?" Meredith grabbed his sleeve.

"I'm going to talk to him."

"But we only met him once."

"So?" Kaydin pulled away. "Every person you have ever known, at one time, you'd only met once."

Meredith didn't get to object further. Kaydin was already across the street at the door of the inn.

CHAPTER FIVE

DUEL

When Airith walked into the whitewashed inn, he smelled warm bread, roast chicken, ale, and wood smoke. In the center of the room, a large, unlit chandelier hung from the high ceiling. Many merchants frequented the establishment as the inn was only a few blocks from the docks and merchants' warehouses.

Airith chose a corner table.

A young maid approached to take his order. After she left, he watched patrons coming and going. He learned a lot by observing the way people acted, spoke, and walked. His grandmother, when she was alive, had once asked him what he was doing and he had simply said, "Watching."

Later, he had heard her say to his father, "High, that boy of yours is going to come to no good, mark my words. At his age he should be doing something with himself."

His father had, in that familiar way, turned to Airith and frowned disapprovingly. He rarely paid attention to his youngest son, and when he did, it was because Airith had done something wrong. "You are right, Mother," his father had said. "It is high time he applied himself." Airith had started sword fighting and schooling a week later.

Learning sword fighting was the one decision Airith was grateful to his father for. He threw himself into it until he had mastered the skill.

As he shook his head to dispel his thoughts, Airith became aware of two young people, a boy and girl with tousled auburn curls and deep green eyes, who had entered the room. They seemed somewhat familiar. When they headed his way, he recognized them.

Kaydin greeted him and asked, "You have not forgotten the sword fighting, have you?"

"No, I have not." Airith grinned at the boy. "I was actually just thinking that it is a good thing I brought my sword with me. In fact, I have two swords. I think you could use one of them. They are in my horse's pack." He stood. Lunch could wait. "Come outside and we shall see how good you are with a blade." He headed for the door.

"Right now?" Kaydin gaped.

"In the street?" Meredith's eyes widened.

Shocking her felt strangely satisfying. "Why not?" Airith flashed his lopsided grin and gestured for them to follow.

They crossed the street and Airith spoke to his servant. The man handed Kaydin and Airith the swords.

They took their positions, facing each other. A small crowd began to gather. Some started to whistle and shout, making bets, mostly in favor of Airith who was older and taller. Meredith was pressed to the back of the crowd.

Kaydin took the first move. Their blades met.

Airith held back his strength, judging Kaydin's abilities.

Kaydin thrusted downward. Airith lifted his sword in an arc to free it from Kaydin's blade. The younger boy lunged for Airith's leg, but Airith expected it. He simply sidestepped and Kaydin nearly fell over with the force of his own attack. He recovered just in time to block Airith's counterattack. The older boy used all his strength this time, enough to make Kaydin stagger and give Airith the footing he needed.

Pressed back, Kaydin tripped and tumbled to his back, a sword tip at his throat. He was heaving for air while Airith was barely breathing hard.

The crowd cheered and men thumped Airith on the back as he sheathed his sword. Several offered to buy him drinks, which he declined. He offered a hand to Kaydin.

"Wow! You are awfully good." Kaydin took the hand and brushed the dust off his clothes.

Airith laughed. "It is only because I have had more practice. Practice makes—"

"Perfect, I know. Thanks for going easy on me." Kaydin returned the sword.

"Why do you think I was going easy on you?"

"I could feel it."

"You were pretty good. Better than I expected. How old are you?"

"We're fifteen."

Airith searched for Meredith. "Wait, are you two—"

"Twins, yes. People always think we're younger than we are."

"I apologize for assuming you were children."

Kaydin shrugged. "We're used to it."

The crowd dispersed, and Meredith pushed her way to her brother's side. Her eyes briefly met Airith's then slid away.

Why did he want her striking green eyes to meet his again? He didn't deserve her attention.

"I cheered for you, Kay." Smiling at her brother made her face light up.

Could he make her smile like that? He commanded the thought to leave.

"Thanks, Mere, but I think you were the only one," Kaydin said.

"You know what?" Airith held out the sword Kaydin had borrowed. "Keep this. I have others."

Kaydin shook his head and took a step back. "I can't! If anything, you should receive a trophy. You won."

"Well then, take it as an offering to seal our peace, for I would hate to have caused you embarrassment at the expense of my victory." Airith held out the sword again.

Kaydin hesitated.

"It would make me feel better," Airith encouraged.

"Very well." Kaydin took the weapon, eyes shining as he held the hilt and admired the blade. "What is its name?" he asked.

"It doesn't have one."

Kaydin arced the blade and thought for a moment. "Swan. Sword Without a Name."

"Fitting," the older boy agreed.

"What blade is it that you have?" Kaydin gestured to the sword sheathed at Airith's side.

"Cala Man. It has been in my family for many generations, passed down through the youngest sons. I would never part with it. The legend is a youngest son of my ancestors raised it in battle against the Witch-Queen." He showed the twins the black hilt embedded with silver filigree.

Meredith spoke up. "Cala Man ... Silver Hand, isn't it?"

"You know the old language?" Airith's eyebrows lifted, impressed.

She blushed. "Van'N taught us. He is our guardian and teacher."

"Who taught you how to sword fight?" Kaydin asked.

36

"My oldest brother taught me when I was young, but after he left home, I did my own training." Airith sheathed the sword. "Have you two ever been to Boldwind before?"

"No." Meredith shook her head. "We've been living at Quire Castle for three years and this is the first time we've come to the city."

"Come with me then, and I will show you the sights."

"We saw you speaking to someone earlier. Do you have to wait for anyone?" Kaydin asked.

"My brother, Cowin?" Airith laughed. "He can get himself lost for all I care. Come on! Follow me." Airith beckoned them toward the docks.

CHAPTER SIX

PIRATE TALES

Meredith and Kaydin glanced at each other questioningly, unsure if they should follow a new acquaintance around an unfamiliar city.

"Why not? Van'N will be busy for a while yet." Kaydin shrugged.

Meredith nodded her agreement.

They ran to catch up with Airith.

At the docks, Airith introduced them to great merchant vessels as if they were old friends. The ships came from all over Quith and the Calldian Sea.

As they passed a rather large military ship, Kaydin asked, "Do you come here often?"

"Sometimes. When I want to get away from home, I either go hunting or come to the docks."

They spent an hour watching and commenting on vessels being loaded or unloaded, setting sail, and entering the harbor.

"I want you to meet someone," Airith told them.

He took them to a rundown section of the docks, inhabited by fishermen and no grand vessels. Airith stopped before a small fishing boat streaked with water marks and caked with salt.

"She's been through countless storms and gales and seen many seasons on the sea," Airith said with pride. Then, he called out, "Calldo!"

An old shack sat next to the jetty where the ship was docked, and perched on a barrel on the sagging front porch was a middle-aged man mending nets. His clothes were patched and mended beyond recognition, and his black beard was flecked with gray.

"Airith! Ya scallywag!" chimed Calldo. "Haven't come ta see mae in quite some time. I was a-gettin' worried somethin' had happened to ya. Who may dese noble youngsters be?"

The three of them stepped onto his porch. "This is Kaydin and his sister, Meredith," Airith introduced. "Kaydin and Meredith, this is Calldo Sambull, he is related to Pirate Patterson."

"Ah, but dat is naught ta be spoken of. Patterson was my great-uncle's fifth cousin's aunt's son, on his mother's side. Sit 'ere beside mea. Give mea a moment and I'll fix ya up some victuals. Fried fish sound good ta ya?"

The twins nodded. "It'll go well with the lunch we bought," said Meredith.

Calldo disappeared into his shack while Airith sat beside the barrel and pile of nets. The twins followed his example. Soon, the aroma of frying fish wafted from the shack.

"Airith?" Kaydin broke the silence.

"Yes?"

"Are you planning to become a sailor and head out to sea?"

"Since I am a youngest son, I don't get an inheritance. My father is going to send me to King Daltaine's court in

Yalefen next year when I turn eighteen. He plans to arrange a wedding with some noblewoman I have nothing in common with. I'll become one of those pampered nobles, bowing and scraping to the king, brimming with vapid smiles, and going on hunts with floods of people who scare away the game. I'll be obliged to listen while old men tediously argue over politics and youths boast over their conquests. Exhilarating. If I'm lucky, I'll get the king or some rich noble to reward me for valor in battle." Airith finished bitterly.

Calldo returned with the fried fish, preventing any response from the twins.

Meredith felt bad. She didn't have to worry about her future. She and Kaydin had been promised equal inheritance from their father, though Stellmear's lands and title would fall to Kaydin.

After they had finished a satisfying late lunch, Calldo lit his pipe. He leaned against the wall of his shanty and proceeded to blow large smoke rings that slowly drifted upward out of sight.

Airith whispered to the twins, "Whenever he's going to tell a story, he takes out his pipe."

Calldo launched into the tale of how he and his brother were drafted into the king's army when they fell asleep in a tavern after too much wine. They fought against one of Sisinta's ships and lost. Calldo survived, but his brother had died in his arms after he was dealt a violent blow to the head. Because of this, Calldo told them, he was opposed to fighting, and he had decided to settle down as a fisherman to the end of his days.

Calldo told five additional erratic short stories. The tales were interesting, but the sailor really got their attention when he started talking about silver dragons.

"I 'ear one was sighted not ta long ago, right 'ere in 'igher Quith! What are t'ings comin' ta these days?" Calldo leaned closer to his audience as if about to share a secret. "Dey say Sisinta keeps 'em alive with Shadows and demons. Dey can't die, even if ya drove a sword in ta deir 'earts. Dey won't die till it is dey're time. Twenty years afore the diseases starts ta take 'em, den dere ain't no way of savin' 'em 'cause da very blood in deir veins turns agin 'em. Give 'em seven years, den dey be dead."

"What about the other dragons?" Airith asked. "The ones who are not silver?"

"Dey lives mostly in da Dragon Mountains, wid Dragonose rulin' 'em. Dat's why Sisinta wants ta kill Dragonose, den she can get da otha dragon's ta serve 'er as well." Calldo puffed on his pipe.

"I don't think Dragonose exists." Airith snorted "He's just an old legend or bedtime story."

"What would you know about it?" Meredith demanded.

Mere ... Kaydin silently warned.

Meredith pressed her lips together.

Airith flashed her a confident, wry smile.

She quickly looked away. Was he amused he'd got a reaction out of her?

Calldo fell silent after an hour's worth of stories, and they watched the brilliant red sun sinking low on the horizon, dancing off the harbor's waves.

"It's beautiful," Meredith murmured.

"Meredith, Van'N is probably wondering where we are." Kaydin stood and thanked Calldo for his hospitality.

Meredith kissed Calldo's cheek. "Thank you very much for your hospitality, sir."

Calldo colored and mumbled, "T'was nothin', nothin' a'tall."

"I'll show you the way back to the market," Airith volunteered.

The twins spotted the city tower, but they both liked Airith's company, so they didn't protest. All three waved goodbye to Calldo.

He called after them, "Make sh're ya come back and visit mae!"

"Do you still believe in those children's stories?" Airith asked the twins. "The ones about Elyon cursing the dragons and Dragonose protecting Quith?"

"How are they children's stories if many adults believe them to be true?" Kaydin demanded.

"They are stuck in the past, hoping in a fantasy that will never come true."

"Then why do we fight Sisinta?" Kaydin pressed. "Is Elyon not the very reason we defend Quith? How is it that he is shown in the very ways we speak and live? The war with Sisinta, the battle on the Ammon Plains, the curse on the silver dragons, and countless poems and stories that are as old as the world. All of it is in the Great Books, which are far older than any legend."

"You're just a boy, Kaydin. When you're older you'll understand." Airith waved his hand dismissively. "Believe in your nursery rhymes for now, I won't hold it against you."

Meredith tried another topic. "Do you have any other brothers or sisters besides the one we saw earlier?"

"Yes, I do. That was Cowin, he's twenty-four. Shar is twenty-three, and my sister Kenta is fourteen. My brother Rasfell died when he was four." Airith's voice was even when he spoke, but the twins felt a spike of guilt when he mentioned his dead brother. "We have another brother, the oldest, but I have not seen him for several years. He joined Elyon's army, and my father was furious. He doesn't want any of his sons 'throwing their lives away' simply because they think they need to 'fight for what is right.' In his opinion, that is 'the peasant's job.'" Airith stopped walking for a moment, then added, "You would like Kenta. No one can help liking her."

"It would be nice to meet her," Meredith agreed.

"The Harvest Games are a week from today," Airith told them. "I'll be entering the sword fighting competition. Kenta should be there. You two should come and watch."

"If we can persuade Lady Quire and Van'N, we might be able to come," Kaydin said.

They had arrived at the Merchant's House. Cowin stood outside the inn talking with the servant who had been watching the horses.

"Airith, where have you been?" Cowin demanded. "I've been waiting while you run off with children and waste my time."

Airith replied calmly, "Meredith and Kaydin, this is my brother, Cowin."

The young man continued to address Airith only. "You know how Father feels about socializing with peasants."

Fire leapt into Airith's eyes. "I don't care what Father thinks. And, for your information, they're not peasants *or* children."

"Say goodbye now. We have to go." Cowin mounted his horse.

The way Airith's black eyes flashed and his fists clenched made Meredith almost afraid of him. There was so much hate in his eyes—a look that could kill.

"Maybe we will see you at the Harvest Games?" Kaydin spoke up.

Airith nodded vaguely in farewell, but didn't take his dark eyes off his brother as he untied his horse's reins.

Kaydin and Meredith started for the tower to meet Van'N.

"Did you see the look in Airith's eyes?" Meredith shivered.

"What look? What are you talking about?"

"Never mind." Meredith tried to forget about it. *His face is nice enough to look at the rest of the time,* she mused. Heat flared in her face, and she glanced at her brother, hoping he hadn't caught her thought. His face remained neutral, and she chose to believe she had managed to keep the thought to herself. Airith probably considered her too young despite their age difference of only two and a half years. She knew her features were considered delicate. She felt her small, pointed chin and rounded cheeks. She brushed the mop of curls out of her eyes to gaze at her simple, boxy dress. This wasn't the first time she wished she looked her age. Why should Airith pay any attention to her?

"Children! There you are." Van'N beckoned them. "We should head home now. Did you find anything interesting in the marketplace?"

Kaydin chatted about the harbor, Pirate Patterson, and Calldo. Meredith added in what Kaydin missed, soon getting caught up in the story. Her uneasiness over Airith left for now.

CHAPTER SEVEN

THE HARVEST GAMES

Dawn on the day of the Harvest Games appeared promising. A fair wind blew and rustled the rich, vibrant leaves—warm for late autumn—and the citizens of Boldwind and the surrounding countryside were in high spirits.

Airith maneuvered his horse carefully through the city streets, avoiding pedestrians. Sellers moved through the crowd, shouting their wares—breads, pastries, ale, wines, and apple ciders. Other peddlers sold an assortment of charms, trinkets, and baubles. Market day was noisy, but the Harvest Games were even more so.

He wore his padded deerskin leggings—best for fighting—and a red tunic bearing his family's coat of arms—Cala Man surrounded by six stars—a representation of the six sons of the first Lord Shaver. His hand subconsciously closed around the sword hilt at his side, its metal cool, familiar, and reassuring.

After some time and struggle, Airith reached the end of the street and joined his sister and brothers. Cowin, Shar, and Kenta took after Lady Shaver with their blue eyes and fair hair. Kenta was as beautiful and gentle as their mother.

Airith was the only one among them who boasted his father's black hair and dark eyes.

Kenta was at a stall studying a pretty, pale blue shawl, while Cowin and Shar inspected the next booth's daggers in various sizes and weights. The keeper of the clothing stall was young, sending the occasional ridiculous wink and grin Kenta's way. She seemed oblivious to the merchant's flattery. Airith's arrival drew her attention.

"Did you enter the fencing competition?" she asked.

Airith nodded. He turned to his brothers as they approached. "I also entered you two in the archery contest."

Cowin merely nodded.

Airith frowned. They were too lazy to brave the crowds and sign up for themselves and wouldn't deign to acknowledge the favor done for them. He didn't need their thanks. He turned back to his sister. "Are Mother and Father here?"

"They left together. I'm not sure where," Kenta told him.

"The competition starts in half an hour, so we had better head toward the fighting ring," Airith told them.

"We'll take the back streets," Cowin said. "It's too crowded."

They started down a small alley in a roundabout way toward the city square. Kenta skipped alongside Airith and linked her arm through his. "I know you're going to win the competition," she whispered to him.

"It's nice that someone has faith in me," Airith grumbled.

"You are the best!"

"I'm not the best."

"If you're not the best, then tell me, who has beaten you at swordplay these past two years?"

"No one. But that is not the point."

"Well then, what *is* the point?"

"You don't understand. Just being good at sword fighting is not what I want."

"What do you want?" she asked softly.

Airith said nothing.

She continued gently, "Airith, Father is very proud of your skill."

How did Kenta always know what was on his mind? He craved his father's support, but he would never believe his father gave it unless Lord Shaver told Airith directly, which he never would.

"I never said I wanted Father's approval for anything," he defended.

Kenta sighed, then spoke in a lighter tone. "You will win, I'll bet on it."

"You're not allowed to bet."

Kenta rolled her eyes. "It's a figure of speech, Airith. And besides, you've bet before."

"You didn't tell Father about that, did you?" Airith glanced to make sure his older brothers hadn't overheard.

"No, but you shouldn't do it."

"Ha! Who says?"

"Father. And for good reason."

"And why do I have to listen to Father?"

"Because he is your father."

"And *you* happen to be my little sister. I don't have to do what you say. Ah, there's the fighting ring." Airith used the excuse to escape.

Kenta followed him anyway.

***

"Airith!" Kaydin called as he and Meredith entered the fighting ring.

The older boy lifted his hand in greeting and hailed them over.

Airith and Kaydin exchanged bows. "This is my sister, Kenta Shaver. Kenta, this is Kaydin and his sister Meredith, uh ... I don't know your family name."

"Amara," Kaydin lied smoothly. He took Kenta's hand and smiled. "I'm blessed indeed in meeting one so fine."

Laying it on thick, aren't you? Meredith silently mocked.

What? Just practicing my manners, unlike you who stares shamelessly at Airith.

What! I do not! He's just ...

Nice to look at? Kaydin filled in.

You weren't supposed to hear that.

Oh, believe me, I tried not to. Can you please think about something other than his 'chiseled' jawline and 'swoon-worthy' hair?

Meredith struggled to keep her expression neutral. *I do not think of him like that.*

It is surprising that you've managed to note his handsome features when you can't bring yourself to meet his gaze for more than two seconds at a time.

Meredith wanted to whack her brother in the arm, but years of practice had taught her to keep her expression neutral when mind-speaking. She couldn't blame Kaydin for his interest in Kenta. She was a beautiful, upper-class lady. Her nose was straight, she had hair in golden curls to her waist, and her eyes were a deep blue. She wore a white dress, pleated from the waist, gold ribbon crisscrossed over the bodice. Meredith felt plain in her simple red dress. She had outgrown all her nice clothes, and Aunt Seala had no money to buy more. Until her father sent money, she had to deal with short hems and mended sleeves. At least she'd stopped growing. The clothing she'd worn at Stellmear Castle had marked her as nobility. Her mother had ensured that. Meredith swallowed the lump of grief in her throat.

"Is your father the Duke of Amara? Airith asked. "I thought you said he was just a lord."

"No, the Duke of Amara is our great-uncle," Kaydin gave the preplanned answer.

A crier took his place on the stone pillar to announce the start of the competition. The excited crowd gathered around the fighting ring, and Airith joined the other competitors. The twins and Kenta sidled up to the edge of the ring to watch.

Kenta told the twins, "My oldest brother has won this competition five years in a row! He was even sent to compete before the king. Everyone said he was the best swordsman in all Tayose. He taught Airith." A brilliant smile lit up her face when she added, "Airith is also an especially great swordsman."

Kaydin laughed in agreement. "I know. I've been at the losing end of his sword."

Meredith filled her in about the sword fight at the Merchant's House.

"That certainly sounds like Airith." Kenta sighed.

"So, tell us how the competition works," Meredith requested.

"Every time a competitor gets a hit, he gains ten points. After fifty points, the match ends. If the competitor floors his opponent, it is an automatic fifty points. The winner of each round moves on to fight the winner of the next round. The winning score is based on accumulated points. Does that make sense?" Kenta asked.

Meredith nodded. "I think so."

The trio watched the fighting for two hours before the final round. The many matches, defeats, and victories were greeted with shouts, whistles, and calls from the crowd. Airith progressed steadily through the ranks. He was an obvious favorite, though some onlookers seemed eager to watch him fail.

If you ever find yourself a damsel in distress, Airith is skilled enough to rescue you, Kaydin teased.

Meredith's attempt to elbow him only made her brother's grin widen.

★★★

During the final round, Airith stepped into the ring with Cala Man in hand. He eyed his opponent intently. Solvan of Waspan was bulkier and taller, lacking dexterity, but making up for it in brute strength. Having beaten all other opponents thus far, Solvan wore a smile of sure triumph.

Airith boasted a wiry frame that masked his toned muscles. Based on size alone, the match seemed unfair. However, Airith had spent time between matches watching his adversary's techniques and was certain he could predict Solvan's movements.

"Let the match begin!" announced the crier.

Airith bided his time. He stood in a ready position and waited for Solvan to attack. Eventually, Solvan stepped forward to strike, but while he was still out of lunging range, Airith sprang forward and brought up his sword, startling Solvan who had barely enough time to parry. Despite the deflection, Airith's sword rose rapidly and struck Solvan's shoulder. Solvan took an unsteady step back, and Airith used the moment to advance with quick, unrelenting strokes that kept Solvan on the defensive, leaving no room for counterattack.

When Solvan found an opening, he attacked Airith's padded legs. Airith easily jumped back. While his adversary was still recovering, Airith twisted around and hit the larger boy with the flat of his sword. He leapt away from Solvan's counter.

Airith's and Solvan's blades locked, both boys straining in strength against strength. After what seemed like an eternity, Solvan used his bulk to shove Airith away and freed his weapon. Airith immediately sprang back, successfully dealing a blow to Solvan's right leg. Solvan's face reddened.

Airith needed to deal only two more blows. Solvan charged, but Airith thwacked the bottom of his padded arm with the flat of his sword, continuing upward into an arc that knocked Solvan's arm away. The shouts and calls of the crowd began to register, and Airith glanced out of the corner of his eye. *No sign of Father.* He'd hoped his father would have at least come to see his final match. The sick feeling of disappointment in his stomach transformed into a flash of rage. Of course his father wouldn't be watching.

He jumped forward and locked swords with his adversary. Just when it seemed Solvan's strength would overcome him, Airith's foot shot out and tripped Solvan. The abrupt release of force almost sent Airith down with him, but he staggered back and regained his footing. Standing over his defeated opponent, Airith brought his sword to Solvan's throat. Seconds later, the cheering and booing from the crowd was so loud that Airith could not hear his own thoughts. He looked up to find his father's piercing black eyes and expressionless face across the ring. Airith's hate melted into guilt.

He withdrew his sword and stepped back, holding out his hand to Solvan. The older boy glared and pushed it away. Solvan stood on his own and stalked out of the ring.

"Airith! Airith! Airith!" His three devoted fans waved and called excitedly. Airith joined Kenta, Kaydin, and

Meredith. The girl gave him a shy smile. He wiped away the sweat dripping into his eyes and began unbuckling his padding.

The crier stepped into the ring and held out his hands for silence.

After a moment, the eager crowd quieted.

"My good people," declared the crier, "has it not been a truly thrilling contest this year?"

There were shouts of agreement and some grumbling from those who had lost bets.

The crier held out his hands again. When silence returned, he addressed the contestants, "You all have done very well and fought admirably, and I will now present the prizes for the three highest scores."

The crowd murmured as a page boy ran to the crier with results from the scorekeepers. While the crier reviewed it, a hush descended.

At last, the crier announced, "Gald of Ranshire in third place, Solvan of Waspan in second, and Airith of Shaver in first."

The yelling and cheering were deafening, and all three winners were pushed into the center of the ring where the crier presented a purse to each contestant.

Airith grinned when he accepted his.

Kenta bumped his shoulder and teased, "So, he *can* smile."

To celebrate the victory, the four friends perused the sights of the fair and the city. When they stopped to watch a play by traveling actors about a battle between a silver dragon and a knight, Airith asked his sister, "Where is Father?"

Kenta shrugged. "I didn't see him, why?"

"I thought I saw him watching the match."

Kenta thought for a moment. "I don't recall seeing him. He must have come and gone again."

Airith's eyes clouded as he ran his hand through his hair.

"You won the competition and ninety silver coins, Airith! I'm sure Father is proud." Kenta tried to encourage him, but Airith did not smile again, maintaining his dark mood for the rest of the day.

★★★

Later that evening, the Shaver family gathered in the library after supper.

Cowin was repairing his hawk's leather hunting hood, their mother was sewing with Kenta, and Shar was reading a book on botany. Lord High sat in front of the fire in his favorite high-backed chair, staring into the flames.

"Father, did you see Airith today at the competition?" Kenta asked. "He had the highest score!"

Lord High stared at her for a moment, then turned to Airith who was cleaning his sword.

Airith proudly met his father's gaze.

Lord High turned back to Kenta. "Yes, I saw him today. His opponent was tired from the previous matches, and Airith had the advantage of energy. If he'd fought the same number of matches his opponent had, he would have lost." High resumed watching the flames.

Kenta opened her mouth to say something else, but Airith's stormy expression closed it. She continued her sewing in silence.

CHAPTER EIGHT

SEVEN MONTHS' TIME

Winter's first snowfall cloaked the world in pure white set with diamonds. Airith stopped his steed under the branches of a willow tree decorated with clusters of icicles. The trees stood sentinel over the sleeping world, guarding the silence and beauty. He surveyed the amazing transformation of nature from the dead browns of late fall to the undefiled white desert of winter.

"Isn't it beautiful, Pallindo?" Airith asked his horse.

Pallindo lifted his head to nibble at the bark of the willow tree.

"Don't eat that, boy." Airith laughed at the horse, reining him back so he couldn't reach the tree. "Why are you always thinking of your stomach?"

Pallindo turned his head to Airith mournfully.

"Don't look at me like that! You're not getting any bark." Airith pulled his fur-lined leather coat closer around himself and watched his breath whiff out in small clouds.

Pallindo pulled on the reins, ready to leave.

"All right, all right."

Pallindo needed no urging to break into a trot and then a gallop. Airith let him have his head, not caring where he went as long as it was away from home and his brothers. He dreaded being cooped up in his father's castle for the winter.

At last, he slowed Pallindo to a stop.

A half mile in the distance, he could see a small village with a castle beyond it. The willow tree must have been the entrance to Willow Road, which meant the town was Juventall and the castle beyond it, Quire. He wondered if he should stop in and see Kaydin and Meredith but decided against it. It would be awkward and seem like he was desperate for friends.

He was prepared to return home when a snowball hit him square in the chest and another in the leg. Airith looked around for his assailants but found no one until he looked up into a maple tree. In one swift bound, he was off his horse and just out of range of his attackers. He scooped up a handful of snow and packed it into a ball, easily hitting his target in the tree.

Kaydin yelled and spat snow.

As Airith prepared more ammunition, he called, "Why is it I keep meeting you in trees? Are you afraid to touch ground?"

"No," Kaydin answered defiantly. "We decided not to take your advice. We're staying here all winter."

Another snowball hit Airith in the arm.

Meredith giggled.

"You don't play fair." Airith hit Kaydin again. "I'm not allowed to hit girls."

Airith used Pallindo as a shield. The old horse stood calmly and tolerated the assault.

At last, Kaydin and Meredith dropped from the tree.

"It's a truce," Kaydin declared.

"I'll take your word for it." Airith took Pallindo's reins.

Meredith and Kaydin shook the snow from their cloaks.

"What's brought you here?" Kaydin asked, holding out his hand.

Airith shook it readily. "Nothing really, I was just out for a ride."

"He doesn't seem to scare easily." Meredith put her hand on the horse's neck.

"No, he doesn't. Pallindo has been my faithful companion all my life, but he's old, going on ... twenty-five years now."

"What will you do with him when you can no longer ride him?" Meredith asked.

"I'll keep him, let him graze the fields for the rest of his days. He will most likely die of overeating. Hey, Pallindo? You old, fat thing." Airith fondly slapped Pallindo's rump.

"I'm cold." Kaydin shivered. "You must be too, Airith, after getting snow down your back. Why don't you come to Quire Castle with us?"

"I suppose I could ... I have no reason to head home yet."

As they walked, Kaydin asked, "What have you been doing since the Harvest Games?"

"Nothing. I'm waiting out the winter until my father sends me to the king's court in the spring."

"How long do you have to stay there?" Meredith asked.

"Until my father sees fit to call me home. Or, I might never come back if the king decides to marry me off," Airith said gloomily. "Then again, it might not be that bad, to get away from Shaver Castle and my brothers."

"Kenta would miss you," Meredith reminded him.

Airith frowned. "I suppose so, but she'd be the only one. Well ... besides my mother."

"I just hope Father comes for us soon," Kaydin complained. "Quaeor, the steward of Quire Castle, is terrifying, and Aunt Seala keeps insisting we read boring poems by boring people."

"I'm so glad my schooling finished last summer." Airith laughed dryly.

The gate to Aunt Seala's castle stood open, and the twins led Airith to the stable. Pallindo entered the stall next to Aunt Seala's skinny, chestnut mare.

"If you aren't doing anything this winter, do you think you could teach me sword fighting?" Kaydin asked.

Airith thought for a moment. "I think you're pretty good for your age."

"I don't care if I'm good—I want to be better." They had reached the door, and Kaydin banged on it until he heard footsteps inside.

Airith nodded slowly. "I'll help you as best I can."

The short, old doorkeeper, Dallbim, let them in and took their cloaks and gloves.

Kaydin led the way to the large, unused banquet hall. "We can practice here," he said.

The two boys fought until sweat ran down their faces while Meredith attempted to sketch the two combatants. Finally, they collapsed into chairs next to Meredith, gasping for breath.

"You two are great entertainment," she said.

"It's a lot harder than it looks," Kaydin growled.

"Are you sure? Airith makes it look easy." She smirked and closed her sketchbook.

Satisfaction lifted Airith's chest. When he smiled in her direction, she ducked her head shyly.

"I'm sore all over." Kaydin groaned. "I think you twisted my wrist, Airith."

60

"If I hadn't, you'd have struck me in the leg," Airith retorted.

"Couldn't you let me get a small strike in every once in a while?"

"No, that would give you a false sense of confidence. Your enemy won't go easy on you."

"I know. I just wish I'd improve faster." Kaydin sighed.

"You will eventually, believe me. You'll never regret learning how to better defend yourself." Airith paused. "I was thinking, if I'm as good at swordplay as everyone says I am, when I go to court, I might ask the king to make me a knight in exchange for service. I could offer to lead his men on dangerous campaigns, and he might even grant me lordship," Airith said.

"But could you do it?" Kaydin asked.

"Could I do what?"

"Kill people. Mock swordplay battles are one thing, but to take a life ..."

"I could do it. It would be fending off the enemy. Let's stop talking about this, I'm not going anywhere for several months yet."

"Well, I do hope Father comes for us before you go," Meredith said. "You're the most interesting person we've met here. It'll be that much more unbearable without you." She sank into her seat with a sigh.

Airith furrowed his brow. What did she mean? He was gloomy company at the best of times. If he tried to dissect her statement, he would enter unknown territory. He latched onto a different point. "Are you sure he hasn't just dumped you here so he doesn't have to take care of you? You've been here, what, four years?"

"Three and a half. And yes, we still hope," Kaydin said. "He sends us letters and visits us when he can. He's a busy man, and he's worried whoever killed our mother is going to find us. He hasn't found a better solution than Quire. If your father promised you he'd come back, wouldn't you believe him?"

"No, I wouldn't," Airith snapped. "My father would never make me such a promise. He doesn't even look me in the eye."

"Why not?" Meredith whispered. She clutched her sketchbook to her chest. He'd upset her, and, surprisingly, his own behavior annoyed him.

Airith shrugged. "I'm just not worth it." He paused, then added, "I'm sorry about your mother. Do you know who did it?"

"Maybe. I don't really want to talk about it." Kaydin crossed his arms and sat back in his seat, matching Airith's moodiness. The trio sat silently in the large room, until eventually, Airith mumbled a goodbye and left.

★★★

During the remaining fall and winter months, Airith gave Kaydin, and occasionally Meredith, fighting lessons as often as he could. Every minute he could spare was spent at Quire Castle, fencing, hunting, and conversing with the twins. For the first time in his life, he had friends. Together, they convinced Van'N to travel with them to Boldwind where they visited Calldo Sambull regularly.

Despite complaining about leaving for court, Airith wanted to get away as soon as possible. His brothers took their cues from their father and treated him with increasing disdain, making the king's court sound more and more appealing. He couldn't wait to leave.

CHAPTER NINE

A HUNT GONE BAD

Banging on the door woke Airith.

"Hurry up, Airith!" came Shar's voice. "Father wants us to go with him to Boldwind. We need to ship those horses to the king."

Airith rolled out of bed and groaned, "Why can't he get the servants to do it?"

"He doesn't trust the servants."

"Tell Father I'm not going!"

Cowin's footsteps retreated down the hall.

Airith rubbed his eyes and staggered to the washstand where he splashed water on his face, sucking in his breath against the shock of icy cold. He dressed in his leather hunting garb and grabbed his quiver and bow. When he descended the stairs, he found his father and brothers waiting.

"What's taken you so long?" Father roared. "We've been waiting over half an hour! I told you yesterday to be ready."

Airith forced himself to stay calm. "I said I didn't want to go."

"You're coming whether you want to or not!"

"*Tasa!* I'm not going!"

"Don't swear at me, boy!"

"It's not swearing!"

"Just because it's in another language doesn't justify it! I'll tan your hide if you don't keep your mouth shut and obey!"

Cowin and Shar smirked.

"Go ahead! Beat me! I don't care. I'm still not going!"

"Airith, please listen to your father," His mother's gentle tone pierced the din.

"I won't listen to anyone but myself!"

"You will listen to me even if it means I have to drag you to Boldwind!" His father's eyes flashed.

A bolt of fear struck Airith, but his own anger overrode it. With a scowl, he stalked out the door.

"Where do you think you're going?" Lord Shaver's face was red with fury.

"Hunting!" Airith yelled back.

★★★

After all the shouting, the room was strangely quiet.

Lady Shaver put her arms around her husband.

He shook with barely restrained anger. "I knew he was rebellious, but this is the first time he's shown it outright."

"Do you want Cowin and me to bring him back?" Shar asked eagerly.

"No," High snapped.

"But Father, he defied you!" Cowin declared.

"Go check on the horses!"

Cowin and Shar hurried away, nearly tripping over each other.

"Please don't send Airith to the king's court, High," Lady Shaver pleaded. "If he's rebellious, it'll only make things worse."

"*I am* going to send him. I'm convinced now more than ever!" Lord Shaver yanked free of her grasp and marched into the library. He sat at his writing desk and took out paper and ink.

Lady Shaver followed him.

"I will tell the king to put him to good use, work out the bad in him, and take him off my hands." High took up his pen and began writing furiously.

"High, he's your son!" Lady Shaver protested. "You cannot throw that responsibility away. What will sending him to the court do for him? You think that will *fix* him? No one can affect a boy like his father!"

"I don't want that responsibility!" High growled.

"Whether you want it or not, you have it."

"I don't want him! I never did! No one can ever replace Rasfell." High slammed down his quill.

"Rasfell is dead! Airith cannot replace him, and no one can ever replace Airith. You act as if I cared nothing for Rasfell! What you forget, husband, is he was as much my blood as yours! I loved him and have reconciled with his death, but you refuse to let him go. I accepted the gift of Airith as comfort in my grief. High, what is the matter with you?" Emerald's lip trembled and tears swam in her eyes as she whispered, "I never thought you so heartless."

"Emerald, I ..."

Emerald turned and left.

High put his head in his hands and groaned. He did not hate his youngest son—he hated what he represented— death and his own failings as a father. What sort of man was he that all his sons had rebelled against him? Airith and his eldest brother might have done it openly, but Cowin and Shar did it subtly. He resented the reminder of his loose grip on his own family. High clenched his jaw and picked up his quill again.

***

Airith leaned against the wall next to the library door. After wrestling for several minutes, he had returned with the intention of apologizing to his mother—he would never forgive himself for grieving his gentle, kind-hearted mother. Then, he'd heard his father's declaration. So, it was true. His father had never wanted him.

His parents hardly spoke of Rasfell, and his brothers did not remember him very well. He did know Rasfell had been his father's favorite. Airith's birthday was never celebrated as his father had declared it a day of mourning. His mother had convinced his father to allow a celebration the day after.

Angry tears filled his eyes. He was doomed, haunted by Rasfell's ghost, who even now was reaching out from the grave and stealing what should have been his. Airith silently cursed his dead brother and fled the house.

He ran to his partly-saddled horse, his hunting hawk perched on the saddlebow. Airith quickly finished saddling Pallindo. The hooded hawk flapped its wings and dug its claws into the leather. Airith pressed his arm to the hawk's chest, and the majestic scout stepped onto his gauntlet.

Once he was out of the stable and in the spring air, he kicked Pallindo into a full gallop. After a few minutes, Pallindo was breathing hard and sweat ran off his haunches. Airith was forced to slow down so as not to overheat the poor horse.

When he slowed, he realized several things—he was crying, he didn't know where he was, and he never wanted to go home again. He was a man—he didn't need anyone—

and he was not going to cry, ever again. He brushed away the tears and buried his hurt and anger deep inside himself. His conscience had forced him to return to apologize and had caused him to hear his father's scathing words. He burned his conscience.

Admitting he wanted his father's love tormented him even more than not having it.

Why was he ever born? What was he ever going to do that would mean anything to his father? Death would be a relief for his misery. He was, after all, worthless, useless, and unwanted—it would not make a difference if he died. Rasfell must be laughing, wherever he was. Airith gritted his teeth and hissed curses upon his dead brother, his father, himself, the day he was born, and his life. Pallindo's ears twitched nervously in response.

A scream ripped the air and turned Airith's blood ice-cold. Pallindo froze and the hawk cocked its head in the direction of the sound. Something bright, living, and large plummeted to the ground and disappeared among the trees nearby. Airith debated if he should investigate. Part of him called for caution, but a greater, reckless desire urged him on. Finally, he threw caution aside and directed Pallindo toward the woods. The frightened horse did not share Airith's recklessness, and several times tried to deviate from the path.

The trees were thick, but Airith followed a deer path, fighting Pallindo every step. He was not exactly sure where the creature had fallen, and he was beginning to despair of ever finding it. Another cry reverberated, more subdued than the last. This time, it was a cross between a whimper and a scream, but still loud enough to ring in Airith's ears.

Airith turned Pallindo toward the sound, and shortly, he broke into a clearing. However, as soon as he did, Pallindo bucked for the first time in his life. The hawk sprang from Airith's arm and landed on Pallindo's saddle. The horse thundered away with the hawk clinging to the saddlebow. Airith, sprawled on the ground, stared in amazement after his fleeing horse and its unconventional rider. "What's gotten into them?" He rose and brushed leaves and dirt off his tunic.

A rasp of heavy breathing stopped him.

Turning slowly, he saw the creature prone on the forest floor. Airith's breath shortened, and he had an overwhelming urge to run.

In front of him was a dragon, the size of a very large house.

CHAPTER TEN

SILVER BLOOD

Airith had never seen any living thing so big and beautiful. Large, white, glowing eyes pierced him with a soft blue light. Spikes gathered in a crown on the dragon's equine-shaped head and ran down the long muscular neck. Its massive wings spread out like the petals of a wilting flower around its lanky frame. The creature's tail—the same length as its body—was also lined with spikes. The dragon's overlapping silver scales caught the morning sunlight.

He looked closer and saw the reason for the dragon's outraged cries. A five-foot-long shaft protruded from its belly. A thin purple ribbon hung from the javelin's butt—the king's colors. Was it from the ballista in the guard tower near Boldwind?

Sweat beaded Airith's skin. He had enough hunting experience to know the worst time to encounter an animal was when it was wounded. He tried to back away slowly, but the dragon growled, following him with its eyes. There was no chance of getting away unnoticed.

He remembered something about dragons speaking through their minds, but since he didn't know how to do that, he started talking to it in a low and—he hoped—soothing tone. "I didn't mean to barge in on you. I'm going to go now, okay?"

The dragon let out a pitiful cry, a plea in its eyes.

Airith took a deep breath. "You want me to help you?" Maybe it was a trick. "Do you promise not to kill me?" Airith didn't know why he was talking to this creature. It probably didn't understand a word he said, and even if it did, what use was the word of a wounded, hungry dragon?

The dragon met his gaze and looked away first—a sign of submission.

Airith grabbed the shaft. "This is going to hurt, so please try not to kill me." Airith pulled. The shaft didn't budge.

The dragon groaned.

"I think it might be embedded in bone. Whoever hit you did a very good job." He placed his hands farther down the base of the shaft. He closed his eyes, took another deep breath, and summoning all his strength, yanked with his full weight, grunting as he did. The shaft released with such force that he tumbled, landing on his back once again.

Then, there was blood—a gush of silver liquid. The dragon tried to back away, but Airith stood, pulled off his tunic, and pressed it to the wound. The silver blood soaked through and dripped along his arms.

The dragon sprang away, and a voice boomed like a thunderclap, "Fool! Stay away!"

"You can speak! Why did you not do so before?" Airith asked.

"I speak only when I must. Your language is so small and tiny in my throat." The dragon licked its wound and watched Airith out of the corner of its eye. The blood flow stopped as quickly as it had begun.

Airith decided it probably wasn't going to eat him, considering he'd given aid. The dragon also seemed to be trying to stay away from him.

He glanced at the dragon's blood sparkling on the ground and on his arms. He spotted a small trickle of a stream tumbling over rocks nearby. Kneeling next to it, he plunged his arms, leather gauntlet, and tunic into the icy cold water, scrubbing vigorously at the silver gore. The fabric and leather washed off easily, but the bare skin of his left hand seemed to have absorbed the silver blood. He scrubbed at it until his fingers felt raw and his joints ached with the cold. In the end, he gave up. It would have to come off on its own eventually. He rung out his glove and tunic and laid them in a patch of sunshine to dry.

The dragon bumped its nose against his left arm.

Airith cringed and almost tipped backward, afraid his arm would soon no longer be part of his body.

"Have you never heard of Silver Blood, boy?"

"Yes. It's a curse Elyon put on the silver dragons."

The dragon nodded. *A curse it is indeed.*

Airith yelped. The creature had spoken directly into his mind. "How did you do that?" Airith watched the dragon warily.

It tilted its head and studied Airith much like a cat when it considers a human to be curiously stupid.

"Can I do that?"

Maybe.

"How?"

The dragon's laughter started in its throat as a low rumble and grew into a thunderstorm. *You like to ask a lot of questions.*

"No, I like answers."

I like you, which is a great compliment. I usually cannot tolerate humans.

"You were raised around humans?" Airith asked.

Yes, but they and my clan have abandoned me, so I've run away.

"I don't blame you," Airith mumbled to himself, then added louder, "Teach me to mind-speak."

You are very demanding, boy.

Airith straightened to his full height. Though he wasn't especially tall, he had passed his father in stature, and that meant something. "You obviously don't know much about men. I'm a man." Or he would be in a few weeks.

The dragon laughed again, but this time it was in Airith's head, and it didn't make his heart pound or his ears ring. *You're right, Airith, perhaps I don't know everything about men.*

How do you know my name? I didn't tell you. Wait. He was mind-speaking! Airith realized his mind was now naked and exposed to the world.

The dragon felt Airith's surprise and was amused, something Airith realized was being relayed to him mentally. *See? I said you would learn. I know your name because your mind is unprotected, anyone can read it.*

How do I protect it?

You can learn.

You like saying that. You're very frustrating, has anyone ever told you that?

Yes.

How's your wound? Airith asked.

Fine.

Let me look at it. Airith took a step closer.

No. The dragon moved farther away.

Why not?

I am fine. The dragon growled.

If you don't get some help you will die.

During the silence that followed, Airith tried to reach into the dragon's mind, but met something hard and cold, like a brick wall. He attempted to peer under the dragon's leathery wing but couldn't glimpse the wound at all.

The dragon shuffled away and watched him with moon-shining eyes. At last, it said with sorrow, *I'm sorry.*

Sorry for what? Was the dragon going to eat him after all?

Do you still not know, boy?

Know what? Airith started backing away.

Look at your hand, boy!

Airith glanced down at his blood-stained hand. *I-It's your blood. It'll wash off eventually.*

Nothing will ever wash it off. The dragon conveyed a mental lament.

Wh-What do you mean? Numbness crept up his arm.

It hasn't washed off, and I can smell it in you. You have what I do. Sorrow permeated the dragon's voice.

What do you have? Airith swallowed. His hands itched to run through his hair, but he resisted the urge.

Silver Blood, the curse.

No, I can't! I'm not a dragon. Silver Blood is a curse for dragons! It's probably only stained my skin.

There is ancient lore of shape-shifting dragons who took the form of men. Some say that is how the Sillians and Paladalls gained their magic. I warrant somewhere in your bloodline there are a few drops of dragon blood. It would explain how quickly you learned to mind-speak. The dragon's claw shot forward. A curved talon pierced Airith's stained arm and retracted.

Airith cried out as warm blood spilled over his skin. He touched the wound and studied his blood-stained fingers in disbelief. His blood was as red as poppies, but there were distinct flecks of silver in it. He closed his eyes and told himself he was dreaming—that at any moment, he would wake and find himself in his bed. But when he opened his eyes, the dragon's head was a foot from his face.

You hurt me! Airith mentally accused.

Would you have believed me if I hadn't shown you the blood?

No.

The dragon retreated.

Airith examined his arm again. The blood was already clotting and the wound scabbing over. *I suppose having a silver arm isn't that bad,* he mused.

No, perhaps not, but having Silver Blood is.

Why?

It makes you invincible, even if you are stabbed through the heart. It also causes you to heal faster. The longer the disease progresses, the faster the healing.

And how is that bad? As Airith considered the benefits Silver Blood would have in battle, memories of Calldo's stories began to filter through.

The bad part is after seven years, the disease consumes your entire body and your heart stops.

"What?" Airith's voice came out as a squawk. All Calldo's ominous tales came flooding back to him.

Your days are numbered, so to speak.

"I can't die! I'm still young! I have more than seven years ahead of me!" Airith, in his panic, forgot to mind-speak. "Help me get rid of it! I don't want it, even if it does make me invincible!"

Can't. Impossible. It has already entered your bloodstream. Even if I bit off your arm, there'd still be silver bits floating around in you.

"Why didn't you stop me from touching your blood?" Airith shouted.

I didn't ask you to stanch the wound. I only wanted you to pull the thing out. Airith caught a faint waft of guilt from the dragon. *Anyway, at least you have seven years!*

Airith calmed somewhat. *How long have you had Silver Blood?*

My whole life. I was born with it. My end is looming.

How old are you? Airith asked apprehensively.

I've seen nearly twenty-seven years.

Oh, well, that's not so bad. That means I still have twenty-seven years. I won't exactly be an old man, but—

The disease activates around twenty years of age, the dragon interrupted. *The progression leads to death roughly seven years after that. The fact that it's already swimming around inside your blood means it's active.*

Is there nothing we can do? Airith attempted to suppress the panic building inside him.

There is one thing, but it would mean going back ...

Going back where?

To Sisinta. She offers all silver dragons a longer life in exchange for service. Do you know nothing of history, boy? The dragon let him feel its annoyance.

Of course I know that. I just forgot. What's Sisinta's offer?

You ask too many questions, the dragon grumbled.

Tell me, Airith demanded.

A Shadow enters your mind to grant you power and prolong your life, usually by an additional seven years.

A Shadow?

Yes, a demon, a shade, a devil, a Shadow. The dragon rolled its eyes in exasperation.

Don't you want to go back? What are you doing here? Airith asked.

All dragons approaching their twenty-seventh year have to duel for the right to a Shadow.

And?

And I lost! The dragon bared its white, pointed teeth. *I was the smallest born in my year. The dragon I fought was the largest. My kin were pleased that I failed. I was banished by my clan. I knew I was going to die soon, and I thought it'd be nice to see the world a bit before then. I flew too low and was spotted, and here I am now.*

Doesn't Sisinta want as many silver dragons on her side as possible? Couldn't you speak with her and ask her for a Shadow yourself? Airith felt a tinge of righteous indignation at the thought that this magnificent creature had been denied its right to live.

Sisinta doesn't interfere with feuds among the dragons, she respects our laws and traditions.

If I were to possess a Shadow, would it give me the power to prolong your life as well as mine?

Maybe ... who knows the limits of a Shadow's abilities? Well, I suppose Sisinta does.

Do you know where Sisinta is? Airith asked.

Yes, but I already told you: I've been banished.

Are there others like me? Men with Silver Blood?

No, the dragon said wearily, *you are the first that I know of. Oh! I recall a memory of an ancestor who knew a Sillian with Silver Blood. He died.*

You recall a memory of an ancestor? The mention of ancestors drew his curiosity.

Ah, yes. I forgot. Humans do not remember as dragons do. All dragons inherit the knowledge of their ancestors. Hmm ... I believe Sisinta would think you quite valuable. Airith could see a plan forming in the dragon's mind. *Although ... she thinks no one valuable,* the dragon mused. *She wants only what she can use for herself.*

Would she think me useful? Airith asked hopefully.

Yes, I suppose so, but why would you go to her? Haven't you been raised to hate Sisinta?

Yes, but if those who taught you to hate her turned and betrayed you, wouldn't you start to wonder otherwise?

Yes, I too have been betrayed by my clan. The dragon paused. *Perhaps we can help each other.*

Airith grinned. *We would be companions? Two friends independent of everyone but ourselves, watchful for each other's needs? Our lives belonging solely to one another?*

The dragon studied him for a moment, and Airith flinched as he felt it sifting through his mind, searching for any falsehood. Airith could hold nothing back.

At last, the dragon nodded. *I think you and I might benefit each other. We shall swear on it, the promise will be binding and sealed with blood.*

CHAPTER ELEVEN

A CHOICE MADE

On the day of Airith's departure for court, a servant readied Pallindo in the courtyard of Shaver Castle at dawn. The worthy old horse had found his own way home after the episode in the woods. Airith had successfully hidden his silver arm under his leather hunting glove the whole week without notice.

Everyone but Lord Shaver woke early to see him off. His mother and sister cried while his brothers slapped him on the back, telling him to conquer the world.

Maybe I will. For the first time in his life, Airith was going to be on his own without the restraint of his family.

His mother had overseen the packing of provisions for the journey to Yalefen, but it would not be enough to get him where he *really* wanted to go. *No matter. My winnings from the Harvest Games will be more than enough to buy what I need.* He did not forget Cala Man, certain he would need the sword.

He mounted Pallindo, leaving his past behind while the world, spread out before him, eagerly awaited.

As soon as he was out of sight of his father's castle, he cut across the fields and made straight for Willow Road.

When he reached Quire Castle, Airith dismounted in the courtyard, and the stable boy ran over to take Pallindo's reins. Airith asked the boy, "Do you think you could deliver this note to your Master Kaydin and his sister?"

"Yes, Master Shaver, that I could."

"Good boy. Here's a silver for your trouble."

The boy's face lit up and he hurried to stable Pallindo and deliver the letter.

★★★

From her window, Meredith saw Airith arrive. She hurried downstairs to greet him but met the stable boy instead. He handed her a letter.

"Master Shaver has left already, but his horse is still in the stable."

"Thank you."

The stable boy bobbed his head and left.

Confused and disappointed, Meredith called for her brother as she opened the seal.

> Kaydin and Meredith,
>
> I leave for court today, and I have been thinking about what I should do with Pallindo. I have decided to give him to you, trusting he will continue to thrive in your care.
>
> Your friend,
> Airith Shaver

Kaydin arrived just as Meredith finished reading the note. "It's from Airith. I wish he had come in to say goodbye."

"He did yesterday, remember?" Kaydin frowned as he read over his sister's shoulder. "I'm confused, though. I thought he was taking Pallindo with him."

"I suppose not. Do you think Quaeor will let us keep him?"

"No. But if we go to Aunt Seala and ask first, Quaeor cannot prohibit us," Kaydin suggested.

"Then we should ask Aunt Seala right now before he finds out," Meredith urged.

Kaydin and Meredith went straight to Aunt Seala's sitting room. Kaydin knocked.

Aunt Seala's eyes lit up when she saw them—the only part of her they could see clearly. She sat in her high-backed chair by the fire, wrapped in several layers of blankets, and resting her feet on a coal-filled heater. "Come to see your old aunt, have you, my dears?"

"Oh yes, Aunt Seala," Meredith began. "Kaydin and I were worried about you. We heard from one of the servants that your joints were bothering you again."

"Oh my, yes, they are. Every day, my old joints get worse. They pain me especially on cold days and stormy nights." Aunt Seala proceeded to give the usual five-minute speech.

When she was done, Meredith smiled sweetly. "Aunt Seala, I think that the joints of the old mare in the stable bother her too."

"Really, dear? Well, I can sympathize with her. She's been here for quite a few years." Aunt Seala nodded grimly.

"She has no companion to keep her mind off the pain."

"That is true, I do have that advantage. Quaeor is ever so nice to me," Aunt Seala admitted. "I would get another horse for her, poor old thing, but they cost too much these days."

"Do you remember Airith, Aunt Seala?" Kaydin asked.

"Yes, I do. He's been coming here for some time now. Nice young man."

"Yes, he has been a good friend to us. Now he has left for the king's court and entrusted his horse, Pallindo, to our care," Kaydin told her.

"Well, then, it all works out." Aunt Seala settled herself deeper into the mound of blankets.

"We can keep him, then?" Meredith asked.

"Of course you can, my dears. When you go out, tell one of the servants to bring me some hot tea. That's a good girl, Meredith." Aunt Seala closed her eyes and, within a moment, was snoring.

"She really isn't doing very well," Meredith whispered to Kaydin as she quietly closed the door behind them.

"She's been keeping to herself more often and asked for us only twice last week," Kaydin acknowledged.

I'll miss Airith, Meredith silently admitted.

Me too. He did promise to write. So, at least there's that.

You're great company and all, Meredith added, *but it was nice to have someone else around to talk to.*

Don't worry, I'm not offended. Kaydin squeezed her in a side-hug. *I don't like talking to myself all the time, either.*

You know that's not what I meant. Meredith poked him. *I just hope he doesn't forget about us.*

***

Midmorning, Airith arrived at his destination in the clearing. The silver dragon was sleeping, its head resting on its front claws. Airith wondered if he should wake it.

The dragon's eye popped opened, and its head shot forward.

Airith yelped and fell backward.

The dragon laughed.

You really enjoy knocking me over, Airith mind-spoke, not at all amused.

I was only pretending to be asleep. I waited for you all morning. The dragon made its amusement known mentally. *I find you extremely entertaining, Airith.*

I'm not here for your entertainment! Now, how do I attach the provisions to your back? Airith demanded.

Sisinta's men used to put a saddle on me.

Well, we don't have one, so I'll have to improvise.

Airith took two ropes from his pack. He wrapped them around the dragon's belly, tying them to its neck spikes, and securing a blanket on its back. He tied the bundle of provisions to the rope, pulling it as tight as he could. Satisfied with his work, he climbed onto the dragon's back.

The dragon stretched and shook out its wings. No trace of any wound remained. *Hold on and don't fall off. I might be able to catch you, but I would rather not have to.*

That's comforting, Airith mind-spoke dryly. *I've ridden a horse often enough that I can manage not to fall. Though, you* are *a little wider than a horse.*

The dragon snorted. *I'm* certainly not *a horse, and if I were you, I would take care not to refer to me as one.*

Sorry, I didn't know it was a touchy subject. Are we going to go now?

As soon as you stop making wisecracks.

Okay, okay. I promise not to refer to you as a horse again.

Good. The dragon pulled its wings back and, in one powerful stroke, launched into the sky.

The wind whistled in Airith's ears and pulled at the hood of his black cloak. His stomach seemed intent on being left behind, unable to catch up to the dragon's speed. The wind continually whipped his eyes, but shortly, the dragon leveled out and slowed to a steady beat with his powerful wings. The wind was not as strong and Airith's stomach settled.

He watched the world fly by. Half an hour found him already farther away from home than he had ever been. For a moment, he pondered if this was a mistake—there had to be another way to avoid an early death. There was no going back. He had made his decision, and he could not undo it. Watching the ground racing by made him dizzy, and he closed his eyes.

I have a question, Airith said.

I have not known you long, but so far you have had no end of them.

What's your name?

It is unpronounceable by the human voice. The men of Sisinta's army referred to me by a number.

You have the right to a name. I will give you one.

The dragon tried to hide its eagerness, but Airith caught some of it.

Airith mused for a long time before saying, *Kappin.*

That's a very short name. Can I have a longer one?

Why would you want a longer one?

Because all the important dragons have long names.

Well, then you'll be the first important dragon with a short name.

Kappin flew silently as he thought about it. After an hour, he declared, *I accept the name.*

The sun remained hidden behind clouds, making it difficult to predict the time of day. Airith lost all sense of time and place. In the sky, nothing existed but the biting wind and the wet, heavy clouds. Alone with his thoughts and the sky, he dozed.

He woke when Kappin began to descend. Night had fallen and the full moon, overcast with occasional clouds, was an ethereal light above them. They landed in a farmer's field bordered by a stone fence and sparse trees.

You nearly fell off in your sleep. Kappin sounded disgusted.

Airith clumsily dismounted. "I'm not the one who can sleep for a hundred years and stay awake for centuries," he mumbled.

Only some dragons do that. I can go without sleep for a few years, though. Kappin hit a nearby rotten tree with his claw, and it smashed to the ground. He pushed it into a large pile. *It's your turn to do something useful. Make fire.*

You mean use a tinderbox? Airith sleepily rubbed his eyes.

Yes, if that's what you call it.

Can't you breathe fire on it? Airith waved his hand at the woodpile.

Of course not! What kind of dragon do you think I am? Kappin indignantly pushed the pile closer to Airith.

Airith rummaged in his bag until his hand closed on the tinderbox. *If you don't breathe fire, what* do *you do?* Airith asked while striking the flint against a small pile of dry grass.

Silver dragons are wind dragons. I call the wind, and it hears me! I whisper to the currents, and they obey! He held his head high.

But wouldn't you rather be able to breathe fire? A thin trail of smoke rose from the rapidly growing flame. Airith sat back on his haunches and admired his handiwork.

Certainly not. Silver dragons are the swiftest warriors in battle—the most agile of the clans. We fly the farthest distances.

Can you tell me more about dragons? Airith asked. He took the pack off Kappin's back and prepped his bed roll.

Hmm ... Kappin settled by the fire, curling his body in a half-moon around it. His silver scales appeared red and orange in the dancing light. *We are divided by clans and the elements of our attacks. We are not terribly sociable—some dragons live their whole adult lives entirely alone. The wind and ice clans usually live high in the mountains where there is snow.*

What about Dragonose and the Council of Dragons? Airith recalled Calldo Sambull mentioning something about them.

We silver dragons have nothing to do with them. Dragonose was put in charge of the Council back when Elyon erected the Dragon Mountains to protect Higher Quith from Sisinta after the Blood Battle on the Ammon Plains. Apparently, they have been successful because Sisinta still finds herself confined to Lower Quith.

You believe the legend then? That Elyon once ruled all of Quith?

There is evidence to suggest it. None of my ancestors have clear memories of that time, but then again, our clan was in a panic over the Silver Blood curse back then. Memories passed down do fade with each generation, so I cannot discount his existence.

Airith thought about that information as he took some dried meat from his pack. *What are you going to eat?*

I'm not hungry. I ate five cows last week. Kappin stretched out his claws and shook his skin to even out the kinks in his scale armor.

Airith sat next to the dragon and watched the mesmerizing flames curl around the blackened tree. After Airith ate, he leaned against Kappin's warm side and closed his eyes. Just as he was drifting off, he asked sleepily, *How far away is Sisinta, Kappin?*

About four weeks' travel.

Airith fell asleep to the sound of Kappin's great heart beating.

CHAPTER TWELVE

RANSHIRE

Flying by day and sleeping in secluded places at night, the days blended and Airith didn't care. He had nothing to worry about. Somewhere in the back of his mind were disquieting thoughts about the deadly disease he carried and the realization he was on his way to meet Sisinta, the Witch-Queen. He knew he would die if she rejected him. He pushed those thoughts to the furthest point of his mind.

The only thing he held onto was Kappin. The dragon was an anchor in a sea of chaotic troubles and worry. They were both in the same situation and knowing that helped Airith contain his panic. Kappin taught him how to protect his mind and not let things leak out when his emotions were high.

One day, during early morning travel preparations, Airith opened the sack of provisions to find only enough food for breakfast.

Can't you go without for four more days? Kappin asked when Airith told him. *We have only to cross the Dragon Mountains, and then we will be in Lower Quith.*

I'm human, Kappin. I need food or I'll die, get sick, faint, become weak—

Enough! Why humans are so weak, I will never understand. I'll place you outside the next village we pass, but I don't want to be seen. Do you have coinage?

Yes. And I could use the exercise of a good walk. I'm saddle sore.

Walking is slow and an unnecessary waste of energy.

Airith laughed at Kappin's forthrightness, he was growing fond of the dragon's quirks.

After Kappin dropped him off, Airith started walking at a brisk pace. At first, he hid by the side of the road whenever he saw someone coming. An irrational fear formed—he would be recognized and sent home. Eventually, the nonsensical fear made him angry—he was too far from home for anyone to know him. He was not afraid of anyone, and he was not going to hide anymore. After that, he made better time. People walked by him without a second glance.

A small sign declared the village to be Ranshire—a large fishing town on the banks of the Enduring River. Most men of the village and their sons were out fishing on the river, leaving the roads uncrowded. The morning air was foggy, and the only people about were some children playing in the streets and fishermen's wives leaning out their windows, chatting with one another.

Airith found a general goods vendor and bought an extra rope and a large piece of leather. Kappin's sharp, rough scales had pierced holes throughout the saddle blanket. The leather would create a more durable saddle. Across the street, he entered a butcher's shop and bought a freshly-killed chicken and strips of dried meat.

The squat butcher eyed Airith as he paid. "Newcomer, right? Do you know the tale of the Ranshire Paladall?"

"I don't," Airith admitted.

"In Ranshire, one can never see the other side of the river, even on a clear summer's day. A Paladall once called the fog to protect him and hide from his enemies. The fog remains to this day." The butcher gave a knowing nod, as if the legend was fact.

Airith politely thanked him and left.

Curious if the tale were true, he walked to the river and stood at the end of the pier. The fog was so thick, he could barely see the water lapping against the shore.

For a moment, Airith felt homesick and lost. His heart ached in his chest. He never thought he would miss his family. But he had gone too far now to turn back. On the other side of the river were the Dragon Mountains and then Lower Quith. Beyond that? He didn't know.

A prickle on the back of his neck gave him the impression he was being watched. His eyes darted about to see who it was. A man stood a few feet away. Airith couldn't see his features in the mist, and dread filled him. An involuntary shudder shook his body—the man was looking into his soul, seeing past the careful walls of self-preservation Airith had built.

Airith ran. Back down the pier and through the streets. He slowed only when he was out of the town, and even then, he glanced back nervously several times to make sure he hadn't been followed. Why was he always running away?

Airith struggled to rid himself of the eerie feeling the man could see both through him and into him. Had the man been real at all? The figure could have been merely a figment of his imagination brought on by the mist and the butcher's tale.

You were gone for three hours, where have you been? Kappin mind-spoke when Airith returned.

Airith didn't reply. He placed the provisions into the pack and mounted Kappin.

The dragon didn't press him.

***

Late the following day, they reached the mountains. As they flew over the first few foothills, Kappin said, *Guard your mind. Perhaps we can cross into Lower Quith without anyone noticing. When I first crossed, I went around by way of the sea, but that would take us a month off course, and I don't know how much life I have left in me.*

Who would notice us? Airith asked.

There prowl many a colored dragon within these mountains. If you search with your mind, you will feel theirs. But I think it would be wise to focus all your energy on blocking everything—your thoughts leak sometimes. Remember, I'm one of the cursed, and you are a traitor to them. They'll probably catch us, and we'll probably die.

That's not a promising prediction. Airith squirmed.

I figured you'd want the truth, Kappin responded.

Despite Kappin's predictions, they remained unnoticed the whole way.

Airith did his best to empty his mind and think of nothing while simultaneously holding up mental barriers. A few feather-light touches of other consciousnesses brushed against his, but they glided over, like water in a stream splitting and rejoining on the other side of a stone.

At the end of the day, they were still flying over mountains. White-capped peaks with lush green foothills covered the landscape as far as the eye could see. Kappin did not stop for the night, and when the sun rose, Airith spotted a break in the mountains. Not long after, Kappin soared through the gap and over the Ammon Plains.

Airith thought he would be glad to leave the mountains, and he was at first. But he soon tired of nothing but flat grasslands with herds of wild horses, deer, and wolves. The occasional tree stood alone, twisted into strange shapes by savage winds. Rare villages dotted the terrain with farms. At one point, he noticed black cat-like creatures running low and fast, headed toward the mountains.

What are those creatures? Airith asked Kappin.

Vagwhar, probably carrying out Sisinta's orders.

Airith watched the black cats until they vanished into the horizon. *Where in Quith is Sisinta?* he asked.

In Baleful, the capital city of Ironcall. Ironcall is on the shores of the Calldian Sea, where the land is fertile.

Airith appreciated the geography lessons. His tutor had barely touched on Lower Quith, claiming Airith would never need to travel there. It was home to savages and Sisinta-worshippers.

Gradually, the ocean came into view on their left. Sandy beaches and rocky cliffs bordered the hazy gray-blue line. Fishing villages dotted the seaboard.

Baleful is not exactly a pleasant name, Airith remarked.

Sisinta named it to strike fear into her enemies. I don't know its previous name. We will reach it soon.

To Kappin, "soon" could mean an hour or a week. So, Airith was surprised to see the outskirts of the city after only a few minutes. Its name was fitting. Overgrown fields and the ruins of farmhouses bore witness to its past prosperity.

It doesn't look very well-off, Airith observed.

Wherever Sisinta goes, the army follows. And the army consumes the land. The land is there to serve Sisinta, not the other way around. If she is satisfied with her hosts, she might cast spells to revive the land. She also handsomely rewards any nobles who support her.

A large encampment surrounded the city. From the sky, Airith thought the soldiers looked more like ants than men. They appeared defenseless and insignificant.

Then, he felt the minds of the dragons. Several hundred impressions battered Airith's mind, and he struggled to protect himself from the onslaught. A moment later, he saw them, silver dragons arranged in ranks, smallest to largest, in the field on the far side of the city. He could read their awareness of the outcast dragon and his rider in the sky above them.

Kappin banked sharply and began to descend at an alarming rate. Airith clenched his thighs and clung to the dragon's neck spikes with both hands to keep his seat.

What are you doing? Airith mentally shouted.

Kappin leveled out moments before colliding with one of the largest dragons. He easily glided over the dragons' heads and landed gracefully before the city gates.

CHAPTER THIRTEEN

THE WITCH-QUEEN

Atop Kappin, Airith saw his dragon was a full head shorter than most of the others. All but the largest dragon backed away. Was this the dragon Kappin had been forced to fight? No wonder Kappin had lost. Airith had difficulty separating his anger from the dragon's.

Not dead yet, are you, weakling? I thought I told you never to return! the giant dragon growled through mindspeak for everyone to hear.

Kappin's nose rose haughtily. *I have a blood oath with this human. I no longer answer to you.* Kappin stated the dragon's name.

Airith tried to arrange the syllables in his head, but the dragon's name was more of a concept than a specific word. Swift flight, shivering winds, moonlight, the scent of iron, the scent of a fresh kill. His human mind couldn't comprehend how all those colliding images and impressions came together as one. He decided to give up trying.

Impossible! Silver dragons do not make oaths with men. Our loyalties lie with the Witch-Queen. The large dragon circled Kappin, sneering with a gaping maw populated by too many teeth.

I never gave my oath to Sisinta, remember? You robbed me of that opportunity. Kappin's rage simmered like a clamoring pot about to boil.

Airith jumped from Kappin's back and spoke aloud the speech he had discussed with Kappin, "This dragon is bound to me. We have sealed our vow with blood." He dramatically removed the leather glove concealing his infected hand and raised his arm into the sunlight. Its gray tint glittered.

He is cursed! a dragon hissed.

Did the human know the risks before you tricked him into making this vow? the large dragon demanded. *Did you explain he was more likely to die than succeed? Have you told him that your lives—and deaths—are now linked? You have condemned the human to an early death.* The dragon faced his kin and mocked Kappin.

But there was something wrong about the tone of the dragon's speech. Airith was by no means an expert on mind-speaking, but he sensed perhaps the dragon was jealous or afraid.

Airith attempted to mentally address the assembly, but the multitude of minds and the strength of their walls led him to retreat. He decided to speak aloud, "I was not tricked when I made the vow." Airith focused entirely on the truth of that statement, not the partial lie. Kappin hadn't warned him of the Silver Blood until it was too late, but he had willingly sworn the oath of friendship with Kappin. He didn't need to prove to anyone that the traditional mingling of their blood was done before the fact.

The large dragon snorted but didn't seem to have caught the lie Airith mentally strained to conceal. He addressed Airith this time, *I am a captain of the Cala Drani, Sisinta's dragons. Who are you to speak to me?*

Airith laughed.

The large dragon hissed and took a threatening step forward.

Airith felt no fear. With rueful acceptance, he acknowledged he owed his father and brothers thanks for that. He'd practiced suppressing his fear so many times that sometimes, it really did simply ... vanish. He mind-spoke, *You don't deserve to know my name, but rest assured, this is not the last you'll hear from me. I will not forget how you have treated my dragon. Now, will someone direct me to Sisinta?*

Not one dragon spoke.

Agitated, Kappin pounced on a younger dragon who was grinning at him. He easily knocked the smaller dragon on its back. *Where is Sisinta staying, you insignificant bug?* Kappin hissed.

"There is no need for violence!" A young man a few years older than Airith ran into the dragon assembly. His hair and eyes were a washed-out, dull shade of brown.

Bland, Airith thought while he pulled on his glove.

The young man wore a black tunic with Sisinta's emblem on the back: a silver dragon gripping a map of Quith in its claw. "My name is Vobad," he said. "I am Sisinta's messenger. You two," he shoved a finger in Airith's and Kappin's direction, "weakling and boy, Sisinta is expecting you. Come with me." The messenger turned toward the city gate.

Airith frowned. He was not a boy, and Kappin was not a weakling.

Kappin privately pleaded with him, *He's a personal servant of Sisinta, Airith. You want to be in his good graces.* Kappin prodded Airith forward. *Come on.*

Airith grudgingly followed Vobad.

When they passed through the city gates, passersby stared and frowned.

Aren't they used to seeing dragons around here? Airith glared back.

The dragons keep to the encampment. The citizens do not like dwelling so close to us. We tolerate each other only because Sisinta demands it. The exceptions are the Black Knights who ride the dragons into battle.

Airith observed many soldiers among the citizens of Baleful. They gathered in clusters on street corners and spilled out of taverns. A couple of them seemed to have ganged up on a local carpet merchant and were close to blows.

When they are not at war, they have nothing to do, Kappin explained. *They spend most of their time drinking. They are entitled to free lodging and sustenance by order of Sisinta.*

Beggars lurked in the alleyways and eyed passersby from darkened doorways. Airith wrinkled his nose at the smell of the filth. The people of the city did not trust anyone. They warily glanced sideways at one another as they passed. Even when they greeted friends, they did so with distrust and an apprehensive vigilance behind their smiles.

As the trio approached the middle of the city, the houses and streets became cleaner. Vobad led them past twelve guards into the courtyard of the keep. Vobad motioned Kappin and Airith to stay. They watched him cross the lawn to an opulent tent. Its sky-blue curtains fluttered helplessly, unable to escape their pole tethers. Inside, Airith spotted various officers and lords congregated around a table in an intense discussion. Their voices didn't carry far enough for him to make out anything more than murmurs and cadences.

Vobad waited near the gathering until it dispersed, leaving only a few attendants and guards. He approached a tall woman with piercing blue eyes, glittering like ice. Sisinta. Her eyes, black hair, and bright red mouth were a striking contrast to her pale skin. She wore a pure white robe that fell to her feet. Despite her pale complexion, she appeared to be the very embodiment of energy and life. She smiled darkly in Airith's direction as Vobad spoke to her in a low voice.

"Come here," she called to Airith.

He took a deep breath and glanced at Kappin for courage. The dragon watched Sisinta nervously. Airith took slow, deliberate steps toward the tent and forced himself to meet her gaze.

"Give us a moment." She waved Vobad and her attendants away. They took a short walk across the courtyard and out of hearing distance. Sisinta appraised Airith. Amusement glinted in her eyes. "You are young, Airith, but I will tell you something. It is the young who own the future."

"How do you know my name?" Airith asked warily. He tried to remember all the terrible things he'd been told that she'd done, but his mind blanked.

When she met his gaze, an image of comparison rose in his mind unbidden—a black wolf, newly risen from the kill, blood on her lips. Deadly and beautiful. Was his own mind making sense of her, or had she projected into his thoughts?

"You told me your name, and I have spies everywhere," Sisinta responded coolly.

"I didn't tell you my name," Airith insisted.

"You have much to learn, Master Airith." She smiled her dark smile again. "Come now, you will learn all the important things in time. Give me your arm." Sisinta held out her hand and Airith very slowly stretched out his. She grasped him by the elbow, yanked off the leather glove, and pushed up his sleeve. In the sunlight, his silver skin was almost as bright as Kappin's scales. She dropped his arm and returned his glove. "I accept your terms."

"My terms? But you don't know what they are!" Airith's brow wrinkled.

"Oh, I know the desires of all men's hearts. I've decided to give you yours. Prolonged life? Power? Acknowledgement? A place in this world? Love?" Sisinta smiled winsomely and tugged the collar of his tunic into place. Her fingers brushed against his collarbone, and he shivered. A deep, damp chill washed over him. On a cold day, the cold would induce trepidation, but on a hot day it was relief. This day was hot.

Power rippled off her—barely perceptible, except when her form shimmered ever so slightly. Was he imagining it? Or was she really brimming with an overwhelming force of magic?

"And a Shadow for Kappin," Airith added meekly.

"That I cannot do. I made a pact with the Cala Drani. I do not interfere with their ways. We can compromise, however. This blood vow between the two of you can serve as a link. Both of your lives will be sustained."

Airith sighed with relief. Kappin was all he had now, and the dragon's death would leave him alone and surrounded by strangers. Plus, he had to admit, he cared for the dragon.

"You will be great, Airith. I am willing to place some faith in you." She waved Vobad over. "See to it he gets food, drink, and new clothes. Bring him to me at sunset." She entered the keep with her attendants following at a respectful distance.

Embarrassment descended as Airith realized his clothing was dirty and travel-worn.

"Come on, boy." Vobad frowned and gestured for Airith to follow.

"I'm not a boy. You're not much older than I am."

Vobad stopped midstride. "What?"

"I'm not a boy, and Kappin is not a weakling."

"Ha, ha, ha!" Vobad's brown eyes filled with mirth, making their dull sheen almost worth noting.

"Weaklings do not have names."

Vobad stopped laughing and grabbed Airith by the front of his tunic. "Learn your place and don't speak to me like that again." He shoved Airith away and started toward the gate again.

Airith, Kappin warned, *you shouldn't have—*

Airith tackled Vobad. The messenger fell hard onto his face. They became a tangle of fists and limbs. Kappin roared in protest. People in the street and the guards at the gate gathered, yelling advice and cheering on the fight. Two guard captains were trying to control the situation and kept giving contradictory orders. In the end, Kappin ended the fight by holding down each of them with a claw. Airith fought furiously against the weight of it, but Vobad just grunted angrily.

"Stop!" Everyone startled violently at the sound of Kappin's thundering spoken voice.

Airith ceased struggling and silence fell over the crowd. After a moment, Airith demanded, "Let me up!"

Kappin allowed him to push the claw off his chest.

Standing, Airith brushed off the dust. He tasted something warm and metallic in his mouth and quickly wiped away the small trickle of blood. It appeared red but he was afraid someone might notice the silver flecks. "You hit hard," Airith grudgingly admitted to Vobad.

"You're worse," Vobad replied as Kappin let him up. He had a black eye and bruised knuckles.

"What's the meaning of this?" a gruff voice demanded.

"General Nadmen!" Fear widened Vobad's eyes.

The general was a tall, older man dressed in full black armor and carrying his helmet. A scar from the top corner of his right eye to the corner of his lip caused him to squint and smirk.

Cringing, Vobad jerked his arm across his chest in salute. "It's my fault, General, sir."

"That's not true! It's my fault, I tackled him," Airith interjected.

"I will take the blame, Airith," Vobad hissed in frustration.

"Blame me, sir," Airith snapped.

"Well ..." the general mumbled, glancing uncertainly at the watching crowd. His gaze alighted on Kappin, and he burst out, "What's a dragon doing in the city?"

"Sisinta requested his presence. I was just escorting them back to the encampment, sir!" Vobad snapped to attention again.

"I'll ask Sisinta. And I'll deal with you later!" The general's bellow sounded squeaky and worn compared to Kappin's roar.

What's with you two? Kappin silently asked Airith, disgusted. *One moment you're ready to kill each other, the next, best of friends.*

Sisinta gave her word I will have a Shadow. Our bond ensures your life will be sustained as well. Vobad's no threat, so I may as well just let him be. Airith shrugged.

I will never understand humans. Kappin sighed. After a pause, he asked, *The Witch-Queen really promised you all that?*

Nearly word for word. Airith grinned at his friend.

Kappin conveyed a sense of overwhelming relief.

Airith touched the dragon's shoulder, unsure what else to do in response.

Now the general was yelling at the crowd to disperse, threatening to personally feed them to the crows. People left one by one, murmuring as they went. General Nadmen turned back to the two culprits again. "What are you waiting for? Go! Now!"

I'm going to fly out, Kappin informed Airith.

Airith nodded. *I'll meet you at the encampment.*

Kappin drew back his silver-white wings. With two powerful upward strokes, he shot into the sky.

Vobad ran out of the courtyard.

Airith followed at his leisure. After he passed the guards, Airith smiled and called back to the general, "Glad to have met you, General Nadmen!"

Vobad was waiting for him, brown eyes narrowed. "What took you so long?"

"Just saying goodbye to the General." Airith was still smiling to himself. He'd met and made a deal with the Witch-Queen without dying. If what Kappin had told him was true, his curse was unique in a human, and the Shadow would give him power.

"I'll take you to the encampment." Vobad motioned Airith to follow.

As they walked, Airith asked, "How did you come to join Sisinta?"

"My father was a soldier, so I am too. I have been a messenger since I was ten. Sisinta might promote me soon ... hopefully."

"Is that all you do? Sit around hoping for a promotion? That's pathetic." Airith snorted with disdain.

"Why? You have a better idea?" Vobad growled.

"I'm not going to answer to anyone but Sisinta. I have something only I can offer, and I will settle for nothing less than what I want."

"Really?" Vobad grunted dryly. "You are going to make some dangerous enemies with that attitude among the generals and captains who could suggest your promotion to Sisinta." Vobad shook his head. "Airith, we are barely men. Maybe in a few years we could be something, but for now, we have to wait."

"I don't believe that. It's the young who own the future," Airith quoted.

"That sounds great as a slogan, but when you're striving for years to rise in the ranks, simply wanting something better won't make it happen. Patience and perseverance, friends in high places, Sisinta's favor, that's what works around here." Vobad waved his hand dismissively.

They passed through the city gates unhindered by the sentries.

Thousands of tents, wagons, horses, campfires, and men spread in every direction. Airith remembered what it had looked like from the air—little ants running around small brown blots. Now on the ground, he swelled with pride at the thought of being part of it. Men shouting to one another, and horses' whinnying echoed in the open air. The smell of garlic and sage, food cooking over a thousand fires, reminded Airith he was very hungry.

Vobad led him to a tent near the edge of the camp.

"You can stay here with Sadgal." Vobad indicated an old soldier sitting beside the fire in front of the tent. "He'll not bother you. I'll come get you when Sisinta asks. Oh, and I'll be back with clean clothes."

Airith thanked Vobad, and the messenger disappeared into the sea of tents and men. Airith nodded to Sadgal in greeting, but the old man barely gave him a glance. A few minutes later, Vobad returned with black trousers and a tunic embroidered with silver.

Kappin descended swiftly and landed by Airith at the edge of the camp. A small tremor shook the tent when he touched ground, and Sadgal flailed his arms in surprise. All the soldiers nearby moved away, shooting Kappin nervous and fearful glances.

"The dragon's camp is on the other side of the city." Sadgal grunted and retreated into his tent.

Airith was hungry. He would have liked to hunt, to settle both his stomach and his nerves, but he didn't want Sisinta to ask for him while he was away, and the likelihood of game in this man-trampled countryside was minimal. Vobad had forgotten to bring him food, so he ate the remaining provisions from their journey. He changed into the clothes Vobad had brought him and buckled Cala Man to his belt. Airith sat against Kappin's warm side.

Kappin, he asked, *do you think we did right by coming here?*

What else could we have done? Give up and die? I suppose I'm one to talk, I have considered it would be a release to die, to leave behind the worry that each moment will be my last.

I don't know what I'd do without you. I would have no reason to live, Airith mourned. *I promise, Kappin, as soon as I'm able, I will link our days. If you die, I die.*

Kappin lifted his head and fixed Airith with a deep, encompassing stare. *Does my life mean that much to you?*

Yes. My father gave me up for dead long ago. I won't make the same mistake. Your life deserves acknowledgment. Together, our lives will impact the world.

Airith, Kappin said gravely, *I would not die in peace knowing that I would drag you down with me.*

Let's cease this talk of death. It's a long way off. After a thoughtful pause, Airith declared, *I'm going to do everything in my power to gain the highest rank possible. One day, I want my father to hear my name and fear me. When I rise, you will also.*

"Airith!" Vobad approached again. "Sisinta will see you now."

"What about Kappin?" Airith asked.

"He can wait in the keep courtyard."

Airith glanced uncertainly at his dragon.

Go, Airith, and change the course of both our fates, Kappin said.

CHAPTER FOURTEEN

A PRISONER OF THE SHADOWS

Vobad delivered Airith to a guard dressed in Sisinta's livery. The man barely acknowledged him as he led him inside through corridors, up staircases, and through multiple doorways until they reached a pair of double doors with two guards standing watch. They solemnly let Airith enter alone.

The room was a long rectangle with a grand fireplace at the far end. The floor was worn oak, and the walls were gray stone. The room was utterly empty except the fire snapping in the fireplace. Sisinta stood beside it. The golden glow of the sinking sun shone through three windows along the west wall. Through those windows, Airith caught sight of Kappin in the courtyard below. He could feel the tug of the dragon's mind. The doors closed with a crash behind him. Sisinta stared at the sunset.

"Come here." Her tone suggested she expected obedience.

A shiver of anticipation streaked down his spine. He started toward her, every step ringing through the floorboards and echoing off the walls. When he finally reached her, he stopped a few feet away and waited for what seemed an eternity.

The sight of her cold, breathtaking beauty stunned him again. Her piercing gaze suggested she was dangerous in a thrilling way that sent his heart racing. He could understand why so many followed her to death and glory.

"Seven years of prolonged life for you and your dragon, power, and acknowledgment in exchange for one of my Shadows. Airith Shaver, do you accept this contract with me?" Sisinta asked. When she turned and looked at him, his breath caught. "And ... do you, here and now, pledge your allegiance to me?"

Images filtered through his mind of Kenta's smiling face, his mother's loving eyes, and the many times he had shared thoughts and words with Kaydin and Meredith that he had never dared to voice with anyone else. Returning to them was impossible. Airith forced the memories into the deepest recesses of his mind. "Yes."

"Kneel," she commanded.

Airith fell to his knees and stared at the lines and whorls in the wood, refusing to look up even if the roof and walls fell on him.

Sisinta drew a sword from a sheath at her side.

His heart began to pound. She wouldn't kill him now, would she? All the stories said she was ruthless.

Her blade changed from silver to black.

He refused to be ruled by the fear snaking down his spine.

"I now knight thee a Black Knight of the Order of Sisinta." She touched one shoulder, then the other with the black blade.

As soon as she lifted the sword, darkness erupted around him, billowing across his vision. He fell into nothing. Deep, penetrating darkness. Complete and utter silence. His body slammed into the ground. He was blind in the dark but could feel the floor against his cheek and touch its surface. It was smooth and cold. Gingerly, he rose. Silence rang in his ears and his eyes watered as he strained to see in the nothingness.

A whispering voice approached, bouncing off the walls of a huge cavern.

Airith shivered. He was naked in the dark.

The whispering voice inched closer every moment—low, rasping, and raw.

Something brushed against him, and he leapt away, stifling a cry.

The thing stopped before him. The voice asked, "Why have you disturbed the Shadows of the deep?"

"I-I have come t-to ask for your help," Airith stammered.

"Mmm ..." the Shadow purred.

Airith clenched his fists to calm himself and carefully chose what to say next. "I have been cursed with Silver Blood." Confidence growing, he continued, "Give me your power and grant me and my dragon longer life."

"Hmm," the thing murmured. "You want power and long life?" Mockery tinged its tone.

"Without you, Kappin and I will die!" Airith yelled into the dark.

The Shadow laughed, long and loud. Airith grit his teeth against the sound. "You are young, angry, and strong. That is good. I will give you what you ask, seven more years of life, but you must first sell me your soul."

"That sounds like a bad idea." Doubt gathered at the edges of his resolve.

"It's a small price to pay for what you ask. You're not doing anything with it, are you?" It stroked his hair, barely moving the strands, but it made him weak in the knees.

"One doesn't really *do* anything with a soul." Airith scrambled to hold onto his faculties but found he could barely form a sentence with the Shadow breathing down his neck.

"Exactly! Give me yours, and you lose something you don't need to gain what you do."

"How?" Airith asked.

"By saying yes," it drew out the word, sibilating even more than before.

Airith paused. But why? He'd decided before getting to this point, hadn't he? "Yes," Airith said, nodding resolutely.

"So be it."

A presence flooded his mind, dug deep into his memories, found all his emotions, and discovered all his fears. He clutched his head and shrieked, trying to fight, but the harder he fought, the more it burned.

It riffled through his emotions like a deck of cards, tossing each one in his face before he had a chance to recover from the last.

Too much. Too much anger, too much hurt, too much sorrow, too much pain.

He pulled his hair and screamed.

The Shadow sorted through his memories, his wants, his anger, his ambitions, and any love he had left. The being forced Airith to experience each one before ripping it from him.

Airith groaned and surrendered. He fell to his knees and allowed the creature to do what it wanted. He had no strength to move and even struggled to stay on his knees.

He was truly alone.

Airith closed his eyes, and gradually, the pain in his head faded, then disappeared completely. It was replaced with a sudden knowledge of the things he *could* do, power pumping like adrenaline through his veins.

Now, he was not alone.

When he opened his eyes, he was surprised to find himself still kneeling in the hall before Sisinta.

She helped him to his feet. "What is your name?"

A voice in his head replied, "Tyrannus." It took a moment to realize he had said it aloud.

"Thus you shall now be known. Airith Shaver is dead."

Tyrannus became aware of Kappin's mind. He was frantic. The dragon had experienced some of the turmoil Airith had been through when the Shadow had entered his mind.

All is well, Kappin, I'm fine, he assured. Then, he felt Kappin's relief.

"Go and rest. You are to stay here in the keep," Sisinta told Tyrannus.

The doors opened and the guard waited for him.

"He will lead you to your room," Sisinta said. "I look forward to seeing your progress and whether you fulfil your ambitions, Tyrannus."

★★★

Tyrannus woke in a real bed the next morning. He lay for some time thinking over the events of the previous evening. He had no trouble changing his name to Tyrannus—a new life, a new name. Maybe he'd shorten it to Tyran. Airith Shaver was dead, and he didn't mourn his passing.

Banging against the shutters drew his attention. He reluctantly left the warm bed. As soon as he'd unbolted the shutters, Kappin thrust his head through. The dragon mind-spoke, *Where have you been? I knew you were lazy, but really, should you be sleeping the day away?* Was Kappin smirking?

Tyran grinned at his dragon. *I will be coming out soon. Give me a few minutes.*

"Hey! Are you coming?"

Tyran looked to the ground where Vobad stood next to the dragon. Tyran waved in acknowledgment and closed the shutters. Not long after, he joined them in the courtyard.

"I've been told to take you to the blacksmith for a suit of armor," Vobad informed him.

He led Tyran to one of the gray stone buildings built into the walls surrounding the city's keep. The door was open to the cool morning breeze, but as soon as they entered, a wall of heat from the forge caused sweat to break out on their faces.

"The blacksmiths here make everything in the armory," Vobad explained.

"What have we here?" a blacksmith asked as he wiped sooty hands on a rag.

"Tyrannus, this is Jackdowel, head blacksmith." To the blacksmith he said, "Sisinta wants a suit of armor for Tyrannus."

"What rank?"

Tyran recited, "A Black Knight under the Order of Sisinta."

"She made you a Black Knight!" Vobad's mouth dropped open.

"Yes ... what is that?" Tyran asked hesitantly.

"Black Knights are independent of all ranks and answer only to their commanding captain and Sisinta. They are the ones chosen to bond with and ride the Cala Drani into battle. A privileged few become the Witch-Queen's elite guard. Being assigned a Black Knight so suddenly will put you in a precarious position in the ranks. There are many who will strongly object." Vobad paused to breathe after his rapid explanation.

Tyran was pleased—Sisinta *did* have faith in him—faith he could defend his rank and shoulder the responsibility she'd entrusted to him.

"I have a suit of armor for a Black Knight. I'll have to repair and modify it, but it should fit." The blacksmith led them through a door in his workshop.

In the armory, chainmail, swords, battle axes, knives, daggers, maces, spears, and shields—all stamped with Sisinta's emblem—lined the walls. There was armor for horses, dragons, hunting dogs, vagwhar, and other animals trained for war.

"Here." The blacksmith indicated a full suit of black armor on a platform in a corner. "Try it on, and I will see what adjustments need to be made. Don't worry about the hole in the breastplate, I can repair it."

Tyran eyed the puncture wound and its inward curving edges. The previous owner had been impaled. The cold, clammy hand of fear ran its fingers up his spine. But after a moment, he relaxed and grinned. Being impaled wasn't something he needed to worry about, he was invincible after all.

Tyran placed his sword to the side as Vobad helped him don the armor. The armor had been forged from an unfamiliar type of black steel. Vobad handed Tyran the helmet. Two side pieces almost touched at the chin and another piece came down the center to the end of his nose. The armor was adorned with a thin line of gold along the seams and edges and formed Sisinta's emblem on the back.

"Modifications to the breastplate and arm bracers, plus repairing the damage shouldn't take too long," the blacksmith said.

Tyran's eyes heated. A voice spoke then. It wasn't Tyran's voice, and it wasn't his words, "Unnecessary."

Vobad and the blacksmith took a step back.

Tyran closed his eyes. The armor shifted, shrinking and expanding to fit his form perfectly. The metal groaned and strained as the gaping hole filled in and smoothed over.

Vobad's jaw hung open, and the blacksmith eyed Tyran nervously. "We had better get you a sword." The blacksmith inched toward the wall of swords.

"I have one." Tyran picked up Cala Man in its sheath. He buckled it to his waist with practiced ease.

"May I see it?" the blacksmith asked.

Tyran's fingers hesitated, then drew his sword and handed it over.

"This is an amazing sword. May I borrow it to study its craftmanship?"

"No." Tyran shook his head firmly. "Even if you tried, you'd fail to copy it, not because you are unskilled but because it was blessed. Cala Man was welded by one of my ancestors in the Blood Battle. I cannot consent to diminishing its glory by making more like it." Tyran purposely left out which side his ancestor had fought for, a detail that amused the Shadow. Its encroaching alien presence was like a snake that had settled into his mind and curled its length around his thoughts. Tyran grimaced.

"Very well." The blacksmith returned Cala Man. "'Tis a pity there are not more like it. Take the armor—it is yours."

Tyrannus removed the armor and carried it to his room in the keep with Vobad's help.

Vobad paused at the door on his way out. "I don't know how you managed to convince Sisinta *and* a Shadow to grant you such a high rank and power, but I think you might end up doing some of those things you said after all."

CHAPTER FIFTEEN

UNWELCOME REVELATIONS

"Gah!" Kaydin snorted in frustration. "Swan's gone rusty!"

Meredith looked up from a book on the myths of Quith. "You must have forgotten to clean it when you put it away last."

"I haven't had cause to take it out since Airith left. It's been rusting for a full two months!" He growled in disgust and buffed the blade with an abrasive cloth.

Meredith ducked her head into the book again. Her gaze slid over the curly letters and illustrations in the margins. A moment ago, she'd been engrossed in the account of the extinct keepers of vagwhar. Now the finer points of the story were lost on her.

"What do you suppose he's doing now?" she murmured.

Still applying his efforts to grant Swan its former luster, Kaydin replied, "Hunting, most likely."

"You're probably right." She sighed.

"Master Kaydin? Lady Meredith?" A servant girl stood at the library door. "You have a visitor. Lady Kenta Shaver here to see you." The girl gave a quick curtsy and admitted Kenta.

Kenta entered with graceful strides. Her long blonde hair was up in a large, braided bun and she wore a bright blue riding dress, the same shade as her eyes. "It's been a while since we last met." Kenta curtsied.

She's so elegant. Meredith caught the stray thought from her brother. She couldn't argue with him—Airith's sister moved like a ripple in water.

"Yes, it's been too long." Kaydin bowed, one arm across his chest and the other behind his back.

Meredith resisted the urge to roll her eyes.

"Please take a seat." Kaydin indicated a large velvet couch across from Meredith's chair.

"Thank you." After settling, she took a deep breath and began, "I'm afraid this isn't simply a social call. I wish to know if you have any idea of my brother's whereabouts."

"Cowin's or Shar's?" Kaydin frowned.

"Airith's."

"Isn't he at the king's court?" Meredith asked, eyebrows raised.

"I'm afraid not. Until yesterday, we thought he was. My mother sent him a letter through my uncle with whom Airith was to stay. Yesterday, she received a reply saying Airith had never arrived. Apparently, my brother sent our uncle a letter two months ago claiming our father had changed his mind, and he wasn't coming."

He lied about going? Meredith and Kaydin mentally shared the same shocked revelation.

"H-He never said anything to us about it," Meredith stammered.

"He often complained about having to go but never indicated that he wouldn't," Kaydin added.

"He gave no hint at all what his plans could be?" Kenta's eyes dimmed and her lips turned down.

"We did think it was odd he left Pallindo with us," Meredith told her.

"Pallindo is here?" Kenta's eyes lit up.

"Yes. I'll get the note he left." Meredith retrieved her sketchbook from the writing desk. Skimming the pages, she found where the note marked a drawing of Airith in a dramatic fighting stance. It was the best likeness she'd ever done of him. Meredith studied the determined expression in his dark eyes before snapping the book shut and handing the note to Kenta. How could someone they'd known for only seven months have impacted her so much?

Kenta's brimming blue eyes swept over the page. "He was supposed to take the horse with him!"

"I'm afraid Pallindo isn't doing well," Kaydin said quietly. "He's very old, and the stablemaster says he might not live much longer."

"Airith loves that horse." Kenta quickly wiped away her tears.

Meredith noted with a hint of envy that Kenta remained beautiful even when she cried. But she couldn't harbor any ill feelings toward Airith's sister—it wasn't a crime to be beautiful.

"Why would Airith just disappear like that?" Meredith whispered. A miserable truth sank in—he'd lied. What else had he not told them?

"My father and brothers haven't exactly been easy on him." Kenta stood. "Forgive me, but I must tell my mother the news."

After Kenta had taken her leave, the twins sat in stunned silence for a minute.

Do you think he's dead or lost? Maybe he'll come home eventually?

There's no point in asking those questions because there's no way to find out the answers, Kaydin said.

You mean we'll just have to spend the rest of our lives wondering where he's gone?

Why are you asking me? I don't know. Kaydin sighed and added, *"Sorry, I know you're worried. I am too. There is someone who knows where he is, though.*

Hope lit in her chest. *Really? Who?*

Elyon. Remember the saying, 'Elyon knows all'?

Well, I wish he'd come and tell us.

CHAPTER SIXTEEN

PARTING

Two years and ten months later

"You're going to do what?" Thia Tieren sat by the largest window in the solarium of her father-in-law's castle. Rain fell in torrents over Ironcall and dripped in streams down the windowpane.

Her husband, Randarin, was pacing. He stopped to check the door handle was locked, and then glanced around nervously before dropping to his knees before her. He whispered earnestly, "I'll be gone only as long as it takes to find out if the rumors are true."

"We've been married only three months, and you want to go off gallivanting after something you aren't even sure exists?" Thia hissed.

"What if Elyon does exist? What if I had a chance to save my people but didn't take it?" He rose and paced again. He clenched his fists and turned back to her. "I can't stand it, Thia! My people are dying! Sisinta is stealing their food and destroying their peace!" He struggled to keep his tone down.

"Why don't you let your father worry about those things?" Thia pleaded.

Randarin didn't stop his pacing. "He's getting old and tired. He's told me he thinks it best to allow Sisinta to do what she wishes, and he'll clean up the country after she leaves. Yet, in the meantime, the people die!"

"Your father has a point," Thia muttered.

Randarin stopped and stared in disbelief.

She hurried to explain, "Rand, think about it—who could ever stop Sisinta? If you start a rebellion, what do you think will happen to you? She would easily crush it then execute you just like all the others."

"I thought you of all people would understand, Thia."

Randarin's dismay and the hurt in his eyes shamed her. She had failed him. He counted on her encouragement, yet she refuted his most passionate beliefs. Thia knew she was being selfish in asking him to stay in Baleful—she wanted him to herself. Instead, she had to share him with all of Ironcall. Sometimes, she wished he wasn't so dedicated to his country.

Thia met his eyes and sighed. "What if Elyon does exist? Why would he help us?"

Hands clasped behind him, Randarin walked to the solarium window. "I'm not sure. Maybe if I could explain to him the state of our nation, he would aid us." The desperation on Randarin's face made him look much older than his twenty-one years.

"What if you don't come back?" Thia whispered the words and tried to hide the tears welling in her eyes. The thought of losing him proved to be too much—her tears overflowed.

Randarin took her small hands and pulled her to her feet. He let her cry against his shoulder. "I promise I will come back. I promise," he whispered into her raven-black hair.

"If you're not here at court, then I don't want to stay," Thia mumbled into his shirt.

"If you want," Randarin lifted her chin, "you can stay at the old castle near the coast—the one Father gave me."

"Alone?"

"No. You can bring our servants and Faylin if you want. My sister enjoys your company. Will you keep my whereabouts a secret as long as you can? Don't even let my father know. I'll tell him I'm touring the outposts."

Thia considered briefly. Faylin was barely thirteen years old and already caught the eye of anyone who saw her. She, like her brother, sported golden hair and bright sky-blue eyes. Faylin was a mere doll to her father—something to possess and be done with as he pleased. Thia nodded in agreement. Faylin would be good company, and it would be a good idea to get her away from the court. "I will." Resolutely, she wiped away the tears.

Randarin hugged her tightly again.

"I'll miss you, though," Thia mumbled into his tear-soaked shirt.

"Me too, but I'll write to you when I can and let you know where I am. If you need to send a letter, send it through the appropriate hands and address it to 'Rand of the Islands.'"

★★★

Several minutes later, Randarin stepped into the hall and closed the heavy oak door behind him. *Elyon,* he silently pleaded, *if you really do exist, please find me.*

★★★

The rain over Ironcall persisted for three days straight. Tyran had been on patrol and only just returned to Baleful. His nerves were raw from the constant gray and gloom.

He was also perpetually damp—an annoyance. Tyrannus occasionally caused the moisture clinging to his clothes to evaporate in whisps of steam, but sometimes the Shadow refused to do what Tyran wanted. Tyrannus insisted his powers were mostly caught up in keeping Tyran alive, but Tyran believed the Shadow used that as an excuse. It enjoyed his discomfort.

Tyran watched the water pouring off the eaves in sheets from the shelter of the gatehouse across from the keep. Only he would ever go out by choice on a day like this. Somewhere in the back of his mind was the knowledge that inside the keep was a warm bath and his large, luxurious bed, but he wouldn't allow himself to be ruled by niceties and comfort. No, he would prove he was not dependent on anything, even his Shadow's abilities. He would stay in the cold and the damp and the misery until he was bored. The only problem was this gave him an inordinate time to think.

He was not deaf to the rumors about him—they had started the day he had become a Black Knight and had only grown since. His rise in rank warranted amazement: What usually took years of training, he had gained in less than a day. In one year's time, he had bested and killed General Nadman in a duel and taken his place as the commanding general of Sisinta's Black Knights. This made him the youngest knight to ever hold the title of Sisinta's second-in-command. He was aware of the hostile glances thrown his way. The nobles and high-ranking officials were jealous and afraid of him. He was Sisinta's favorite and held more power—politically and physically—than all of them combined. Tyran knew Sisinta picked favorites to cause dissension among her men and to keep the noblemen, kings, and generals from uniting and rising up against her. Only a privileged few knew of his Silver Blood—most believed the Shadow miraculously healed him time after time of his numerous, otherwise-fatal wounds. Each thin silver scar crisscrossing his body was a reminder of the battles he had fought and the disease slowly consuming him.

Being hated came with power, and Tyran had accepted it. His only real friends were Vobad and Kappin. People who said he was too young never said it to his face—he had killed men over less. Rather than punish him for murder, Sisinta applauded such ruthlessness.

I don't love killing, but it isn't unpleasant, Tyran mused. *It's life. The weak fall behind while the strong grow and command.*

Tyran leaned against the stone wall of the gatehouse, crossed his arms, and bowed his head to think. The reason for his turmoil—he decided—was entirely due to what day it was. His birthday. When he said his age out loud, it sounded so young—twenty-one. He felt a hundred or ninety was a better age to account for how much he knew and had seen in his short life. What had happened to the boy once so young and eager? He had died with Airith. No. He had died before that. Unnoticed, he had slowly faded into nothing. Tyran barely believed he had ever existed.

Lightning flashed. Above the noise of the rolling thunder, he heard running footsteps across the yard. Vobad. Tyran had promoted him from messenger to captain, and though there had been grumbling from the other generals, no one had dared to challenge him outright.

Sure enough, Vobad dashed under the cover of the gatehouse, dripping wet. His hair was matted to his head, and he shook it.

Tyran regarded his friend silently, reading Vobad's mind and why he had braved the storm to see him.

"Whew! This is some storm!" Vobad grinned despite his soggy state.

Tyran remained blank-faced.

Vobad's smile faded. "You know why I came." He sighed and his shoulders drooped. "Why do I even bother delivering messages to you when you already know them?"

"It makes me feel loved," Tyran said dryly. He pushed off the wall and stalked through the rain toward the keep.

Vobad hurried to catch up.

Inside, Tyran paused while the guards saluted him.

He realized he thought of himself as two different people: Tyran and Tyrannus. Tyrannus held the power, and Tyran enjoyed the effects. But they were the same person, or at least he thought they were. *I am thinking too much today.* Sisinta was waiting and he had to push aside all other thoughts.

He and Vobad parted ways, and Tyran made his way up staircases, down halls, and through doorways. He remembered when he had first arrived and couldn't find his way around the keep. Now it was automatic.

Tyrannus heated Tyran's skin, so by the time he reached Sisinta's apartments, his hair and clothes were dry. The guards outside Sisinta's rooms bowed, but he ignored them and pushed open the doors himself.

Sisinta stood over a table covered with papers, pens, and precious artifacts from her allies in the Outlands and campaigns throughout Lower Quith.

He regarded her with an irritated air.

She stared at him for a long moment before she spoke. "Something troubles you, Tyrannus."

Tyran averted his gaze and stood by the fire instead. "It is my only weakness, my confounded life before this." Tyran ran his fingers through his hair and stared hard into the fire, studying every coal and flame. He sighed and finally met her gaze. Her beauty never ceased to take his breath away. "I was thinking of how the day my older brother died was also the day of my birth." He wished Sisinta would cast a spell on him so he could forget the past and, if he still had one, his soul. His Shadow had refused to do it. Sisinta had told him his past had brought him there, to forget it was to forget his purpose.

Sisinta weighed him with her gaze. At last, she said, "I suppose you are wondering why I called you here."

"I confess that thought crossed my mind, but then again, you know already." Tyran chuckled. He picked up a spherical glass paperweight from Sisinta's desk and held it up to the light of the gilded lamp. A large poisonous beetle had been entombed in the glass. Its outer shell changed colors with every turn. He recognized it as a memento of Sisinta's military campaigns in the Outlands. Like the native tribes, the skittery, poisonous creatures had a nasty habit of springing out of the sand and stinging anyone who entered their territory.

"Actually, Tyrannus, it has been growing harder to read your mind."

Tyran replaced the bug. "What do you mean?"

Sisinta smiled proudly. "You've been growing mentally and physically."

Tyran struggled to hide the grin that wanted to spread over his face. "Thank you."

Sisinta put her hand on his shoulder. "You are all that I wished you would become—and more. Now, take a seat." She pointed to a chair across from hers.

Tyran obliged.

"It has come to my attention Prince Randarin has been missing for some time, six months at least. I suspect he is not simply inspecting outposts as his father claims."

"Treason, my lady?"

"It is possible. If you have learned anything at all, Tyrannus, I hope it is to trust no one. Send an informer to Randarin's estate. I believe his wife knows more than she admits."

CHAPTER SEVENTEEN

THE LETTER

Days passed slowly for Meredith and Kaydin. Several years had gone by with the occasional secretive visit from their father, but those lasted only a couple days before he would be whisked away on Council business. He occasionally sent them letters, explaining the danger of writing more frequently and why they were safer staying in Tayose. When they completed their education, they would join him.

"He knows we're almost eighteen, right?" Meredith asked her brother after one such letter. "What more does he expect Van'N to teach us?"

"I think he'll always think of us as children until we prove otherwise," Kaydin theorized.

Quire had slowly, unintentionally become their home. Meredith sometimes tried to recall memories of the winding corridors in Stellmear Castle. She did her best to remember winter evenings by the fire in her father's lap while her mother sang songs about Rackdarians and Sillians.

At least we still have each other, Mere, Kaydin would tell her whenever he caught wind of her drifting thoughts.

What is to become of us, brother? Meredith had asked him more than once.

He would smile and reply, *Great things.*

★★★

One quiet afternoon while engrossed in a book on the habits of rare birds, Meredith rounded a corner and bumped into a servant. They both yelped and plates of food crashed to the floor.

"I'm sorry." Meredith helped the maid pick up the broken dishes. They looked like Aunt Seala's lunch dishes. The food had barely been touched. Meredith bit her lip, worried by her aunt's bedridden state.

"That's all right, ma'am. Ya didn't mean no harm."

Meredith put the last of the broken pieces on the tray and returned it to the girl.

The maid turned to go, but then stopped and asked, "I know it ain't my business, ma'am, but I was wonderin', who was da letter for? Da one dat came taday. 'Twas from Boldwind."

"I didn't know a letter came." Would her father dare to send a letter directly to Quire? He'd never done so before.

"Oh. Well, sorry ta have bothered ya, ma'am." The servant girl bobbed a curtsy and left.

Letters were a rare thing in Quire Castle. Quaeor insisted he inspect all letters first for "security reasons." Meredith couldn't decide if Quaeor was malicious or nosey. Thankfully, Van'N posted and collected letters from their father in Boldwind instead of having them sent to Quire.

Dallbim sat faithfully on the small bench next to the castle's heavy oak door. His ears were keen, and his vigilance had not waned in all the years he'd worked for Aunt Seala. He smiled at Meredith.

"How are you this afternoon, Dallbim?"

"Very well, m'lady. Though, the rain drilling on the roof last night kept me up for some time. And how are you?"

Meredith smiled at her old friend. "I'm fine, thank you. The rain was rather loud, wasn't it?" She paused. "I have a question Dallbim. The letter that came today, who was it for?"

"'Tis a curious thing. It was for Master Quaeor."

"For Quaeor?"

"Yes, m'lady."

"That's odd. I didn't think he had any connection with the outside world."

"Neither did I. Another thing, the letter was from very far away. I asked the carrier, and he said it had changed hands several times."

"Well, thank you for your time, Dallbim." Meredith turned to go.

"Anything for you, m'lady."

Just then, Kaydin burst in. His face was red from the spring air, and his curly hair was in disarray. "It's a beautiful day outside, Mere. You should have come with me on the old mare." Kaydin had recently bought a stallion with money Aunt Seala had given him for his last birthday. He called the horse Vasgo—"wild one" in the old language.

"On that unfortunate animal?" Meredith laughed. "She's had her fill of years, poor old girl."

"Do you want to fence with me in the great hall? My fencing instructor can't make it today. I'm a bit rusty, so you'll have an advantage. All this fresh air has put me in a restless mood."

"I fenced with you last week, and you were not at all rusty!" Meredith scoffed.

"Can I help it if I'm better than you?" Kaydin smiled innocently as he took off his riding coat and gloves.

"Yes, you can. All right, I'll fence with you. Give me a minute to return this book to the library."

"I'll see you in the hall," Kaydin called.

★★★

When Meredith entered the library, Quaeor was writing at the cherrywood desk in the center of the room. A large dictionary sat open beside him. He furiously scribbled and muttered under his breath, repeating words, shaking his pale head, and flipping pages impatiently.

"What are you writing?" Meredith asked as she replaced the book on the shelf.

Quaeor glared at her. "That's no business of yours."

The servant girl ran in, out of breath. "The cook 'as beaten the stable boy for stealin' an apple, and we are all sure he's 'alf dead!"

"I wish you wouldn't come to me with your petty problems," Quaeor growled. He rose and stuffed his papers in a robe pocket and stormed out of the library, the servant following.

Meredith was about to leave when she spotted a wayward page on the floor. She picked up the sheet and read:

> To her Most ~~Divine~~ Excellent Highness, Sisinta Queen of ~~Lower~~ Quith.

Meredith gaped at the first line. Quaeor was writing to Sisinta! She read and reread the opening line three times before she forced herself to read on:

> ~~I must flatter you on your excellent letter.~~ I have received the letter you have sent me, and I will carry out your ~~orders~~ requests as soon as possible.
> Lady Quire's health is failing daily. She cannot outlast the month. When she dies, ~~Kaydin~~ Dragonose's son

will inherit all as the only male heir. I will secure any other future heirs of Dragonose by marrying the girl. After which, her brother will be dispatched in a ~~secretive~~ discreet manner. As such, the boy will not become the next Dragonose and you ~~can~~ may use his sister to draw Lord Stellmear out of hiding.

Though it was some time ago that we agreed on a reward for my faithful and ~~extraordinary~~ constant loyalty, I trust it is still pleasing to you? Quire Castle, the girl, and protection in your ~~takeover~~ rule of Higher Quith? That is all I humbly ask.

May you succeed in your endeavors and have many victories.

Your devoted ~~and admiring~~ servant,

Future Lord of Quire,

Master Quaeor

A wash of hot and cold crashed over Meredith's skin. She touched her forehead in an attempt to secure her reeling thoughts. A spy for Sisinta! Quaeor was slimy and abhorrent, but how could he betray his country? And plot her brother's murder while planning to marry her and steal Kaydin's inheritance! How did he know who she and Kaydin were? Had he always known?

Black crowded the edges of her sight, and little pinpricks of light burst in her vision. She had to tell herself to breathe or she would pass out. What could she do? Aunt Seala would never believe her, and the servants could do nothing. Van'N had left to visit relatives. If she showed anyone, Quaeor would simply deny he wrote it and claim she was attempting to defame him.

Meredith stuffed the letter into her pocket and ran from the room. She did not stop running until she reached the hall. Her brother was waving Swan around experimentally when she arrived. Gasping for breath, she grabbed his shoulders.

"Kaydin ..." Meredith swallowed. "Quaeor ... wants to kill you ... marry me ... and Sisinta ... your inheritance ... I read the letter ..."

"Calm down, Mere. Sit." Kaydin led her to a chair. "Now say it again slowly. What is this about Sisinta and getting married?"

She pulled out the crumpled letter and handed it to him.

Kaydin read it while Meredith willed her racing pulse to slow.

When he reached the end, Kaydin nodded slowly. *I wish I could say that I'm shocked, but frankly I've always thought Quaeor capable of any and all despicable acts.*

"What are we going to do?" Meredith fairly wailed.

Shh! Meredith. Don't speak aloud, Quaeor might hear. Kaydin gripped her arm. *Let's write Father a letter.*

That could take weeks to reach him!

We could tell Van'N, Kaydin suggested.

He's not here, remember? He left for Rivenwall last week, and we don't know when he's coming back! Meredith conveyed a mental moan.

We could write him a letter, Kaydin proposed.

What if it doesn't reach him in time? Meredith countered.

If Aunt Seala dies, and he's not back the next day, we could escape to Rivenwall.

The healer said she doesn't have long. Meredith wrung her hands.

Kaydin rose and said, *We have to trust.*

Who?

Elyon.

He seems so very far away. Meredith sighed.

Seeming and being are two different things. Kaydin grasped his sister's hand and pulled her to her feet. *Now, we're going to keep a level head and be responsible. I'll write the letter to Van'N while you look out for Quaeor. May Elyon show us the way.*

You sound like Father. Meredith groaned.

I know, Kaydin agreed, hiding a smile.

I like it. Meredith added hopefully, *Maybe Aunt Seala will live to see many more years.*

★★★

Lady Seala Quire died three days later during the night. Quire's title and lands were willed to Kaydin.

The next day, the twins were so anxious and worried they both agreed to mentally block each other. They remained in the library, out of sight, jumping at every sudden noise and servant's entry.

We leave tonight. Kaydin's mental tone was resolute, but Meredith saw fear in his eyes.

CHAPTER EIGHTEEN

A ROYAL AUDIENCE

King Daltaine of Tayose decided he was old. As he sat at a desk overflowing with letters, decrees, trade agreements, and tax reports, he seriously considered abdicating his crown to his eldest son.

"Cardlin has the vigor of youth, he'd manage just fine," he muttered to himself while searching through the fluttering pieces of his kingdom for a quill. "Unlike myself!" he grumbled louder as he finally seized his prize, only to find it had a broken nib. Frustration raised his voice, "I've not got the mental agility for this anymore!" He tossed the quill. It fluttered lazily to rest peacefully among the birds woven into the ornate blue carpet.

"Sire!" His manservant popped around the large oak door of his study.

"What is it now? I'm busy." Daltaine shuffled more piles of crisp white pages in search of a functioning quill. He stopped with a sigh of defeat. He'd ruined any sort of organization his steward had employed.

"There's someone requesting an audience with you."

"Does he have an appointment?"

"No."

"Then tell him to come back when he has one or on a petition day." Daltaine waved his hand dismissively.

"He insists his petition is timely. He also claims to be royalty. He won't give his name, only to you in person."

Daltaine let out a puff of air and stared up at the intricate plaster ceiling. It needed a good dusting. "How many people come here demanding an audience with me every week?" His eyes followed the curve of a dragon's plaster spine sculpted on the ceiling. Its tail wound around the base of the chandelier and the tip pointed downward along the iron anchor.

"Too many to count, Your Majesty."

"Then why bother me with this one?"

"He looks the part, sire."

Daltaine frowned and moved his gaze to the manservant. "How so?"

"He's in tailored armor inlaid with precious metals. And ... he has a bearing, sire. He claims to have proof of his identity. He has a slight accent, perhaps a diplomat?"

Daltaine stretched and stood. "All right, let's see this person of interest. I'll meet him in the feast hall. I'm done with my paperwork anyway."

The manservant eyed the overflowing desk skeptically.

Daltaine narrowed his gaze at the man, daring him to contradict his sovereign.

The servant bowed and left.

"Yes, I think Cardlin would make an excellent king," Daltaine repeated as he made his way to meet the stranger. This was a much-needed diversion. He liked diversions.

Daltaine had no sooner settled into his seat at the head of the great table when the door opened, and the young man entered.

He strode with sure steps, and his height was accentuated by perfect posture. The armor was impressive, though in a style Daltaine didn't recognize. It was all edges and points whereas Daltaine's knights sported armor with a bulkier fit and smoother edges.

With practiced indifference, he watched the blond-haired, blue-eyed man approach, bow appropriately, and speak in the common tongue with a slight accent. "My Lord King, I pray you will forgive the uninvited intrusion, but I accept your attention with gratitude." He pronounced his words in crisp, short tones and more precisely than a native would.

"My attention is in short supply these days. Sit and make your case." Daltaine indicated the seat next to him.

The man's brows rose in surprise, and he tilted his head in acceptance. "It would be my honor." The man's armor wasn't meant for lounging or sitting in antique chairs. Daltaine hadn't particularly loved his great-grandfather's style choices, but sentimentality had overruled. If a chair gave out now, he could finally choose proper replacements. With a slight measure of disappointment, he watched the armored man sit elegantly. The chair held.

The man removed his gauntlets and placed them on the table. "I wish to form an understanding between our houses. If you would answer a few questions for me, I would be entirely in your debt and your kindness would not go unremembered."

"What sort of benefit is your house to me? You've given me no name and no reason to trust you."

The man dipped his head in acquiescence. He removed a large signet ring from his middle finger and placed it on the table with a clink against the dark oak. The coat of arms was set in a thick gold band.

Daltaine recoiled like he'd opened a box to find a viper inside. "I know that symbol!" He pointed at the offending object between them. "How dare you enter my palace! My kingdom even! Who let you in here?" Sweat broke out on Daltaine's wrinkled forehead.

"You did, my Lord King," the man responded calmly.

Daltaine took stock of all the weapons in the vicinity. An old ceremonial knife on display—too far away. He could shout for the guards, but the man was close enough to hold him hostage before they arrived. He could defend himself, but he doubted he'd hold out against this younger, armor-clad enemy.

As if he had read Daltaine's mind, the man continued in a calm tone, "I have no weapons, Your Majesty. Your steward took them before I entered. A sensible policy."

Was the man mocking him? Daltaine took a calming breath and met the man's stunning blue eyes. He tightened his features. If he was about to be assassinated, he would not go out a coward.

"I have no intention of harming you, your house, or your kingdom. I ask only for information. Please hear my inquiries before you judge my reasons." The young man's face seemed to glow with honesty, but Daltaine remained skeptical.

He leaned back in his chair, crossed his arms, and clenched his teeth. "Well then, ask them! I cannot guarantee an honest answer or my cooperation."

"Keep in mind, oh King, that I have not threatened you in any way. I showed you the seal of my family's house in the hopes of establishing truth between us."

"Hurry up and ask your all-important questions and leave," Daltaine snapped.

Again, the man tilted his head in humble acquiescence. "I have heard it said that the High King has been seen here in Tayose. Do you know where I can find him?"

Daltaine stared blankly. "The ... High King? Who do you mean?"

"The man-god they call Elyon. I believe he is considered a source of divine magic among your people."

"Elyon?" Daltaine couldn't hide his astonishment. "Isn't he an enemy of your so-called Witch-Queen? What do you want with him?"

"I wish to employ his assistance."

"I hardly think he'd look favorably on the request of a house loyal to Sisinta since the Blood Battle. Well, except for that incident with the Cala Drani."

"I realize that. But I hear he is just. I wish to appeal to his sense of fairness."

Daltaine sighed. "I won't try to convince you one way or the other, if you're determined enough to cross the mountains into Higher Quith and speak to me, I doubt I'll dissuade you."

"You are correct. Except for crossing the mountains. I sailed around them."

"Around the South Cape? Surely the storms and water dragons would have prevented that route."

"Yes, at one point, we were beset by a terrible storm. When I was sure we would die, a voice spoke the name of my purpose into my heart—*Elyon*—and I knew we would live. A favorable wind took us wide of the cape and no lives were lost."

"There are more of you? Where are your men now?"

"I do not know. I bribed the captain to make the trip. He is his own man. I assume he has a cargo of contraband."

Daltaine opened his mouth to demand the names of the smugglers, but the man raised a hand. "He risked his life to get me here, I will not insult his confidence."

Daltaine huffed. Legend said Elyon cursed the capes to the north and south of the Dragon Mountains with storms and wind currents that sank or carried ships far out to sea. He also set water dragons to guard them. Sisinta had never successfully launched a naval assault on Higher Quith, but infrequent smugglers managed to survive the trip. Since Tayose was the first kingdom along the southern coast, Daltaine had to deal with them. He decided to let this one go—his intelligence network estimated at most two ships per year managed to round the cape.

"Remind me again what your question is." Daltaine reigned in his thoughts.

"Elyon has been seen in your kingdom. Where can I find him?"

"Has he? I haven't heard of it. Who told you he was here?"

"Fishermen under my father's employ were wrecked along your coast. They met a man on the beach who called himself Elyon. He clothed and fed them, then offered to find them new homes in Higher Quith. He claimed to have caused the storm so they would be brought here. All but one accepted his proposal. The only one who didn't crossed the mountains on foot. After a year, he arrived home and related his story to my father. I was in attendance when he gave account."

"Oh. Yes. I remember now. That was two years ago. Those men presented themselves to the lord of the lands where they'd landed, and he agreed to accept them as tenants. I was informed. I personally did not see the High King. In fact, I've never seen the man."

"Is he a man? There is very little information about him. Sisinta has banned all mention of him in the history books. His name is used as a curse in my kingdom." The young man leaned forward, eagerness sparking in his blue eyes.

"Well, er ... I suppose he isn't *just* a man—he's immortal. As a boy, I was told he's the only one of his kind."

"How can I learn more about him? How can I speak with him? Do you know of someone who can tell me?"

Daltaine thought for a moment. "There are many books by various philosophers on the subject of who or what he was. I don't ascribe to a specific view myself. If I were to take a public stand, I might lose support."

The man tilted his head and furrowed his brow.

Daltaine felt compelled to explain himself. "There is a view that if Elyon is announced as a *literal* High King versus a *figurative* High King, then the kingdom's laws would be subject to his rule. Some of his laws haven't always been ... popular. My job is to follow the majority. They make up the bulk of my subjects, you see?"

The young man shook his head. "I don't believe that to be true. The majority of citizens in my country follow Sisinta, and their poverty-stricken lives are miserable. It is the role of the king to lead by example, regardless of common sentiment."

"Ho, ho! A little self-righteous and naïve, aren't we? Just wait until you've ruled a country filled with opinionated, obstinate subjects and lords. It's impossible to keep them all happy all the time. Compromise is the only way to keep the peace."

"Shouldn't truth reign supreme?" the young man pressed.

Daltaine turned away and waved his hand dismissively. "You're one of those sorts, are you? An idealist willing to argue a point until you're blue in the face. I'm too old for this. I'm comfortable with my view, you can keep yours."

The young man fell silent, his brow furrowed.

Daltaine pushed back his chair, the legs scraping loudly against the floor. He stood and peered at the pensive man, then sighed heavily. "Look, I appreciate you want to better your country. I can also appreciate you're willing to follow your cause through near-death to meet with me, but I'm afraid I have nothing to offer you. Everything I know about the High King is handed down to me. Privately, I consider him to be an ideal. It's said that he wanders Higher Quith, dealing out justice and giving hope to the weak. He can't be found in one place. I don't doubt he existed at some point in history, but I think he died, and his memory and ideals live on without him. I support the sentiments his name invokes. Perhaps your fishermen saw this ideal in the man who saved them—a new life free from Sisinta's tyranny— and attributed it to Elyon?"

The young man bowed his head in apparent disappointment.

"I cannot offer hospitality to an enemy nation, but I will grant you safe passage out of my home. After you pass the castle gates, I can promise no protection. But might I suggest you note the state of my people. They are happy and content. Take that knowledge and the sentiments of the High King back to Ironcall."

The young man stood and retrieved his gauntlets and signet ring. "What good are sentiments to my people when a tyrant rules them, and my hope is placed in what you would call an ideal? Ideals do not defeat evil." He bowed sharply. "I am grateful for your time. Respectfully, I will disagree with your version of Elyon. I do not believe Sisinta would ban the mention of someone unless she feared him. She manipulates ideals for her gain. Elyon is something more, I am sure of it."

CHAPTER NINETEEN

FLIGHT

The doorkeeper's diligence in oiling the hinges of the castle's main door and the lack of a guard at the gate allowed the twins to sneak out of the castle with ease.

They took inventory of their supplies as they packed Vasgo's saddlebags—four blankets, a rope, Kaydin's sword, a knife, two sets of their plainest clothes and warmest cloaks, two waterskins, a small handful of coins, Meredith's sketchbook, and enough loaves of bread, apples, and strips of dried meat to last them several weeks.

The horse's name meant "wild one," but in the middle of the night, Vasgo was hardly wild. He was reluctant to be roused from sleep and did not appreciate being saddled. He pulled at the lead and pawed the ground. Kaydin walked Vasgo over the fields for the first half mile, afraid someone would hear hoofbeats on the road and inform Quaeor.

When the twins mounted, Vasgo was wide awake and pulling enthusiastically at the reins, but Kaydin held him back until sunrise. Meredith held tightly to her brother as he let the horse have his head. They galloped across the countryside until Vasgo was no longer interested in mad dashes, his initial energy spent. For his sake, they stopped at a small lake to let him graze and drink. After the refreshment, they found the road and continued toward Rivenwall.

The journey was not as easy as they had hoped. The biting insects of late spring would leave neither man nor beast in peace. Vasgo suffered most of all. The only defense the horse had against the swarming army of tormentors was his tail and hooves. The nights were too cold, and the days were too hot. Their clothes remained soaked by frequent spring downpours, even when the sun shone. Mud slowed their pace. On the first day, a passing traveler told the twins that Rivenwall was a week's travel away. When two weeks had passed and the road became a path that petered out in the middle of a dark forest, they were forced to admit they were lost. Kaydin stopped Vasgo and the twins dismounted.

"If we cut across country," he suggested, "we might find the main road again."

"That may make things worse," Meredith responded. "I've been thinking it over, and I'm guessing we've gone west when we should have gone north. I think we could even be in Dolsulbane!"

"We should have grabbed a map instead of assuming we knew the way," Kaydin acknowledged. "I haven't seen any sign of civilization for two days now!" He stretched high and ducked low, peering around the trees in all directions, but stopped and sighed, defeated. They could not even spot a way out of the maze of menacing black trees, and it would soon be dark.

"What are we going to do?" Meredith grumbled. Her exhaustion was mounting into frustration.

"It looks like we're staying here for the night," Kaydin said hopelessly.

"I don't know if I want to stay here." Meredith shivered. Threatening trees stood between them and safety. What kinds of creatures came out at night after the last rays of sunlight disappeared? All the stories she had heard of people vanishing in the wilderness and never returning crowded her mind. What made it worse was the dead silence. Nothing moved. No birds singing, no squirrels or rodents, none of the expected woodland creatures, not even the wind.

Kaydin felt her uneasiness and told her, "I dislike this place just as much as you do, but I would rather be sitting by a campfire when it gets dark than wandering through these woods all night looking for a way out."

"I suppose you're right." She reluctantly agreed to help him build a fire in the tiny clearing.

They ate the last of their food.

"I thought about hunting a couple days ago," Kaydin said, "but we haven't seen any game, and the only experience I have are those times we tagged along with Airith on his hunts."

"Maybe we've scared off the game?" She paused, then added, "Hunting with Airith was exciting."

Kaydin nodded. "It was. I like to imagine he's found the life he wanted—lord of his own land, acknowledged and respected for his swordsmanship. Hunting to his heart's content."

Meredith's troubled emotions spilled into Kaydin's. "I asked after the court politics in Tayose when that visiting dignitary stopped in to see Aunt Seala last fall. He'd never heard of Airith. Maybe he became an adventurer or mercenary?" she suggested. "Or a sailor? He liked Calldo's stories about the sea." She began to hum under her breath as she stared into the fire. The familiar flames dancing about the glowing red coals and the shifting shapes calmed her worried thoughts. *Kaydin?* she mind-spoke.

Yes?

Do you remember when Father used to shape the fire into people, animals, castles, and flowers? Meredith smiled.

I remember. Mr. Wiggles, the little singing and dancing fat man, was my favorite character, Kaydin recalled with a smile of his own.

Meredith started to sing to herself again, a simple and haunting melody.

I know that song, Kaydin said thoughtfully.

You should, Mother used to sing it to us before bed.

As the words resurfaced in his memory, Kaydin sang, slowly and softly:

> When the stars have gone away
> When there is no light in the day
> When fear is your only companion
> And your soul wanders alone, below in dark canyons
> Remember me when all you see
> Is the sun always setting and never rising.
>
> In your heart I will always be
> The light in the dark
> To help you see.
> I am always with you when all else is gone
> The one who stands beside you
> The one whose hand guides you.
>
> In your heart I will always be
> The light in the dark
> To help you see.

Kaydin took a deep breath.

The song lingered in the air, making the darkness outside the firelight even lonelier.

"I think she was singing about Elyon," Meredith whispered.

And about herself, in a way. She will always be in our hearts. Kaydin mentally replied. *How long has it been since she died?*

Five years and seven months.

Oh ... I hadn't been keeping track. Kaydin lifted his head to watch the fire.

Meredith thought for a long moment. *Elyon has never talked to me. Do you think that means he doesn't know I talk to him?*

When we were little, you used to say he talked to you all the time.

Well, yes, but I don't know if that was just my imagination. I wanted so badly to be like Father and Mother, and they spoke to him often.

Kaydin gazed at her intently. *Maybe you stopped seeing him because you stopped looking.*

The Great Books say he will never abandon us no matter what. How is it, then, that when I stopped looking, he stopped being there?

I don't think he stopped being there, Mere, you just stopped wanting to see him.

Meredith's brow furrowed. *I don't remember not wanting to see him.*

Kaydin took another deep breath and said out loud. "I think Elyon is replacing pieces of my heart with burning coals. He's pulling out the roots I have wrapped around everything I love. Sometimes, I feel so much anger in me, it scares me. Mother was taken from us *and* Father." Kaydin's voice was trembling. "But everyone loses someone. What right do I have to mourn when people are murdered by Sisinta every day? And you ... you just sit there and take it all, and you don't say a word. I've failed Father. He told me to take care of you and here we are, starving in the wilderness." Kaydin put his head in his hands, his breath ragged with emotion.

Meredith stared at her brother with astonishment. She couldn't remember the last time he'd allowed himself to be so vulnerable with her. *Kaydin, you're strong, stronger than I am. You always keep a level head when things go wrong,* she silently attempted to encourage him.

Kaydin snorted. *What happened to us, Mere? I've missed you. Your real, deep down, inner thoughts. We shared those with each other once. Why did we stop?* Kaydin met her eyes.

Meredith saw the hurt and hopelessness in his face. She wrapped her arms around him and closed her eyes. *I think it started when Mother died, to protect each other from our grief. You put up a mental wall that's still in place.*

Well, my self-preservation seems to have harmed us. He took a shaky breath and said aloud. "We cannot survive on our own, Mere. We're going to die here, and it will be all my fault." His voice cracked.

"It will not be your fault," Meredith said firmly. "You did your best, and I have never felt safer in anyone else's hands."

"My best is not enough," Kaydin whispered.

"'Remember me, when all you see is the sun always setting and never rising.'" Meredith quoted. "Don't succumb to despair, Kaydin. There's a light in the darkness. All you have to do is look for it."

Vasgo whinnied and pulled at his tether.

Kaydin shot to his feet. He shoved the moisture from his eyes with his sleeve as he approached Vasgo.

A low, long growl sounded just outside the firelight.

Kaydin froze halfway to Vasgo, his sword in sight on top of the saddlebags. He glanced at Meredith sitting on the log by the fire. The growl had come from behind her.

Meredith sat perfectly still and held her breath. *What is it?*

I don't know, but don't move. Kaydin edged slowly toward the saddlebags.

A large, black cat with glowing, white eyes watched him from behind Vasgo.

Kaydin froze.

The horse continued rearing and yanking at the rope.

The big cat kept its eyes trained on Kaydin.

Another glance at his sister revealed a second vagwhar behind her in the shadow of the trees. Kaydin spotted two more in the woods on the other side of the fire. They were surrounded.

Meredith ... he warned.

I see them, Kaydin. What do we do? Meredith responded.

Kaydin's eyes darted around the small clearing.

Something crashed through the underbrush.

Both twins turned toward the sound.

A man with shining golden hair on horseback burst into the clearing, brandishing a sword. He wore full armor except his helmet, which dangled with a horn from the saddlebow. His mount—a huge, white warhorse—reared. A fearsome sight. His manner was threatening and his face wild. He raised the horn to his lips and sounded it.

The poisonous cats screeched and scattered in every direction.

Kaydin and Meredith remained frozen in place.

A moment later, the man quieted his horse and dismounted. "Are you two well?"

Kaydin nodded dumbly.

The man was tall and fair with a handsome face. His immaculate posture and formal speech revealed his high social class. His manner—terrifying moments before—was now relaxed and easygoing.

"What are you doing here?" Kaydin asked warily.

"I think I could ask you the same question." The man laughed, a merry sound. "I was tracking those vagwhar."

"My sister and I are traveling to Rivenwall to visit a friend, but we've gotten lost," Kaydin explained.

"Lost! I should say! As far as I know, the nearest road is three days from here!"

"Do you know exactly where we are?" Meredith asked.

"Actually ... no. I'm new here myself," the man admitted. "But I do have a map I've been following."

"My name is Kaydin Amara, and this is my sister, Meredith."

"Pleased to make your acquaintance." The man bowed. "My name is Rand."

The twins waited for him to elaborate, but he didn't.

"I do not know this area well, but I do know how to get out of these woods and to a road," Rand said finally. "Why are you traveling alone?"

Meredith answered quickly, "Our mother died, and we're no longer welcome in our father's house. He also died some time ago, and all his wealth went to a relative. We are traveling to Rivenwall to live with a family friend."

"You do not act or speak as common peasants. Who was your father?" Rand queried.

"Nor do you," Kaydin countered.

Rand laughed again. "You are right, fair sir. A deal it is. I shall not tell you my origins, and neither shall you."

"That is not what I meant," Kaydin said hastily. "What my sister said was true ... at least, part of it."

"Ah, yes. And I'm a prince." Rand snorted with a smirk. He tied his horse's reins beside Vasgo who had calmed since the vagwhar had departed.

"We didn't ask you to believe us," Meredith snapped.

"Ah, but you did!" Rand explained. "When you told your story, you were implying the details were true. Yet, I can read guilt all over your faces. Who are you really running from?"

"We are not lying," Meredith insisted. "We're running from the relative who took my brother's inheritance. He was going to murder Kaydin and marry me!"

"I can see you are in a predicament," Rand responded humbly. "I did not mean to upset you, and I apologize that I did. I would be willing to escort you to Rivenwall."

"You're headed in that direction?" Kaydin inquired.

"More or less. It would not be an inconvenience."

"Can we stay here until daylight, please?" Meredith nearly begged.

"Indeed, 'tis foolhardy to roam these woods at night," Rand agreed. "You children should not be out here alone. We can leave in the morning."

Meredith bit back a retort that they were nearly adults. It was not the first time someone had misunderstood their ages based on appearances. They needed a guide. If perceiving them as children added to his desire to see them safely to Rivenwall, they'd just have to accept it. Meredith took a deep breath and reminded herself he didn't mean to be condescending. She smiled and said, "We're no longer alone now that you're here."

CHAPTER TWENTY

THE MINSTREL

They set out at sunrise. Rand led the way down a twisting path out of the woods. When they finally emerged from the dark forest, the sunlight brightened everyone's spirits.

At noon, they stopped by a wide river to rest the horses and eat. Rand unsaddled the horses and shared some of his provisions—dried fruit and smoked ham. Kaydin and Meredith sat on the riverbank while they ate.

"Rand?" Meredith spoke up.

"Yes?" Rand responded while adjusting his horse's saddle.

"Could this be the Enduring River?"

Rand looked out over the river. "I-I do not know."

"I think it's the Enduring River," Kaydin said. "If we are where I think we are, it makes sense. What do you think, Mere?"

Meredith surveyed the dark waters and distant shore. "I think it is! We used to play by the river as children. Only the Enduring River has shimmering black waters. I remember Father said it was because of some mineral in the riverbed. I can't remember what it's called."

"Mica," Kaydin filled in.

"So ... you two know how to get to Rivenwall from here?" Rand asked.

"The source of the Enduring River is in the Dragon Mountains," Meredith explained. "If we travel downriver, it flows into the Calldian Sea. Rivenwall is by the harbor at the mouth of the river."

"Okay, we will go that way then," Rand said cheerfully.

"You really aren't from around here, are you? You didn't know about the river." Kaydin gestured toward the swirling, shimmering water.

"No," Rand acknowledged.

"Where are you from?"

Rand finished securing the saddlebags before speaking. "I thought we had agreed not to question each other on that subject."

"I don't know if we should continue with you if we don't know anything about you," Kaydin stated firmly.

After a moment, Rand said, "I am from the Islands. I am the son of a warlord."

"You look far too clean-shaven and finely-dressed to be the son of a warlord." Meredith crossed her arms and eyed him suspiciously. *I don't believe him for a second,* she added silently to her brother.

Well, we did agree not to share details, Kaydin said. *We're hiding our origins from him too.*

"I will take that as a compliment." Rand mounted his warhorse.

Kaydin mounted Vasgo and reached to pull Meredith up behind him.

As they followed the river's edge, Rand asked, "Have you ever heard 'The Song of Camaly'?"

Meredith shook her head. "Not that I can remember."

"Sing it for us," Kaydin urged.

Rand took a deep breath and began to sing a merry song in his pleasant tenor:

I know a girl who only wears pearls
And dandy is she.
She loves to whirl and twirl, she loves to dance for me.
She can only wear silk and she can only wear satin
And she is lovely to see.
Her mount is the wind and her chariot the sun.
Her home is a castle in the sky and her heart is the sea.
And she loves only me!
I promised her that she was mine and always would be.
And on my journeys across the sea,
I always remember Camaly.

He wore a small smile when he finished.

Kaydin and Meredith laughed, delighted by his strong singing voice. After that they exchanged songs and stories. He claimed each song they sang to be new to him as well. They soon learned he preferred merry tunes to melancholy ones and love songs to battle ballads.

"Have you ever been in a battle, Rand?" Kaydin asked.

"I have not, though I can hold my own in a fight."

"I thought you said your father was a warlord." Meredith frowned.

"Our tribe is at peace right now. My father is old and less eager to start wars. As a result, our tribe members and land are slowly being usurped by another warlord, and my father will do nothing. That is why I am here. To find Elyon and ask for his help."

"You're searching for Elyon?" Meredith perked up.

"Yes, do you know where he is?" Rand's tone was eager.

"No." Kaydin shook his head. "Not many have seen him since the Blood Battle, six hundred years ago. He's called

High King of the ten kingdoms, though Quith is currently only five united kings. Some claim to have seen Elyon and that he walks among us."

"You doubt he lives?" Rand asked. "I have heard Sisinta killed him."

"No, no," Meredith interjected. "We know he's alive. It's just that not everyone in Higher Quith has seen him."

"I hope he is. Elyon is the last hope for my people," Rand said grimly. "No one knows where he is?"

"He is everywhere, unconfined. Some say, he used to be spotted in Lower Quith and even the Islands, where you are from," Kaydin said.

"Yes," Rand murmured thoughtfully, "I have heard that said as well. Why does he not reveal himself as king over all Quith once again? If he is so powerful, why does he not defeat Sisinta?"

Meredith recalled the passages she'd read in holy books. "When Elyon created Sisinta, he promised to give her a kingdom to rule for a set time. She tried to take more than he gave her, and that led to the Blood Battle. Sisinta killed Elyon and spilled his blood on the battlefield. Elyon's blood created a massive explosion that wiped out her entire army. When the dust settled, Elyon revived himself. My mother told me Elyon never lies, and since he'd promised Sisinta would rule, he would not rescind his word. Instead, he confined her to Lower Quith and erected the Dragon Mountains. At the end of her allotted time, he will dethrone and punish her."

"No one has ever told me that before," Rand mused. "I heard only the part in which Sisinta killed Elyon. I was told all of Quith is rightfully hers. It has never made sense to me that an immortal, invincible, all-knowing being like Elyon could be killed." He paused thoughtfully. "I would like to see the day Sisinta is dethroned and punished for her deeds. I do not believe evil will go unchecked forever."

"I would also like to see that day," Meredith agreed soberly.

★★★

Two days later, they spotted a road on the far side of the river, but the water was too deep to wade. They spent several hours riding along the riverbank in search of a ford but found nothing passable.

In the red light of sunset, Rand noticed a blotch of bright color under a tree at the river's edge. He dismounted to investigate. A young teenage boy slept on the riverbank beside a beached raft. He was skinny and wore a mishmash of bright colors. He had an unusual hat with a feather that drooped over his eyes. A flute was secured to his waist with a leather cord. Around the big toe of his bare foot was tied a fishing line.

Rand called Kaydin and Meredith over. He shook the slumbering boy.

The boy stretched and yawned, then rolled over and went back to sleep.

Rand grabbed the boy and shook him harder.

"Go away!" the boy grumbled angrily, pulling his hat even farther down his face.

"We just want to borrow your raft," Rand told him.

"Take it, and leave a fellow to sleep!" the boy growled.

"All right, thank you." The raft was large enough for all of them. "Help me here, Kaydin." Rand grunted as he struggled to push the raft into the river.

Kaydin dismounted and handed Vasgo's reigns to Meredith.

"Hold on a moment!" The boy was on his feet. "What are you doing with my raft?"

They all looked at him, bewildered.

"Crossing the river with it," Rand said.

"Why are you dressed in those cockamamie clothes?" Meredith asked from atop Vasgo.

"They are *not* cockamamie. They are appropriate for my profession." The boy's chest swelled with pride, and he threw his head back in a dramatic pose.

"Which would be ..." Rand prompted.

"A minstrel. My name is Zray, son of Urran the Minstrel." The skinny boy bowed, sweeping his hat in a grand arc.

"And what, Sir Minstrel, would someone like you be doing in a place like this?" Rand asked.

"A man stole my money, so I took it back, but then he pursued me to get back what I had taken from him, which he had originally stolen from me. So, now I am in hiding."

"I see ..."

"Well, it was nice meeting you," Kaydin said, returning to the task of pushing the raft into the river.

"Wait a minute!" Zray shouted.

Kaydin sighed. "Listen, Zray, son of whomever, we are tired and hungry, and we would prefer to be on the other side of the river before dark."

"I know, I know. You can go as soon as you pay for the raft," Zray announced.

"Pay for it! You told us we could borrow it!" Kaydin snorted.

"I was not fully aware of the situation."

"How much?" Rand asked as he untied a purse from around his neck.

"As much as I need money, I need something else more. Take me with you."

"They are going to Rivenwall," Rand pointed to the twins, "and where I am going, you cannot come."

"Take me with you to Rivenwall," Zray declared, "or the raft stays here."

Rand lifted his eyebrows in question to the twins.

Kaydin shrugged.

"All right, we will take you with us. Only as far as Rivenwall," Rand decided. "Now help us with this raft."

All three men pushed the raft into the river with guiding poles. They crossed the river with the horses tethered to the raft and swimming alongside. Night had descended by the time they reached the far shore. Kaydin started a fire, and they settled around it to eat Rand's dried fruit and stale bread. When they laid in their bedrolls, sleep came quickly.

★★★

Waking Zray the next morning took Kaydin fifteen minutes. An even longer process commenced, trying to convince the minstrel to wear Kaydin's extra set of clothes.

"Your bright clothing will draw too much attention," Rand patiently explained.

"And why shouldn't they?" Zray haughtily turned up his nose. "A minstrel should always be easy to spot in a crowd."

"Because someone wants to kill us." Meredith said.

Zray looked interested. Meredith fed him the same story they'd given Rand. He kept asking for very specific details. When he asked the color of their mother's eyes, Meredith had enough.

"Why do you want to know?" she demanded.

"For the ballad I plan to write on your behalf, of course. I'm assuming you'd compose it yourself if you could. As it stands, you're not a minstrel, *I* am. I'll write it for you."

"That's not—"

"No, no," Zray interrupted. "No need to ask for payment. I'm always game for a good tale."

She didn't bother trying to change his mind after that. At least he agreed to change his outfit.

Their patience was tried again when Zray refused to ride with Rand. He agreed only when Rand promised to buy another horse as soon as they reached a town.

Not long after following the river road, they started to see people and houses again.

By crossing the Enduring River they were back on track— traveling through the kingdom of Dolsulbane and heading for Rivenwall.

Zray was grating on everyone's nerves. He complained constantly, questioned everything, and argued often.

It's one thing to complain to yourself or to me, Meredith mind-spoke to Kaydin from her place behind him on Vasgo, *but he complains to everyone about everything. If I catch him standing by the river, I'll push him in so he will have something legitimate to complain about.*

Kaydin laughed aloud. *I could see you doing it too, Mere.*

Kaydin's laughter interrupted Zray's current tirade on how underpaid minstrels were. Rand and the minstrel stared at the twins, puzzled by the outburst.

Toward midafternoon, Zray offered to tell a story of the Duke of Gasbal and his nephews. "This story was my father's specialty in his travels across Quith," Zray bragged.

The travelers exchanged glances but could find no reason to refuse. Zray's voice took on a different tone and drew them into the world he described.

Meredith imagined she could look behind her and find the Duke of Gasbal and his knights riding hard in pursuit of his runaway nephews whom he had plotted to kill, but who had outwitted him and escaped his grasp. They asked Zray for another story after he had finished the first.

As twilight dimmed the sky, Rand suggested they keep their eyes open for a place to spend the night. Kaydin spotted an abandoned barn, and they stopped to see if it was habitable. The hay had turned to dust and the wooden frame creaked as if it might buckle at any moment.

"It's perfect!" Kaydin called happily from the loft above. The wooden ladder was missing rungs and was impossible to climb.

"How did you get up there?" Rand called.

"I climbed the loft supports." Kaydin grinned. "Come on up!"

"I shall not, under any circumstances, do any such foolhardy thing," Zray declared, arms akimbo.

Meredith inwardly lamented that her dress prevented her from joining her brother.

As Rand climbed the post supports, he noted, "This building is very unstable, I do not think we should stay here."

"Why would it choose tonight to fall down?" Kaydin asked.

"One swift storm is all it would take."

"There are no clouds in sight." Zray peered between the wooden planks of the wall.

"All right, staying one night should not do any harm," Rand finally agreed. "You two boys bed down the horses and get us a big pile of firewood."

"Why don't you or the girl do it?" Zray grumbled as Kaydin and Rand climbed down from the loft.

"Because Meredith is a lady, and I am going to get us our supper," Rand told him. He retrieved his bow and arrows from the saddlebags. "Unless you would rather do it, boy."

"I'm not a boy," Zray muttered angrily under his breath.

The two young men followed Rand's instructions.

"I can get some water from the river," Meredith suggested.

"Stay nearby. Do not wander far," Rand warned on his way out.

CHAPTER TWENTY-ONE

BANDITS' CAVE

"Zray, where is your father now?" Kaydin asked. He tossed aside the gnawed pheasant bones, remnants of Rand's hunting success.

"Prison, last I heard." Zray shrugged and kicked a wayward coal back into the flames.

Rand jumped to his feet. "Did you hear something?"

"No." Zray shook his head.

"Not at all," Kaydin agreed.

"I think I heard something," Meredith whispered.

The flickering shadows cast by the fire on the barn's walls seemed to be ghosts, reaching out long gray fingers to snatch at them. The younger three held their breaths as Rand strode determinedly to the door and peered into the darkness.

When nothing happened, he mumbled, "I must have been wrong."

Just then, a man's hand pressed a knife against Rand's throat. "Unfortunately, you weren't."

Zray squeaked and tumbled off his log seat.

The twins surged to their feet.

The man stank of ale as he threatened the travelers. "Don't any of you move, or I'll slit his throat."

Five more dirty, surly-faced men emerged from the shadows, armed with knives and clubs.

Meredith couldn't figure out if they had truly materialized from the shadows or simply been hiding.

"What do you want?" Rand demanded.

The man behind him answered, "Well, now, let's see … everything you have of value."

Rand clenched his fists, and Meredith saw a muscle jerk in his cheek.

"You two," the bandit leader gestured toward two of his men, "get their horses. And you other two, tie their hands. You, boy, search their bags."

The bandits obeyed. Two tied up Rand and Kaydin. The boy rifled through Rand's bags and pulled out cloth bundles. He unwrapped them to reveal pieces of armor inlaid with precious metals, glinting in the firelight.

The leader grabbed them from the boy. "I'll take those." He stuffed them into a sack.

"Hey! Who said you could choose what you get? It's an even share for each of us!" another bandit protested.

"That's right!" the other men agreed.

"I'm the leader! I'll do what I please! Are you fools challenging me?" The bandit leader glared at his men. "I suppose you have forgotten what happened to Frag? Elyon rest his soul."

The men shuffled their feet, gazes down.

"It's all yours, Baldgave. You take it," one man said meekly.

The others agreed in subdued murmurs.

"That's better. Now hurry up, and let's get out of here," Baldgave barked. "Come on, you lazy hogs, hurry and finish tying them up."

As soon as the bandits finished tying up the travelers, they silently slunk back into the shadows. A minute later, they heard nickering and hoofbeats as the bandits presumably rode away with the horses, the armor, Kaydin's and Rand's swords, and all their provisions. The bound travelers listened intently in case they came back.

Do you think they were hiding in the shadows or came out of them? Meredith silently asked her brother.

What do you mean? What's the difference? Kaydin asked.

Meredith didn't get to explain her question because Zray broke the silence. "Well, this is jolly rotten!"

"Why, aren't you enjoying yourself?" Kaydin asked.

"Thank you, Zray, for stating the obvious." Meredith rolled her eyes.

"Come on, you three. Stop sitting there and help each other out of your ropes." Rand struggled against his bonds.

"How?" Kaydin asked.

"They made a mistake by tying us up separately. Make your way to your neighbor, back-to-back, and untie each other."

Kaydin shimmied to Zray, and Rand to Meredith. Within minutes, Meredith and Rand were free, but Zray and Kaydin were arguing, making no progress with the knots. Rand untied Kaydin first and then Kaydin tried to untie Zray.

"You are strangling me!" Zray whimpered.

"Zray, you cannot strangle someone by the wrists," Meredith chided.

"Will you stop squirming?" Kaydin growled.

"I'm squirming because you are hurting me!" Zray complained.

"Here." Rand reached into one of his high leather boots and pulled out a knife.

Zray flinched.

"Hidden pocket," Rand explained.

"You're going to kill me!" Zray moaned pitifully.

"Stop squirming, or you will cut yourself," Rand ordered.

As soon as he was free, Zray jumped up and rubbed his wrists. "You are all unfeeling and hateful."

"Come on, we must go!" Rand urged as he dumped water onto the fire.

"Wait, wait," Zray stopped him, "you aren't planning to do what I think you are ... are you?"

"I am not going to let them get away with our weapons and only form of transportation." Rand gestured for them to follow.

Zray groaned. "I think I would rather stay here."

"If you are going to travel with us, you listen to me. That means you are coming too." Rand firmly grabbed Zray by the shoulders and pushed him out the door.

★★★

The moon illuminated the way for the travelers. They heard the bandits before they saw them—arguing over who could ride the horses. Baldgave insisted that, as leader, Rand's horse was his, but the others said Rand's armor was his share of the loot, the horses and the swords were theirs. They finally agreed to sell the armor and split the money.

The twins, Rand, and Zray followed the bandits at a distance, hiding behind bushes, trees, and rocks. Finally, the small band stopped by a stream to rest and drink.

"I can't see anything!" Zray said in a loud whisper.

The others scrambled to cover his mouth.

Zray made some muffled protests but fell silent when Kaydin whispered threateningly into his ear, "I swear, I'll leave you behind for good or dunk you in the river if you don't keep your mouth shut."

The four followed the bandits across the stream and into a rocky gully that ended in a cave. Three women sat around a fire with food.

Rand gathered the travelers in their hiding spot behind some rocks and whispered, "Okay, this is what we are going to do. As soon as they fall asleep, we will sneak in and take back our belongings. Kaydin and Meredith, you get the horses and saddlebags. They have not removed the saddles for the night." Rand sounded disgusted at the bandits' lack of horse knowledge. "I will get the swords and armor. Zray, keep watch."

"For what?" Zray asked.

Rand sighed, exasperated. "For three-toed wallabumps that fly."

Zray stared at him blankly.

"The thieves, Zray! The thieves!"

"Oh." Zray acknowledged vaguely.

Two hours later, the bandits were asleep. The sack of swords and clothes lay next to Baldgave. The horses had been tied to a tree near the cave entrance. The twins skirted the camp toward them while Rand slipped silently and cautiously into the cave. The fire had reduced to glowing coals. Meredith waited with Kaydin while Rand eased the bag from Baldgave's side. The armor was wrapped and didn't make much sound, but the swords clinked together. Meredith's anxiety flared and she grabbed her brother's arm. Rand froze. Baldgave stirred in his sleep and rolled over.

They waited a full minute, before Rand took a deep breath and motioned for the twins to continue with the horses. Meredith had no trouble with Vasgo, but Rand's horse didn't trust Kaydin. When he tried to lead the warhorse away, it reared. A bandit woke and cried out.

"Rand, Kaydin needs your help!" Meredith shouted.

Rand raced toward his horse. He mounted the steed in one leap and pulled Kaydin up with him.

All the bandits were awake now and yelling after them. In the confusion, Baldgave tripped over a bucket and cursed as he fell over, barely missing the fire.

Meredith and Zray mounted Vasgo. A bandit with a long beard near the fire blinked out of existence and rematerialized next to the horse's head. Meredith shrieked. Vasgo reared, and Zray slid off the horse's rump. The bearded bandit grabbed the bridle in one hand and reached for Meredith's foot with the other. She screamed again and kicked the cold, clammy hand away. One by one, five bandits stepped into shadows across the fire and materialized around the horses. Baldgave was on his feet again, brushing ash and dirt from his trousers.

"They've got magic!" Zray shouted while attempting to scramble into the underbrush. "There's something glowing in their hands!"

Meredith didn't have a chance to process the information as Vasgo reared and kicked while she held on for dear life. One blow from the horse connected with a bandit's chest, another with a head.

The youngest bandit grabbed for Zray's outstretched legs.

Zray screeched an octave louder than Meredith and kicked with all his might. His kicks made contact. The young bandit's legs were knocked out from under him, and he landed with a thud—his head connecting with a rock mere inches from Zray's face.

Meredith managed to regain control of Vasgo, but he still danced sideways uneasily.

Rand drew his sword from the sack and shouted, "Back! Back! Or I'll take a part off you!"

The two remaining bandits backed away, arms raised in surrender.

Zray dove for Vasgo's stirrup and tried to claw his way into the saddle.

Meredith did her best to help him while still holding Vasgo in check.

"Go!" Rand told Meredith. He kept his sword pointed at the bandits and did not break his threatening gaze.

Meredith carefully walked Vasgo toward Rand and Kaydin, avoiding the three men groaning on the ground, two clutching their heads and one, his chest. Once Vasgo cleared them, both horses galloped away.

They didn't stop until they had passed the barn and reached the road again.

"Are you crying, Mere?" Kaydin reached for her shaking shoulders.

She lifted her head, laughing uncontrollably. "That was intense! Did you see Baldgave's face?"

"You must be in shock." She felt Kaydin's relief.

Rand smiled.

They all began to chuckle and then laugh. The anxiety and stress faded with each peel of joy. They were alive!

"We should do that again!" Zray cheered.

The laughter ended.

"Ah, no." Rand shook his head. "I prefer to be on more equal footing next time."

Zray shrugged. "It was just a suggestion."

"You know, Zray, you are the most interesting person I have ever met," Meredith told him.

"Thank you, my lady." Zray made a mock bow on the horse. The minstrel reached into his outlandish coat and presented a broach set with a large, red gem.

"What is it?" Rand examined it in the moonlight.

"I grabbed it from my assailant's vest. I think it has something to do with the magic they were using. You know, to teleport through the shadows?"

"Is that really what they did?" Kaydin asked skeptically.

"Yes." Zray and Meredith spoke in unison.

"It was glowing," Zray explained.

"How did some lowly bandits come in possession of something so powerful?" Rand mused, turning the broach over in his hand. "It's red glass, not very valuable." He returned the broach.

"How does it work?" Zray shook it, but nothing happened. "I think it's broken." He sighed and placed it in his coat pocket.

"We should keep going," Rand said. "The bandits can still catch us if we stop here. There is no telling how far they can travel with those ... magical shadow broaches."

Zray mouthed the words "shadow broaches" and nodded in approval of the name. "This whole affair will make for a fantastic scene in my great epic." He beamed.

"Your great epic?" Meredith's eyebrows rose.

"Yes. The great epic of my life. I've been recording it all up here," he tapped his temple, "and one day it shall be sung in every tavern, at every fair, in all the kings' courts, across all of Higher and Lower Quith!" He flung his arm out dramatically as if expecting applause.

Kaydin snorted.

Zray proceeded to recite lines of verse about bandits, caves, and shadow broaches.

The others ignored his rambling for the next few hours while they traveled into the night.

★★★

Kaydin woke while it was still dark, sensing someone else was awake. He sat up slowly, curling his blanket tighter against the cold. Rand sat at the river's edge. "Is something wrong, Rand?"

A long moment later, Rand replied in a hoarse whisper, "They are still tracking us."

Kaydin swallowed hard and asked, "Who?" but he knew. Over the past few days, he had sensed unfamiliar animalistic minds hovering just outside his consciousness.

"The vagwhar we met before. Why are they in Higher Quith? Sisinta is getting too sure of herself ... or desperate."

Kaydin sat next to Rand. "What do we do about the vagwhar?"

"I figure if we can reach Rivenwall safely, we can lose them. They do not like civilization." Rand looked to the horizon. Dawn approached. He pulled from his pocket a worn piece of paper that had been folded and unfolded so many times it threatened to fall apart. He traced the edges of the paper with his fingers.

"What is that?" Kaydin asked.

Rand smiled to himself. "A letter from my wife."

"You never mentioned you're married." It struck him that Rand was merely a few years older than he was. He hadn't yet considered the possibility of marriage.

Rand nodded absently and then smiled broadly. "She is going to have a child."

"Congratulations!" Kaydin thumped Rand on the back.

"His name will be Randurren. I wish I could hear from her more often, but my travels make it difficult for her to get word to me."

"How do you know the baby will be a boy?" Kaydin asked.

Rand shrugged. "All firstborns in my family are boys." He looked at the letter again, sighed, and returned the letter to his pocket.

A few minutes later, the others woke.

Kaydin couldn't hide his unease from his sister and she mentally questioned him.

He told her about Rand's wife and the vagwhar still following them.

I think Queaor told Sisinta where we'd likely be, and she's sent the vagwhar after us.

You might be right, Kaydin agreed.

Two days later, Rivenwall was at last in sight.

CHAPTER TWENTY-TWO

THE CAPITAL CITY OF TRADE

"Look at all the people! This is the biggest city I've ever seen!" Kaydin exclaimed.

The buildings towered into the bright spring sky, several stories higher than anything in Boldwind.

"It's the largest city in Higher Quith," Zray informed him as they passed through Rivenwall's main gate. He happily launched into the history of the city. "The buildings are made of black stone mined from deep within the Six Peaks mountains. Seven hundred years ago, the stone was hauled over a hundred leagues all the way to the mouth of the Enduring River to build this famous city. The king of Dolsulbane had searched the world over to find the best architects and engineers to build the Capital City of Trade." Zray paused for a breath, glancing at the others, and looking pleased to have their full attention. "Though the city itself is amazing, the people are even more interesting." Zray gestured to the pedestrians. "They are from many nations. Sillians with faces pale as full moons, covered in robes and cloaks to avoid the bright sun. Occasionally, you might see a Rackdarian, but they do not care for cities and come only to trade."

"What about Paladalls?" Meredith asked. "I have always wanted to see one do magic."

"They are rare, and most serve Sisinta."

"I have heard they are very beautiful."

Rand asked, "Where does your friend live?"

"Van'N?" Kaydin started. "Well ... we do not know—"

Meredith finished for him. "He's staying with his son Jad'N down by the docks in the merchant district."

"How do you know that? I didn't know that." Kaydin frowned.

"He told us. *You* just forgot." Meredith smiled smugly.

"Maybe we'll find him if we ask around the merchant district," Zray suggested.

"That sounds reasonable," Rand agreed.

A large section of the city was devoted to fostering the merchant trades. Two miles of docks faced the main harbor, while merchant homes, storehouses, and shops lined the surrounding blocks. Looking for Jad'N proved difficult. One sailor told them they were "looking for a needle in a haystack" as "the merchants in this city are more numerous than the beggars." The sailor suggested they visit city hall. Records of all citizens could be found there, along with the names of the merchants who had purchased trading licenses. However, when they found city hall, the guards refused entry after sunset. When they argued that the sun was still above the horizon, the guards threatened to throw them in the dungeon for the night.

"They just want to end their shifts," Meredith commented as the travelers left city hall.

Rand sighed, echoing their collective weariness. "We will continue looking for him until we find him."

"Kaydin and I can find him by ourselves," Meredith offered.

"That is out of the question." Rand balked. "I promised to deliver you to your destination, and I will abide by my promise."

"You've brought us to Rivenwall. You fulfilled your promise!"

"I will not leave you until you are in safe hands. There will be no more said on the subject. Let's find a horse dealer."

Three city blocks were dedicated to horse dealing. True to his word, he bought Zray a horse. He also told Meredith to pick one. She argued that she was happy riding with Kaydin, but Rand insisted because Vasgo was worn ragged carrying two riders all these weeks. Meredith agreed and picked a white mare.

"I think I'll call her Moyna, *cloud* in the old language," Meredith said.

"My steed is Lightning," Zray announced.

"Lightning! Zray, that is a common name for a horse," Kaydin admonished him.

"Exactly, it'll be an easy name to remember. But don't insult my horse by assuming he is common." Zray patted the bay's neck. "You are an exceptional beast, Lightning, and don't let anyone tell you differently."

Kaydin rolled his eyes.

Rand found an inn near the waterfront, paid for one large room, the stabling fee for their horses, and bought them supper.

They visited city hall first thing in the morning, but it took quite a few hours before they found the name Jad'N listed under "wool merchants."

To their relief, Jad'N answered his door when they knocked. He was tall and—unlike his father—balding. He carried himself with an air of importance but not arrogance. His burgundy and green wool robe had the standard cut and style of his profession.

"May we please speak to Van'N?" Meredith asked eagerly.

"How do you know my father?" he asked, narrowing his eyes.

"He's our tutor," Kaydin explained, then introduced themselves. "Has he never spoken of us?"

"He has, but I thought you were in Tayose, not Dolsulbane."

"We were, but something happened," Meredith explained in a hurry. "We need to find him as soon as possible. Is he here?"

"He returned to Tayose a week ago."

Kaydin groaned.

"Do you know when he will be back?" Meredith asked.

"No." Jad'N shook his head. "I'm sure you know he doesn't journey here often."

"Well, thank you for your time." Meredith hung her head as they left.

"Oh, wonderful," Kaydin complained. "Now we're in a strange city in a strange country with nowhere to stay and nowhere to go." He switched to mind-speech, *We cannot go back to Quire Castle either, Quaeor might kill us before we get a chance to speak with Van'N. Our best bet is to find Father.*

Let's go back to the inn and we'll worry about it later, Meredith replied.

As they walked, Rand had them stop at a courier's office to check for word from his wife. The man had a letter for "Rand of the Islands." Rand's face lit up.

"Rand of the Islands is rather a broad term," the courier protested. "How do I know the letter is for you?"

"It is signed by a woman named Thia," Rand told him.

He opened the letter and scanned the page. A slow grin spread over the courier's face as he read. "It's a love letter!" he howled.

Rand's face burned bright red. "If it is signed by Thia, please give it to me."

"All right, all right." The man closed the letter again and handed it to Rand who stuffed it into his shirt. "The color of your face was all the proof I needed." He chuckled.

"How did the letter get here? I thought spring storms made trading with the Islands unsafe this time of year?" Meredith asked as they walked away.

"Some Paladalls have a magical system for sending letters," Rand explained. "If you pay them, they'll write on a spelled page, and the contents appear on another magical page far away."

"That's fascinating ..." Meredith considered that information for a moment before excitedly mind-speaking a revelation to her brother, *That's how Quaeor must be communicating with Sisinta!*

What I'd like to know, Kaydin mind-spoke back, *is why Rand is acquainted with Paladalls. I'm sure there are some who don't serve Sisinta, but those would be an exception to the rule.*

★★★

At the inn later that night, Kaydin, Meredith, Rand, and Zray stayed up late by the fire in the common room. Drunk men sang songs and shouted to each other. Zray eventually complained of fatigue and headed to bed.

Rand turned to the twins, "I will not leave you two alone. Is there nowhere else you can go?"

Kaydin glanced at Meredith. "There is someone ..."

"Kaydin ..." Meredith warned. She caught herself when she realized she had spoken aloud.

Kaydin continued, "Our father. He's probably somewhere near the Dragon Mountains."

Rand frowned. "I thought you said your father was dead."

"He was ... is, in a manner of speaking." Kaydin chose his words carefully. "He went into hiding four years ago after our mother died."

Rand took a deep breath and stared into the fire.

"You don't have to take us to him, Rand," Meredith told him. "We can find our own way."

"No," Rand said sharply and met their eyes in turn. "I am going in that direction. You will continue with me. It is time I returned home. I have not found Elyon, and I have been away from my wife and my people for too long."

"We don't know exactly where our father is," Meredith protested. "We might be wandering for a while before we locate him."

"We can ask one of Father's friends, Meredith," Kaydin offered.

"What friends?"

One of the dragons, he mind-spoke, giving her a very deliberate look.

"Oh, yes! You mean someone like Stavon."

"Exactly."

"Who is Stavon?" Rand asked.

"Someone who lives in the Dragon Mountains. Father used to visit him regularly," Meredith told him.

"*In* the mountains!" Rand exclaimed.

Kaydin cringed and nodded uncertainly. "Ah ... yes."

Rand thought for a moment then said slowly, "I see. Well then, it's settled. As much as I love sleeping in a warm bed and eating proper food, we must leave tomorrow after buying supplies. Now, go get some sleep."

The twins didn't argue. There was a sense of relief having someone they could trust, even just a little bit.

Meredith said, "I feel like I ought to clarify something."

"Hmm?" Rand turned to her.

"I think you're under the impression we're younger than we actually are."

"Oh? I'm sorry. I didn't presume to ask your ages."

"I think you're presuming how old we are anyway. So, I want you to know we're nearly eighteen."

"Oh!" Rand's brows shot to his hairline. "I'm sorry if you feel like I've been treating you like children. I honestly thought you were fifteen or sixteen at most!"

"You're not the first one to make that mistake. But please don't feel so burdened with responsibility in our regard. Have a good night."

As they ascended the stairs, Meredith looked back to see Rand take out the letter from Thia. She hurried after Kaydin, giving the man some privacy.

CHAPTER TWENTY-THREE

THE DEAD CITY

The monotony of trees, roadside streams, swaths of rocky plateaus, and sheep fields created the illusion of endlessly traversing the same road. It was as if they had never been to Rivenwall or slept in soft beds or eaten warm meals in front of fireplaces. Now and then, Meredith flipped through her sketchbook to remind herself of Boldwind's clock tower, Quire's crumbling outer walls, and Rivenwall's impressive architecture. Every night by the fire, she did her best to draw whatever had caught her eye that day. She rarely allowed herself the pleasure of flipping to the front of the book where painful questions rested between the crinkled pages and marred the sketches of a dark-eyed boy.

Zray remained a nuisance, but a nuisance they soon could not imagine living without. When they were tired of the weather, the insects, or the rock-hard bread, the minstrel would bolster their spirits with history, legends, and merry tunes. Sometimes, they would groan and protest, but once he had finished, they would reluctantly agree he did have talent and maybe he should tell another story. He was lazy, always hungry, too hot, too cold, constantly complaining, and talking himself into trouble, but he was lovable in his own way.

Rand kept mostly to himself, sharing little, but often asking questions about the history and songs that mentioned Elyon and Sisinta. The others had grown up with them and didn't quite understand how they could be new or even exciting to Rand. Zray didn't complain on that front—he enjoyed having an attentive listener. Rand didn't talk about his past. None of them did. Meredith had the impression everyone was hiding something, but none of them dared ask the others about it and risk being asked in return.

Some weeks after leaving Rivenwall, while passing through open countryside, Kaydin spotted a large, manmade structure in the distance. "What could that be?"

Zray replied, "I do believe that's the Dead City."

"The Dead City?" Rand puzzled over the name.

"You mean the city that was abandoned after a plague killed over three quarters of the population?" Meredith asked.

"Yes." Kaydin nodded. "It's called the Dead City now because they say the spirits of the dead walk the streets at night."

"We better not be going near that place." Zray shivered. "It scares me."

Kaydin rolled his eyes. "Everything scares you, Zray. You're afraid of the dark."

"I am not! I never said I was!"

"You didn't have to."

Rand cleared his throat. "Let us not argue. There is no reason why we should go near the city."

Kaydin shrugged and glanced at Zray who mumbled something less than complimentary under his breath.

Rand pulled out the map from his breast pocket and squinted at it.

Meredith spoke up, "It's going to be dark soon, and there is nothing around for miles."

"You're right," Rand agreed. "I really do not like spending the night without any protection."

"Protection from what?" Zray asked.

"Well, the weather, for one," Kaydin said.

"What are those?" Zray pointed behind. "They seem to be running toward us."

The others reined in their horses and turned to look.

Three feline creatures streaked toward them. Their eyes glowed brighter as they advanced in the fading light.

"It's the vagwhar! Run!" Rand kicked his horse into a gallop.

"It's the *what*?" Zray screeched.

Meredith and Kaydin followed Rand. Zray galloped behind, shouting questions that went unanswered.

The black cats quickened their pace and began to close the gap at an alarming rate.

The Dead City loomed closer every moment, and the fleeing party soon realized their only hope lay in reaching the city.

Their horses were wet with sweat and shivering with exertion when they finally arrived at the city's outer wall. Despite the city being abandoned, the walls were in excellent condition and there didn't appear to be a way through them. There was a large gate, but it was barred on the inside. Rand led them along the city wall, looking for another way in.

"I see a door in the wall, but it's rotted away!" Meredith shouted.

"We cannot go in there!" Zray protested. "Didn't you hear the part about the ghosts inside?"

"What do you suggest then? We try to outrun them?" Kaydin retorted.

Rand drew his sword and knocked down the old door in three strikes of its pommel. The door was narrow but tall and they were able to pass through on horseback.

Rand dismounted before his horse had come to a complete halt. He ran to the doorless hole in the wall and called for the others to help him fill it in. They grabbed rubble, rotten boards, broken roof shingles, large sections of stone fallen off the wall, and loose cobblestones from the street.

"Use whatever you can!" Rand urged as he picked up the biggest stone he could lift and, staggering under the weight, dumped it in the entrance.

The others followed his example and began frantically piling rubble in the doorway. Within a minute, the entire opening was almost filled.

"They're nearly here!" Kaydin shouted.

A second later, first one vagwhar and then another slammed their bodies into the rubble.

"Kaydin!" Meredith yelled.

He jumped back just in time as one vagwhar forced its poisonous claw through a gap.

Zray grabbed a stone and jammed it into the opening, crushing the animal's claw.

Its horrific scream made all the companions cry out in pain and cover their ears. The four horses reared, and then ran whinnying shrilly into the city.

"Come on!" Rand yelled over the sound of the vagwhar's screams. "We must get the horses!"

They hurried in the general direction their mounts had taken. They'd run a great distance into the city before the vagwhar's angry cries faded and then disappeared completely.

Night was falling, and every moment, the air grew steadily wetter as mist began to settle over the city. Within minutes, the fog claimed their vision. Meredith couldn't help imagining that the mounds of rubble looming before them were misshapen people and creatures—trolls, a small child, figures lying in the street.

Her impressions carried over to Kaydin and he mentally shouted, *Stop it! You're making me jumpy!*

Sorry, I can't help it! Zray's emotions are wearing off on me.

After a few minutes, they were forced to a walk.

"We're never going to find the horses in this mess! I can barely see a few feet in front of me," Zray whined.

"He is right." Rand sighed. "We should find shelter. We can look for the horses in the morning."

"Here!" Kaydin called them over to a stone house. "It still has a roof and doors."

Rand tried the door. "It is locked. I'll have to knock it down, but then it will be useless to stay in."

"Wait!" Meredith picked up a flat stone of pink quartz. Under the stone was a key, rusty with age. She handed it to Rand.

His eyes widened in amazement.

"The stone was different from all the others and seemed purposely placed," she explained.

"I think this will work much better than knocking the door down." Rand smiled. With some effort, the key turned, and the door opened reluctantly on squealing hinges.

Meredith thought the house loathed to let them enter, like it feared they'd wake the long undisturbed memories inside.

The lone room stood empty. Dust covered the floor and windowsills. It was too quiet.

Meredith shivered and Kaydin felt a great sadness for the place.

Zray spoke first, "I wonder who used to live here."

Rand closed the door and locked it behind them. "Do you have your tinderbox, Kaydin?"

"No." Kaydin shook his head. "It's in the saddlebags."

"Oh, great. No food, no tinderbox, no horses. What are we supposed to do?" Zray groaned.

"Just go to sleep, I suppose," Meredith said.

"I'm so hungry." Zray moaned.

"You are not the only one, Zray," Rand reminded him.

"I'm sure I'm the only one who cares!"

"Just because we don't complain doesn't mean we don't care about anything!" Kaydin retorted.

Zray opened his mouth but shut it again. He frowned and sat in a corner where he threw menacing glares in Kaydin's direction.

"Fighting will not help us any," Rand admonished. "Come now, Zray, will you not tell us a story?"

"No, I will not." Zray sulked.

"Very well, then, I shall tell you something from my country." Rand sat on the stone floor near a window and started in a clear strong voice. "There is a legend, a prophecy of sorts, in my country. It tells of a prince who will free our people from Sisinta's tyranny and stand as one after Elyon's own heart." Rand paused and gazed at the others. "Have you ever heard of this?"

The others shook their heads.

"I suppose it is strange to have one such prophecy from any place other than Higher Quith. After all, Elyon is not our king, he is yours. Yet we long for him to see us as well and come to our aid. We do not deserve it, I suppose. What hope do we have?" Rand sighed and leaned against the wall.

"Do you mind me asking about the letter you received in Rivenwall?" Meredith asked.

Rand's eyes lit up and a small smile lingered at the corners of his mouth. "Thia is well. The baby is due next month."

A low, long, eerie sound echoed in the streets.

Zray's face contorted and Meredith and Kaydin glanced fearfully at each other.

"What was that?" Meredith whispered.

"Ghosts," Zray rasped. He glared at Rand. "I told you we shouldn't have come here! Now we'll never be heard from again!"

"Calm down. It is just the wind. Besides, if you became a ghost would you torment people?" Rand asked.

"I might ..." Zray let his voice trail off mysteriously.

"Oh, come on, Zray! Don't be superstitious," Kaydin reprimanded.

The ghastly sound came again.

Rand opened the shutters and looked outside. The others joined him. The fog was thick, drifting in clouds that obscured their view of the street.

"Did you see that?" Zray cried, jumping back in fright. He pointed randomly into the mist.

"No, Zray, we didn't. We cannot see anything." Kaydin sighed, frustrated.

A figure emerged ten feet away. Shaped like a large man, its eyes shone brilliant blue and its skin glowed ethereal white.

Rand slammed the shutters shut and locked them. "Get back!" He pulled Meredith and Kaydin away from the window, across the room where Zray had already taken refuge.

"Why?" Kaydin asked. "It didn't look dreadful at all. It almost looked beautiful."

"Looks are deceiving. That was a Shadow, a demon," Rand whispered.

"How do you know?" Zray also spoke in hushed tones.

"I have seen them before. Men are powerless against them."

"Men are, but not Elyon," Meredith spoke loudly.

Rand and Zray cringed at her tone.

"They cannot harm us," she added quieter.

"She's right," Kaydin said. "They can do nothing. My father told us they are afraid of Elyon. The saying goes that he 'bound them to the earth and the night.' Though I don't know what that means."

"Are you daft? Keep your voice down!" Zray snapped.

"We're subjects of High King Elyon. Stay away from us!" Meredith shouted.

As soon as she spoke Elyon's name, thousands of screeches pierced the night. It remained a constant, high-pitched scream.

Rand yelled over the noise, "I understand you believe that they cannot hurt us, but you need not anger them."

"They'll be gone in the morning," Kaydin shouted back. "My father said they can't come out during the day without a host body. All we can do is wait."

CHAPTER TWENTY-FOUR

THE HALL OF TWELVE TREES

Meredith slowly cracked open the front door. Perfect silence. Traces of the night's fog drifted low to the ground. She looked east across the abandoned city and glimpsed the sky fading from ebony to navy blue. She withdrew into the house again, closing the door behind her.

The others were still sleeping. The demon Shadows had kept them awake for most of the night with their screeching and moaning. Meredith took a deep breath of relief. Now she wanted to go back to sleep without the sounds of nightmares in her head, but she knew if they wanted to find the horses and leave the accursed city before dark, they had to get up now.

Meredith woke Kaydin first. She closed her eyes and pushed carefully against the door of his mind. He resisted at first but a few seconds later, his eyes fluttered open. He sat up and rubbed the sleep out of his eyes. *Are they gone?*

Meredith nodded. *The sun is going to rise soon. You wake Rand and I'll see to Zray.*

The minstrel was harder to wake than a bear in the dead of winter and snored as loud as one too. Meredith shook him but he didn't stir, so she grabbed the hat with the ridiculous feather off his head. Almost immediately, Zray jerked awake and jumped to his feet. He snatched the hat from her hand.

"Never," Zray shook his finger at her, "never, touch my hat." He jammed it back on his head and stomped to the other side of the room.

Kaydin laughed at the sulking minstrel. "What's with you and that hat anyway?"

Zray glowered in response.

A few long minutes later, the sun rose, and the small group ventured into the Dead City. When they spoke to each other, their words echoed off the city walls and spread through the empty streets. They had to pick their way carefully through the debris-strewn streets—fallen roof tiles, rotted wood, crumbling and tumbling stones.

A bucket with a rusted hole in the bottom creaked from the end of a chain hanging over a communal well. Meredith paused to look down into the well's inky blackness while the others walked on. A streak of blue-white light flashed in the darkness below. She gasped and jerked back, sending loose stones from the well's lip clashing down its gaping maw. She took two shaky breaths before stepping forward and peering into it again. Only blackness. No splash of water meant it must be dry.

Don't mention it. Zray will panic, Kaydin cautioned. *Let's just get out of here as quickly as possible.*

Meredith took another shuddering breath and nodded. She ran to catch up, minding the terrain.

"Do you notice something odd about this place?" Zray asked.

"Everything about it is odd," Kaydin said.

At the front of the line, Rand called for a halt to catch their breath when they arrived at the top of a steep mound of rubble.

"No, I mean *really* odd," Zray insisted.

"I give up, Zray, what is so odd about this place?" Meredith said between gasps for breath as she sat on a large boulder.

"There are no plants."

Rand cast his gaze over the landscape. "He is correct. Nature should be taking over."

"I bet it's those demons." Zray smirked triumphantly. "They keep anything good from growing, and nothing can survive."

"You have to hand it to him, Kaydin, he could be right." Rand shrugged.

"Only this time," Kaydin grumbled under his breath.

Why are you always picking on Zray? Meredith mentally rebuked her brother, but found he was already miserable.

I really don't know. I tell myself to be nicer to him, but the wrong words come out.

Then, think before you speak.

I've been trying.

I think you're just taking out your frustration over our situation on him.

"We should keep going," Rand said. "We are more or less rested now."

A faint, shrill cry caught Meredith's ear.

"Wait," she said.

"What is it?" Kaydin asked.

"Listen." Meredith held a finger in the air.

They strained their ears.

Rand said slowly, "Was that our horses whinnying?"

"That's what it sounded like to me!" Meredith jumped off the rock and climbed down the other side of the rubble as fast as she could.

The others followed, and they broke into a run once on the road.

Meredith rounded a bend, then called out, "Over here! I found them!"

The others arrived an instant later. The horses were trapped in an alley. The animals' eyes were wild, and they reared and snorted frantically.

"What's the matter with them?" Zray asked.

"It seems last night's ordeal has made them delirious," Rand observed. "Aldaydo!" he commanded.

Aldaydo nickered in recognition.

Rand snatched the horse's dragging reins.

The warhorse immediately stilled. When Aldaydo calmed, so did the others.

Kaydin and Meredith easily caught their horses, but Zray was terrified of Lightning's skittish behavior. He tried to grab the reins trailing on the ground, but with every step forward, Lightning took a step back. Zray stopped and the horse stopped. Zray looked to the others for help.

"Do not look at us, we have to hold our horses," Kaydin said with a grin.

"We will encourage you, though." Meredith smiled.

Zray rolled his eyes and looked at his horse. Lightning eyed him back. "Okay, horsey, it's just you and me. Save me a lot of trouble and just come over here."

Lightning stayed where he was.

The others snickered.

Zray whipped his head around.

Rand was checking the buckles on Aldaydo's saddle, Meredith was staring up at the sky, and Kaydin was picking at an interesting bit of fluff on his sleeve.

Zray frowned at them, then stared down his ornery horse.

"I'm sure you'll stare him into submission, Zray." Kaydin laughed.

Zray charged the horse. Lightning was momentarily stunned, but quickly recovered enough to bolt. Zray managed to put his hands up in time before slamming into a stone wall. He rubbed his wrists, sore from the impact, and turned to find Kaydin holding Lightning's reins. Zray stomped over and grabbed them from him. He mounted and started to ride away.

"Wait for us, Zray!" Meredith called as she and the others hurried their horses after him. When they caught up, she added softly, "We didn't mean to hurt your feelings, Zray."

"Don't bother mentioning this incident again," Zray said flatly, refusing to look at her.

"Zray, don't take it personally."

"Wow!" Zray halted Lightning abruptly, and Meredith had to pull Moyna to a quick stop. "Look!" Zray pointed ahead.

Meredith peered around the minstrel. Rand and Kaydin stopped on either side of her.

"What is it?" Kaydin asked, breathless.

"It is the most beautiful thing I have seen in a long time," Rand said with wonder.

The six-story structure ahead was almost completely covered in green, growing vines that reached clinging fingers and arms upward in a verdant embrace. Flowers nestled among the leaves in little bursts of color. In contrast with the Dead City behind them, the building was an oasis. A warm wind rocked the leaves in a slow, calm rustle, revealing glimpses of the stone underneath. Meredith caught glimpses of dragons, animals, warriors, mountains, and a myriad other images and messages carved in multiple languages and symbols.

A large stone archway granted entrance. Its inscription read: "Gal est et gal fay. Gal ba et gal may. Gal soy da et gal toy past Oy villa."

"What does it mean?" Zray asked. He leaned as far back in the saddle as he could.

Rand eyed him nervously, like a bird watching its fledgling about to topple out of a nest.

"It means, 'Here is and here lives. Here are and here was. Here will be and here ever shall he dwell,'" Meredith translated.

"You can speak the old language?" Rand's eyes brightened.

"Yes." Meredith smiled. "Can you?"

"Indeed." Rand nodded. "I spoke it for the first twelve years of my life."

"Hey! You three! Are you coming or not?" Zray had tied Lightning's reins to the base of a thick vine and stood under the arch. The others followed.

They entered a massive hall that spanned the length of the building. The floor was made of smooth, white marble with hints of gray, like clouds with vague outlines. The marble was nearly perfect except straight down the middle where the roots of twelve sprawling trees had cracked and buckled through the pavement. Their mighty limbs obscured the glass ceiling above. The girths of the trees suggested they were thousands of years old. A pool of clear water glistened in the center of the room between the two center trees. A shaft of light fell through the glass ceiling and penetrated the pool's surface and mottled its tiled floor. The four humans marveled in silence. Meredith took a deep breath and smelled life in the damp, heavy air.

"What sort of place is this?" Rand asked in awe.

"There's something pure about it." Zray gaped at the ceiling above. "I definitely need to write a ballad about this."

A melody, light and pure echoed off the high stone walls.

"Do you hear a bird?" Meredith turned about to locate the creature.

"Over there." Kaydin pointed where tree branches spread over the pool.

An unidentified large bird perched in the branches, alert and watching them. It chirped a few notes every few seconds. A bright blue tail, several feet long, spread out behind it. A green crest crowned its head. It spread huge turquoise wings, tilted its head back, and warbled like a bubbling brook.

"Could this be a piece of the old world?" Kaydin asked. "Things were different before the Witch-Queen. Perhaps the curse she uttered at her birth did not touch this place?"

"Her birth? What do you mean?" Rand's eyebrows pinched.

"Sisinta was 'reborn' as the Witch-Queen when she uttered a curse that spread across the world and started the war with High King Elyon," Kaydin explained.

"I have never heard that story." Rand shook his head.

"It's a fascinating legend. I'll tell it to you some time," Zray offered as he continued to survey the room.

Meredith looked at her reflection in the pool. Its bottom was covered in sapphires. A breathy whisper filled her ears. She leaned even closer, inches from the water's surface. *The jewels are whispering. I can't quite make out what they're saying,* Meredith mind-spoke to Kaydin. She reached into the pool, and a cool shock creeped up her arm.

"'Tis not for you! 'Tis not for you!"

Meredith snatched her hand back.

The bird stared intently with eyes like the stones in the bottom of the pool.

"Did it just speak?" Kaydin's tone wavered.

"I think it did." Rand nodded.

"A talking bird!" Meredith exclaimed. "I've always wanted to see one. I've heard they can mimic the words of men."

The bird flew to perch on the pool's edge. "'Tis not for you! 'Tis not for you!" It bobbed its head as it spoke and fixed its eyes on Meredith. "The holiest of secrets can become a curse when it is not meant for you! Not meant for you! Not meant for you!"

"I think it's saying you shouldn't touch the stones," Kaydin offered.

"Here is and here lives. Here are and here was. Here will be and here ever shall he dwell," the bird squawked.

"What does that mean?" Zray eyed the bird suspiciously.

"I think it means Elyon is somehow here, and you cannot touch him," Rand suggested.

"You cannot get out! You cannot get out!" The bird bobbed its head. "Evil lies at every turn!"

"I don't like this!" Zray's voice shook. "It sounds like it wants to trap us here! This creature is in league with those Shadow demons!" He turned to run.

Meredith grabbed the back of his tunic.

Zray scrambled on the stone before regaining his balance.

"Elyon leads! Elyon leads!" The bird warbled.

"I don't think it would speak the name of Elyon if it was planning to kill us," Meredith assured. "Elyon isn't evil."

Zray pulled himself from her grasp and smoothed his ruffled tunic.

"Follow the sun and go by the moon! Follow the sun and go by the moon! Wherever you travel ever shall there be one of these. One of these! One of these!"

"Okay, the repeating thing is getting on my nerves," Zray snapped at the bird. "If you need to say something, just say it! Don't make us lose our minds and die of vexation!"

The bird continued, "Follow the river and chase the wind! Follow the river and chase the wind!" It returned to its perch and sang its warbling song.

"We should go now," Rand reluctantly told the others. "We do not want to spend the night in the city again."

"Follow the sun and go by the moon! Follow the sun and go by the moon! Follow the river and chase the wind! Follow the river and chase the wind!" the bird sang again.

Rand, Kaydin, and Zray left through the archway, but Meredith stopped just outside and picked a small section of vines growing around the arch.

"If I were you, I wouldn't touch those," Zray warned.

"Why?" Meredith twisted the small vine into a necklace and tied it around her neck. "I want to take some of this place with me. I don't think it's evil."

Zray eyed her warily for a few minutes, as if he expected Meredith to turn green and fall over dead, or a black cloud to descend and consume her for her profanation. When nothing happened, he shrugged and said, "It's your funeral."

"The sun is low on the horizon," Kaydin observed.

"We were in there all afternoon? How can that be?" Meredith asked in surprise. "We didn't look around for more than ten minutes!"

"Perhaps time moves differently inside that place?" Zray shivered under the gaze of the Hall of Twelve Trees.

CHAPTER TWENTY-FIVE

RIDDLES, RUINS, AND ROADS

The companions continued through the Dead City toward the outer wall. After two hours of navigating streets and alleyways, sidestepping large piles of rubble and debris, Kaydin asked, "Are we going in the right direction?"

Rand halted Aldaydo to look around. The others stopped behind him.

"I have no idea," Rand admitted. He spurred his horse into a gallop down the street.

The others followed. After a few minutes, they rounded a bend and found themselves on a main road. Rand followed it and shortly stopped his horse at the edge of the city square.

"How did you know where this was?" Meredith asked.

"The keep is taller than most other buildings. It'll be a good vantage point to gauge our location." Rand led them to the stone keep where they tied the horses to the rusted rings in the wall. Rand tried the door, and it opened easily.

Inside was a hall with another door at the end. A stone staircase to their left spiraled toward the roof. The air smelled of dust and mold and the walls were damp with condensation. Cobwebs hung from the high corners of the ceiling. There was no window, and the only light came from the setting sun through the door behind them. Rand took a burnt-out torch from a tarnished metal ring in the wall.

"Kaydin, grab your flint," Rand requested as he cleaned the torch.

Kaydin obliged. Rand held out the torch and Kaydin struck two rocks together. A few sparks fell but did not light—the oil-soaked cloth was too damp. However, after a few more tries, the fire caught, and the torch leapt to life.

Rand held it out as the twins and Zray followed him single-file up the narrow staircase. Every fourth step featured arrow slits carved into the stone wall.

A lot of good arrows would have been as a defense against an overwhelming plague, Kaydin silently commented to his sister.

Meredith almost slipped on the worn, slick steps. Kaydin grabbed her arm. They stopped to catch their breath.

Have you noticed the grooves in the steps? Meredith scuffed one foot on an indent. *At one time, these stairs were so well used the people who climbed them wore away the stone.*

The whole city is still filled with evidence of those who once lived here.

"Are you well?" Rand had paused for them.

"Yes, we're coming," Meredith confirmed.

At last, they reached the top of the stairs. The door at the top groaned terribly when Rand opened it, and the handle crumbled in his hand. A gust of fresh air filled their lungs as they stepped onto the rooftop. In turns, they gave gasps and groans of disappointment. In every direction were lifeless streets and roofless or caved-in houses. In the square below were the dilapidated remnants of merchants' stalls and animal pens.

"I had no idea the city was so huge," Meredith whispered, disheartened.

"The Hall of Twelve Trees was taller than this keep, yet I cannot see it," Zray observed.

"Neither can I." Kaydin shook his head. "It's like it disappeared."

"That is odd," Rand agreed.

"Or creepy," Zray muttered and added, "Maybe it was a figment of our imaginations brought on by some kind of residual demon magic? This city must be steeped in evil magic." Zray shivered and pulled his cloak tighter about himself.

"We know for certain it was real." Rand pointed to Meredith's necklace. "Meredith still wears the vine."

"We'll never be able to get out of here tonight!" Zray wailed.

"Follow the sun and go by the moon," Rand murmured. Then, his tone brightened. "Follow the sun and go by the moon!"

"What did you say?" Kaydin asked.

"West! Follow the sun! The sun goes from the east toward the west!"

"Are you all right in the head? I think you've started babbling nonsense." Zray asked.

"The bird! It was telling us how to get out of the city!" Rand explained.

"But what about everything else it said?" Meredith asked. "'Wherever you travel there will be one of these,' and the part about following the moon and the river and chasing the wind?"

"I am not sure," Rand leaned on the battlements and closed his eyes in concentration. "What is usually there with you wherever you go?" he wondered aloud.

"The sky?" Zray suggested.

"Elyon?" Kaydin offered.

"The wind?" Meredith added.

"Air?" Zray tried.

"Air! Really, Zray that is ridiculous!" Kaydin scoffed. "How are we supposed to follow air?"

"Well, like Meredith said, the wind. The bird said, 'follow the river and chase the wind,' so we should follow the wind."

"But the direction of the wind changes all the time," Meredith countered.

"No, no." Rand opened his eyes and shook his head. "None of those options make sense. It is a riddle. We must look beyond the obvious."

"Grass?" Zray offered.

"Clouds?" Kaydin suggested.

"The earth or land?" Meredith asked.

"Wait. Wait." Rand started pacing the roof, his brow furrowed in thought. "The ground ... the ground. What is here in the city that is usually everywhere else?"

"Houses?" Kaydin asked.

"Stone?" Meredith wondered.

Rand stopped before Zray. "You are a minstrel, you tell riddles. What does it mean?"

Zray was silent for a long moment. "The ground ... roads ... streets." Zray grinned. "'Wherever you travel there ever shall be one of these.' There are usually streets wherever you go, especially in a city."

"So," Rand resumed pacing, "we go toward the sun." He stopped again and turned to the others. "And follow the streets? What if ... sun, moon, river, and wind are all names of streets?"

"Yes!" Zray cheered.

"But there are hundreds of streets! How will we know where those specific streets are?" Meredith asked.

Rand faced the sun. "The sun street is toward the sun. Come. Let's return to the square." He led the way down the steps.

They mounted their horses and hurried to the west side of the square, then surveyed the three streets that branched off on that side.

"Do any of you see street signs?" Rand asked.

They each chose the head of a street.

"This one says 'Kas heel,' Fish Street," Kaydin called.

"This one does not have a name!" Zray complained.

Meredith helped him look.

"My street is called 'Nus heel,'" Rand said.

"What does 'Nus' mean?" Kaydin asked Rand. "I don't think it's the old language."

"'Heel' means street, but I do not know what 'Nus' means." Rand agreed.

"It spells 'sun' backward!" Zray declared as he and Meredith approached.

Rand laughed and reached over to ruffle Zray's hair, knocking the boy's hat askew. "I knew you were good at riddles, Master Minstrel!"

Zray fiddled with his hat to hide a smile.

Rand pushed Aldaydo into a gallop down the street and the others followed.

"Look out for Moon Street!" Kaydin called.

"Or Noom Street," Zray reminded. "I am glad these street signs are carved in stone. Wooden signs would have rotted away a long time ago."

A little while later, the sun was setting. The twins and Zray glanced at each other, wondering if they should remind Rand. He seemed unaware, caught up in reading street signs in the sun's fading light.

The road came to a fork. One way was "Noom Heel" and the other "Way's Street." They took Noom Heel then Virda Heel, or River Street. In the meantime, the darkness grew deeper, and the air was damp again. The fog was not far behind.

"Rand, maybe we should stop and find a safe place to spend the night," Zray voiced their collective worry.

"I said we would not spend another night in this city, and I meant it!" Rand countered. "Besides, the bird has been right thus far, and we have only one more street to find."

With the darkness came the fog, cold, and wet. The lack of visibility forced them to slow the now-troubled horses. Piles of rubble appeared without warning in the fog and the horses had difficulty maintaining a steady pace.

"The vine!" Zray cried, pointing at Meredith's neck. "It's glowing!"

A halo of soft green light surrounded Meredith's neck and face.

"I have never seen a bioluminescent plant before," Rand remarked.

Zray glanced fearfully at Meredith and her glowing vine. Eventually, the nearly non-existent visibility and the terrors of the occasional screech in the distance drew his attention away.

Meredith didn't *think* the vine was possessed by evil magic—it felt *right* around her neck and it had come from a place that had possessed that sense of *rightness*.

"Rand, if there is another street, we will not be able to see it!" Meredith called to him. Her voice did not carry, oddly dampened in the dense fog.

Rand did not answer, and no one else spoke. Everyone concentrated on keeping the person next in line within their sights.

Mere, came Kaydin's voice in Meredith's mind.

What is it?

I thought I saw something.

Meredith saw nothing but white-gray mist. *I can't see anything!*

It was just for a moment, and now, I am not sure it was there at all.

Meredith noticed Zray on his horse to her right and not behind her where he usually was. "Zray!" she called to him.

"I'm right here!" Zray's voice sounded behind her.

"Then, who is that?" She pointed to her right, but the rider was gone.

"Probably just the fog, it makes you see things." Zray's voice trembled slightly.

I see a rider too, Meredith. Kaydin mind-spoke. *On my left. There's no fog around him.* A moment later Kaydin added, *He* saw *me. I can't explain it, but I think he was looking at ... my soul!*

What did he look like? Meredith whipped her head around, searching for the figure.

I don't know, I couldn't see his face. All I know is that he was *looking at me. He's gone now.*

"I think there's a Shadow demon following us!" Zray said with a tremor.

Sure enough, a tall, man-like figure with the glowing eyes of a Shadow watched and followed them from a distance.

"There *is* a Shadow following us!" Meredith yelped.

"Why does it not attack us?" Rand wondered. "We cannot kill them with our swords, and we are alone."

"I don't think we are," Kaydin said solemnly. "Meredith and I saw other riders, and they didn't look like Shadows."

"We need to get out! Has anyone seen the wind road yet?" Zray's tone teetered on the edge of panic.

"Right there! Look!" Meredith cried. "The fog is clearing and I can see a gate!"

The fog was indeed clearing and the small gate ahead became visible. They spurred their horses forward, and a moment later, were attempting to lift the heavy beam barring the gate.

After a few minutes of struggling, they forced the gate open. Clean air greeted them with kisses of cold, invigorating energy. The moon's blue-white light illuminated the plains.

Meredith stepped over the threshold and the vine's green glow blinked out.

None of them had time to enjoy the clear air and freedom. Instead, they took on their respective roles as quickly and efficiently as possible. Meredith was to lead the horses in a pack chain, while the men carried the large wooden beam.

If the Shadow creatures could have left the city, they would have long ago. An unknown force doomed them to their prison of empty houses and streets. But barring the door still seemed wise.

Just before closing the gate behind them, Rand spotted the unknown rider.

The robed and hooded rider inclined his head slightly in recognition, then turned his horse and galloped away, leaving a trail of clear, fogless air behind him. The horse's hooves made no sound.

"How in the world did we manage to find the right street in that fog?" Zray wondered breathlessly. He was trembling, bent over with hands on his thighs while he gasped for air.

The others said nothing but suspected the unknown rider had something to do with it. Rand helped Kaydin and Zray lift the heavy wooden beam into the gate's outer slots. They all hoped it would stay barred forever.

CHAPTER TWENTY-SIX

SLEEPLESS

Days of travel bled into weeks of mindless drudgery.

How long has it been since we left Rivenwall? Meredith asked Kaydin at one point.

Kaydin squinted at the noonday sun and furrowed his brow. After a moment, he shrugged. *I've lost track of time.*

Me too. Meredith sighed internally.

They had stopped at inns whenever they happened to encounter one, but most nights were spent on the sides of highways with only a fire and their now-threadbare blankets for warmth.

Slowly but surely, Meredith had come to think of Rand and Zray as more than traveling companions. She thought, perhaps, they could call each other friends now.

Rand periodically reminded them to keep an eye out for signs of the vagwhar. Zray had tried getting information about the cats after the Dead City incident, but no one offered an explanation. He'd eventually stopped asking, and instead dedicated hours to composing an epic poem about their near-death experience. To pass time around the fire at night and get over her fear of the black cats, Meredith sketched their snarling faces and sleek feline figures in her sketchbook.

At one point, they met a passing caravan from Athlon. The travelers pulled over to the side of the road and watched. The Sillian merchants wore robes and tunics of turquoise and orange, made from unique got cloth using secretive dyeing and weaving techniques. The haughty individuals rode gottle birds bareback with thin ropes tied about the animals' beaks. The large birds were man-height with long, blue legs and large, taloned feet. They squawked periodically and fluffed their vibrant crests when their riders directed them where they didn't feel inclined to go. Several Sillians narrowed wary, almond-shaped eyes at the travelers as they passed and let their hands drift to the finely-worked knives tied to their cloth sashes.

Do we really look that threatening? Kaydin mind-spoke the question.

Meredith surveyed their travel-worn clothes and their horses' neglected coats. She ran her fingers through her snarled brown curls. They certainly did look like disreputable company. Zray still wore his hat with the large feather in it, but he had stopped trying to convince the others to let him wear his colorful minstrel's outfit. At that moment, Meredith thought that if he had been wearing it, he would have looked more sophisticated than the rest of them.

Meredith ducked her head in embarrassment and wondered if she should ask Rand for money to buy a new dress next time they reached a town. It seemed like a vain, selfish thought after Rand had spent so much of his money on them already.

Kaydin caught her thoughts. *Don't disparage yourself, I think you look fine. If it makes you feel better, compare your dress to my socks.*

Meredith watched her brother pull one foot out of his boot and wiggle his toes through large holes in his sock. Meredith's mouth quirked to hold in a snicker that inevitably escaped. Kaydin's own laugh joined hers.

"The way you two carry on, I'd think you're reading each other's minds," Zray complained.

The twins sobered immediately. Kaydin cleared his throat and kept his eyes straight ahead, while Meredith avoided his gaze and picked at the loose threads on her sleeve.

★★★

One night, after a particularly long and hard day of traveling, they made camp in the woods. After starting a fire, Rand and Kaydin went hunting, but returned unsuccessful.

"It is very odd," Rand said as he sank down in exhaustion, "there are no birds or squirrels or pheasants. When we were riding earlier, I saw many. We seemed to have scared them off."

"Or maybe this area has already been heavily hunted and cleared of game?" Kaydin suggested. He groaned and removed his sole-worn boots before stretching his feet toward the fire.

"It just means we will be having dried meat instead of fresh." Meredith tried to sound cheerful while rummaging in the food pack.

"You need not remind us, Mere," Kaydin grumbled.

"I don't like this," Zray groused. "Why didn't we stop in that village this morning and buy more food?"

"Zray! It's not our coin. You shouldn't demand to use it," Meredith chastised.

"No, he is right," Rand conceded. "I should have stopped and bought provisions."

"What is done is done. We cannot go back, so we'll just have to be happy with what we have," Meredith said firmly. She did her best to find edible greens and berries so when they drifted off into an exhausted sleep after supper, they were moderately satisfied.

★★★

Kaydin woke sometime after midnight. The fire burned low, and moonbeams found their way through the treetops to the ground around him. He tossed and turned for some time. Frustrated, he sat up. Something glowed near Meredith where she slept a few feet away. The vine around her neck. After leaving the Dead City, Meredith had shared her suspicion that the vine's glow indicated some sort of danger nearby.

Heart racing, Kaydin stretched his mind around him for a moment until he sensed all three minds—Meredith, Rand, and Zray. He sighed in relief.

Then, four unknown minds drifted into his consciousness.

Kaydin froze. The thoughts from the new minds were a constant stream with no context of past or future. He recognized the common theme of animals' senseless thoughts, slaves to their instincts and impulses. The woods were thick and filled with shadows. No matter how intently he peered into them, he couldn't see any hidden vagwhar.

There! A pair of eyes, glowing white, just beyond the light of the dying fire.

Then a second and a third. And yet another.

Kaydin's heart fluttered with fear and anxiety. He grabbed the largest stick within reach and thrust it into the fire, stoking the flames. As soon as the fire sprang up, the animals leapt away from the light. Kaydin shouted with mind-speech and his voice simultaneously.

His companions woke. Rand had his sword in his hand before he was even on his feet. Kaydin scrambled back to his bedroll and snatched up Swan. Meredith rolled to her feet, collecting dried leaves and dirt in her mussed hair. After sleepily stumbling upright, Zray began asking incoherent questions. The horses were bucking and neighing in terror. Kaydin also realized he'd used the last piece of firewood.

"To the horses!" Rand called. He raced for Aldaydo and mounted the panicked horse.

The others followed, and soon, all four travelers galloped down the road.

Kaydin looked back and saw the black cats silently loping after them. It was only a matter of moments before the cats caught up. He had to lead the vagwhar away from the others. Without stopping to think over the consequences, Kaydin turned Vasgo off the road and into the woods. The four cats followed.

Kaydin dug his heels into Vasgo's side, urging the horse to move faster. Vasgo was already at his maximum speed, fueled by terror. A black cat leapt at the horse's flank and fell short by only a few inches. Horse and rider burst into a clearing and found themselves facing a natural rock wall. Kaydin swung Vasgo about and pushed him to follow the stone wall, which he soon discovered was a ridge. The horse was having none of it. When Kaydin dug in his heels, Vasgo reared and threw him. The horse's hooves crashed down inches from his rider's head. The impact threw dirt in Kaydin's face. He rolled before Vasgo could rear again. With Swan in his hand, he barely missed slicing himself on the blade. Vasgo whinnied and fled into the woods.

Kaydin lay stunned for a moment, then forced himself through the shock and onto his feet. As he took a defensive stance, the vagwhar formed a circle around him, one crouched, ready to spring, while the others stalked back and forth. Kaydin took a steadying breath, and then leapt forward. The moment his sword sliced through the crouched vagwhar, he cringed. Flesh and bone gave way beneath the well-maintained blade. His hands trembled. Another cat roared and pounced. Kaydin thrust his sword into the animal's chest before it could reach him. The beast's dead weight knocked him to the ground. Fueled by the rush of the fight, he threw all his might into pushing the thing off and rising.

The two remaining vagwhar continued pacing, keeping him in their sights, and occasionally advancing lightly only to retreat again. Breathing hard, Kaydin watched them wearily—his energy ebbed. If his strength failed, they would overwhelm him and he would surely die. Just like his mother: alone and poisoned.

Kaydin tried to ignore the despair pressing in on him. His father had frequently taught him of the strength bestowed from the High King. "A benevolent king," he'd called him. Kaydin could certainly use such help now. In his mind, he cried out with as much concentration as he could spare. How *did* one summon an all-powerful being?

At that moment, the vagwhar on his right stepped toward him. Kaydin ran the last few feet and brought his sword down on its head. The cat screamed and jerked its head back and forth. Kaydin sliced again and felt Swan go through bone. A second too late, he realized he would not be able to turn around before the remaining vagwhar could attack his exposed flank. As he swung around to face it, the animal slammed its body into his, knocking him over, and pinning him with its front paws. Kaydin scrabbled for Swan just beyond his reach. The vagwhar snarled and extended its claws into his chest. He cried out and grappled with the vagwhar's head, attempting to wrestle it off. The black cat remained unmoved. Every streak of its claws burned like fire.

Kaydin heard a cry of rage and both he and the cat froze.

CHAPTER TWENTY-SEVEN

BLACK POISON

Meredith stood over the vagwhar with Kaydin's sword in both hands. She drove it into the animal's back. The cat collapsed onto Kaydin.

"I can't breathe!" he gasped, struggling to shove off the vagwhar.

Meredith dropped to her knees, and together they rolled it away. The animal flopped on its back, gave one last shudder, and then lay still.

"Are you all right?" Meredith worried.

"No." Kaydin grunted as he pushed to his feet and leaned against a tree. "My chest is on fire."

"You're covered in blood!" Meredith cried. She pulled his ripped shirt open to assess the damage.

"It's not that bad," he tried to reassure her.

"Kaydin!" she cried.

He looked down at his chest. Each tear in his flesh was black, like the wriggling legs of spiders, pulled off their host but still animated.

"You've been poisoned!"

"I forgot about that." Kaydin struggled to speak.

"Forgot? Kaydin! How could you forget? What are we going to do?" Meredith wailed.

"I don't know." Kaydin looked confused. "Maybe we should find the horses." He took a step away from the tree, but promptly fell over. Meredith rolled him onto his back, and he looked up at her with glazed eyes.

"Moyna ran off as soon as I dismounted," she told him.

He began to shake. "Meredith, I'm so cold. S-So c-cold." His teeth chattered. He grabbed her arm and squeezed with all his might. She yelped in pain. "Don't leave me, Mere! Don't leave me! I don't want to die alone like Mother!" His arm dropped to his side.

"I'm not going to leave you, Kaydin." Meredith took off her cloak and put it around him.

How long did they have before he succumbed to the poison? Her mother had died so quickly. But her poisoning had been worse, hadn't it?

"What do we do?" Meredith asked fearfully.

"Ask Father." He closed his eyes.

"Father isn't here!" Meredith shook him until he opened his eyes again.

"You're right." Panic flickered across his face. "Father isn't here! Where is he, Mere? Where did he go? Mother?"

"No, Kaydin. I'm not Mother! Stop talking like this!" She knew it was irrational to scold him in his state but she couldn't seem to get a clear thought into her head.

"I'm so cold, Mere! Why is the sky black?"

The sky was dark, but the moon was bright.

"It's night, Kaydin."

"Everything's so dark. Why, Mere? Why am I so cold? It hurts, Mere! Why does it hurt?" He whined like a child and writhed in pain. He began to claw at his chest but as soon as Meredith grabbed his wrists, he sagged against her in defeat. His eyes were glazed and darting back and forth. His body was soaked in sweat. The claw marks had stopped bleeding, but lines of black poison creeped under his skin and through his veins. How was she supposed to get it out?

"I want to go to sleep." Kaydin abruptly closed his eyes and went limp.

"No! No! Kaydin, stay with me! Do *not* sleep." Meredith shook her twin until he opened his eyes, but he soon closed them again. His breathing shallowed and he jerked irregularly in his sleep. "Don't leave me!" Meredith sobbed. She put his head in her lap and whispered into his hair, "I cannot lose you, not you Kaydin ... not you too." Her tears fell on him. "Don't take him away from me. He's all I have left."

Meredith's shoulders shook as she cried out, "Please, help! Someone! Rand! Zray! Anyone!"

Nothing.

She broadcasted her thoughts in every direction, *Please, help! Is anyone there?* Meredith bowed her head and sobbed. "Anyone?" she repeated in a whisper.

Footsteps sounded next to her, and she jerked her head up, hopeful. A man stood next to her. She found him impossible to describe. Human words were inadequate to explain a being who was decidedly *not* human. He was shaped like a man, but when she reached for his mind, his impression was alien and terrifying. She withdrew her mental touch immediately.

"Why do you weep?"

Meredith found the question odd. He was reading her mind, and he knew why. He had slipped past her mental defenses as easily as if they hadn't even existed. It dawned on her that he wasn't just referring to her worry for Kaydin's life.

"I'm afraid," she whispered. "I weep because I'm afraid to be alone. I cannot survive in this world alone. Without him, I'm only half of myself, half alive. I'm so tired, tired of hopelessness, tired of always searching for home. I'm tired, and Kaydin helps me carry the weight of my life. I'm selfish, he can't die because I'm selfish." Each word brought her fears to light and with them, painful relief.

The man caressed her hair. It reminded her of a gesture her father had bestowed on her as a young child. His voice moved, breathless and light—a soothing wind in her ear. "Your soul loves but is not bound in worth to his. You are never alone."

She took a deep, shuddering breath of relief and closed her eyes. Did she dare to assume that her doubts stood any chance against his certainty? She opened her mouth to guess at the man's name—*Elyon*—but a great rush of feathers caused her eyes to fly open in curiosity.

The man was gone.

Had she hallucinated? No. The peace he'd given her— that she was an individual with a purpose—had stolen her panic and fear.

She heard the distinct sound of great wings above. A large creature descended—not a dragon. Only after it landed with its eagle wings did she realize it was a gryphon. She had never seen one before. It was twice the size of a horse, and its golden eagle eyes seemed to glow at certain angles. It sported a tawny lion's body and tail.

A man wearing a black tunic and britches jumped from the saddle. Something was decidedly familiar about his movements, face, dark hair and eyes.

He bent over the unconscious Kaydin and placed a hand on his forehead. "Where is he wounded?"

Meredith was so startled she couldn't speak coherently.

The man uncovered Kaydin and examined his wounds. "How long has it been since he was attacked?"

Meredith roused herself and answered, "About five minutes."

"We need to hurry. Help me hoist him into the saddle."

With effort, they lifted Kaydin, where he slumped precariously over the gryphon's neck. The man mounted and wrapped one arm around Kaydin's torso to secure him in place. Kaydin cried out, his back arching in pain, and he fainted again.

The man held out a hand to help Meredith mount. She hesitated. She did not know this man, but there was nothing else she could do and no other guarantee of help. She took his gloved hand and mounted behind him. The gryphon spread its wings and launched into the air.

The sudden rush of air reminded Meredith of riding Stavon with her father, but her pleasant memories were crowded out by worry for her brother. They were not in the air for very long before the gryphon landed on level ground. They touched down on the outskirts of a small village.

"Help me," the man ordered. "Hold him until I get down."

She grasped her brother's limp form while the man dismounted. He carried Kaydin, with some difficulty, toward the nearest house—a small, crude mud hut with lit windows.

CHAPTER TWENTY-EIGHT

A HAND TO TAKE

Once inside, Meredith's eyes needed a moment to adjust to the room's brightness. Lit candles adorned various spaces—the chandelier, windowsills, the large table in the center of the small room. A fire with a large cauldron over it added even more light and heat. Bottles of many different colors and shapes littered the table and shelves among books and random objects. The bottles had odd labels: Dogoner, Fly Caps, Bug Meals, Free Games, and other names that made no sense to Meredith. Dried herbs hung from the rounded peaked roof.

The man placed Kaydin on a bed set in the wall and surrounded by an array of curtains in various colors. An old woman dressed in a brown robe emerged from a small room to Meredith's left. The old woman was as strange as her hut and its contents. Her white hair was wild, frizzy, and tied with a cloth of mismatched patches.

A broad smile wrinkled her ancient face when she saw the man in black. When she spoke, her voice was worn with age, yet comforting. "Falcon! My, my, but it has been a long time since I saw you last! How goes the front? Any news of the war?"

Falcon smiled affectionately and said, "I was on my way to see you, Gelsda, when I received a summons to search the woods. I ran into these two children." Falcon motioned to Kaydin and Meredith. "The boy has been poisoned by vagwhar."

The old woman studied Kaydin's face and the black claw marks on his chest. "He doesn't appear to have much of a chance."

"Is there nothing you can do for him?" Meredith begged. "Please hurry. Our mother died within minutes of being poisoned. He might have only moments left!"

"Now, now child." Gelsda patted Meredith's hand as if consoling a small child. "She must have been given a higher dose of poison. I will do my best for the boy, but if Elyon has called him to attend his great feast, I can do nothing. Now, deary, hand me that bottle, please." Gelsda pointed to a book-and-bottle-filled shelf.

Meredith picked up a black bottle. "Do you mean this one?"

"Which other one would I be pointing to?" Gelsda huffed.

Meredith handed it to her, and Gelsda set to work mixing solutions and dried herbs. She treated Falcon as her errand boy, and he did what she asked. If she admonished and lectured him, he simply nodded and apologized. Finally, Gelsda poured her potion down Kaydin's throat and slapped him on the cheek as if that would help. Next, Meredith helped Gelsda bind Kaydin's wounds with poultices.

Gelsda said, "Now, all we can do is wait." The old woman shuffled to the fire and poured three cups of tea. She passed them around, then sat in a chair by the fire. "The only thing you can do now is wipe him with cold cloths," Gelsda instructed. "You will find a bucket of cold water by the door and cloths in a basket beside it." Promptly, the old woman fell asleep. Snores soon issued from her partly open mouth.

Meredith could not drink her tea with all her attention on her dying brother. Kaydin tossed in his sleep and murmured things she could not hear. His fever was high, but she kept cold cloths on his hot forehead. She tried very hard not to cry in front of Falcon. He also sat by the fire and watched over his cup of tea.

Meredith began to sing under her breath:

> When the stars have gone away.
> When there is no light in the day.
> When fear is your only companion,
> And your soul wanders alone, below in dark canyons,
>
> Remember me when all you see
> Is the sun always setting and never rising.
> In your heart I'll always be,
> The light in the dark
> To help you see.
> I am always with you when all else is gone,
> The one who stands beside you,
> The one whose hand guides you.
>
> In your heart I'll always be,
> The light in the dark
> To help you see.

Don't die on me now, Kaydin, Meredith whispered fiercely into her brother's mind. It was a jumble of thoughts and restless dreams. *We've gone through so much together, why should you leave now?*

"Meredith?"

She startled.

Her brother's eyes were open, glazed with fever. "Where am I, Mere?"

Meredith sighed and smiled. "You're somewhere safe."

"Is Mother here?"

Meredith gasped and shook her head. "No." It sounded more like a sob than an answer.

"Oh." Kaydin closed his eyes again and sighed. "I could have sworn I heard her singing." He fell into a deep sleep.

"Leave him be now." Falcon came to the bedside. "Let him sleep." He took her arm and led her to the fire where he made her sit in his chair. He handed her the teacup. The tea was cold. Falcon remained beside her, watching intently. "Are you all right?" he asked.

Meredith nodded. "I'm just so afraid for him." Meredith bit her lip as she gazed at her sleeping twin.

"He is your brother?" Falcon asked.

"Yes. He's all I have."

"You have no other family?"

"Well ... not really. Our father is missing, but other than him, we have no one else. We were traveling with friends to find him, but we got separated when the vagwhars attacked. They have been following us for some time."

Falcon frowned. "Why are they even here?"

Meredith said nothing.

"What are your names?"

"My name is Meredith, and he is my twin brother, Kaydin. I'm so grateful to you for helping us. I was terrified he would die in my arms."

"'Twas Elyon who sent me to you," Falcon said.

"Elyon? You spoke with Elyon?" Meredith's tone rose slightly.

"Yes. Have you?"

Meredith thought before answering. "Yes, I have. I'm ashamed to say there have been times I've wondered if he even existed."

"We all have our moments. I am happy in his service now, but there was a time when I drifted through my life, wondering what I was supposed to be doing with myself, or what I could do to serve my country. Elyon showed me, and I have never been happier." Falcon smiled pleasantly, and in that moment, he looked so familiar that Meredith's heart leapt in her chest. However, she couldn't recall where she could have met him and the likeness slipped away.

"Do I know you?" she asked.

"I do not think so, why do you ask?" Falcon took a drink from his teacup. Something so delicate in such large, battle-scarred hands struck her as humorous.

"I'm not sure, but ever since I first saw you, I've had this feeling I somehow know you."

"Well, I cannot imagine there being two of me." He chuckled. "Perhaps you are mistaken?"

"I suppose so." Meredith watched the fire and smiled. The dancing flames reminded her of Mr. Wiggles, her father's fire character.

"What are you thinking of?" Falcon asked.

"Just old times, when my father was with us."

"I have a father." Falcon paused. "I think." He smiled that smile again. "I have not seen him for many years. He does not approve of what I do."

"What is it you do?"

"Put simply, I work for Elyon. Sometimes, I do not understand the missions he sends me on, but every now and then, he shows me their purposes."

Meredith sighed. "I used to wish I could meet Elyon. I thought if I could just see him, all my problems would be cleared up. But now that I have, I still have so many questions."

"He will answer all your questions. You might not be happy with some of the answers, but they *are* the real answers." Falcon placed their empty cups on the overcrowded table. "You should sleep. I will watch over Kaydin."

Meredith opened her mouth in protest.

"If there is any change, I will wake you."

She was very tired but wasn't sure she could sleep. She did consent to lay on a mat by the fire and quickly became drowsy. Before long, she drifted into an exhausted sleep.

★★★

Kaydin dreamed.

He was standing beside a fire with Meredith, Zray, and Rand. Plains surrounded them at night with the stars far above. A dark cloud gathered on the horizon, and he knew it was coming for him. Vagwhar led the black cloud forward.

"Ghastly, isn't it?" A familiar figure stood beside him, gazing into the growing darkness.

"Airith? What are you doing here?" Kaydin felt confusion clouding his reason.

"I'm dead. Haven't you realized that by now?"

"No." Kaydin shook his head. "I don't want to believe that."

"Keep your chin up." Airith turned his wry smile on Kaydin. "You'll be joining me soon enough." Airith's form burst into shadows, scattering in all directions. Kaydin tried to run, but his feet were rooted to the ground. He opened his mouth to warn the others but had no voice. The dark cloud reached him and blotted out all light. It took away his friends. He was utterly alone in a sea of darkness.

So cold. Blackness molded into different shapes and shades of black all around him. His soul was exposed, screaming in the wide open dark. Even when he closed his eyes, the darkness was in his mind. It coursed through his veins and laughed at his pain. His heart was in anguish, his mind was tormented, and he could find no light. He was falling. There was no solid ground.

"Elyon, I asked you to help me!" Kaydin sobbed.

A speck of light grew in the distance, banishing the darkness as it approached, until everything was light. It warmed him inside out, caressed his aching heart, and calmed his crying soul. His feet found firm ground again.

"There is no promise I make that I do not keep." A voice like thunder filled the world. "Your time has not yet come, Kaydin."

A hand appeared, and Kaydin took it.

CHAPTER TWENTY-NINE

SPIDER WING TEA

When Kaydin opened his eyes, the aches throughout his body consumed all thought. Elyon and his beautiful light were gone.

He slowly turned his head. How had he arrived here? He raised one aching arm to feel the bandages wrapped around his chest. Early morning light filtered through an open window.

"So, he wakes!" A strange man rose from his seat by the fire.

Meredith was at Kaydin's side in a moment. "You're all right!" she nearly squealed.

"Yes, yes, I'm all right. Can someone tell me what happened? My chest hurts terribly, and my head feels like somebody has been kicking it."

Meredith sat on the edge of the bed and explained the vagwhar attack. She introduced Falcon as the one who had rescued him. He was sinewy, had black hair and eyes, and looked to be in his early thirties.

"Kaydin Amara." Kaydin held out his hand, and Falcon took it with a smile.

"Pleased to meet you. I would like to stay, but I must leave you for a little while. Stay here with Gelsda, and I will return shortly," Falcon said. He bowed and left the hut.

Outside, he whistled a peculiar call. Through the window, they saw the gryphon drop down beside his master. Falcon mounted and flew away.

"Was that a gryphon?" Kaydin asked in amazement.

Meredith nodded. "His name is Firefledge. He carried you last night, but I guess you don't remember." She crossed to the fire.

"I remember bits and pieces, I think," Kaydin said.

"Do you want some gruel?" Meredith put a spoon in the pot over the fire and tasted its contents. "Gelsda put some strange things in it, but when you're very hungry, it doesn't taste that bad." Meredith filled a bowl and brought it to her brother.

Kaydin struggled to sit up, then took the bowl from her hands, and began to eat eagerly. "Who's Gelsda?" he asked between mouthfuls.

"A healer. This is her house. She left an hour ago to collect something in the woods." Meredith watched her brother for a long moment. "You almost died, Kaydin."

"I know," Kaydin was still eating, "I felt like I was dying, until ... I saw the light ... and him." Kaydin paused with the spoon halfway to his mouth, staring past Meredith.

She glanced over her shoulder, then at her brother again.

Kaydin shook his head to clear his thoughts and continued scarfing down the food.

"Who did you see?" Meredith asked.

"Elyon." A look of wonder played on Kaydin's face.

"Me too!" Meredith exclaimed. "I can't explain what it was like."

"I also saw Airith." Kaydin frowned. "He told me he was ... dead, and I'd be joining him."

Meredith's hand shook as she smoothed out the wrinkles in her skirt. "That was just a dream, right? We don't know that he's ... that he's ..." She couldn't bring herself to say the word.

"I think it was my fear talking," Kaydin said.

"Sometimes I dream about him too," Meredith admitted.

"I know. You wander into my blissful dreams, dragging him along with you."

"Sorry." Meredith grimaced. "Sometimes, I spend hours lying awake at night wondering where he is and hoping one of these days, we'll walk into an inn and see him there, or he'll pass us on the road."

Just then, Gelsda entered the hut with a wicker basket over one arm. Her old face broke into a grin when she saw the twins together. She patted Kaydin on the head. "I knew you would make it, child. My, you two look alike! Now I must feed the crows. Take this." Gelsda handed her basket to Meredith.

Meredith opened the lid and almost dropped it. "Worms!" she gasped.

"What else would they be?" Gelsda snorted.

"We're not going to eat these, are we?" Meredith asked, horrified.

"Of course not! They glow at night, so I put them in the lamps outside." Gelsda picked up another basket and headed toward the door. "Put the lid back on the basket, dear. They will die exposed to the light like that."

Meredith closed and put the handbasket on the table.

Kaydin grinned at her.

"What?" Meredith frowned at him.

"Eating worms, Mere?"

"She does strange things!" Meredith defended.

Kaydin laughed too hard and started to wheeze. He clutched his chest in pain.

Crows called outside. They looked out the window and spotted the little old woman with her basket. She was throwing breadcrumbs into the air while hundreds of crows swooped for them.

"They're rapid crows, used to carry messages. I've seen them before," Meredith said.

"Help me."

She helped her brother to his feet.

He closed his eyes as a wave of pain swept over him, and he swayed on his feet.

Meredith watched him fearfully. "Maybe you shouldn't get up yet, Kaydin. Gelsda said your chest would take some days to heal completely, and it will be a while before you're back to full strength."

Kaydin opened his eyes and forced himself to smile. "I want to get up. I'm fine, it's just some cat scratches."

"Very bad scratches," Meredith reminded him.

"We have to find Rand and Zray, then find Father." Kaydin grabbed the back of a chair and lowered himself into it slowly, trying to avoid jarring his aching body.

"Speaking of which ..." Falcon stood in the doorway.

"You weren't gone long," Kaydin observed.

"I had some help, as it turns out. The people I was looking for were looking too!" Falcon stepped aside to reveal two figures behind him.

"Rand! Zray!" Meredith ran forward and hugged a surprised Zray and a relieved Rand.

"I can see I found the right people." Falcon chuckled.

"We were so worried when we realized you were no longer behind us," Rand said.

"We went back to look for you and found the dead vagwhars and your horses unharmed but riderless," Zray continued. "Rand was sure you were dead, and it was his fault, but I knew otherwise." He pressed his thumb to his chest and smirked with pride.

"Kaydin *did* nearly die," Meredith told them.

Rand approached Kaydin. "How are you feeling?"

"Not great, but I suspect I'll survive," Kaydin replied.

Gelsda returned and her face lit up. "A whole party! This is wonderful! Now, we all can have spider wing tea!" None of them knew what spider wing tea was but it didn't sound like anything they wanted to drink. Gelsda was already at the fire, adding seemingly random ingredients from her bottles to the pot of boiling water.

"Shouldn't we continue toward the Dragon Mountains?" Kaydin asked.

"I'm not sure you should be traveling in your condition," Rand said. Concern wrinkled his forehead.

"What if our father is there now, and by the time we get there, he's gone again?"

"A few days won't make a difference either way, Kay," Meredith placated.

"It made a difference when we looked for Van'N in Rivenwall," he retorted.

"Did you say you were heading for the Dragon Mountains?" Falcon inquired.

"Yes," Rand affirmed.

"Could you use a guide? I'm familiar with the area."

Rand looked to the others.

Zray shrugged.

"Why not?" Kaydin said.

"Then it's settled. When do you want to leave?" Falcon asked.

"Six days. We could all use a short rest. I think Kaydin's wounds will be stable then." Rand looked to the little old woman for confirmation.

Gelsda nodded. "But no hard riding, and he must rest often." She wagged her finger at them.

"Of course." Rand bowed.

CHAPTER THIRTY

UPRISING IN THE NORTH

Tyran woke to find a messenger with an order from Sisinta to see her immediately. He found her waiting for him in the keep's courtyard, sitting in a chair under a pavilion. Her eyes followed him as he approached and saluted, bringing his arm across his chest to his heart. After giving a slight bow he inquired, "You called for me, my lady?"

"Yes, yes, I did." She seemed distracted. "Are you well, Tyran?"

Tyran shifted uncomfortably. She never called him "Tyran," nor asked after his health. He must have done something wrong. But how was he to confess to something he didn't know he'd done? "I'm fine, my lady. Have I done something wrong?"

"No, you've done nothing wrong. I'm just worried about you, that is all."

Tyran sighed in relief.

"Are you lonely, Tyrannus?"

"I have friends."

"That is not what I asked." Sisinta rose and moved to a small table where she poured wine, then handed the goblet to Tyran. "I think you are."

"Are what?" Tyran sipped the wine.

"Why have you not married yet, Tyrannus?"

Tyran gulped the wine and began to cough violently. When he caught his breath, he answered, "I never considered it, my lady. Women are nothing but trouble, so I am told."

"Only if you let them be. If you keep them in line, you will have no trouble at all." Sisinta returned to her chair. "What about X-Sayda Bloodgo?"

Tyran placed his goblet on the table and growled. "She only loves my position. Besides, I hate the woman."

"You didn't before."

"Things change," Tyran declared. "Marrying was never really a desire of mine."

"If you don't find yourself a wife, I will." Sisinta smiled darkly.

"I don't desire to be chained to one place by marriage," Tyran responded irritably.

"She would come here and stay with you."

"I think I would prefer not to, my lady." Tyran tried to use as much respect as he could muster.

"X-Sayda is already here. Engage with her. That is an order," Sisinta snapped. Then, she added softly, "It's for your own good, Tyrannus."

Tyran groaned inwardly. Only a short time ago, he would have fallen at X-Sayda's feet. What a fool he had been.

"We have some trouble in the north, a rebellion," Sisinta said.

"Oh?" After slaying so many in the last rebellion this past year, he thought the people would have learned their lesson by now. "The stupid fools. How many of them must die before they realize it's useless?" Tyran shook his head in disbelief.

"You need to take fifty Knights to Ladle's Ridge. Raze their villages and leave none alive. We cannot risk the children following in their fathers' footsteps. You leave at daybreak." Sisinta dismissed him.

"I will do as you ask." Tyran saluted again and bowed.

Vobad was at the gate.

"Send messengers to the generals and captains of the Black Knights," Tyran told him. "I want to see them in my rooms in half an hour."

Vobad nodded and left to obey.

"Why, it is Tyrannus Black!"

Tyran cringed and mumbled a curse under his breath. He turned to X-Sayda Bloodgo, the only daughter of Seldan Bloodgo, one of the most powerful chiefs in the Outlands.

X-Sayda curtsied deeply, her head bowed. Her dark eyes snapped up to meet Tyran's as she straightened to her full height. She was tall and dark-skinned with straight black hair. Blue tattoos wound around her wrists and crowned her forehead. She wore a deep red, ankle-length gown, the color of her family's house.

Tyran's breath caught in his throat. Wild and stunning, she was beautiful. However, her dark eyes held a flash of red. He wondered why he had ever thought that look meant she loved him.

"It's been a while since I saw you last. My, you *have* improved." X-Sayda smiled coyly.

"X-Sayda, I'm busy, so if you don't mind ..." Tyran tried to sidestep, but she blocked him.

"What happened to last summer? You liked me then." X-Sayda moved very close to him, but he took a step back. When she tried to touch his face, Tyran grabbed her wrists and pinned them to her sides.

"What happened? You married your cousin, that sniveling chief," Tyran growled.

"He's dead now. Poisoned by some rival. I never really loved the fool. I always loved you, though." The coy smile returned.

A thought flickered through his mind, a hope. Maybe she wasn't lying? Maybe she really did want him? But no, she had used her flattery on him before, and he had always regretted it afterward. "I don't care for you anymore, X-Sayda. You lost me when you left. Your actions proved you never loved me, and you don't love me now."

A flash of dangerous rage filled her eyes, and she struggled in his grasp. "Let go of me, you possessed dog! You're hurting me!"

Tyran released her wrists, and gently but firmly, pushed her away. Turning on his heel, he walked to the keep, past Sisinta and the guards at the door, and slammed the door shut behind him.

★★★

Half an hour later, Tyran called the meeting to order. Various generals and captains deemed worthy of Tyran's confidence surrounded a table where he had spread a map of Lower Quith.

"The informant said they were gathering at Ladle's Ridge. We leave at daybreak for a surprise attack. It will take three days of hard flying, so I need you, Captain Vobad, to ensure we have fifty silver dragon mounts saddled and ready by the morn. The rest of you will oversee the army here. Sisinta wants to move the army back to Aster. I will not let this disrupt our plans. Understood?"

Affirmations sounded from all sides.

One young captain spoke up, "My lord, will fifty Black Knights and dragons be enough against a thousand peasants?"

Tyran's eyes flashed at his defiance. "You underestimate Sisinta's elite guard and the silver dragons. You also overestimate the peasants. They are farmers and young boys. You were recently promoted, is that right, Captain?"

The young man straightened with a proud smile. "Yes, sir."

"Well, then, I'm afraid you will have to work your way up again."

"What do you mean, sir?"

"I'm demoting you."

Horror crossed the man's face. "But I have worked hard to be here!"

"You will have to work harder. You are all dismissed." Tyran opened the door to the hall and the young man walked out with slumped shoulders. The others followed, but Vobad lingered.

"At the risk of being demoted," he started cautiously, "I'd like to point out you were harsh on the boy."

"I have no use for boys. This will motivate him to grow up and keep his mouth shut. Unlike you." Tyran glared at the captain.

"I take my leave and say no more." Vobad bowed before exiting.

Tyran closed the door and sank into a chair with a sigh. He ran his fingers through his hair and silently mourned the looming loss of his freedom. X-Sayda was a menace, and if he could help it, he would have nothing to do with her. He was looking forward to the battle and the chance to release his anger and frustration.

"I want you to take her with you."

Tyran lurched to his feet. He automatically drew his knife, ready to thrust it into the person who had dared invade his privacy and personal rooms.

Sisinta stood before him.

He let out an angry grunt and reluctantly sheathed the knife.

"I did not mean to startle you." Sisinta smiled.

"How did you get in here?" Tyran demanded.

"My dearest Tyrannus, you should know by now I do not need doors."

"I had forgotten," Tyran mumbled. He entered his bedroom.

Sisinta followed. "I know you are not on good terms with X-Sayda, Tyrannus. Spend more time with her and reconcile. I want you to take her to fight at Ladle's Ridge."

"My battles are my own! I don't need anyone to help me fight them!" Tyran fumed as he tossed his black coat onto the closest piece of furniture. He stalked to the balcony. The sunset was a brilliant gold, and the sky blood-red promising fair weather for traveling tomorrow. "I already have two voices in my head—I don't need someone else telling me what to do." Tyran allowed Tyrannus to the forefront of his mind, causing his black eyes to glow yellow.

"I'm ordering you, Tyrannus. Her father is a wealthy chief in the Outlands, and she has gained more wealth since her husband's death. If you marry her, you will gain a very strong position among the savages." The authority in Sisinta's voice was clear.

Tyran smoldered.

Sisinta concluded, "It's settled then."

Tyran gripped the rail of the balcony until his palms ached. He swung around to state his refusal but found only air. Tyran murmured angry curses. He hated X-Sayda with all his being, but she would be coming tomorrow whether he wanted her to or not.

★★★

Tyran rose before dawn the next morning, and the Black Knights were in the air within a quarter of an hour.

Tyran was in a good mood—he had been looking for an excuse to get away from Baleful. Fulfilling petty orders— taking care of matters too small for Sisinta but too important for anyone else—wasted his days. Matters like signing death warrants and relocation orders. None of the five kings were allowed to put anyone to death without Sisinta's permission, and that included the hundreds of petty criminals wasting away in the kings' dungeons awaiting execution. Tyran spent hours signing papers from the five kingdoms. In his opinion, he saw no reason for these legal niceties—just put them all to death unceremoniously! What did he care! Every time he visited another city, beggars, harlots, and criminals polluted the streets.

What happened to your goodwill and mercy? Kappin mind-spoke.

Goodwill and mercy are not a requirement. Letting someone continue in their misery and wretchedness is not mercy. It is cruel and unfeeling, Tyran told his dragon.

The decision to end someone's life is not up to you, Tyran.

Perhaps not, but the person who can make that decision isn't doing their job, and I'm the substitute.

Kappin shook his head in disbelief. *You really are very proud, Tyran.*

I disagree. However, there is no harm in being proud, except when it makes a man overconfident. I don't think I am overconfident.

Kappin fell silent, unable to sway Tyran from his opinions.

CHAPTER THIRTY-ONE

LADLE'S RIDGE

An hour before dawn, Zaylin surveyed the many tents and fires of the encampment along the outskirts of Ladle's Ridge. So many had come from the surrounding villages. They'd have a chance against Sisinta this time! However, last night's council meeting weighed heavily on his mind.

When he had voiced his hope, an elder had spoken up. "It is not enough. In all my years, I have seen thousands upon thousands of men slaughtered, their villages burned, and the women and children enslaved or murdered. No, it is not enough." The old man had shaken his head, grief-stricken.

"Then what is enough?" Zaylin had demanded.

"When we stop trusting in men and look elsewhere for help."

"Where else can we find help? Higher Quith? Ha! They would sooner spit in our faces and laugh at our defeat than help us. Do none of you recall the Blood Battle? The dragons refused to help." The young farmer had slammed his fists on the table in frustration. "Sisinta should not be permitted in Aster. I had to watch my two young sons die while Sisinta's men feasted on the food I had worked day and night in blood and sweat to provide for my children."

"We've all lost friends and family, Zaylin," another farmer had said.

"You still have your eldest son," the elder had said. "Will you watch him die because of your quest for revenge? Go home. All of you, back to your homes and lands. We can perhaps negotiate with Sisinta for provisions. We have no chance against her armies."

Zaylin now stood watching the encampment and thinking of all the old man had said. The fool! There was no reasoning with Sisinta.

The sun peeked over the horizon. Then, he saw them. His face drained of color, and he gripped the door frame to keep from collapsing.

His wife opened the door behind him. "Zaylin? What's the matter?"

Zaylin could only cry out in fear. Silver dragons glinted in the sky, heading for the ridge! Zaylin sprinted to warn the army of farmers. At the camp, he yelled frantically and pointed to the sky.

A moment later, the dragons' battle roars filled the sky.

Men scrambled in every direction.

The Black Knights atop the dragons' backs aimed flaming arrows and fired. The dragons fanned the flames with their wings. In a matter of moments, the entire encampment was ablaze.

Zaylin was rooted to the spot in disbelief and horror. All around him, men on fire screamed and threw themselves to the ground to try to extinguish the flames.

The ground shook as fifty dragons landed, and the Black Knights dismounted. They cut down anyone who was standing, and then moved into the town. A Black

Knight near Zaylin had glowing yellow eyes. The infamous Tyrannus, the leader of Sisinta's army, her right hand. A burning hate grew in Zaylin's heart as he watched the man drive his sword through every living thing. The demon created hell wherever he went. The wildfire blazed over the farmers' fields.

Stooping to grab the nearest sword, Zaylin charged Tyrannus in a blind fury.

In a flash, something black shot through the air and knocked the sword from Zaylin's hands.

A woman jumped off a dragon's back and charged into him with a wicked smile.

Zaylin stumbled and tried to shield himself with his hands to no avail.

She drove a dagger into his heart.

The last thing Zaylin saw as he lay dying was his house, containing his wife and son, going up in flames.

★★★

X-Sayda turned from her kill. "I suppose this means you owe me your life."

"I could have killed him myself had you not interfered!" Tyran roared furiously. He pushed past her and continued into the village.

Kappin followed his master, killing anyone whom Tyran had not already picked off.

"You cannot ignore me forever!" X-Sayda shouted after him.

"Watch me," Tyran shouted back.

In full light of the sun, the dragons and Black Knights walked among the fallen figures, finishing off anyone still alive. Tyran stood in a charred doorway and surveyed the pitiful house. Only ashes remained. He had fulfilled his mission. He removed his helmet and, closing his eyes, let the wind cool his sweaty, soot-covered face and toss his black hair.

Kappin sat in his familiar cat-like position behind Tyran. *So, you have done it again. 'Cleaned the world of filth' as you put it. Have you fulfilled your bloodlust yet?*

You forget, dragon, it is just as much my deed as yours. Tyran met Kappin's gaze with bright yellow eyes.

Kappin looked away in submission. *It is as you say, but I do not rationalize it as you do. I fully admit to its horror.*

A nearby commotion turned their attention to a group of Black Knights.

Tyran handed his helmet to a Knight next to him and went to investigate. "What is it?" he demanded.

They moved aside to reveal a Black Knight standing protectively over a small boy and a woman. She was weeping and holding the man whom X-Sayda had killed earlier.

"You killed my husband!" the woman cried.

"Why has no one killed her yet?" Tyran demanded.

"We tried to, sir, but he will not let us." The Knight who spoke gestured to his fellow Knight protecting the woman and boy.

"Why aren't you carrying out orders?" Tyran asked.

"Sir, this woman is my wife's sister. My wife would never forgive me if I killed her."

Tyran looked at the woman, then the boy. He drew Cala Man and swiftly ended her.

The Black Knight paled and uttered a cry of despair.

Tyran turned to the boy.

He was barely six years old, burnt clothes clung to his frail frame, and his huge brown eyes were filled with terror. "Why?" he squeaked. "Why did you—"

Tyran flung his dagger into the boy's chest.

The boy looked down at the knife and the red blood pooling around it, confusion etched across his face. He took several uncertain steps back and tripped over his mother's body, then lay still.

"Now your conscience is clear," Tyran told the distraught Knight. He retrieved his helmet. "I acknowledge this was a difficult situation to find yourself in. You have done well in the past so I will forgive you for your insurrection ... this time." Mounting Kappin, he ordered the others to mount up.

All followed suit except the Black Knight who continued to stare at his dead sister-in-law and nephew. "What do I tell my wife?"

"Tell her you were not the one who killed her. I ordered you to mount, Sir Knight, didn't you hear me?"

The knight slowly obeyed.

"We ride for home! A feast awaits us, no doubt!" Tyran cried.

They took to the sky, leaving the peasants of the surrounding villages to claim and bury the dead.

CHAPTER THIRTY-TWO

AFTERMATH

The events of Ladle's Ridge haunted Tyran's thoughts. He had just returned to Baleful from the three-day journey and now sat alone in his rooms. The other men were celebrating and feasting in the great hall below—he could hear them laughing and drinking, unaffected. Even the Black Knight with the dead sister-in-law seemed to have moved on. Maintaining indifference and freedom from culpability was exhausting.

He watched the flames hungrily lick the wood, burning every bit until there were only charred remains, just like the village at Ladle's Ridge. Images of the blackened remains and dead bodies lying cold on the ground, unburied and left to rot, riddled his mind. He was the cause. Their blood was on his hands. His upturned palms looked red in the firelight. He clenched his fists and looked away.

Killing had never presented a problem before. He had killed at least a hundred men or more in battles and duels and ordered the deaths of thousands more. Why was it only bothering him now?

He thought his conscience dead—hadn't Tyrannus seared it out of him? Yet, it was back from the grave and taunting him relentlessly. Before his eyes swam the faces of men he had killed—horror, terror, and panic on them all. Nearly all were nameless to him. The cry of the mother at the discovery of her husband's death, the screams of orphaned children calling out for their parents—they haunted him. The light dying from their eyes as he drove his sword into them, ending their lives and watching each one fade into empty corpses at his feet.

That boy's large brown eyes would not leave him. His question still rang in his head: "Why?" He had no answer. Why had he killed them? What had they ever done to him? Why, why, *why!*

Tyrannus, Tyran concluded. The Shadow in his mind! It controlled and manipulated him. It whispered dark things to him when he was alone and numbed his empathy.

They're just as much my deeds as yours, Tyrannus mocked Tyran with the same words he had used on Kappin earlier.

It's because of you that I've become what I am! It's because of you I came here! Tyran countered.

I didn't force you to come to me or take me in, no one did.

It was my only choice!

You just said it yourself. It was a choice—and you made it.

Anger boiled inside. He was tired of the Shadow using his own words and thoughts against him. *Where else was I to go? I was too young to die!* Tyran shot back.

So then, why blame me?

Because you give me the power to kill and murder! Tyran accused the Shadow.

I never gave you that power. I only fed what was already there. Tyrannus laughed.

I'm not a murderer! Tyran raged.

Then what are you?

I was fighting for Sisinta! I was merely carrying out her orders! I kill in war. Tyran knew he could not justify himself.

Silence followed.

Tyran ran his fingers through his hair and put his head in his hands.

Do you really believe you are good deep down inside? Tyrannus baited.

"No. There is nothing good in me," Tyran whispered to the empty room.

What are you then? Tyrannus repeated. The Shadow was enjoying their exchange.

Yes, fine, I admit it! I'm a monster! Tyran shouted in his mind.

And that monster isn't a murderer?

"Leave me alone! Get out of my head! I don't want you anymore!" Tyran yelled aloud.

You cannot live without me. Glee tinged the Shadow's words.

"Just watch me!" Tyran snapped.

You have no power over me, and I choose to stay.

"Get out of my head!" Tyran yelled wildly and pulled at his hair in frustration.

No.

"Leave me alone!" Tyran jumped to his feet and shoved his chair. "Get ..." Tyran smashed a vase on the mantelpiece, "out ..." he threw a small table at the wall, "of my ..." he pulled down the drapes, "head!"

Tyrannus just laughed, an echo endlessly bouncing around his skull.

In desperation, he grabbed a knife from his belt and drove it into his chest. He gasped as it sliced through his skin, between his ribs, and into his heart. His heart beat feebly, then stopped. Cold spread over him as he stumbled to his knees. A second later, burning fire replaced the cold, and his heart began to beat again in force. He looked down at his chest, soaked in silver blood. He grasped the knife by its hilt and slowly extracted it. He moaned in pain.

You can't even kill yourself, Tyrannus whispered scornfully.

The knife clattered to the floor. Tyran lay his head in his blood-covered hands. Sobs racked his entire frame. He looked up and found his reflection in the full-length mirror beside his bed. The face staring back at him had eyes glowing an ugly yellow and limp, pitch-black hair in stark contrast to his pale skin. He looked like death. A demon from hell. With both fists, he smashed the mirror. Shards scattered around him. His fists dripped with silver blood.

"Curse you! Curse you!" Tyran sobbed and collapsed on the floor, unmoving. Exhausted, he found himself in a half-slumber, his mind drifting into nightmares and images of his victims.

★★★

Tyran stared out into a thick mist, this way and that—it was all he could see. He shivered in the cold air. The dampness seemed to seep into his bones. He thought he could hear the gentle lapping of water against a dock.

"Hello?" he called out. His voice was muffled in the fog. How had he gotten here? He couldn't seem to remember.

Turning about, he looked for any sign of life. He caught sight of a dim figure approaching in the fog. The man stopped a few feet away, his features obscured by the white mist. He suddenly remembered a scene like this one, a long time ago as a boy. Where was it? He struggled to recall the memory. It was in Higher Quith, by the river. He had seen a man in the fog in that small village he had stopped in for supplies.

Tyran swallowed nervously. "Who are you?" he wondered aloud.

"You know who I am," was the reply.

"Have we met before?"

"Many times. You dream of me often, but Tyran steals the memory away."

"I don't know what you're talking about. I'm Tyran."

The man reached out and grabbed Tyran's arm. An explosion of insecurity hit him. He was stripped bare of all defenses, his soul exposed. He cried out and yanked his arm free, turning to run away blindly into the mist.

The air was sucked from his lungs when the ground seemed to give way beneath him. After a few seconds, he realized he had fallen over a cliff. and a cord was wrapped about his waist and fastened to something out of sight and above him—the only thing keeping him from falling. He glanced down and saw a river crashing violently against rocks far below, just waiting for him to be hurled down into its raging waters and deadly course.

The man appeared above him, standing at the cliff's edge.

"This is your life's thread, Airith. When it breaks, you will die."

"Help me!" Tyran cried.

"I will, Airith Shaver, son of High," the figure reassured him.

"How do you know my name?"

"Your soul is mine. I know all who are mine by name."

"I don't have a soul. I sold it. It isn't yours!" Tyran shot back, angry at the figure's confident statement of ownership.

"Your name, do you know what it means?" the figure calmly asked.

Tyran glanced down and his heart lurched in his chest. "What has my name to do with anything?"

Next to the figure, the fog swirled and shifted, creating a perfect replica of his mother, dressed in a white nightgown that reached her bare feet. Her long, blonde hair fell in waves of gold down her back. She cooed and rocked a baby-shaped bundle in her arms. She looked up and her eyes locked with his. Tyran was perfectly still, transfixed by her beauty and the love and guilt that welled up inside him at the sight of her.

"The redeemed. Don't you remember, Airith? Didn't I tell you many times over? You can't have forgotten." The sound of her voice caused him equal measures of pain and joy.

"She named you with the name I placed in her mouth the day you were born." There was tenderness in the figure's voice.

The image of his mother turned and vanished into the whirling mist.

"Wait!" Tyran's attempt to reach in her direction was futile. The rope swung wildly about, and in a panic, he clutched it with both hands.

The figure bent down and grasped the top of the rope—the swinging cord immediately stilled. "Your life's thread will break under the strain of your struggles, Airith, and when it does, it will be too late. You know I'm your only hope. Why do you run from me?"

"I don't know! But I do know I'm more afraid of you than I am of dying," Tyran admitted. The rope threads began to pop and fray, one by one in quick succession. "No! I'm not ready to die!" Tyran howled.

★★★

Tyran opened his eyes and lay still for a long moment. Glass surrounded him. His heart was hammering in the aftermath of a vivid dream. Already, the memory had begun to fade into a vague sense of terror. The room was dark, save the light of the full moon hanging in the black sky through the open balcony door.

Tyran struggled to his feet. His ripped shirt exposed his chest and made him shiver. Dried and crusted silver blood flaked from his skin, but there was no sign of his self-inflicted wound. Bits of glass had cut his face but had healed in triangular silver lines.

He stumbled to the washbasin. He removed his shirt and splashed water over his face and chest, washing away the blood. He stopped and stared at himself in the mirror above the basin. His face dripped water, and his hair was a mess. His wild eyes were black, no trace of yellow.

"Perhaps he's finally gone," Tyran murmured, unconvinced, as he ran his fingers through his unruly hair.

You can never be rid of me, Tyran Black, came the Shadow's gleeful whisper.

Tyran closed his eyes and didn't move. "You're right. You've won again, but please, just leave me be!" He didn't need the Shadow to make himself miserable—he did that quite well all on his own.

CHAPTER THIRTY-THREE

THE DRAGON MOUNTAINS

Meredith, Kaydin, Rand, Zray, and Falcon stayed the six days with the old healer. She told them all manner of stories from the "days before the mountains" and had them grinding, chopping, and cooking while she talked. Meredith tried her best to pay attention to the details the woman offered on what herbs helped with what ailments, but the information was imparted with short explanations and the ingredients of potions rattled off so rapidly that most of it went over her head. She gave up memorizing, and instead sketched the plants Gelsda said were useful.

On the morning of the seventh day, they rose early, saddled the horses, and dressed for travel. Rand tried to pay Gelsda, but she insisted it was a gift, and the only way to repay her would be to come back and visit again. Having slept under a roof and eaten warm, homemade meals, it was difficult to be satisfied with dried meat and fruit, riding all day on dusty roads, and sleeping on the damp ground at night.

Falcon proved to be a valuable guide. While the others had relied on general direction rather than roads or cities of the unfamiliar countryside of Dolsulbane, Falcon had been all over Higher Quith. He assured them, with good weather and time, they should reach the mountains in one week.

When they finally climbed to the top of the first foothill they stopped to admire the view.

"Wow," Kaydin exclaimed.

"They're incredible," Meredith breathed.

"Amazing!" Rand agreed.

"Awe-inspiring," Falcon said.

"Astonishing!" Zray added, rolling his eyes. Peak after peak scraped the sky and each white-capped mountain rose as a sharp point among a sea of others. They created a palisade of impenetrable dragon teeth. Zray remained unimpressed. "Why nature built these, we will never know, but crossing them is dangerous and promises almost certain death."

"Nature did not build them," Falcon corrected the young minstrel. "Elyon did, after the Blood Battle as a defense against Sisinta."

"Whatever." Zray shrugged. "One must now ask the question, where are we going?"

The question fell to the twins.

Kaydin glanced at Meredith and said uncertainly, "Well ... ah, we still have to find and talk to my father's friend."

"It will be dark in a few hours. I have a Rackdarian friend who lives in that village." Falcon pointed to a small village in the valley below. Other than a few curls of smoke twisting from some of the houses, no other life stirred.

Zray declared, "I still want to know how we are going to cross the mountains! Our horses are not exactly the best transport through here."

"I think I might know a way through," Falcon said hesitantly.

"Can we go down to the valley and stay in the village?" Meredith suggested.

The others agreed, and they began the descent. A single road passed through the tiny town with houses built against the stone walls of the mountains and hills. Each house had steps leading to a wooden platform before the front door. Many of the platforms had urns, baskets, brooms, and racks of drying animal skins and wool on them. The street was eerily quiet.

"I marvel they would dare to dwell so near the mountains with the dragons guarding them," Rand remarked. "I've heard there are other creatures living here too."

"The Rackdarians raise sheep and goats, and some of them are miners," Falcon explained. "They are not warlike but cautious. They have an understanding with the dragons. If you get past their initial distrust, you will find loyal friends. Though, I would advise against crossing them. They carry grudges that can last generations."

"Are there more villages like this?" Rand inquired.

"A good number. Although only along the edge of the mountains. They do not dare wander farther in. There are many more Rackdarians who live in underground cities."

"Why does everyone fear dragons so much? Aren't they on your side?" Rand asked.

Meredith caught her brother's eye. *Why would he say 'your side' and not 'our side'?*

A slip of the tongue? Kaydin shrugged. *He told us he's from the Islands, but I think we know by now that's not true.*

Then where could he be from? Over the sea?

Not likely. Kaydin conveyed a sense of disappointment.

No, he's not from Lower Quith! Meredith's eyes widened. *I can't believe that. I mean—I don't want to believe that.* The twin's emotions jumbled together in confusion and anxiety.

Falcon's voice pulled their attention back, "The dragons prefer to be left alone. They prevent anything in Lower Quith from getting into Higher Quith and the other way around."

Cloth flapped in the wind, and the travelers saw a woman shaking out a large woolen blanket on the wooden platform of her house. When she noticed them, her expression changed first to fear, then to annoyance. She threw the brown blanket over her shoulder and picked up her skirts as she retreated into the house, closing the door firmly behind her.

"Not very friendly," Zray remarked.

"Come." Falcon beckoned them to follow him. He led them to a house at the end of the narrow road. He mounted the steps and knocked on the large wooden door studded with metal rivets.

The door creaked open a crack, and he saw a head with a pair of dark eyes and bushy red eyebrows peeking out, framed by the golden glow of a fire inside.

"What do you want?" a gruff voice demanded.

"Basal Greed, you have not forgotten an old friend, have you?" Falcon asked.

"Falcon?" He opened the door a little further. "It's been some time. What brings you to this forsaken place?"

Meredith could see Basal's face clearer now, and he looked just like his voice—gruff, worn, and suspicious. His beard and hair matched the hue of his eyebrows. Van'N's voice reciting facts echoed in her head: "The Rackdarians are somewhat shorter than humans and have thicker bones."

"What do you mean? Never is a place forsaken," Falcon told the mountain man.

"I would beg to differ," Basal rumbled. He noticed the other travelers. Alarm crossed his face.

"All is well, Basal," Falcon said in a rush. "They will do no harm."

Basal said nothing but continued to eye the others with suspicion.

"Will you leave us standing here in the growing darkness?" Falcon asked.

Basal remained silent for a long moment before finally stepping aside and fully opening the door.

Falcon beckoned the others. They tied the horses to a railing in front and followed him into the house.

The house was a large, one-room, thatched dwelling with a high-pitched roof. A large fire burned in the center hearth. A woman dressed in a plain wool gown and apron stood by the fire, stirring a large iron pot with a wooden ladle. Seven children sat on blankets on the far side of the room. One older girl combed her little sister's long brown hair, while the oldest boy was whittling a small block of wood. The others stopped their playing and silently watched the strangers with wide eyes.

Basal closed the door behind his visitors and walked to his wife. He tapped her on the shoulder. Her hair was a mess under her small cap, and dark bags hung under her eyes. When she saw Falcon, her tired face brightened into a big smile. "Falcon!" she cried happily. She wiped her hands on her apron before taking Falcon's face in her work-worn hands, kissing him on each cheek and patting them affectionately. "The very sight of you does me good," she told him fondly.

"As does the vision of your beautiful face." Falcon returned a kiss on her cheek.

She blushed and laughed. "Your pretty words will make a woman very happy one day, my dear boy." The woman turned to her children. "Surely you remember Falcon, children? Come and greet him."

A slow smile spread over the oldest boy's face. He approached and heartily clasped Falcon's hand. The other children's shy countenances turned to smiles, and they ran to Falcon with the younger ones wrapping their arms around his legs. They all started talking at once, competing for his attention.

Falcon held out his hands for them to calm down, and he picked up the youngest, a toddler, and placed a kiss on his plump cheek. "My, you have grown! When I was last here, you were barely a few days old."

"Yes, he'll be two summers soon," an older girl told him.

"What were you whittling?" Falcon asked the eldest boy.

"A handle for a knife," the boy told him proudly. "I'm going to sell them to the traders when they come."

"*If* they ever come," Basal threw in.

Everyone fell silent. Basal's words had spread a blanket of gloom over the room.

Falcon glanced at Basal but received no explanation. He put down the toddler and introduced his companions. "This is Rand, Kaydin, Meredith, and Zray, a minstrel. This is Basal and Frana."

"A minstrel! We have not had one here in ages!" Frana beamed. "You'll entertain us after supper, I'm sure. You all must be very hungry." She picked up a stack of bowls and served stew from the pot. She handed one to each of them in turn.

Everyone sat on benches around the fire and ate mashed turnips and lamb. Afterward, Frana sent the children to their beds—mats and blankets on the other side of the room. When they protested they had not yet heard the minstrel, Zray consented to play a few songs on his flute and recite a ballad. Zray's clear voice and flute filled the room with haunting melodies.

After the children fell asleep and the horses had been tended, Falcon turned to Basal. "What troubles you, my friend?"

Basal frowned and rubbed his hands together. "Raiders."

"Again?" Falcon's brows lifted.

"Yes." Basal sighed heavily. "Again. They will not leave us be. The traders have not been coming for fear of them."

"Have you sent a messenger to the Sillian emperor for help?"

"Of course, but what can he do? The raiders come so suddenly and stay for such a short time—they are long gone by the time the emperor can send soldiers."

"When did they strike last?"

"Two days ago—a village only ten miles away. It's been worse to the north. Those murdering thieves!" Basal clenched his fists. "They don't serve anyone but themselves, not even Sisinta. They think they can get away with anything."

"Have you tried to ask the aid of the dragons?" Falcon asked.

"No. It's been so long since anyone called upon them for assistance. If we start discussions with them again, it'll result in arguments and loss of land."

Falcon and Basal continued to talk between themselves in low voices.

Frana asked the twins, "Where are you from, dears?"

"Near Boldwind, in Tayose," said Meredith.

"My, that is very far, I have only heard of the place and have never been there." Frana turned to Zray. "And where do you come from?"

He blinked and his eyes widened. "No place, really. I traveled with my father everywhere. All of Quith is my home."

"What about your mother?" Frana asked.

Zray stared at his hands and fidgeted. "I-I do not know."

"You don't know who your mother is?"

"No, I know who she is, it's just ..." Zray glanced at the twins. "I ... ah ... have a little sister." The words came out strained, as if he were admitting the hardest thing possible.

Frana gazed warmly at him.

Zray looked away. "My ... father was not a good man. He drank away nearly all the money he made and stole whatever he could. My mother had to do something. She loved him, but she finally had enough of his ways and told him to leave. At that time, my father was my hero. I thought being a traveling minstrel was the only profession worth having, so when my father came one night to take me away with him, I went."

Zray took a deep breath and continued. "I traveled with him for several years. He taught me everything he knew, including stealing. One day, we got caught, and they threw him in prison. I was still very young, so the judge sentenced me to a beating and told me to go home. But I didn't want to. I knew my mother would be angry with me for leaving her, and I hated the fact I'd let her down. I've been on my own ever since. I do my best to honor my mother by doing only what would make her proud, but I fear I fail more often than succeed. You remind me of her." Zray jutted his chin toward Frana.

"This hat ..." Zray removed the hat from his head and ran his fingers along its brim lovingly. A small smile tugged at the corners of his mouth. "My mother made me this hat when I was younger. It was too big for me then. She knew how much I idolized my father and my desire to be like him. She told me I'd grow into it."

Frana took the young minstrel's hand. She looked him in the eye. "I tell you this as a mother who knows the pain of her children's foolish decisions. Sometimes, the only way children learn is by their own faults, but when they come back to me and tell me they were wrong, anger is the furthest from my mind. Joy at their return is all I feel. If your mother loves you, which I am sure she does, she will be glad you have realized the error of your ways and returned to her."

Zray frowned and looked at the floor. "I am not so sure."

"You will see." Frana patted him on the knee.

Zray flushed and donned his hat.

"You all must be very tired. I'll make up beds for you near the fire." Frana moved to a trunk and searched, pulling out some blankets and closing the lid.

The twins, Zray, and Rand settled down to sleep while Falcon, Frana, and Basal stayed awake, speaking in hushed tones. Zray fell asleep quickly, but Kaydin and Meredith mind-spoke, taking extra caution to hide their conversation from other minds.

Rand and Falcon will not stop pestering us until we tell them where we need to go, Kaydin started. *We cannot let them know who we are! We have to contact Stavon and ask him for help.* Kaydin communicated a sense of urgency.

And exactly how do we find Stavon? Meredith asked.

We have to find a dragon and ask.

Have you felt any dragons around?

Several.

Where?

Everywhere.

Did you ask any of them where Stavon is?

No, they're too far away to ask, but if we travel about fifteen miles farther into the mountains, we should be able to speak with them. I sensed one in that direction.

Falcon and their hosts had finally gone to bed, and they saw the chests of Zray and Rand rise and fall evenly.

Are you saying we have to leave the others? Meredith asked. A tinge of regret impressed on Kaydin's mind.

What else can we do? I don't want to go without them either. But if Rand is some rich lord from Lower Quith, he could be a spy.

Not a very good one, Meredith responded skeptically. *He's been terrible at hiding his accent and cultural ignorance.*

Kaydin squeezed her hand reassuringly. *The fact remains, we can never reveal our identities to anyone. How many times did Father and Mother tell us that?*

I know. Meredith sighed wearily. *But, it's exhausting to live this way.* She pulled her hand out of his. *When do we go then?*

Tonight, when we're sure they're asleep.

Meredith's heart was heavy in her chest, and her breath ran ragged through her constricted throat. They were betraying their companions. Rand, the noble knight who had taken it upon himself to see two lost people to safety. Falcon, their guide—though they had known him only a short time—had already saved Kaydin's life. Zray, the mistrustful, talkative, selfish minstrel, whose songs had brought camaraderie to their little band. She closed her eyes and tried to convince herself leaving them was the right thing to do. Bringing the others into unnecessary danger was not right. She wished she and Kaydin could tell them everything, but their friendship could not compare to the vow they had made to their parents.

CHAPTER THIRTY-FOUR

SLEEPING HILL

Meredith? Meredith!

Meredith knew she was dreaming, but the voice continued to call her. She opened her eyes slowly and found her brother's face.

We have to go now, he told her silently.

Meredith sat up and rubbed her eyes. The fire had died down to embers, and except for Zray's snores, the night was silent. Meredith put on her leather shoes and her brown cape over her simple, green dress.

Kaydin was already in his traveling clothes—his brown cape over his blue tunic and black trousers. Swan hung from his belt. *Come on.* Kaydin waited for her at the door. He slowly lifted the wooden bar and froze when it scraped against the wood.

One of the small children roused and sat up.

The twins didn't move. Meredith tried to breathe shallowly and prayed that they looked like shadows in the gloom.

The little girl gave a sleepy sigh and lay down again.

Kaydin waited thirty heartbeats before lifting the bar the rest of the way. Meredith followed him out into the night.

Moyna and Vasgo were still tied to the rail. They saddled the steeds as quickly and silently as possible. Kaydin mounted and turned his horse down the road. Meredith hesitated and stared at Basal's house. They were stealing away like traitors or thieves.

Meredith, we have to go, Kaydin said impatiently.

Can we just leave a note for them? Meredith asked as she climbed onto Moyna's back.

No. I don't want to risk waking the others by going back inside to leave one. When we're home, we can send a letter letting them know we're safe. Kaydin beckoned her.

Meredith reluctantly turned Moyna down the street after Vasgo.

The moonless sky and the unfamiliar terrain made the horses nearly stumble frequently. The road split several times and stayed in the foothills, but they abandoned it for a path farther into the Dragon Mountains. The path wound through passes and over more hills, which grew larger and larger as they traveled deeper into the mountains. Just as the sun rose, they reached the crest of a hill where the path ended. The mountains burst into flames of gold as the sun's light stole its fingers across the peaks and lit up the valleys and lakes.

"This place is beautiful," Meredith exclaimed.

"I am not sure where to go from here." Kaydin surveyed the area, finding no signs of life. "The dragon mind I sensed earlier should be close." He cupped his hands around his mouth and shouted, "Hello!" The greeting bounced off the canyons, through the passes, and mountain faces, then faded away.

The twins held their breath. Nothing stirred.

Is anyone there! Meredith yelled mentally.

Silence.

Then ... *Who are you?* a dragon mind-spoke.

Meredith and Kaydin Stellmear, the children of Jade Dragonose, Meredith replied. *We are seeking Stavon, the red dragon.*

The ground rumbled, and the horses became uneasy. The hill before them came to life. A ridge broke away and became a long tail. Rocks on top of the hill lifted and turned into the sharp spikes on a dragon's neck. Finally, a head rose and what had appeared to be dead trees became the horns on its head. One eye opened and then the other to reveal a pair of ochroid eyes with pupils slit down the center. The hill stretched and became the dragon's back. She stood to her full height and twisted her head to iron out the kinks in her neck. Moss and grass clung to her scales, disguising her true color.

She turned and examined the twins. *You are very small.*

Kaydin fought to keep Vasgo in check and asked, *You were here the whole time?*

I was.

Did we wake you? Meredith asked timidly. Her father had told her waking a dragon was considered rude.

No. I've been awake for this past year, listening to the minds around me. You gave me a reason to get up. She yawned and stretched her great claws.

How long had you been asleep? Kaydin wondered.

I am not sure, thirty years maybe?

You have grass growing on you, Meredith pointed out.

The dragon turned to look at herself and laughed. *So I do! I stopped to rest after flying a long way, and I suppose I fell asleep.* She brushed off most of the grass, revealing her shining copper scales. An earth dragon. That explained the abundance of vegetation all over her. She narrowed her eyes and looked them over. *So, you claim to be the children of Dragonose? How can I be sure you are telling the truth?*

I don't think you can, Meredith admitted.

The dragon drew her neck back and sat in front of them like a composed, observant gargoyle. She seemed to think for a long time and attempted to search their minds. At last, she said, *You are young, your minds are not strong. I see you are telling the truth. Dragonose is not here.*

Meredith had felt no mind-reading take place, and their father had praised them for their mind-blocking abilities. Did the dragon want to seem more proficient in her mind-reading abilities then she actually was?

How do you know? You've been asleep for a long time, Kaydin challenged.

As stated, I have been awake for a year. I spoke to a dragon from afar some days ago.

Oh. Meredith and Kaydin looked at each other, disappointment evident in their tone.

The dragon tilted her head and narrowed her eyes as she studied them. *Though I suppose I could take you to Stavon.*

You know him? Meredith asked.

He is on the Council. At least, he was thirty years ago. Every colored dragon knows him.

Please, could you take us to him? Kaydin pleaded.

You will have to walk because of your animals. The dragon looked at the horses with disgust. *I will fly and lead you from the sky.*

Is it far? Meredith inquired.

A few hours' travel with those things. The dragon indicated Vasgo and Moyna. She spread her wings and stretched out the kinks, then shot into the sky, leaving a wake of strong wind behind her and shedding bits of grass and dirt as she went.

Kaydin and Meredith had to kick their horses into a trot to catch up. The sun was too bright to look up, so they followed her shadow on the ground.

She led them over hills and down winding gorges. Huge boulders fallen from the faces of the towering mountains above them were strewn about. The hills soon became mountains, and they had to skirt narrow passes when climbing became impossible.

Every time they asked the dragon to slow down, she grumbled and had to circle back to them because she had gone too far ahead.

Meredith eyed Kaydin multiple times, attentive to his emotions. His face was pale and pinched with occasional pain as he tried to hide his aching wounds.

Two hours of traveling brought them to the foot of a large mountain. The dragon circled the summit, then disappeared behind it and did not reemerge. The twins continued for another half hour before they reached the place where they thought she had vanished. They stood in the woods surrounding the mountain and looked up at the towering peak but found no sign of her.

Finally, you have arrived. I nearly fell asleep waiting, the dragon mind-spoke. *Follow me.* Her copper-colored form rose from among the trees and she began climbing the mountainside. The twins dismounted and followed. The dragon did not fly since they could not keep up with her.

About halfway up, they came to a rock shelf. Though they could climb the many vines growing over the edge, they would be forced to leave the horses behind. Before the twins could say anything, the dragon disappeared into the cliff. They stared at the rock, amazed that the dragon had disappeared into it and unsure what to do next. A moment later, the dragon's head stuck out between the vines next to the horses, causing the animals to skitter away. The twins had to take a moment to quiet them.

Why must I keep after you children to follow? We are wasting time.

The twins moved the vines aside to find a big tunnel, high and wide enough for a large dragon to fit. It was dark and the air cool. The twins led the horses after the dragon. They could see nothing ahead in the darkness. They proceeded for hours, sometimes turning corners and ascending, but mostly descending into the bowels of the mountain. Eventually, the dirt walls became stone, smooth from the many claws and scales of passing dragons. The tunnel was clear of any rubble, and the twins were glad they did not have to worry about tripping over something they couldn't see. They rounded two sharp bends and emerged into an open space, their footsteps echoing on the uneven stone floor.

A loud voice boomed like thunder, vibrating the cavern. "So, they have come!" A flash of light and heat flared in the darkness, and a torch burst to life.

The twins covered their eyes. When their eyesight adjusted, they saw the torch in an iron stand shaped like a dragon's scaly claw. A dragon stepped out of the shadows.

The flickering firelight reflected off his blood-red scales and illuminated the cavern in speckled light. He was larger than their dragon guide and much stronger in both appearance and manner. His tone commanded authority, and his glowing yellow eyes displayed wisdom. His scarlet scales glittered and rippled with the movement of his sinuous body. Neither twin dared speak, holding their breath and gaping at the awe-inspiring creature.

"So, you have come at last," the dragon whispered softly this time.

Kaydin let out a sigh of relief that sounded more like a sob.

Meredith let out a cry of joy, "Stavon!"

CHAPTER THIRTY-FIVE

MISSING!

Zray woke on his own. Something was wrong.

He rolled over and tried to go back to sleep, but something was bothering him. The breathing of the others was low and rhythmic. He bolted upright and strained to look around in the light of the nearly dead fire. The breathing! That was the problem. Someone was missing.

"Falcon," Zray whispered loudly.

The man stirred almost immediately. "What is it?" Falcon whispered back.

"Someone's missing."

"How do you know? I can hardly see in this darkness."

"I just know."

"I'll check." Falcon stirred up the fire and added wood. It flared and revealed the missing twins.

Zray watched him go outside and return a moment later.

Then, Falcon shook Rand awake. "Kaydin and Meredith are missing, and so are their horses. Do you know where they could have gone?"

Rand sat up sleepily and blinked several times. His face creased with worry. He threw off his blanket and rose.

"They talked about finding their father's friend. I don't know why they would have gone without us."

"Did they mention the friend's name?" Falcon inquired.

Rand nodded slowly as he thought. "Yes, they did. It was something like Tavon or Savon ... Maybe Zray remembers?"

Falcon asked carefully, "Was it Stavon?"

Rand's face lit up. "Why, yes, I do believe it was. Do you know him?"

Falcon frowned. "I think I do, and I know where he lives too—far into the mountains."

"What man would ever dare live there?" Rand wondered.

In the meantime, Frana rose and began to prepare breakfast. Basal joined them soon after.

"My, you lot are early risers," Frana remarked as she began to boil water. "It's still an hour before dawn!"

Falcon explained the situation.

Basal raised his eyebrows. "I knew there was something off about those two. Didn't you see how they stared off into space, smilin' at nothing? Or like they were holding some kind of silent conversation? How well do you know them, really? I'll wager they're spies for Sisinta, sent to search out our weaknesses!"

"I do not think that is the case," Rand said. He accepted a wooden mug of warm tea from Frana. "We have traveled with them for many months. I am sure they are not spies. They told me about Elyon. Why would spies for Sisinta speak highly of Elyon?"

"To pass through unnoticed. They knew everyone in Higher Quith speaks of him and didn't want to cast suspicion on themselves."

"I am sorry to contradict you, Basal," Falcon said softly, "but I agree with Rand. I am sure they are not spies. True, everyone knows about Elyon, but not everyone believes in him or speaks about him. They could have remained silent, and no one would have suspected them."

"We have to find them!" Zray pleaded. "They don't know where they're going! What if they are eaten by dragons or get lost and freeze or starve to death?"

The others stared at Zray, various degrees of surprise on their faces.

Zray blushed and mumbled, "You lot are the closest thing I have to family right now, and Kaydin and Meredith are a part of that."

"He's right," Rand agreed, "we cannot leave them to wander into near-certain death. I promised to keep them safe."

"We should go look for them as soon as we have eaten. The journey to Stavon's location is a hard one," Falcon said.

They quickly ate, packed their things, and saddled the horses. After Falcon bought some supplies from Basal and Frana, they said goodbye and mounted their horses. Falcon led them along the road out of the valley and over hills for several hours until they reached the end of the road. When they crested a hill, they overlooked a newly formed crater. Rand and Zray marveled over the strange formation, but Falcon muttered under his breath about dragons and urged them onward.

"How can we go on?" Zray grumbled. "The road ends here and we cannot go any further."

"There is a ravine a short way from here," Falcon told them. "We must dismount and walk to the ravine. The ride will be easier after that." He dismounted and led his black stallion down the rocky hillside. Rand and Zray followed slowly, mindful of the strain on the horses.

After some time, they found themselves in a small hollow of old, dark trees. The underbrush obscured the ravine until they were upon it. While they stopped to rest, Zray stood at the ravine's mouth and peeked in. A cold breeze issued from its maw and made him shudder.

"It's narrow and scary," he told the others.

"It's cut out of solid rock and winds its way through the mountains," Falcon explained. "We will have to travel single file and watch out for falling rocks." Falcon remounted his stallion and started down the dark ravine.

"You certainly cannot mean we are going down *there*!" Zray cried out.

"Why not?" Rand inquired as he mounted Aldaydo.

"It's dangerous!" Zray insisted.

"That's the beauty of it," Falcon said. In one swift motion, he reached down and lifted Zray into Lightning's saddle.

Zray lost his hat and had to grab wildly for the saddle horn to keep his balance. He let out an angry cry and threw a fuming look Falcon's way, but the man had already started down the ravine, his back to the minstrel.

"I don't like him." Zray whimpered pitifully.

"Your injured pride will heal." Rand laughed as he ruffled Zray's hair, then put the hat back on its perch.

Zray straightened his hat and scowled before reluctantly following the older men.

The wilderness of the mountains revealed myriad birds, insects, and small rodents. But also rocky terrain, caves, and cliffs—dwelling places of many strange creatures, including the dragons who ruled the perilous place. The travelers spotted three-toed footprints in the soft, muddy bed of a dried-up stream, and scat much too large to have come from a squirrel.

Every now and then, unearthly screeches from some unidentifiable animal sounded from afar. Zray shivered in his saddle and glanced over his shoulder to be sure nothing was watching them from the crags and crevices. He felt a dreadful sense of premonition. The two men ahead of him showed little reaction to the disturbances, but Zray spotted tension in Rand's shoulders and white knuckles gripping his reins. Zray felt a small sense of relief. No one was perfectly brave all the time. He hated being shown up by everyone with their high and mighty declarations of bravery.

The ravine ended in a valley where Falcon called for a halt. He whistled a peculiar series of notes, like the sound of a large bird of prey. Moments later, Firefledge answered, and the gryphon arrived soon after. Falcon whispered something into the bird's ear, and the creature crackled an indecipherable answer from its curved beak. It spread its eagle wings and departed.

"We can go now," Falcon told his companions.

"What did you tell him?" Zray asked.

"He's going to deliver a message to the Dragon Council. They will ensure our safe travels through these mountains." Falcon started forward. With dread, Zray realized the ravine continued on the other side, and Falcon was leading them into its maw again.

***

At nightfall, Falcon chose a cleft in the rock for their encampment.

Rand offered to search for firewood. He found nothing but shrubs with branches too thin and green to be of much use. Shortly, he spied the roots of a tree ahead and approached cautiously. The wind creaked in the branches of the great oak before him. It towered upward and thrust its limbs above the sides of the gorge.

He pressed one hand against its great trunk and mused aloud, "How long have you been here?" Its immense presence and the surrounding silence filled him with contradicting contentment and terror. He resolved to find the wood quickly and return.

Rand circled the tree methodically, picking up broken twigs and branches as he went. Part of the great trunk pressed itself against the rocks behind. He found a man-sized opening half obscured by the oak's girth. Rand peeked over his shoulder in the direction of camp. To explore or return? Curiosity got the better of him. He placed his bundle of sticks on the ground and climbed the rubble. At the top, he peered into the opening and glimpsed trees and grass. Nothing sinister. He scrambled over the shale and emerged on the other side of the opening.

He stopped and turned in a circle. He knew this place—the woods surrounding his father's castle in Ironcall. He remembered fondly the games he used to play here as a child. He recognized a large rock with the ground hollowed out underneath it. He used to pretend it was a cave that led to the underground cities he had heard of in geography books.

Above him was the huge tree he used to climb and from whose highest branches he could see for miles—the city of Baleful, the fields, towns, woods, and nearby castle. Rand kicked up dead leaves and watched the wind tumble them like the dancers and acrobats who came to his father's court. He'd watched them doing handstands and whirling as they leapt through the air, like they were afraid to touch ground.

What had happened to those carefree days? He'd never worried about his people or his land or seen the suffering and death Sisinta brought. As a child, he'd dismissed things if he didn't understand them. Confusing things were for the adults to worry about.

When he was eight years old, he'd decided he was never going to grow up. But he had. He had witnessed the suffering and desolation of the kingdom, and he'd decided it was time to embrace his responsibility as the crown prince.

"It was beautiful, was it not?" A man walked toward him. The stranger paused and took a deep breath of the clear air. "Why did you grow up and leave this place?"

"I knew I was meant to do something greater than becoming king," Rand responded. "I believed I could help my country better as their prince instead. The king has his place, but he cannot effectively relate to the common people because he does not live among them. I want to save them, not rule them. I resolved to find a better way than what Sisinta offers us."

"How do you plan to save them?" the man asked.

Rand shook his head. "You will think I am crazy, but I am searching for Elyon."

"And did you find him?"

"No ... at least, I do not think so. I have seen so much of him in the culture of Higher Quith, in the faith of its people, and in the stories of his feats. Yet, I have not encountered him personally."

"What would you ask him if you did?"

Rand narrowed his eyes at him. "I would ask him to send his armies to drive Sisinta out of Ironcall and restore peace."

"But what about you?" the man asked. "What about your own heart and the hearts of the people? Without a change of heart, your people will always find themselves submitting to tyrants and witches."

"Is there a way to change a man's heart? It seems impossible to me."

"It is possible, but a man cannot do it."

"If a man cannot change, how can his heart be shifted from its course? How can he save the hearts of others?"

"He cannot, but I can."

Rand's brow wrinkled as he scrutinized the man closely. "Who are you?"

"Elyon, High King of Higher Quith and rightful ruler of Lower Quith, the Outlands, and all the Islands and countries of the sea, earth, and sky." His words rang true and hovered like the peals of a bell in the surrounding air.

"Can you change the hearts of my people?" Rand asked.

"You cannot make that decision for them. That task is mine. But as for you, I can."

Rand's heartbeat quickened. "I can go back and tell my people about you? That there is a power higher than Sisinta's to call on?"

The man's eyes seemed sad. "They will not listen to you. Their eyes are blind to their own corruption, but I promise you, someday they shall listen. One of your own blood shall lead them. He will carry out my wishes and stand as one after my own heart."

"I had always hoped I would be the one to save them." Rand's shoulders slumped.

"I have greater plans for you." Elyon placed a strong hand on Rand's shoulder.

The prince's heart warmed. A pulsing light shone through his skin and all the muscles, bones, and sinew of his body, like latticework backlit by a great fire. With the light, peace swept over Rand.

"Go now, and do not forget what I have told you." Elyon turned to leave.

"Wait!" Rand cried after him. "When will I see you again?"

Elyon smiled. Just as he disappeared into the trees, he called, "Soon, very soon."

Rand turned back to look at the huge tree but found a fire instead. He was back at camp with Falcon and Zray. The woods and Elyon had vanished as quickly as they had appeared. The wood he'd gathered was piled at his feet.

"What are you thinking about, Rand?" Zray asked as he handed him a bowl of soup. "You've been moving about like a man in a dream." The minstrel sat on a fallen tree trunk beside Rand. "A man in a dream ... that would make a good title for a poem I think." He nodded approvingly to himself and stuffed his mouth.

"I was thinking," Rand murmured. He didn't fully comprehend his surroundings. "He found me," he added.

Zray was too busy eating to ask more questions, but Falcon met Rand's eyes and nodded.

CHAPTER THIRTY-SIX

TUNNELS

The twins mentally told Stavon everything that had occurred.

Stavon shook his large head and said, *'Tis strange how Elyon works. How I would like to get into that mind of his and see what he has planned. Your father visited Quire a week after you left and has been searching for you this entire time. I went with him, but eventually, he ordered me to return in case you came here.*

Hopelessness descended on the twins. *If only we had stayed a few days longer in Quire or turned back to Boldwind.* Meredith's shoulders slumped in defeat.

Kaydin thought for a moment. *I wouldn't change what happened. If we hadn't endured all the traveling and trials, we would never have met and shared stories with Rand, Zray, Falcon and Gelsda, seen the Hall of Twelve Trees, survived the Dead City, or bested those bandits. We wouldn't be grateful for our lives if they hadn't first been threatened.*

I hadn't thought of it that way, Meredith mused.

Where is our father now, Stavon? Kaydin asked the red dragon.

To tell you the truth, I don't know. I last heard from him a month ago. I've been here keeping an eye on the Council while he's away.

Can you take us to our father's house here in the mountains? Meredith begged.

It's quite far away. We'd have to take the tunnels. We dragons prefer not to expose ourselves by flying so near Lower Quith. Stavon acknowledged the copper dragon. *Ah, yes, Scara, you have done well in bringing them here.*

Thank you very much for showing us the way. Kaydin said and Meredith echoed her own thanks.

Scara's embarrassment mentally flowed over as she said, *I fear I was not a very good guide.*

On the contrary, you got us here! Kaydin told the earth dragon.

If I may, Stavon, could I accompany you? Scara asked.

Stavon looked her over for a moment. *You are very young, Scara. You might get into trouble.*

Oh no, I will follow behind and make sure nothing attacks us.

What would attack us from behind? Meredith asked.

Wasals, Scara replied cheerfully. *They have three feet, one in back and two in front. They walk in a sort of shuffling motion. They have four eyes and eat—*

That will do, Scara, Stavon interrupted. *There are very few left. We rid ourselves of most of them. All the same, you may come with us.*

Scara beamed. *I have never been to the other side of the mountains!*

It is well you have not, Stavon admonished. *If you ever do—and I strongly advise you do not—never go alone.* He ended the subject with a nod. *We will leave now.* Stavon swept his large body around, and the brazier winked out, sending them into darkness again.

Stavon led the way through the tunnels. This one was littered with stones. Meredith repeatedly ran into Kaydin, and he kept tripping over his feet in the dark. The horses periodically yanked on the reins as they too nearly lost their footing multiple times. Meredith inevitably tripped over a small boulder and bowled into Kaydin, causing Kaydin to trip over Stavon's tail and Scara to nearly fall on Meredith. The horses whinnied in distress and pranced nervously.

This isn't very good at all, Stavon observed.

Can you not see where you are going? Scara demanded as she scrabbled to her feet.

"It's too dark. We can't see anything." Kaydin's voice echoed off the walls and disappeared down the tunnel.

I would have expected the children of a dragon to have better darksight, Scara grumbled.

Our father is not a dragon. He is the Keeper of Dragons, and only he has eyesight like yours, Meredith explained timidly.

The girl is right, Scara, Stavon said. *We need to get a light for them.*

I have a torch. Kaydin felt around in Vasgo's saddlebag and withdrew it.

Stavon blew a small stream of fire and lit the torch. It barely missed scorching Kaydin's arm, and he nearly dropped the light with a gasp, but he quickly regained a secure grip.

There. Now, shall we be on our way? Stavon urged.

Time became irrelevant in the winding labyrinth of unending tunnels and turns. When they were too tired to go on, they slept. When they were hungry, they ate. Scara protested, but Stavon explained that humans need sleep regularly and cannot sleep for several years at a time. Scara reluctantly accepted and kept watch with Stavon while

Kaydin and Meredith stretched out and rested with their backs against the wall to eat and sleep.

★★★

The twins stood on a mountaintop with the world spread out like a map. To the east, they saw Rivenwall in Dolsulbane and Jad'N's house. Van'N stood in a window overlooking the street. With his white beard and faded blue eyes, he looked more careworn and older than they remembered. His countenance seemed tired and worried. Meredith looked northwest and spotted Gelsda in her chair by the fire, her glowing lamp-worms lighting the outside of her hut. Kaydin saw the Dead City, desolate and abandoned except for the cursed Shadows wondering the streets. Standing as a brilliant star amid the night, the Hall of Twelve Trees rose as a promise that even in darkness, there is light.

Meredith looked upon Lower Quith. A man in black armor stood under the stars, gazing upward. Far to the north, a village stood in ruins and the dead lay unburied on the open plain. Kaydin turned to the Dragon Mountains. He could see straight through the stone and earth to himself. He stood beside himself and stared down at his sleeping body with Meredith's head resting on his shoulder. Stavon lay with his head on his claws, his eyes open. Scara lay on her back and stared at the tunnel roof. The vine around Meredith's neck glowed brightly, pulsing.

"Kaydin." Elyon stood before him.

He dropped to his knees and bowed his head. Despite feeling afraid, joy sprang in his chest.

"On your feet." With a grip like iron, the High King pulled him to his feet. "While you sleep, evil has raised its depraved arm and would crush you with it. Wake now. You slumber when you should be watching." Elyon pointed.

Kaydin looked the way he indicated. Racing through the tunnel were the oddest and ugliest creatures he had ever seen. They had three feet, and four eyes in twisted faces. Their hands were claws and their mouths, beaks. They loped and limped in turns.

Kaydin jerked awake. Meredith still slept beside him. The dragons were awake but unmoving and undisturbed. Had he been dreaming? He rubbed his eyes and peered down the tunnel into its darkness.

I had a dream that Elyon showed me horrible creatures coming this way, Kaydin mind-spoke to everyone.

Stavon cocked his head and strained to listen. "Wasals! We must go now!"

Meredith woke at the sound of his powerful voice. She sat up, green eyes darting about wildly. "What?"

The horses cried in fear, and turning tails, galloped down the tunnel without their masters.

"Ah! My sword is in the saddlebags!" Kaydin jumped to his feet and threw up his arms in frustration. "I'm getting kind of tired of our horses abandoning us at the slightest amount of danger. Cowards."

"I don't know if we can fight the wasals here," Stavon said. "It's very narrow."

"There are about thirty of them," Kaydin told him.

"How do you know that?" Meredith asked.

The drawn out scraping of claws on stone interrupted them. A second later, the hideous creatures came into sight. They bared their teeth-filled beaks and charged.

Stavon roared and fire spewed from his open mouth.

Several beasts burned up, but most of them scrambled up the stone walls where the flame did not reach them. More and more poured around the corner.

Go! Run! Scara and I will catch up! Stavon ordered.

Kaydin grabbed Meredith's arm, breaking her stunned state, and snatched up the torch from a crevice in the rock. There were so many wasals that some had been able to slip past Stavon's guard and were fighting with Scara. Five of them circled past the earth dragon and were about to attack her from behind when Meredith yelled a warning. The five creatures fixed their sights on the twins. One snarled, and then, all five of them abandoned their original quarry and lunged after the twins. Meredith screamed, and Kaydin grabbed her hand again and ran.

Neither of them had any idea where they were going. Their days on the road had strengthened their muscles, and they were able to run for some time before becoming winded. The wasals were closing in.

The twins rounded a bend and found themselves at a crossroad of three tunnels with only a few seconds to decide. Kaydin didn't want to wander lost in thousands of miles of tunnels beneath the Dragon Mountains.

"I feel a breeze! Come on!" Meredith chose the far-left tunnel.

At first, this tunnel was the same as before, but gradually, the walls became rougher, and the floor became dirt. They had to dodge around large rocks littered across the path.

Meredith screamed and threw herself to the side as a head-sized rock fell from above and smashed to pieces at her feet.

"Are you okay?" Kaydin gasped for breath and yanked her up. The motion strained his scabbed-over wounds, and he winced.

"I'm fine." Meredith scrambled up and kept jogging.

"The torch is dying!" Kaydin cried out. He kept a hand on his chest, fearing his newly healed skin would split.

"Up ahead! It looks like daylight!" Meredith shouted.

A wasal snapped inches short of Kaydin's heel.

Calling on Elyon, he summoned as much strength as he could find and surged ahead. The circle of light grew larger, and at last, when they both felt they couldn't take another step, the twins burst into the light. The light of sunset temporarily blinded them after spending several days in near-darkness.

The wasals reached the end of the tunnel and stopped short, howling in frustration and pain.

Kaydin and Meredith stumbled through a wood until finally, heaving for breath, Kaydin collapsed on the ground in a pile of leaves, and Meredith sank onto a large rock beside him. Their eyes acclimated to the light, and they looked for signs of their whereabouts. Trees spread out in every direction. Kaydin checked his wounds, surprised they hadn't reopened.

"Knowing you are going to die and fearing you can do nothing about it is the worst feeling ever. I never want to experience that again," Kaydin declared.

Meredith agreed. "How did you know they were there?"

Kaydin gaped at her. "You were there!"

"I was where?" Meredith's brow furrowed.

"In our dream, remember?"

"Oh! The dream we had about standing on the mountain?"

"Yes. Did you see us sleeping and Elyon speaking to me?"

Meredith shook her head.

"I suppose it was meant only for me."

Meredith sighed and slumped. "I'm so tired."

"Me too." Kaydin closed his eyes.

"Van'N told me wasals never leave the tunnels, so I think we're safe now. Let's wait here for Stavon and Scara," Meredith suggested.

"Are you sure Van'N knew what he was talking about?" Kaydin worried.

"You know him as well as I do."

"Well, we should move on if the dragons don't find us soon."

"Mm-hmm," Meredith mumbled, her eyes already closed.

CHAPTER THIRTY-SEVEN

THE CHILDREN OF DRAGONOSE

"I have summoned you here on a matter of great importance." Sisinta perused a large tome as she sat across from Tyran in her new private rooms. They'd recently moved the bulk of the army to the city of Malefic on the Ammon Plains, close to the base of the Dragon Mountains. "It was a matter I had under control, until that fool, Quaeor, messed it up!" She hissed and slammed the book shut. After a moment of fuming, she smoothed back her hair and asked, "You know of Dragonose?"

Tyran nodded. "Who doesn't? He's one of the main reasons we've been unable to pass into Higher Quith."

"Exactly. If there is no Dragonose, there is no dragon resistance. Their defense would weaken, perhaps even fall apart without him. Until six years ago, I could not identify which dragon clan possessed the inherited title. Then, I received a communication from a supporter of our cause, an incompetent fool named Quaeor. He was advisor to some minor lord in Tayose. A distant relative of the man, Lord Stellmear, had visited with his two young children. Quaeor informed me the children were in constant mental communication with each other. It seems I had underestimated the High King's craftiness. I realize now he'd picked a shape-shifting dragon to be the first Dragonose. The dragon's bloodline has mingled with humans!"

"Isn't Stellmear one of the nobles supporting the kings of Tayose, Dolsulbane, and Athlon in their defense against us?" Tyran leaned forward in his seat.

"He is. I discovered where Lord Stellmear lived and sent the black ones. The stupid things only killed Lady Stellmear. Dragonose hunted them down like dogs and eliminated all but one." Sisinta shook her head. "Such a waste. I shouldn't have sent mere beasts to do a job best done myself. Not a week later, Lord Stellmear disappeared. I couldn't locate him, but I was able to keep track of his two children through Quaeor. I instructed him to watch them while I continued to search for Dragonose—unsuccessfully. I decided to try a different approach. I told Quaeor to kill the boy and bring me the girl." Sisinta rose and began to pace the room. "Quaeor let them slip through his fingers. I sent out more vagwhar, and they chased the children halfway across Higher Quith. Eventually, the children killed them with help from two others. That is the problem with vagwhar: For all their tracking and hunting abilities, they remain dumb animals. A mental link with them is worthless."

Tyran resisted the urge to ask why she had not sent him to do the job. He would have succeeded.

Sisinta stopped and smiled. "Today, I received news! Ah! What glorious news." Her laugh tinkled like icicles breaking. "The wasals sent word that two children smelling of dragon blood exited the tunnels into Lower Quith. This is where you come in." Sisinta pointed to Tyran. "I cannot ask just anyone to retrieve them. I want you to take some Black Knights to the Spairen Wood and bring the children of Dragonose to me, alive."

Tyran stood, saluted, and bowed his head. "I will do all you ask, my lady."

Sisinta smiled lovingly at him and cupped his cheek with one hand. "I know you will." She turned back to her overflowing table of papers, pens, books, and numerous artifacts. "You are dismissed." She did not look up.

Tyran walked backward a few steps before he swung about on his heel and pushed the doors open. The motion startled the door guards back to attention. One of the soldiers was shaking but kept his eyes perfectly straight. Other than swallowing hard enough to make his Adam's apple bounce, the other guard showed no emotion. "If I catch either of you lapsing in attention again, I will have you whipped in front of the entire army." Tyran held each of their gazes in turn and found an appropriate measure of fear. Satisfied that his words had their desired effect, Tyran left.

★★★

Kaydin bolted upright, his heart pounding. *Did you hear that?* He shook his sister awake.

Did I hear what? Meredith's thoughts were muddled with sleep, and she groggily lifted her head. All she could see were the dim outlines of trees and rocks.

It sounded like leaves. Kaydin sent her his apprehension while peering into the gloom.

Kaydin, last fall's leaves are everywhere. Meredith rolled her eyes.

But there is no wind to move them.

Then she heard it—the distinct sound of someone or something crunching the leaves. She jerked into a sitting position, spun around, and found herself face to face with a man in full armor. She yelped and nearly collided with Kaydin.

Kaydin grabbed a branch and jumped between the man and his sister in a long point stance. "Get back!"

"Kaydin, what are you doing?" the armored figure asked.

Kaydin stared at the man in disbelief and slowly lowered his primitive weapon.

Rand removed his helmet.

Kaydin dropped the branch and cried, "What are you doing here?"

"I think we can ask you the same question."

Falcon and Zray stepped out from behind a tree.

"How did you get here?" Meredith demanded.

"Tunnels." Zray gestured in the direction they had come from. "Falcon knows some dragons who let us use them. I think he made up the part about the dragons, though, and just tracked you himself. Where did you go? We thought you had been kidnapped or something!"

"We, ah ..." Kaydin glanced at his sister, "found our father's friend who led us through the tunnels."

"What are you doing here, then?" Rand questioned.

"What do you mean?" Meredith asked.

"We're in Lower Quith."

"Are we?" Meredith's face clouded with worry. "We weren't planning to be here, but we were chased by wasals and ended up in this place."

"Was-what?" Zray asked.

"Wasals," Falcon told the minstrel. He eyed the twins. "Right now, I'm wondering how you two know about the tunnels."

"Our father's friend," Kaydin repeated.

"I would like to meet this friend. If he knew anything at all, he should never have let you travel the tunnels alone."

"He hasn't! I mean ... he didn't. We were separated when the wasals attacked. They're going to catch up with us later," Meredith defended.

"They?" Falcon raised his eyebrows.

"Well, yes, you see, there was another ..." Meredith trailed off and then burst out, "Why do we have to answer all your questions?"

"Because you were the ones who disappeared without a word! For all we know, you could be working for Sisinta!" Zray accused.

"How dare you!" Kaydin shouted. He would have punched the cocky minstrel if Meredith hadn't held him back. "We don't have to answer to any of you!" He shrugged off her hold.

"You have to answer to me." Rand stepped forward. "Remember, I promised to take you home, and you agreed to my help. So far, you have led us on a wild goose chase. I think you owe us an explanation."

"We can't give you one!" Meredith proclaimed. "We would if we could, but we made a promise that we can't break!"

"You do not trust us? Have we traveled all this way together only to be separated by secrets?" Rand demanded.

"We aren't the only ones with secrets," Kaydin mumbled loud enough for everyone to hear.

They all fell silent.

"We found your horses," Rand said at last. "We were worried you had been killed."

"Where are they now?" Kaydin asked.

"Back there." Zray pointed behind.

"We just set up camp for the night. Let's sort this out there," Rand suggested.

"We have to wait for our friends," Kaydin said firmly.

"We are your friends. It's not far," Rand insisted.

The twins reluctantly nodded and followed. They reached the camp where the horses were tied. No one ate anything or said a word. They only glanced sideways at each other, passing silent judgements and worrying they had all discovered each other's secrets.

After a few minutes Falcon sat up, alert, and cast a cautious gaze around.

"What is it?" Zray asked.

Falcon held up his hand for silence.

Everyone held their breath.

"A crow," he told them.

"So? There are crows all over." Zray frowned.

"But they are usually asleep at this time in the evening. They would make noise only if something disturbed them."

"T-The vine! I-It's glowing!" Zray pointed at Meredith. "Something bad is about to happen!"

The forest came alive as men in black armor emerged from every direction, armed with swords, and forming a tight circle.

Falcon drew a dagger, and Rand picked up his sword. Falcon launched his weapon without hesitation, and it struck a chink between the helmet and breastplate of a Black Knight. Before the man had time to clutch his throat and fall, Falcon drew his sword. The other Knights sprang forward, and Falcon and Rand rushed to meet them.

Kaydin stumbled to Vasgo and managed to wrestle his sword out of the saddlebag in barely enough time to engage a Knight. The Knight easily knocked Swan from his grasp and held him at sword point. Kaydin spotted the rest of his companions in the same predicament. Only Meredith moved, kicking and struggling in the grasp of a brute at least seven feet tall.

A Black Knight stepped forward and removed his helmet. He grabbed a fistful of her long brown curls and yanked her head back.

Meredith cried out. Tears blurred her vision, but she met a pair of glowing yellow eyes in a handsome face crossed with silver scars. The face of the last person in the world she would have ever expected to see.

CHAPTER THIRTY-EIGHT

OLD FRIENDS

Tyran paled and his eyes widened. He released his grip and stumbled back. "Wh-What are you doing here?" Tyran put a shaking hand to his eyes attempting to compose himself. The sight of her brought back a thousand memories he had tried to forget. When he turned away, he found the green eyes of yet another ghost from his past—Kaydin.

Kaydin stared in horror. Tyran didn't have to read the boy's mind to know he had been recognized. No, Kaydin was not a boy anymore, at least not the boy Tyran remembered. He and Meredith still had light brown hair and deep green eyes, remarkably similar, although Meredith's features were more feminine, and Kaydin was a little taller. Tyran refused to look anymore, lest the memories steal his resolve. "Take them back to Malefic," he ordered.

"Is this what you have come to?" a voice challenged. "Kidnapping and sneaking up on unsuspecting men? I would have expected Airith Shaver to have more honor than that!"

Tyran drew his sword and faced the challenger. Black eyes flashed at him, and he nearly lost his grip on Cala

Man. "Father!" The word slipped out involuntarily. Panic flamed up his spine, then burning rage. A lifetime of hurt and anger flowed through him. The pitch-black hair and eyes were so like Tyran's own, but this man had no gray in his hair and was years too young to be his father. Tyran's eyes narrowed, and he corrected himself, "Falcon."

Falcon smiled, and spreading his arms, took a bow. "I'm glad you recognize me, brother."

"You're no brother of mine!" Tyran yelled. He pressed Cala Man's tip against Falcon's neck. "You abandoned me."

Falcon's smile faded, and he said quietly, "You would challenge an unarmed man?"

Tyran laughed mirthlessly and snarled back, "Imagine that, after all the times I ended up on my back with your sword blade at my throat, now I have bested you, the so-called best swordsman in all Tayose! You have no idea the battles I have won now, big brother." Tyran threw his arms out dramatically then brought his sword back to Falcon's eye level. "You might be our father's son but I, for one, am not."

"Are you so sure about that, Airith?" Falcon's voice held a threat.

"Quite sure."

"Am I nothing to you now, then? Have you no memory of the times I cared for you as a child? Or of the hours I spent imparting all my swordplay knowledge as a labor of love to the little brother who desperately wanted purpose? Have you no feeling left?"

"Feeling? I have plenty, though it mostly consists of hate and anger for those who forced me into what I am. You left me!"

"No one forced you, Airith. I'm sorry I left you when I did. I know Father was harsh on you, but—"

"Harsh?" Tyran's voice rose to a shout. "That's an understatement! Nothing I ever did pleased him! All I ever wanted was to hear him say he loved me or a single word of praise, but no, *I* was the cursed one! The one who was the living, breathing, walking reminder of Rasfell," Tyran spat out his dead brother's name, "his beloved dead son. The only thing I ever did was be born on the day he died. At least you were the best swordsman in Tayose, poised to inherit Father's estate!"

"But I did not," Falcon said calmly.

"No, you did not." Tyran leered. "Instead, you joined The High King." Tyran spat at Falcon's feet. "So now here you are, come to convince me to turn from my 'evil ways' or kill me if I don't. That is what you do, isn't it? You're the High King's cold-blooded assassin."

"No." Falcon shook his head. "I have never killed a man in cold blood, and I didn't come here to kill you. However, I will do everything in my power to convince you to leave the life you're living. I would hate to have to kill you."

"Kill me!" Tyran laughed. "You think too highly of yourself. Don't you know? I cannot be killed! I've even tried it myself."

"Oh, Airith, surely you can see what has happened to you! Why would you try to end your own life if you were truly happy with it?"

"What life could you possibly offer that is better than what Sisinta has given me?" Tyran scoffed and turned away.

Falcon snatched his sword from the guard next to him, knocking the man to the ground with a backhanded strike of the hilt through the Knight's open visor. "Come forward and fight me like a man!" Falcon challenged.

The other Black Knights stepped forward, but Tyran held up his hand. "I was rather looking forward to letting you live. I thought perhaps I could show you the wisdom in turning your loyalty over to Sisinta. She could make you a general to fight beside me, but if I kill you, no such favor."

"That's fine by me. Yours is a life of walking death." Falcon sprang forward.

Their swords crashed with such force, it threw both of them back several steps, but a moment later, they were exchanging powerful blows that caused both to lose their footing.

"The student has surpassed the master." Tyran panted between clenched teeth.

"What is the one thing I said would be your downfall, Airith?" Falcon dodged a blow aimed for his head.

"My name," Tyran smashed his sword against Falcon's, "is Tyran!"

"Pride and overconfidence, Airith."

Tyran's eyes flashed yellow. "I've not become what I am for nothing." Tyran grunted as Falcon's sword locked with his at the hilt. The brothers were eye to eye, Falcon pressing his full weight forward in the lock and Tyran gritting his teeth with the effort of throwing off Falcon's sword.

A moment later, Tyran succeeded, but Falcon's blade crashed down on Tyran's gauntlet and knocked the sword from his hand. Then came a thud, and Falcon dropped at Tyran's feet.

★★★

An hour later, Falcon slowly regained consciousness. With difficulty, he concentrated on the noises around him. There was the slow drip of water leaking and a clinking of metal against metal. Chains? Voices whispered in the rise and fall of conversation, but he couldn't decipher distinct words. He thought the speakers might be very close, but the sound came to him muffled and ringing in his ears. His head ached and pounded. He felt a small, cool hand on his face and opened his eyes reluctantly.

Meredith, who was bending over him, sighed in relief and handed him a cup of something.

When he swallowed it, he had a coughing fit and nearly choked. "What is this, poison?"

"Water. I know it's brackish, but it's all they've given us to drink." Meredith's voice cleared in his ears—he was thankful that sounds were no longer muffled.

Falcon carefully lifted his head and took in their surroundings. Iron bars and a locked door. The others sat on the stone floor of the large dungeon cell. The only light came from a torch in the passageway. Falcon gently lowered his head again so as not to jar his already aching head. "What happened?" he asked.

"When you disarmed Airith," Meredith explained, "one of the guards hit you over the head, and you passed out. They brought all of us here to Malefic. I don't know what they're planning to do with us." Meredith shuddered.

Falcon closed his eyes again and put his hand on his throbbing forehead. "How do you know Airith?"

Meredith was silent for a moment. "He was a friend of mine and Kaydin's, at least ... we thought he was. We didn't know what had happened to him after he disappeared. Did you know?"

"Yes, but not until recently. I write to my mother often. She told me he'd run away, and I've been looking for him ever since. I heard descriptions of Tyrannus, and I knew in my heart who he was. I resolved to go to him and talk him into changing his ways. Elyon told me Airith would not heed my warnings. On my own, I have no influence over others' decisions, but Elyon said I was to go anyway."

"Why would Elyon send you to do something when he knew the outcome could be a disaster?" Meredith frowned.

"He has a plan, and my being here has something to do with it. Even if my brother never changes, at least I can say I tried." Falcon sighed heavily.

"Airith never told me you wrote to him. He said you had joined the army, and your father had disowned you."

"My father doesn't allow my mother to show my siblings the letters I write. He's bitter and sad. I feel sorry for him."

"It's so hard to believe Airith is Tyrannus. How could the boy I knew become a man like that? I was better off thinking him dead. What's that odd yellow light in his eyes?"

"That's the Shadow dwelling in him, keeping him alive. He has Silver Blood."

"Airith? Silver Blood? I thought it was a disease affecting only dragons."

"You're right, usually. For some reason known only to Elyon, he caught it. The scars on his face? Those must be where the Silver Blood has healed him."

"Does everyone know he has it?" Meredith asked. "When I heard about the deeds of Tyrannus Black, no one mentioned Silver Blood."

"I don't think everyone knows. But Elyon told me, and it makes sense. Airith rose to power quickly and has never been wounded in battle." Falcon fell silent, and Meredith didn't press him. She remained quiet at his side, mulling the situation over and attempting to reconcile the frustrated, ambitious, dark-eyed, teenage boy with the scar-faced, raging, murderous man she'd just met.

Zray spoke up, "It doesn't seem likely we'll be getting out of here any time soon."

"If only I hadn't pushed you to take the left tunnel, we wouldn't be here," Meredith said to her brother.

"You couldn't have known what would happen," Kaydin assured her. "If we had taken any of the other tunnels, the wasals could have caught up with us, and we could be dead now."

"Is this any better? We're going to die anyway." Meredith was on the verge of tears.

"Cheer up, Mere, we don't know that yet. Elyon has a plan, you heard Falcon say so." Kaydin tried a happy tone, but it fell flat.

***

A few hours passed, and they barely spoke. Meredith thought being caged and uncertain of their fate was almost as bad as being chased by wasals and knowing she was going to die. She curled up on a pile of straw and tried to sleep, but the sounds of other prisoners moaning and crying flooded her ears, and she found herself crying silently too. Finding Airith now was just as bad as losing him all those years ago. She'd have taken the news of his death better than the news of his identity under Sisinta.

Was there any way out of this place?

Please don't leave us here, Elyon, she prayed.

CHAPTER THIRTY-NINE

A COUNCIL OF WAR

Higher Quith was silent and still. There was no moon and no one to see the dragon flying on stealthy wings above the sleeping world.

Stavon had been searching all day, asking after Dragonose. He'd sent Scara to gather the Council of Dragons. The fire dragon believed he deserved to have his heart ripped out—by failing to save the twins, he'd failed his master. Their blood was on his claws, it might as well drip from his own jaws. He'd followed their scent through the tunnels after he and Scara had killed all the wasals in their path.

He had encountered one of Gelsda's crows flitting about in the forest. It repeated everything it had heard—Black Knights, Tyran, and his prisoners. Stavon needed to inform Dragonose.

The fire dragon spotted Gelsda's hut below and dove. The ground shook when he settled, and he heard glass tinkling and rattling, followed by alternating thuds and shattering.

A moment later, the old lady came out in a huff. "You boisterous old buffalo, do you know how long it took me to collect those ingredients! I ought to tan your hide!" Gelsda waved her stick at the red dragon.

Lord Stellmear emerged from the hut. He gently took the stick from her hands and told her, "I will pay you for the trouble."

"I have to collect some of my herbs all over again." Gelsda glared at Stavon menacingly.

"I'll help you gather them," Jade told her.

"A thousand apologies, my lord, but you cannot," Stavon said.

Dragonose turned to the dragon. "Are the raiders attacking the villages again?"

"No, sir." Stavon shook his massive head. "We killed the last group after they attacked a village last week."

"What is it then?"

Your children, Stavon mind-spoke.

Dragonose put a trembling hand on the red dragon's scaly neck and asked, "Where are they? What's happened? Gelsda tells me they stayed here with her, but they left some time ago."

I'm sorry, my lord, I have failed you, and I have failed them.

"Tell me what's happened, and I will be the judge of that."

Sisinta has captured them along with Falcon and two others.

"Elyon's man, Falcon Shaver?"

Yes, Stavon confirmed.

Lord Stellmear took a fortifying breath and whispered, "Elyon, watch over them." In a normal tone, he asked, "Does the Witch-Queen know who they are?"

"I don't know." Stavon shook his head. "I have summoned the Council."

"This is a matter of war. We must go now." Jade quickly mounted Stavon.

***

By dawn, Dragonose and Stavon stood in the center of the council room in the bowels of a dormant volcano. The sunrise filtered down around his feet. Seven dragons clung to outcroppings and jagged juts of rock. Their names were difficult for him to pronounce, so he called them by names associated with their colors or elements described in the common tongue. There was Malachite, Permafrost, Cinereous, Onyx, Ignis, Bronze, and Cerulean. Together, they represented the elements of their tribes and made up a rainbow that flashed in the dim light.

As a young boy, Lord Jade Stellmear had hatched Stavon. He had not named the fire dragon and, instead, used the name Elyon had imprinted on the hatchling. Stavon meant *helper*, and a helper is just what he needed to rule temperamental, stubborn, opinionated, ancient beings.

Where is Aurelian? Dragonose demanded.

She should be here shortly, Stavon replied. *She's been at Six Peaks visiting her brother.*

We cannot wait for her. I must speak now. Jade mind-spoke his greeting, *My fellow dragons and worthy members of this Council.*

Aurelian chose that moment to enter and take her place next to Ignis.

Dragonose continued, *I have called this urgent meeting because five citizens of Higher Quith have been captured by Sisinta.*

The dragons murmured among themselves.

Two of them are my children.

The dragons all began mind-speaking at once:

I warned you they were not safe anywhere! Cerulean lectured.

How did Sisinta get so far into our land? Bronze wondered.

Where are they now? Malachite asked.

She plans to kill them so there will be no one to rule us and no future Dragonose! Cinereous, barely containing his panic, fanned himself with his wings.

Who are the other three with them? Malachite broke in.

How did Sisinta learn of their whereabouts? Bronze asked.

I say we burn Sisinta's troops and demand she return them! Ignis cried in outrage.

What about us frost dragons? Permafrost offered, *We can freeze the army to get the children out without burning them alive.*

There are fewer frost dragons than fire dragons, the red dragon retorted.

And there are more light and water dragons than fire dragons! Permafrost retorted. *This isn't a competition!*

Why should we do anything? Cerulean interrupted. *Sisinta is obviously using them as bait. We should wait until she sends a ransom message. In the meantime, she's probably lying in wait for us.*

"Silence!" Onyx roared aloud, booming in the huge mountain hall. "Our master is speaking!"

The other dragons cringed and slunk back until the reverberating sound waves dissipated.

Stavon, please explain, Dragonose told his dragon.

Stavon stepped forward. *The twins were on their way to the house of Dragonose when they were chased by wasals and lost in Lower Quith.*

Didn't we get rid of those beasts a long time ago? Ignis questioned.

Apparently not, Permafrost sneered.

They were in the tunnels we rarely use, Stavon clarified.

Dragonose cleared his throat, and they all fell silent again. *Sisinta captured them when they entered Lower Quith.*

Uneasy silence lingered, until Bronze said what they were all thinking, *I'm afraid we'll have a hard time getting them back. She can claim they were on her land and are therefore her subjects and prisoners.*

What of the three others you say Sisinta has? Aurelian asked.

They were not with the children when they passed through, Dragonose said. *Falcon led them down different tunnels. Onyx granted him permission to use them.*

I don't think I was wrong to trust Falcon Shaver, Onyx defended. *He's in your good graces, Dragonose, and has come on Elyon's business to the mountains before.*

Perhaps he's betrayed us to Sisinta! We would all be doomed if Falcon tells all the secrets he's been entrusted with! Cinereous worried.

Malachite told the rock dragon, *You always panic and assume the worst before you hear all the facts.*

He's one of the oldest dragons, he has a right to be here! Cerulean exclaimed.

"Silence! None of you will speak unless spoken to!" Onyx roared aloud.

After order was restored, Aurelian requested to speak, and Jade granted it. *If I may, my Lord Dragonose, how do you know all this?*

That doesn't really matter, Jade declared.

Because I was there, Stavon said.

"Stavon ..." Jade started out loud.

It's my fault that they were taken.

No such thing, Jade declared. *You did what you thought needed to be done, and let us leave it at that. Now, let us get to the reason I called you all here. I believe Sisinta is trying to use my children as bait, but I have a plan.*

CHAPTER FORTY

REVEALED SECRETS

"It's been at least a full day since we came here, and the only person we've seen is the jailer!" Zray complained from his place against the damp stone wall, his hat low over his eyes. "Are we going to have to stay here for the rest of our lives simply because they found us in Lower Quith? The only one who should be here is Falcon, the rest of us are innocent bystanders."

The twins shared a concerned glance.

"You have no right to speak ill of our guide," Rand rebuked. "He was only helping us look for Kaydin and Meredith."

Zray pushed his hat higher to glare at Rand. "Some guide! Look where he got us." He turned toward Falcon. "Why did you never tell us who you were?"

Falcon opened one eye, then the other, fixing his eagle-like gaze on the young boy. "I told you I worked for Elyon, and that is all you needed to know. Anything else was personal." Falcon closed his eyes again.

"Humph." Zray snorted, then pulled his hat over his eyes.

"Why are you here, Zray?" Kaydin spoke up. "I think I remember you said you were planning to travel with us to Rivenwall. After that, you came of your own accord."

"I didn't have anything better to do with my time," Zray snapped.

The main prison door creaked and crashed open. None of the group looked up anymore, accustomed to the jailer's comings and goings. However, more than one set of footsteps drew their interest.

Tyran stood at their prison door.

They scrambled to their feet, except Rand, who was already standing.

Tyran looked them over, starting with Falcon and ending with the twins. He turned to the jailer and told him something in a low voice.

The jailer nodded and then barked an order to the two soldiers with him. After unlocking the cell door, the soldiers entered.

"You two," Tyran ordered the twins, "come with me."

Panic crossed the twins' faces.

Rand and Falcon stepped forward to stop the guards.

"If you value your lives or theirs, you will step away," Tyran growled.

The soldiers grabbed Meredith and Kaydin by the arms and pulled them into the hall. After Tyran exchanged a word with him, the jailer nodded and locked the cell door. The twins were led away with Tyran behind.

Meredith looked at her brother for reassurance, but he had his head bowed. Her escort yanked at her arm to keep her eyes forward. *Kaydin—*

Don't. Don't say anything. We don't know who could be listening.

Meredith's building panic was amplified by the absence of her brother's comforting presence in her mind. It brought back memories of the lonely days following their mother's death.

The prison door banged closed, and the twins found themselves in a damp, narrow passageway sparsely lit by torches. The guards hurried them along through locked doors and down halls until they mounted a set of stairs, which brought them to ground level. Sunlight illuminated the hall, streaming through a pair of open doors on their right. Freedom ... but it was foolish to assume they'd be released that easily. They were forced to hasten toward a second pair of double doors across the hall where four soldiers stood guard. Their black tunics embroidered with map-clutching silver dragons marked them as Sisinta's men. They came to attention and bowed before Tyran. In unison, both doors opened dramatically.

Meredith cast a longing gaze at the open doors, the outside, the free world. After passing through the guarded doors, the sunlight vanished.

Pillars and columns supported the high ceiling and gilded roof of the throne room. The twins tilted their heads back to observe many figures of animals, dragons, Paladalls, gryphons, men, and hundreds of plants and flowers carved into the stone. Meredith nudged Kaydin and nodded toward the far end of the room.

A group of nobles stood around a throne on a raised dais—Sisinta's most trusted men and women. They wore a variety of colors, likening themselves to over-fledged birds. Their eyes followed the twins' entrance like a frigid, piercing wind on a miserable day, while their judgmental frowns and rigid backs overcast the room with a cloud of disapproval.

Kaydin tried to hide his quick inhale when he saw the powerful, alabaster woman on the throne. She stood out like the pale moon in the night sky. Her presence demanded attention without resorting to the pomp and colorful accessories of her court.

The guards pushed the twins to the foot of the dais. They were forced to their knees, then the guards stepped away.

Kaydin and Meredith tried to stand, but Tyran placed his hands on their shoulders and forced them down. Their knees cracked on the marble floor. Meredith could not hide the cry of pain that slipped through her clenched teeth. Kaydin grunted.

"Stay on your knees if you want to live," Tyran warned in a harsh whisper. He bowed before Sisinta, then spoke in a booming voice that shattered the silence in the hall. "Here are the prisoners you asked for, my lady."

Meredith shivered, and Kaydin groaned inwardly.

Sisinta assessed the twins for a long moment, then turned to the man standing closest to her. "What do you make of them, King Pavilion?"

King Pavilion was a middle-aged man with a gold crown and a richly embroidered tunic. But the crown was simple, and his clothes were slightly worn, testifying to the poverty of the once-wealthy kingdom of Aster. The king studied them with large, lazy brown eyes. He puffed out his chest in the most ridiculous way. "They look like ragged vagabond children who would do better working in the mines than here, my lady."

"That," Sisinta pointed at the king, "is where you are wrong." She turned her frigid, dark smile on the children. "They are the key to winning this never-ending war."

"How is that, my lady?" Pavilion appeared mortified to find his opinion was wrong.

Sisinta descended the dais steps. She walked in a circle around the twins, who kept their eyes downcast. "These are the children of Lord Jade Stellmear, Dragonose, the Keeper of Dragons."

A chorus of gasps rose among the nobles.

Neither of the twins could hide their mental distress.

One noble stepped forward to get a better look at the twins. He was a true northern nobleman, tall with dark skin. His handsome face was crowned with a high forehead, but the glint in his eyes betrayed his depravity. "This is fortunate indeed," he said. "We can lure out Dragonose with them, and even if we do not capture him, we have his children, and therefore the future Keeper of Dragons."

Sisinta smiled at the man. "That thought had crossed my mind, Lord Sazecall, but I would prefer to have both Dragonose dead *and* his son under my command."

"I would never do it!" Kaydin jumped to his feet and snarled at Sisinta. "I will never submit to you and your perverted schemes!"

Sisinta struck Kaydin across the face, sending him sprawling.

Meredith let out a cry and lunged toward her brother.

Kaydin sat up, wiping blood off his lip.

"I can easily kill you and keep your sister," Sisinta hissed.

"I would never do as you say, either!" Meredith asserted.

"No," Sisinta smiled wickedly, "but your son would. There are many who would be more than willing to marry a pretty young thing like yourself."

"I would never marry anyone who served you!" Meredith spat back.

"Who said you would have a choice?" Sisinta laughed wickedly. She turned to Tyran. "Bring me the other three prisoners. I'm curious to know what sorts of people the children of Dragonose associate with."

Tyran nodded and disappeared.

Meredith helped her brother to his feet. He winced in discomfort.

Tyran reentered with a bewildered Zray, an apprehensive Rand, and a calm Falcon. All three were marched to Sisinta. Tyran ordered them to kneel.

Falcon refused. "I will not bow before anyone but my king."

Tyran raised his arm to strike, but Sisinta stopped him. "Let him have his little rebellion. I have heard of your deeds, Falcon Shaver." To Tyran, she said, "I must congratulate you, Tyrannus, not many men would turn in his own brother. I'm honored by your loyalty to me."

The nobles began to murmur, looking between the two brothers.

Tyran ran his hands through his hair, betraying his agitation. Meredith could still read him after all this time. "I disowned him long ago."

Sisinta approached Zray standing between Falcon and Rand. "And who are you?"

Zray looked positively pitiful—his face was pale and his hands shaking. A breath of wind could knock him over. He glanced at the twins as if for advice, but he paled further when he saw the blood on Kaydin's face.

"Who are you?" Sisinta demanded again.

"I am, ah ... Z-Zray s-son of, ah ... Urran. I-I am a-a minstrel."

"Only a minstrel." Sisinta snorted. "What are you doing here?" Sisinta didn't give him a chance to answer, instead turning to Rand. At first, she studied him on all sides, then recognition crossed her face. "Prince Randarin Tieren, how fortunate! I have men out searching for you."

Rand winced. Falcon and Zray stared at Rand like he was some foreign creature from another world. The twins gazed at him, open mouthed.

"You're the crown prince of Ironcall!" Zray exclaimed. He stepped away fearfully. "You said you were from the Islands!"

"I think you owe me an explanation, Prince Randarin." Sisinta narrowed her eyes. "I was told you were touring the outposts."

Rand cast his gaze about the room. He closed his eyes and took a deep breath. "I never went on a tour of the outposts. I told my father that so he would not follow me. I have been seeking an audience with Elyon."

Gasps and cries of, "Betrayal! Treachery! Treason!" spewed from the nobles. The noise grew into arguments among the nobles until no one could be heard over the din.

"Take them away! I will deal with them later!" Sisinta called to the guards, who stepped forward and escorted the five prisoners out of the throne room.

Even after the doors were closed, the outraged voices could still be heard until the captives were returned to the underground prison.

CHAPTER FORTY-ONE

DEMANDS

Torch in hand, Tyran stood outside the dungeon door. Should he go in or leave well enough alone? He ran his fingers through his hair. He had so many unanswered questions, but did he dare ask them? What if he gave in to his meddling conscience and interfered with Sisinta's plans? No. He could not take that risk.

Tyran had made up his mind to leave when the prison door was unlocked from the inside and the jailer stepped out. The man saw Tyran, bowed, and held the door open for him.

I may as well, Tyran decided.

He looked down the long corridor of prison cells. There were rarely any prisoners important enough for him to bother with. "Take the prisoner called Falcon Shaver to a questioning cell," he ordered the jailer.

The man obeyed. Tyran followed him to the interrogation cell.

In the cell, Falcon stood with his arms crossed, calmly watching Tyran.

Tyran opened his mouth to speak but stopped. He turned his back to his older brother and stared up at the high, stone ceiling and tried again. "I was wondering about Mother," he blurted, then held his breath, waiting for an answer.

"She was well when last I heard from her," Falcon responded.

"You spoke to her?" Tyran turned in surprise.

"I've been writing to her since I left home. Father never allowed her to tell you."

Yellow light began to glow around Tyran's black pupils, and his voice held a faint echo. "If I had the chance, I would kill him!"

"Don't say such things. He cares for you. He humbled himself and wrote to me after you disappeared. He asked if I knew where to find you and if I could convince you to come home."

"Home? This is my home now!" Tyran hissed.

Neither spoke for a little while.

The yellow light in Tyran's eyes faded. Finally, he inquired, "Kenta?"

"She's sixteen now and might be married next year."

"To whom?" Tyran's brow furrowed.

"Hasdell."

"He's not good enough for her."

"Hasdell is not the same boy you remember. He's only a little younger than you. His father died, and he is now Lord Hasdell."

"No one will ever be good enough for Kenta," Tyran insisted. "Did Father talk her into it?"

Falcon shrugged. "She is a strong and wise woman. No one is going to trick her into something she doesn't want."

"Unless she believes it will make Father happy," Tyran murmured.

Falcon did not respond.

"How are Cowin and Shar?" Tyran asked half-heartedly.

Falcon sighed sadly. "Not well. After you left, Shar fell in love with a peasant girl, Brayla, a maid. They wanted to get married, but Father refused his blessing on account of her low birth. Shar married her anyway. Father disowned him, and Shar is now working on his father-in-law's farm."

"Ha!" Tyran laughed dryly. "Soon he will have no more sons left to disown. What about Cowin?"

"Cowin has gained the reputation of a rogue. He gambles too much, has been in love with five women at once, and is always getting into fights. He also killed a man in a duel."

"I never thought he had it in him."

"I wish he didn't."

Silence again.

"You know you are going to die?" Tyran stated it as a question and gauged Falcon's reaction.

"I know." Falcon nodded. "I assumed as much when I came here."

"Then why did you enter Lower Quith? You could have left me alone and saved yourself!" Tyran fumed.

Falcon stared at his brother. "You should know better than anyone."

"I don't want your sympathy," Tyran said. How could Falcon act like it was normal to sacrifice his life just to speak with him?

"I know," Falcon responded quietly.

"I have to go." Tyran turned sharply and swung the door open. His eyes glowed bright yellow as he slammed the prison door and locked it. "See you, Brother." Tyran's tone was pointed and sharp and he didn't turn back to look before disappearing down the hall.

★★★

"How do you feel about the new prisoners, Tyrannus?"

Tyran looked up from the message he had been reading.

Sisinta watched him intently from across the table.

"I think they will cooperate if we approach them the right way." Tyran tossed the paper to the table and pointed at it. "That letter demanding them back proves we have Dragonose in a corner, but we must be careful. If we push him too far, he may react dangerously."

Sisinta nodded slowly in agreement. "That's all true, but how do you feel about the prisoners?"

Tyran ran his fingers through his hair and shrugged. "I'm not sure what you mean, my lady. They are, after all, just prisoners."

"Do you doubt me, Tyrannus?" Sisinta challenged.

"Never." He picked up a goblet of wine.

"How are things going with X-Sayda?" Sisinta raised a brow.

Tyran was halfway through a gulp and had to splutter to avoid dissolving into a coughing fit. Why was he always drinking wine whenever that woman was mentioned? "I hate her."

"She loves you."

Tyran snorted. "She has confused her love for me with love of herself."

Sisinta sighed. "What am I going to do with you? You must understand, if you want to maintain your power, you need to marry into a powerful family."

Tyran growled in response.

"There's always the daughter of Dragonose. Does she appeal more to you? She'd be more of a handful than X-Sayda and wouldn't marry you willingly. Dragonose would grant you none of the lands and wealth she's entitled to, but your children would become powerful players in our war."

Tyran was struck dumb. He opened his mouth to respond but didn't know what to answer. A version of the old Meredith came to his mind—she'd looked at him with interest once. But the new Meredith, one not based on old memories, took over that image—a shocked, horrified version of the green-eyed girl he once knew. "M-Maybe?" he stammered out.

Sisinta presented him with a worn, leather-bound book. Tyran took it. "What's this?"

"It was among the things we confiscated from the prisoners."

He turned it over in his hands, frowning. There was something familiar about it. A leather cord wrapped and bound the book. Loose pages threatened to spill out.

"Open it," Sisinta ordered.

A few pages fell when he did. He bent to retrieve them and was surprised when he saw his own face looked up at him. A younger version with no scars, holding a guard stance. He slowly placed it back on the table. Even as he asked, "Who drew that?" he knew the answer. He could picture Meredith now, bent over the little book, casting furtive glances across the room while he and Kaydin sparred. She'd shown him a couple of her drawings once, but those had been of his horse and Quire Castle. He felt sure she would be embarrassed that he'd seen this particular sketch.

"You knew them," Sisinta stated.

Tyran nodded and forced himself to return the book. "I didn't know who the twins were at the time. Search my thoughts, and you'll know it's true."

"I already have. No need to feel guilty." Sisinta eyed him thoughtfully. Then, she stood and rounded the table.

Tyran eyed her warily.

"I need you to deliver this to Dragonose." Sisinta held out a letter sealed with her coat of arms.

"Can no one else do it?" Tyran dared to ask.

"No. All the soldiers are afraid of the mountains. I know I can trust you."

Tyran reluctantly took the letter. "Where do I deliver it?" he asked.

"Dragonose specified there would be a colored dragon waiting at the edge of the woods, near where you found the prisoners."

Tyran nodded slowly. "I will go now." He saluted and bowed.

Upon entering the courtyard, Tyran called Kappin mentally. Shortly, the silver dragon appeared in the sky above him.

Half an hour later, Kappin landed in the small clearing where Tyran had apprehended Falcon, Rand, Zray, and the twins. The extinguished fire was still there after two days, black and dead. A slight wind stirred the trees. The sky was overcast, and the air was humid and damp after the rainfall the night before. Tyran looked up at the threatening clouds, but feeling Kappin stiffen under him, he quickly snapped his head down and looked around apprehensively.

The largest dragon Tyran had ever seen appeared from among the trees. Kappin was a mere child compared to him. The silver dragon took a step back, and Tyran did his best to calm him mentally.

I believe you have a message for me, the red dragon mind-spoke with disdain.

Tyran drew out the letter from the pouch around his waist.

The dragon pinched it between two claws and launched himself into the air.

They watched the dragon disappear over the treetops.

Well, he was nice, Kappin remarked sarcastically.

I never knew colored dragons were so big, Tyran replied.

Kappin spread his wings and returned to Malefic. *Colored dragons are larger than we silver dragons only because they have longer lifespans. Dragons never stop growing. Even with the Shadows in our minds, we live only to about twenty-seven. Shorter lifespans, smaller dragons.*

Tyran remained silent the rest of the way, calculating in his head. If the Shadow expanded his lifespan by the promised seven years, and added to the seven years of Silver Blood, he was left with roughly eleven years before he'd succumb to his disease. If he wasn't currently in Sisinta's employ and under the power of Tyrannus, he would have four years left. The thought of eleven more years of fighting suddenly wearied him.

He daily found himself tossed between three different states—acceptance of his fate, complete panic and horror at the end looming in the distance, and stubborn rebellion against any acknowledgement of his inevitable demise. The latter was his preferred state of being.

What if he had not come to Sisinta? What if Tyrannus had never entered his mind? Where would he have been now? Tyran forced the questions away. He had to make the best of the years he had left. Somehow, railing against everyone and everything made him feel just a tiny bit better.

★★★

"This is an outrage!" Stavon's voice resounded off the walls of the underground cavern.

Lord Stellmear held the letter his red dragon had brought back from Sisinta.

"A complete outrage!" Stavon added, his voice like a roaring river, deafening to the ears.

"It was to be expected," Dragonose murmured. "Never expect Sisinta to have integrity. I was hoping she did not know who Kaydin and Meredith were."

She cannot really think you would go through with her demand of your life for theirs! Does she?

She would be a fool if she did.

What are we going to do? Stavon asked.

"This could actually give us an advantage," Jade said. "She will not expect me to turn myself in, but what if I do? It would certainly put her off guard." Jade's voice rose in excitement. "We could still carry out our original plan and rescue them while there is chaos."

No. Stavon shook his head and firmly pressed his answer into his master's mind. *You know Sisinta would never keep her word of returning the twins safely, and we cannot risk losing you.*

"But she will not kill me right away. She will want to gloat over her victory first."

No. Stavon flatly refused again. *You forget when you put yourself in danger, you put all of us in danger. Your calling is to rule us, and without you, we are vulnerable despite all our strength. We cannot risk it. We stick to the original plan as agreed.*

"Those are my children out there, Stavon." Jade could not hide his distress.

I know.

Jade shook his head and covered his face in grief, then mounted the stone steps to his house carved into the stone wall of the mountain. "She might kill them, Stavon." Jade spoke without turning.

Stavon shook his head sadly, but his resolve was still strong. He could not let Jade surrender to Sisinta even if there was a small hope he might save the prisoners and escape.

Stavon had watched the young Dragonose grow into a man. He knew many of Jade's daring feats and was not shocked by Jade's plan to give himself up to Sisinta. But Stavon was drawing the line. He worried his master might get himself into something he would not survive.

CHAPTER FORTY-TWO

INNER BATTLES

Tyran paced his rooms. He tried to sit in front of the fire, but his mind would not rest.

The sun had set. Only the soldiers on guard duty patrolled the streets and called out the watch.

"What's wrong with me?" Tyran growled in the dark room.

You're worried about the prisoners, Tyrannus taunted in his mind.

"I am not! What do you know of them anyway? You know about them only because you stole my memories. I wish I'd never come to this accursed land or pledged myself to—"

Careful, Tyrannus warned. *You're thinking traitorous things.* Tyrannus reported to Sisinta, and Sisinta would punish Tyran if she knew of his disloyal thoughts.

"I have to get out of here." Tyran grabbed his black cloak and left.

The fresh air calmed Tyran a little. He stopped in the courtyard and stared into the star-scattered sky. He tried to look at each star individually, but all together, they dazzled his eyes. There were too many to count and take in. The tiny points of light were so small, and yet they stunned him. Realization dawned on Tyran how small he was in comparison to the world. What right did he have to think himself so great, so high and mighty when the very stars in the sky outnumbered him and had more effect on the universe than he did? He had never examined them or considered them as anything but tiny lights in the sky. Now that he thought about it, they played a great role in everyday life—in navigating the sea, in songs and tales, in the change of seasons, and in lighting the sky at night. Without them, the night sky would have little worth.

"My lord!" A guard ran toward him. "Sisinta wants you to send for the prisoners, she said you would know which ones."

Tyran sighed and did not move toward the castle until the guard had left. He slowly made his way inside, stopping at the gate to send a guard to retrieve the prisoners. He waited for them by the throne room doors.

The prisoners were silent. Except Zray, they walked with their heads erect. They marched into the throne room showing no fear. Tyran didn't know if they were brave or ignorant.

Sisinta stood before her throne with a dangerous smile. The audience of nobility stood behind her. Most notably, the king of Ironcall stood as the guest of honor at Sisinta's right hand. The man was in his late sixties and wore a perpetual frown, which masked all other emotions. He stood completely still, both hands hidden in the opposite sleeves of his shimmering blue robes. With the scale and makeup of the audience, Tyran deduced Sisinta planned a spectacle of some sort, one likely involving blood. A sinking feeling settled in his stomach. She had done it before, only this time, the condemned involved posed a controversial roiling of emotions inside of him.

The prisoners filed in, and the court judged silently, their eyes sweeping over the weather-beaten travelers with haughty glances. *Better you than I,* the silent pronouncement emanated from Sisinta's current favorite courtiers.

Tyran noted the reaction of King Tieren when the prince arrived, bedraggled and shackled. A flicker of surprise, and then the perpetual frown returned.

A gray-robed, hooded figure stepped up behind the king. A Paladall, Tyran realized. The individual placed both hands on either side of the king's temples. The fingers of the robed being sank into the man's sandy gray locks. The king immediately went rigid, his hands falling to his sides, fingers splayed in shock. His deep blue eyes—so like the prince's—rolled back in their sockets, then he crumpled to the floor. The robed figure remained standing, the lower half of a feminine face showing under the deep cowl.

"Father!" Rand burst out.

Sisinta watched impassively until the Paladall gave a barely perceptible shake of her head. "Chain all of them! Except the prince. I want him here, at my feet," she ordered.

The guards obeyed.

Sisinta walked circles around the crestfallen prince, who gazed back and forth between the floor and his unconscious father. After an agonizing minute of silence, the Witch-Queen broke it, "Prince Randarin Tieren, you have committed treason."

Rand swallowed and closed his eyes.

"*You* have betrayed your country, your own father—if my Paladall is to be believed—and your queen!" Sisinta's voice became an angry hiss, "Because of what you have done, your family will pay! Oh, do not think you will be pardoned with their blood, you will also pay."

Rand paled and sweat dotted his brow. "My lady, please! Do not kill them, they knew nothing! It was I alone who sought to free my people. Kill me!" he pleaded.

"True." Sisinta continued to circle the anxious prince. "Your father knows nothing, neither does your sister, but your wife ... now, let me see ... what was her name again? Ah! I remember. Thia." Sisinta stopped her pacing and regarded Rand with a wicked smile. "If I recall correctly, it was I who recommended your union. I was pleased when I learned you had found a mutual affection for each other in such a short time, but she failed to report to me, so you may rejoice that she will be joining you in the afterlife."

"Please." Tears streamed from Rand's closed eyes. "She is with child, and I told her not to tell anyone where I was."

"Ah, yes! Your son. Randurren, isn't it? He was born a short time ago. Your wife has been trying to send word to you since then. I have a mind to raise the child as my own, to teach him to be a loyal, trustworthy king and to never repeat his father's treachery."

Rand opened his eyes, and his glare held utter animosity. "Your days are numbered, Sisinta. Elyon will punish you for all the atrocities you have committed!" Rand's voice rose to a passionate pitch, and his eyes shone. "He told me my country and my people will be free of you."

"You poor misguided man. You have been corrupted beyond saving. What makes you think I would ever let that happen? Or don't you know of the legions I command—dragons, men, Shadows?"

"I have seen him, and he has seen my people." Rand remained steadfast.

Tyran could not explain the fear he felt of this man. Something about this prince made Tyrannus restless and angry. Tyran fought to calm the Shadow, but he could not control the spirit's burning hatred. He could feel his eyes glowing, burning with the Shadow's light.

"Let me kill him, my lady!" the voice of Tyrannus spoke for him.

Sisinta turned to her second-in-command, smiling. "Not yet, Tyrannus. You will have the opportunity for blood soon. But contain yourself for a little longer. I would like nothing more than to kill him now, but first ... bring her!" Sisinta nearly bellowed to a guard.

He stammered in assent and left, returning quickly with a beautiful woman. Her long black hair fell past her knees and her blue eyes were the shade of a clear summer sky. But her eyes were downcast and her once-beautiful white dress was torn and soiled.

Thia uttered a cry of distress when she saw Rand shackled and on his knees before Sisinta. No one stopped her from running forward and sinking to her knees before him. Tears streaked through the smudges of grime on her cheeks.

"Don't cry." Rand tried to speak in a comforting tone, but his voice failed him.

Thia held his cheeks and kissed him with pale, trembling lips. "I'm sorry. Sisinta intercepted some of my letters."

Sisinta growled and a guard jumped forward, hauling Thia to her feet. "I sentence you both to execution by the sword," the Witch-Queen pronounced. "You can be sure your traitorous names will always be remembered with disdain and shame. Tyrannus!" Sisinta pointed toward Rand. A guard stepped forward, ripped open Rand's shirt, and yanked his head back by his golden hair, exposing his throat.

Tyran stared first at the prince, then at Sisinta.

Seconds dragged by painfully.

Tyran drew Cala Man and gripped the hilt with all his strength. Warning bells rang in his head, and a trickle of sweat made its way down his back. "My lady, is this wise? After all, he is the crown prince of Ironcall, and the people will be very angry if—"

"How *dare* you contradict me!" Sisinta's face was a picture of fury and outrage.

Tyran winced.

"You are nothing! A useless boy, a nobody I raised from the ranks of the cursed! You were a walking dead man! I gave you all the power you ever wanted. I handed you your life on a silver platter, and now you dare defy *me*?"

Tyran ran his fingers through his hair and tried to still his shaking hands. "I'm sorry, my lady, I didn't mean to—"

"Kill him!" Sisinta shoved a finger at Rand. "Kill him!"

Tyran swallowed, closed his eyes, and fought silently with Tyrannus. Time seemed to stand still, and Tyran felt strangely removed from his surroundings. He looked at each person in turn—Sisinta stood tall and dark with her beautiful face twisted into a baleful sneer, void of compassion. The twins were so alike, yet so different—fear on Kaydin's face and horror on Meredith's. His brother's tight expression showed sorrow and disappointment. Tears bathed Thia's face, and Rand's was admirably courageous.

Time rushed back upon him, and dozens of eyes bore down on him, waiting for what he would do next. "I-I ..." Tyran was lost. What should he do?

Tyran raised his sword and took one step forward but then stopped. Rand's eyes held a thousand words and pleas, yet there was a calm understanding and acceptance of death. He found himself wishing he could know what gave Rand such courage and concern for others. What had he learned in his search for Elyon that had changed him so? What had he discovered on his journey that had given him that look in his eyes, like one wise beyond his years?

He'd burned his conscience, Tyran reminded himself, and he must use only his head. Sisinta had ordered him to execute this man and he had to do it—he had done it before. But still he hesitated.

"Elyon is greater than you will ever be!" Rand abruptly shouted to Sisinta. "You are not Queen of the Outlands or of Quith, Higher or Lower! You are not ruler of anything. Your only subjects are Shadows, demons, and the forsaken!"

"Do not dare to speak that name to me!" Sisinta raged. "Kill him!"

Tyrannus was infuriated. *Obey and kill!* the Shadow roared.

Tyran felt his grasp on his self-control slipping as he watched his hands move of their own accord. Cala Man thrust forward.

The sword drove into the prince's stomach. He drew it out as quickly as he had forced it in.

Meredith screamed, and Thia shrieked. Thia fought to reach her husband, but a guard kept her at bay. Her voice abruptly fell silent.

Rand was still on his knees. Nothing appeared to be wrong other than his shocked expression. No words came out of his mouth. He fell to the marble floor with a sickening thud.

Falcon closed his eyes and shook his head.

Kaydin stared at the fallen prince.

Meredith yanked on her chains and spat curses on Sisinta and Tyran. "Elyon curse you! I hope you suffer a thousand times more than all those you have murdered and tortured! May the dark ones you rule consume you and rot you from the inside out! And all those who serve you be swallowed alive by the earth and suffer forever in the depths of hell!"

"Meredith! Be silent," came Falcon's soft reprimand. "Elyon will punish, but your words may bring calamity on your own head."

Meredith burst into tears.

Kaydin added, "Have courage, Mere."

Falcon bowed his head and whispered, "Elyon, greet him when he comes to you."

Thia had fallen silent after her first screech. When Tyran turned his attention to her, his breath stopped in his throat. She lay in a pool of her own blood, Sisinta holding the knife that had done the deed.

"Take them away!" Sisinta cried. To Tyran, she added, "I will deal with *you* later."

The guards unchained the remaining prisoners and were about to leave when Sisinta ordered them to wait. The guards froze.

Sisinta studied Zray for a long moment. She ordered two guards, "You two! Take this useless screecher of a minstrel out to the tunnels and feed him to the wasals."

Meredith let out a cry, and Kaydin tried to yank out of the guard's grasp.

Zray remained in shock. He did not even struggle when the two guards dragged him out.

***

Falcon and the twins were returned to their dungeon cell.

Meredith curled up in a ball in the corner and cried silently.

Kaydin sat beside her and leaned his head on her shoulder. Eventually, he broke down too.

CHAPTER FORTY-THREE

DYING WISHES

Tyran was alone in the throne room. Everyone had left, including the king of Ironcall, who had to be supported by two servants. No one had come to take away the dead bodies yet or clean up the blood. He stared at the unmoving figures and felt his heart twist in his chest. The same feeling he'd had after killing that boy at Ladle's Ridge. He acknowledged with dread that his conscience had begun to slowly rise from its ashes.

What had Rand ever done to him? Nothing. Yet here he was, lying in his own blood, the same blood that marred Cala Man. Silver Hand, the sword his ancestors had lifted to fight for freedom, justice, life, and the good of others, in the name of their king, and he had stained it with injustice, murder, his own selfish gain, and in the name of a queen who caused destruction and death wherever she went. And Thia, she would never get to hold or raise her newborn son.

Tyran had not known Crown Prince Randarin Tieren or his wife, but he knew enough about them to know they were well-loved by their people. The people would not take kindly to their deaths—Ironcall had looked forward to Rand's rule. Tyran carefully walked to the fallen prince's side and squatted to turn him over. The man stirred, and Tyran nearly dropped him had Rand not snatched Tyran's black cloak. Desperation swam in his eyes.

"Do not let her have him. Do not let him grow up like me, not knowing the truth! Do not let Sisinta or his grandfather have him." Rand's breath came in gasps, and he struggled to hold on to the small thread of life left in him. Tyran tried to pull away, but Rand tightened his grasp. "Tell him ... tell him ... I loved him very much."

Tyran stared at the man in disbelief. "Don't you know who I am?"

"Yes, yes, I do." Rand closed his eyes and tried to find the strength to speak. "I am dying. Do you know how that feels?" Rand looked up at Tyran, begging for understanding.

A mix of emotions ran through Tyran. He knew the feeling well—the sensation of life draining drop by drop, vision fading, and mind numb, panicked. But Tyran had always been cheated out of the end results and had never met death. He had wished more than once that he could feel its sweet relief from his endless dying. Tyran closed his eyes. "Yes ... I know how it feels."

"Then stay with me until I am gone. I have these ... thoughts running through my head." Rand closed his eyes again and swallowed. "All I can think of is last summer when I saw her ... Thia, she was standing ... in the sunshine, and ... and ..." Rand laughed. "She smiled at me and I saw, in one moment, the greatest thing in the world—I saw love." Rand opened his eyes. "Do you know how *that* feels?"

Tyran fought tears as he whispered, "No, I do not know how that feels. I do not think I have ever felt it."

Rand clutched Tyran's shoulder so hard, Tyran winced. Rand looked him straight in the eyes. "I know where you can find it. Do you know where you can find it?"

Tyran hid his grief-stricken face. His answer came out as a sob, "No."

"Elyon."

Tyran shook his head.

"He has given me … a purpose for living … and dying. He promised me I would see him soon. What are you living for? Your next moment of glory? The next time Sisinta praises you for … for taking another man's … life? I can see … the emptiness you feel … the hopelessness." Rand grasped the back of Tyran's neck and leveraged himself off the ground. He looked into Tyran's eyes and said with the sincerity only a dying man can convey, "I used to feel that way, but I have found hope … and the answer." Rand fell back, exhausted. Tyran tried to lift him again, but Rand shook his head. "I am gone to meet my king and my wife. Will you not … bid me … farewell, Airith? That is your name, is it not?"

Tyran's body racked with silent sobs, and he could only shake his head.

"My name will not last long after I am gone, and neither will yours. What will become of you when you are gone? Can you promise me something … Airith? My son … can you … watch out for him?"

"Yes, I will." A torrent of tears burned drops of hot guilt against his skin. Tyran gripped Rand and wildly whispered, "I am sorry, I am so sorry. Please just hate me! Say you hate me, and I will be satisfied!"

Rand closed his eyes, struggling to speak. With his last breath, he rasped, "I have already forgiven you." He went limp.

"But I cannot forgive myself!" Tyran cried. He put his head against Rand's and wept, "I am beyond forgiveness."

***

Sometime later, Tyran found himself standing in an unlit room at the foot of Randurren's cradle. He did not know how long he had been there. One hour or three? Time was either passing slowly or had stopped altogether. This tiny, sleeping creature had a hold on Tyran he could not explain—so calm and captivating, so small and fragile, yet he held so much promise and intelligence.

Tyran envied his ignorance. This child did not yet know about the pain and struggle in this world or of the evil that had befallen his parents this night. The event had changed the course of his life, and he did not even know it. Randurren had his father's hair, his mother's eyes, and his grandfather's face. Tyran knew Sisinta would either have him put away for the rest of his life or raise him to do her bidding.

"Randurren," he whispered to the baby sleeping in his cradle, "it might have been better if you had never been born." Tyran closed his eyes but could still see the image of the sleeping baby. "I am sorry," he whispered, "but sorry is not enough, is it?" Tyran bowed his head.

A door opened behind him, and the light silhouetted X-Sayda. "There you are, I have been looking for you." Her voice was like a slap of ice water to his face. She stood beside him, barely giving the baby a glance. "Such a pity, is it not? I think he would have been better off dead. Why Sisinta did not kill his mother while she was still with child, I do not know." X-Sayda sniffed.

If Tyran had hackles, they would have bristled. He felt an obligation to protect Durren. Maybe because he himself was unwanted when he was born. Durren had been wanted and would never know it. His parents were gone—there was no one left to love him. His grandfather, wrapped up in power and fear of usurpation, might even kill his own grandson.

"I would beg to differ." Tyran did his best to control his anger. "Go tell your opinions to someone who cares." He spun on his heel and left the room.

X-Sayda's footsteps retreated in the opposite direction.

Tyran didn't know where he was going—he allowed his feet to carry him where they willed. Therefore, he was not at all surprised when he found himself at the prison door. Tyrannus told him not to go in. The Shadow was confused by his feelings. He smiled for a moment when he realized he had won a very small victory over the demon. Tyran pushed the Shadow to the back of his mind and unlocked the door. Tyran strolled down the corridor until he reached the cell he was looking for.

Meredith looked up.

A shock of emotion ran through him when their eyes met. He couldn't name the emotion or even begin to guess what it meant.

Everyone else was asleep.

Tyran saw her initial look of astonishment harden to hate, and his heart sank. Of course she would hate him—he had just murdered her friend right before her eyes. He had no right to expect more from her. Still, there was part of him that didn't want to admit their friendship was dead.

She wasn't dark and shockingly gorgeous like X-Sayda, and she wasn't pale and cruelly beautiful like Sisinta. She was a calm and warm kind of pretty he'd forgotten existed in a world of back-stabbing noblewomen and blood-thirsty chieftain's daughters. She reminded him of autumn hunts, furtive smiles, and long winter days spent by the fire. He'd spoiled those memories for both of them. What was he doing here? In that moment, he knew he could never marry her as Sisinta had suggested. He'd ruin her empathetic heart. He'd steal the light from her smile. Seeing the hate in her eyes every day for the rest of his life would be torture.

Oh, but you'd deserve it, Tyrannus goaded.

Tyran gripped the vertical bars of the cell door. "Can ... can I talk to you for a moment?"

"There is no one preventing you," Meredith replied, her green eyes alight with anger.

Tyran took a steadying breath. "Yes, there is."

She frowned. "Who?"

"Tyrannus."

"You *are* Tyrannus."

"I know." Tyran ran his fingers through his hair. "But I think of myself as Tyran and Tyrannus as the demon who controls me."

"And who is Airith?" Meredith demanded.

"Airith never existed."

She walked to the door.

Tyran stepped back as a nameless fear sprang to life.

Afraid of a little girl, are you? Tyrannus snickered.

"Then, who was the boy I knew?" Meredith challenged.

"He was Tyran in a mask," Tyran said.

"I hate Tyran," Meredith whispered.

She should, the Shadow said. *She doesn't know the half of what you've done.*

"We used to be friends, didn't we?"

"I was friends with Airith, not Tyran. And even Airith never spoke much to me—he was friends with my brother." She assessed him, from his black armor to the silver scars marring his hands and face. Tyran refused to flinch. She wasn't the young girl smiling shyly at him anymore. She was a woman evaluating a man by his actions. He could read in her eyes—he was found wanting.

"I never ignored you!" Tyran cried. "I just didn't know how to talk to ... girls."

You didn't deserve her interest. Tyrannus pulled up a memory—Tyran's acute sense of inadequacy in the face of her admiration.

"You said 'I.'" Meredith's glare was cold.

"I say 'I' because I *was* Airith, but he no longer exists!"

"Do you really believe that?" She crossed her arms.

"Yes."

"What about Sisinta? Do you really believe every drop of poison she feeds you?"

"She is much wiser than you or I."

"And Elyon? He is much wiser than any of us!"

At the mention of the High King's name, Tyrannus roared in his head.

"Stop!" Tyran shouted.

Meredith jumped.

"That name is never to be mentioned here!" He felt more frightened than angry.

The others in the cell raised their heads.

He added weakly, "He does not even exist."

"Then why am I not allowed to talk about him?" Meredith asked. "What is wrong with talking about someone who does not exist?"

"He did exist, a very long time ago, but he is dead now," Tyran growled.

"So, what is the matter with talking about him?" she repeated. "If he is dead, like you say, he cannot do anything to you."

"You deceive yourself by talking about him as if he were alive," Tyran insisted.

"How do you know he is dead? Many people have seen him. *I* have seen him."

"Sisinta killed him!"

"How do you know? Even if she did, could Elyon not come alive again? After all, Sisinta is immortal, why would he not be?"

"Stop this nonsense! You are just a child who believes in fairytales!" Tyran stalked down the hall and slammed the door behind him.

***

In a flash of memory, Meredith recalled a younger Airith using those very same words years ago in Boldwind. Perhaps Tyran had been there all along.

CHAPTER FORTY-FOUR

REACTING DANGEROUSLY

"A useless screecher, she says. Well, I'll have her know, I have earned a living from my profession!" Zray mumbled to himself as he stumbled through the woods at spear-point. His thoughts were beginning to make sense again as the shock of Rand's death ebbed.

The early-morning light filtered through the treetops. Zray tripped over a root and mumbled again, "I happen to have sung for the Duke of Gasbal, and he complimented my pluckiness."

"Would you just be quiet!" the bald guard snapped.

"Let's hurry up and get this done," the other guard spoke fearfully. "I do not like the look of this place. Whole bands of soldiers have disappeared in these woods."

"You don't suppose it was because of dragons, do you? Because that would just be ridiculous ..." Zray's voice trailed off when he saw a huge scaly claw a few feet away. His eyes lifted very slowly, scanning the entire gigantic creature before him. Zray yelped and stepped back. He tripped over his own feet and found himself on his back, staring up at the largest meat-eating animal he had ever seen.

The dragon was brown with a gold sheen to his scales and had enormous, black, cat-like eyes. He brought his head very close to Zray's and studied the minstrel with one of his penetrating, onyx eyes.

Zray threw his arms over his face to protect himself and yelled, "I'll give you anything you want! Please don't eat me! I promise I taste terrible!"

"I can see that for myself." The dragon sniffed and pushed Zray with his snout.

Zray's eyes widened as he registered six colored dragons standing behind the first. The minstrel got to his feet and brushed off his coat. He laughed rudely at Sisinta's guards backing away fearfully.

As the two soldiers scattered in opposite directions, the brown dragon roared and spoke with a thunderous voice. "Catch them! We cannot let them give away our presence!"

Two dragons streaked forward and pinned the soldiers.

Zray put his hands on his hips and yelled after them, "So *now* you run! Cowards! Why are you afraid of a few little dragons? I bet you wish you had *them* on your side, eh?" Zray yelped when he found himself hanging in the air in the brown dragon's claws. Zray started yelling and kicking wildly. Then, he screamed when he was thrown through the air and caught by the dragon's tail. "This is *not* proper behavior for a dragon!" Zray shouted while beating the dragon's tail with his fists.

The brown scales were thick, and the dragon just chuckled at the minstrel's futile attempts. The dragon spread his majestic wings and leapt into the sky followed by the other dragons, including the two carrying the screeching soldiers in their massive claws.

In a short time, they landed in a clearing at the edge of the mountains. The dragon put a dizzy Zray on his feet.

The minstrel clutched a tree to keep from falling over and put a hand on his stomach as he moaned, "I hate heights." He glanced at the woods and started to move toward them when a dragon growled in warning. Zray winced and hid behind the tree.

"What are we going to do with them?" the brown dragon asked the other dragons.

"Just kill them," a red dragon suggested eagerly.

"We cannot kill them without permission from Dragonose," a larger red dragon stated firmly. He appeared to be the leader.

"Then I will call for him, Stavon," the green dragon replied, agitated. "Act now, inquire later."

"Ahem!" Zray cleared his throat, and all the massive, scaly heads turned their attention to him. Struggling to find his voice, he asked the red dragon, "Are you Stavon?"

"What is it to you?" the red dragon asked.

"Well, I was just wondering if you are the same Stavon whom my two friends were looking for, though I thought you would be ... a little more human."

"Friends?" Stavon squinted at the boy.

"Yes." Zray nodded with a smug smile. "The twins, Kaydin and Meredith, claimed you knew their father."

Cries erupted among the dragons, and the brown dragon seized Zray in one of his gigantic claws and brought him close to his huge eyes as he examined the terrified minstrel. "What do you know about them?"

"Nothing, nothing!" Zray wailed fearfully. The brown dragon shook him hard, and Zray screeched. "All right! All right! I traveled with them from Dolsulbane with Rand and then Falcon, but we were captured by Sisinta." Zray was shaking uncontrollably. He added with a whine, "She was

353

about to have me killed, but thanks to you chaps, she did not get the chance!"

"How do I know you are not just making this up to get out of dying?" the dragon growled.

"Because, because ... I have no idea."

"What is this?" a human voice broke in.

The brown dragon dropped Zray, who fell with a bump. The dragons cleared the way for a man dressed in battle armor, carrying his helmet. As he walked toward Zray, the minstrel observed the man. He was middle-aged with brown hair and bright green eyes. All the dragons lowered their gazes as he passed. The man looked familiar. Zray watched in fear.

"Who are you?" the man asked calmly. The tone reminded him of someone.

"Zray, son of Urran."

"Urran the minstrel?"

Zray was pleasantly surprised that someone had heard of his father. "Yes, you know of him?"

"I met him last month in Danelaw."

Zray's smile faded. "You met him last month?"

"Yes."

"Oh," was all Zray could find to say. Had his father escaped from prison or been released? The latter was unlikely, but either way, if his father were free, then he would be looking for him, and Zray was no longer sure if he wanted to see him again.

"What are you doing here, Zray son of Urran?" the man asked.

"Sisinta said I was useless and a screecher, so she told those two guards," Zray pointed to the dragons' prisoners, "to feed me to the wasals." He glared at the frightened men.

"Do you know if my children are all right?"

"Your children? Wait, do you mean ..."

"The twins, Kaydin and Meredith Stellmear," the man finished for him.

"Stellmear? They said their names were Kaydin and Meredith Amara."

Surprise lit the man's eyes briefly, then a small smile crept across his face. "Then they are still alive." He sighed like a heavy weight had been lifted from his shoulders.

"Why would they not be? There is no reason for Sisinta to kill them, but she did kill Rand, and you will not believe it! Falcon is Tyran's brother!"

A confused looked passed over the man's face. He frowned and asked, "Who is Rand?"

"He is dead. He and Thia, gone." Zray was not even sure he believed his own words—realization of Rand's death had not yet set in.

"Who was he?"

"Randarin Tieren, the crown prince of Ironcall." Zray was in a haze, overloaded by emotion. "We never knew who he truly was. He called himself Rand and told us he was the son of a warlord from the Islands. He was looking for Elyon." A presence brushed against his thoughts, and he froze, his eyes wide.

"I see you have much to explain. Let us first get you something to eat. Come with me." The man pulled the still-dazed minstrel to his feet.

Zray followed the twins' father past the seven dragons who fell in line. Zray kept glancing behind to keep an eye on the meat-eaters, and in his case, potential minstrel murderers. They came to a rocky ridge with a tunnel large enough to accommodate the biggest dragon. Zray entered the tunnel apprehensively, sure it was going to be long, dank, and dark like the ones Falcon had led them through.

To his surprise, it was short. They rounded a corner and into a beam of blinding sunshine. The tunnel widened so the dragons were able to pass the stunned minstrel.

The trees were tall and ancient with few to no branches below their spreading canopy, so most of the sky was covered above, but the ground below was clear. There was enough space to shelter the several hundred Rackdarians, Sillians, and dragons who camped under them. The Rackdarians were dressed in furs and patched clothes, like the men Zray had seen in the small village where Basal and his family lived. The Sillians were dressed simply but elegantly in light tones. They seemed to flit like sunbeams with grace and silence while blending in with the forest. The dragons ranged from pitch-black to shining albino white. They all seemed to stay in groups of similar color while still associating with the other colored dragons around them. The light bounced off their scales in a rainbow of radiance.

No one noticed the young minstrel. However, everyone acknowledged the twins' father. Some would nod, and others bowed, but everyone seemed to know him. Zray watched, curious.

The man was talking in low tones with a Sillian. The Sillian was very tall and pale, but not in an unhealthy way—his hair was pitch black, long, and pulled back to reveal his almond-shaped eyes. Zray glanced back at Lord Stellmear. Now that Zray knew the man was the twins' father, he could see the resemblance, almost like an older Kaydin. Jade smiled at him.

"Who is he?" Zray asked Stavon, who had not moved farther into the camp with the others.

"My master." Stavon's deep voice was a growl of endearment. "Dragonose, Keeper of Dragons."

"Dragonose? I thought he was a legend! The twins never mentioned their father was the Keeper of Dragons."

"It was well they did not. We have all tried our best to keep his identity a secret since the very first Lord Stellmear became Dragonose. Unfortunately, Sisinta discovered his name when a spy betrayed them to her."

"You mean Sisinta knows that Meredith and Kaydin are his children?" Zray asked.

Stavon nodded gravely. "We received a ransom note two days ago from Sisinta, demanding Dragonose in exchange for the lives of the twins."

"What is he going to do?" Zray wondered. He could see maybe two hundred dragons and about three hundred men and Sillians, but they would not do much against Sisinta's horde of at least eight thousand men, five hundred vagwhar, and untold number of silver dragons!

Stavon said, "We do not plan to win against Sisinta with this army, and there isn't time to assemble a bigger one. We are planning a diversionary tactic. All but three dragons are going to launch a surprise attack on Sisinta's army camped outside the city while Dragonose and the three dragons free the twins and Falcon. Our best advantage is surprise."

"Who are all these people?" Zray asked.

"Rackdarians and Sillians who have dedicated their lives to protecting Higher Quith. Some have been sent by the kings of the five kingdoms to maintain the front lines, preventing Sisinta from passing the Dragon Mountains or from sailing around them on the Calldian Sea. They answer to the Sillian emperor. The capture of the twins is disastrous for Higher Quith, an emergency."

Zray nodded slowly. *This dragon is free with his information.*

Stavon answered Zray's thought, "That is because I already read your mind and know you've been telling the truth."

"I forgot dragons could do that," Zray muttered.

"You said you were a prisoner with the twins, correct?" Stavon inquired.

"Yes, I traveled with them and Rand for about ... three months now. Falcon joined us while we were in Dolsulbane." Had it really been only that long? How could one of the companions he had known so well, shared so many dangers and joys with, disappear forever?

"Perhaps you should come with us when we rescue them. You would know the basic layout of the castle and how to locate the dungeon."

"I suppose I would." Zray nodded thoughtfully.

"I will speak to Dragonose about it," Stavon told him.

"Are you Zray the minstrel?" a small feminine voice asked. A young mountain girl held out a bowl of roasted grouse and a tankard of ale to Zray. "This is for you."

He took the food and thanked her. He sat on a log around one of the many campfires. As Zray ate ravenously, he wondered what the others were doing and if they were still alive. Guilt washed over him, and he slowed his bites. Here he was eating the best meal he had had in months, while the twins and Falcon subsisted on dry bread and water. He wished Elyon were real, that everything he had ever heard and been told about the High King was true. Then maybe they would have a chance against Sisinta. The likelihood of rescuing his friends safely was slim.

He looked up from his bowl of stew and spotted the two guards who had been ordered to kill him. They were now bound hand and foot to a tree across the fire from him. The bald one glared. Zray shivered and returned to his food, being careful not to meet the guard's gaze again.

CHAPTER FORTY-FIVE

THE BATTLE OF DRAGONS

Zray squeezed his eyes shut, but it didn't abate his nausea. The wind whipping against his face helped a little, but he still dared not open his eyes. He could feel the movement of Stavon's muscles rippling under red, rough scales. The dragon's strong wings beat the air without faltering. The minstrel clung to a spike protruding from Stavon's neck. Despite the firm hold of the Dragonose behind him, Zray was sure he would plunge to his death at any moment. He stifled a whimper and concentrated on convincing himself that such an end would not be so bad when compared to an even more gruesome death at the hands of Sisinta.

I should be used to this by now, he reasoned with himself, *knowing I'm going to die ... but I can't seem to get over it.* His heart still skipped a beat every time he thought about it. He was actually going into danger without kicking and screaming. What on earth had happened to him? Was he gaining some semblance of bravery?

"There it is," Dragonose yelled to be heard over the sound of the rushing wind.

Zray reluctantly opened his eyes and carefully looked down. The unsuspecting city of Malefic spread out beneath them—and beyond the walls lay the encampment.

Zray glanced back at two hundred dragons and their riders in formation. The light reflected off their colorful scales in thousands of tiny points that momentarily blinded Zray. They'd timed the attack with sunset, coming from the west when the sun's glare would hide their approach.

Like Stavon, some dragons carried more than one man. The fire dragon flew in circles high above the keep until Scara and Bronze, who were assigned to the rescue mission, joined them. The other council dragons led the remaining dragons toward the encampment beyond the city.

Dragonose held up his gloved hand, clutching his large sword, then sliced the air. On cue, the other dragons shot down out of the sky. They reminded Zray of the birds he had once watched on the cliffs of Tayose overlooking the sea. The birds had gracefully sliced through the air and into the water in one fluid motion, emerging with their unsuspecting prey in their mouths. It was both beautiful and deadly.

The fire dragons attacked first, shooting streams of fire as they descended on the unsuspecting army camped around the city. Flames spread in waves across the dry fields, consuming everything in their paths.

Then, the sound dragons roared. Zray had to cover his ears to keep his eardrums from rupturing. Luckily for the dragon riders, the dragons had aimed at the ground and the sound did more damage to the ears of the enemy soldiers.

From high in the sky, Zray watched Sisinta's soldiers scramble in every direction, the majority toward the city and the open gates. The water dragons followed soon after, dousing the flames so they could land briefly to allow their riders to dismount. Screeches filled the air, and Zray saw silver dragons on the horizon, flying toward the battlefield. The colored dragons met the Cala Drani with a crash in midair. Claws, teeth, fire, bursts of light, waves of water, and sharp icicles exploded around them. Never before had Zray seen anything like it. The colored dragons clearly had the advantage in size, but the silver dragons had far greater numbers.

"My lord! My lord!" A guard burst into the great hall and stopped, doubled over, and panted to catch his breath.

Tyran sat in his seat next to Sisinta's empty throne, his head in his hands.

"My lord!" the guard said again, he lowered to one knee before Tyran and bowed his head.

Tyran sighed and asked wearily, "What is it?" He had not slept all night in fear of reliving Rand's death in his dreams.

Tyran jumped to his feet. "Where? Who? When?"

"Five minutes ago, sir. Colored dragons attacked the army camped outside the city."

"Tasa!" Tyran cried and paced in agitation "Have we lost many men?"

"Yes, sir, I am afraid we have, but the casualties would be worse if the silver dragons had not retaliated. They are only just keeping them at bay right now."

"How many dragons? Men? How many are there?"

"Two hundred dragons and about three hundred men, sir."

"Two hundred dragons! We have six hundred! If the rest of Quith hears of this, we will be the laughingstock of the entire world!"

"They are much bigger than the silver dragons, sir."

Tyran waved his hand dismissively. "We have superior numbers by far! Three silver dragons could best one colored dragon any day!" He stopped long enough to take a deep breath and added in a calmer voice, "You say they are only just keeping them at bay?"

"Yes, my lord," the guard replied.

"Where are the reinforcements?" Tyran asked.

"Most of them are still at Baleful, four hundred, sir, but there are about three hundred dwelling in the Black Mountains and in the cliffs overlooking the Calldian Sea."

"Have them summoned immediately, but make sure to leave two hundred to guard Baleful. It might be a trap."

"Sir?"

"I am sure there will be more dragons coming."

"Respectfully, sir, I have heard most of the colored dragons had died off long ago."

"No." Tyran shook his head. "They've been keeping to themselves, which has made their numbers difficult to ascertain, but there are definitely more than two hundred." Tyran strode out of the hall with the guard following.

Uproar engulfed the castle and surrounding city. Soldiers dashed to and from their posts, while people panicked in the streets. Many citizens carried armfuls of belongings to the keep and banged on the doors, begging to be let inside. They were met with guards and closed doors.

"Where is Captain Vobad?" Tyran roared.

"Last I heard, he had gone to the encampment, sir," answered a guard at the main doors.

"Before or after the attack?"

"Before, sir."

Tyran frowned. "Has anyone heard from him?"

"No, sir."

"If anyone does, tell him to report to me immediately." Tyran called for his armorer. It took some time to don his armor amid receiving frequent updates on the battle and delivering orders.

"Should I call the generals for a war meeting in Sisinta's throne room?" one captain asked.

"No." Tyran tightened his gauntlets. "There is no time for that. Send out servants to find them and report back on their whereabouts."

The captain nodded and departed.

"Where is Sisinta?" Tyran demanded of a passing servant carrying buckets of water.

"Out on the west battlements, sir."

"Where are you going?"

"To the back courtyard, sir. A building is on fire."

"Carry on." Tyran placed his black helmet on his head.

A soldier arrived and told Tyran Sisinta wanted to see him on the west battlements.

Tyran hurried to the stone tower. He did not stop when he reached the top of the wall surrounding the castle but continued along the crest until he met Sisinta, her guards, and Lord Sazecall—her current favored lord. Tyran took his place at her side and followed her gaze to the horizon. Colored and silver dragons battled in the sky beyond the city walls and soldiers below fled into the city from the encampment.

The Witch-Queen sighed and shook her head sadly. "Such a waste of good fighting dragons. Did you send for more from Baleful?"

"Yes, my lady."

"Good." Sisinta continued to gaze upon the battle.

"My lady?" Tyran dared to prompt.

"Colored dragons have the advantage of size, but surely they realized that our sheer numbers will outweigh their superior strength. I knew they would attack, but I assumed far greater numbers."

"You knew they would attack?"

"Of course. Did you really think they would give up their precious Dragonose or his children so easily?"

Tyran shifted uncomfortably. "Of course not, my lady."

"They are planning to rescue them. That is why you," Sisinta turned to Lord Sazecall, "will stay here with fifty of my Black Knights and their silver dragons. Kill everyone but Dragonose and his two children—I want them alive." She didn't look as she addressed Tyran. "You, Tyrannus, will gather the soldiers who have entered the city and post them in the castle and on the towers. Set up archers along the walls and tell them to aim for the dragons' eyes and throats. Then, take the remaining Knights to the field."

"But my lady, only I command the Black Knights!" Tyran protested.

Sisinta threw him a cold glare. "I decide who leads them. Your actions lately have led me to doubt you."

Sazecall snickered, and Tyran slammed his armored fist into the lord's pretty face. Lord Sazecall staggered backward clutching his bleeding nose. "You will regret that one day, Tyrannus!" Sazecall hissed.

"That is enough." Sisinta's voice was hard. "I ordered you to go."

Both young men held each other's enraged gazes for a long moment until Tyran stalked off.

Because you did not listen to me, Sisinta now mistrusts you, Tyrannus growled in his head. *You are initiating your own downfall. If you want to stay in Sisinta's favor and in command, I suggest you start listening to me.*

I hesitated to kill the prince because I did not want the nightmares. Like that boy.

You are becoming weak, Tyrannus snarled in disgust. *If you listen to me, I promise to prevent your nightmares.*

You cannot do that, Tyran accused.

You continually underestimate what you and I can be together.

I've seen what we can be, and I am starting to detest it.

And what is wrong with that?

"My lord!" Vobad called.

"Where have you been?" Tyran growled.

Vobad's armor was battered and dented, his face streaked with dirt and sweat. He limped and held his right arm protectively against himself. "I am sorry, Tyran, I was visiting the encampment when the attack started. I have only just arrived. We need reinforcements."

"You are in no shape to go back there."

Vobad opened his mouth to object.

"Gather the army inside the city and send them to defend the wall with archers, then see to your wounds. That is an order."

Vobad nodded and limped away.

Tyran determined to fight his hardest, and Sisinta would have no reason to doubt his loyalty. That insufferable Lord Sazecall! Just thinking about the man put a bitter taste in his mouth. What experience did he have? None. The Black Knights were under *his* command. This must be another one of Sisinta's tests. Tyran drew Cala Man and growled to the Shadow in his head, *All right, Tyrannus. I am with you on this one.*

365

CHAPTER FORTY-SIX

ZRAY'S LUCK

Stavon, Scara, and Bronze still circled high above the castle in Malefic, and Zray was becoming impatient. "Why do we not rescue them now?"

"We have to wait for most of the soldiers to join the battle, and Sisinta is still in the castle," Dragonose told him.

"Why not kill Sisinta?" Zray demanded.

"Sisinta will not die."

"Well, we don't have to ask for her permission."

"No, she *cannot* die," Dragonose repeated. "She is immortal, like Elyon."

"How are we going to defeat her then?" Zray complained.

"*We* cannot, but Elyon can."

"I wish he would hurry up about it," Zray grumbled.

"There! Is that not Sisinta's entourage?" Bronze indicated a group of soldiers surrounding someone on horseback. They had left the castle and were traversing the streets toward the city gates.

The dragons slowly descended and landed in the back courtyard. No one stopped them. The sounds of battle raged faintly.

"This is odd," Bronze growled as he looked around suspiciously.

"Perhaps it is just luck," Zray said lightly as he jumped down from Stavon's back.

Dragonose followed.

"There is no such thing as luck," Scara admonished.

Zray shrugged and crossed the deserted courtyard to the door. It opened with ease. "Are any of you coming?" Zray asked innocently. "No? Okay." The young minstrel disappeared through the door.

"That rascal is too cocky for his own good," Bronze snarled. "I would like to drop a mountain of earth on him."

"Peace, friend. He is young and still has much to learn." Dragonose patted the earth dragon's neck and started after Zray.

★★★

Kappin, where are you? Tyran demanded as he led fifty Black Knights on horseback through the streets toward the city gate. He tried not to linger on the fact that there ought to be a hundred Knights and that Lord Stuck-up had stolen half of them.

I am a little busy, Kappin replied, irritated.

Tyran spotted Kappin in the sky, battling a golden dragon twice his size. He was attempting to sink his teeth into the dragon's neck but was foiled by the colored dragon's scales. Tyran reached the gate where streams of soldiers were scrambling to safety. Tyran kicked his horse into a run, and the Black Knights did the same. The men parted quickly before him.

As he passed, Tyran called to the fleeing soldiers, "Follow me, you cowards!"

Most of them fell in behind the Black Knights with battle cries, and those who did not were pushed roughly aside with contempt.

Tyran broke through the gates with the stream of soldiers and Knights behind him. Apparently, the attackers weren't all Rackdarians and men—there were Sillians among the attackers. Their forms shimmered with a magic he had not seen before. They appeared to blink in and out of existence across the battlefield, attacking soldiers unexpectantly with spells formed in their hands.

"Kill them all!" Tyran yelled. The soldiers cheered their agreement and barreled past him. He watched the enemy try to regroup before the soldiers reached them.

Kappin succeeded in bringing the golden dragon smashing to the ground where a flood of soldiers ended him like a caterpillar overrun by ants. Tyran galloped to Kappin's side and jumped from the back of the horse onto his silver dragon.

The clashing of swords, roaring of dragons, shouting and yelling of warriors, seemed to Tyran only a whisper compared to the roaring in his ears. Tyran's Silver Blood raced in excitement through his veins. He did not even bother fighting Tyrannus—the Shadow seemed to consume him as one after another, he and Kappin cut colored dragons down from the sky. They fell to the ground where they were ended by the soldiers below.

★★★

"I could swear the dungeon was at the end of this hall," Zray murmured. He and Dragonose stood in a corridor with doors on both sides.

Dragonose glanced at the minstrel and asked, "Are you sure you remember the way?"

369

"Of course!" Zray scoffed, but then added uncertainly, "I think."

"Start at the beginning." Dragonose looked around. "We came from there." He pointed back down the hall. "Maybe if we backtrack, you might recognize something."

"Good idea." Zray let Dragonose lead the way.

They returned out the door they had come through and ended up in the large hall. Zray scratched his head. This looked familiar, but he couldn't put his finger on it.

"Do you remember where the throne room was?" Dragonose asked.

"I cannot really say. When a fellow is scared half to death and sure he is going to die, he usually doesn't remember to take notes on the route being taken to said death."

"Zray, you do realize we have a very short time before we are discovered here?" Dragonose reminded him.

Footsteps sounded in the corridor.

"We have to hide," Dragonose urged. "Do you recognize any of this?"

"Wait, those doors! I remember going through them!" Zray pointed to the two large doors across the hall.

Dragonose pushed open one of the doors and they slipped through. The Keeper of Dragons kept his ear to the door, listening intently in case they had been followed. Zray leaned against the door beside him, breathing heavily. He stopped breathing for a moment when he took in their surroundings. The minstrel carefully tapped Dragonose on the shoulder.

"What is it?" Jade whispered without turning.

Zray could not find his voice, so he tapped Jade's shoulder again.

"What?" Dragonose turned, and any further words died on his lips.

Sisinta's throne room.

"I remember why the doors looked familiar. I thought I was on my way to die last time I saw them," Zray murmured in an aside.

Sisinta calmly watched them from her seat, a small, dangerous smile on her lips.

"So nice of you to join me, Lord Stellmear. I was expecting you." She laughed. "Black Knights surround this castle, and your three dragon friends have been captured. You did not really think I would let you waltz in and out again with my prisoners, did you?"

"No, I did not," Jade replied calmly. He opened the door just wide enough for the skinny minstrel to pass through. "Go, Zray," he whispered. "Find Falcon and the twins."

Zray had no chance to respond as Jade pushed him through the door and slammed it in the minstrel's face. After a long moment, Zray registered what Dragonose had told him and looked around the hall. There it was—the door to the dungeon!

Across the hall, an old servant calmly scrubbed the floor on his hands and knees, going about his business as if he had no idea a battle raged outside. Zray strode past, and the man did not even look up.

The door was unlocked, and the minstrel made his way slowly down a staircase lit with torches. At the bottom was a narrow hallway with more torches, more doors, and more steps. Finally! The door of the dungeon. He yanked on the handle, grunting with effort. Of course, it was locked. Desperate times called for desperate measures. Despite his "broomstick" frame—as his mother had once described him having—Zray walked to the opposite wall and rushed the door, shoulder first. Before the minstrel could slam into it, the door opened from the other side. He sailed through the opening and landed hard on the floor with a grunt. He looked up at the large figure of the jailer bending over him. It wasn't the jailer he remembered.

"Are ya all right?" he poked Zray in the side. "If ya wanted ta come in, all ya had ta do was knock, ya know. What's da message?"

Zray needed a moment to clear his daze. He stood and swayed precariously. The jailer watched him anxiously.

"A message? You want a message?"

"From da front, do ya have news?" the man asked nervously.

"Ah ... why yes I do!" Zray cried abruptly, and the jailer jerked. "We are losing. The colored dragons have defeated the silver dragons, and the men and Sillians are overrunning the city as we speak! Sisinta has given orders for everyone to flee!"

The man's eyes had grown twice their size while the minstrel was speaking.

"What are you still doing here, man? Run! Flee! Save yourself!" Zray encouraged.

"Oh ... oh!" He turned and ran.

"Oh wait, man! I need your keys! Sisinta told me to let out the important prisoners so the enemy can't get their hands on them."

The jailer did not even pause—he tossed the keyring to Zray before leaving the dungeon as fast as he could.

Zray grinned. What an unexpected turn of luck! He whistled as he walked down the line of cells, looking through the keys as he went. They all had numbers on them, and by the time he had reached the cell where the twins and Falcon were, he had found the key he needed.

"Zray!" Meredith jumped to her feet and the two men followed. "What are you doing here? I thought Sisinta had ordered those guards to kill you!"

"So she did, so she did." Zray chuckled to himself as he put the key into the lock and opened the door. "I think I must be a very lucky man indeed. I will tell you about it later, I think we had better get going before the jailer decides to come back when he realizes I lied to him."

"Is it only you here?" Kaydin asked as he left the cell with Falcon and Meredith. "I heard some colored dragons were attacking the city."

"I am here with Dragonose. He is with Sisinta at the moment, but do not worry a fish's fin about him, he can take care of himself."

"Dragonose?" Meredith squeaked.

"Come on! We have to go." Kaydin grabbed his sister's arm and they ran for the door.

"We have to hurry," Zray pressed.

"Follow me," Falcon ordered.

On their way out, Zray threw away the keys. They landed in a prisoner's cell, and with a cry, the man leapt forward to snatch them.

★★★

Now on the ground, Tyran brought his sword down on a man's head. The helmet did not break, but he did stun the Mountain Man long enough to drive his sword into him. Tyran proceeded to the next man.

Kappin fought at his side, bringing down five men with one swing of his massive claw. A Sillian let loose an arrow, its trajectory aimed at the slit in Tyran's helmet. Kappin threw himself in front—the shaft bounced harmlessly off his scales. Tyran bounded forward and cut down the Sillian, mentally thanking Kappin as he went.

A man walked toward Tyran from the very midst of the battle. He wore a white hooded robe edged in gold, and a mask covered the lower half of his face. He carried a sword that reflected the sun in sparkling stabs of light. Chaos abounded around the man—men shouting, screaming, falling in the bloody mud. Bodies pressed together and heaving their weight against each other as brute strength and swordplay sparred. This particular man fought no one, and no one challenged him. His posture exuded composure and calm amid the raging storm. The man stopped and regarded him with unseen eyes.

Tyran challenged above the sound of battle, "Fight me!"

The man calmly raised his head and met Tyran's gaze from the shadows of his hood.

A chill snaked down his spine. He knew those eyes—the gaze that penetrated the center of himself. A memory—a dream—tugged at the corners of his mind. The man, warrior ... king? Whoever he was, he exuded authority, and it unnerved him.

The man was reading his thoughts, one by one and all at once, shuffling through them like a deck of cards.

Where were the defenses Kappin had taught him to build? The walls he'd spent years constructing around his mind?

"Fight me!" Tyran shouted again, infuriated.

The warrior didn't react.

Tyran attacked.

The warrior parried with his double-edged sword, clashing it loudly against Cala Man and easily pushing Tyran away.

Tyran persisted, but the man's sword stopped him, again and again. No matter how hard he fought, Tyran couldn't wear him down. The battle raged around them, but all Tyran could see was this maddening man before him. Time flew until it seemed he couldn't remember a time when he had not been fighting this man. Nothing else mattered but this fight. How could Tyran bring down a man he couldn't even touch?

He could feel numerous cuts at all the weak points in his armor—between his shoulder plates, his neck piece, and every one of his joints. They weren't healing. He wanted to call Kappin but could not find his mental voice or allow himself any lapse in attention.

For the first time in a long time, Tyran was afraid of death. This warrior could kill him, this man could break him down, this man could end him. He knew his thoughts were irrational, but they rang true anyway. Why wasn't his body healing as it should?

If the warrior could kill him, why hadn't he already done so?

The man in white hooked his sword under Tyran's helmet and threw it off.

Tyran blinked, stunned.

The warrior's double-edged sword was at his throat, its cold, metal point against the exposed, vulnerable skin.

For the first time in his life, Tyran knew he was beaten. As the realization slowly crept over him, he lowered his sword and dropped to his knees. Was this the point of his existence? All his railing against life and death, and here he was, about to die on a battlefield broken down to nothing. Tyran closed his eyes and bowed his head. He'd believed that when the time came, he'd be ready for it, he would be at peace, but in that moment, he knew he'd lied to himself.

CHAPTER FORTY-SEVEN

THE REDEEMED

Tyran gritted his teeth, and his fingers closed around the hilt of a dagger strapped to his boot. He would not go down without a fight. In one fluid motion, he drew and swiped the blade at the man's unarmored legs.

His attack never found its mark. Instead, he stared at his empty hand and then at the warrior who now possessed his last line of defense.

The man took a moment to sheath his sword before studying the simple, unadorned knife, turning it this way and that, as if weighing its metal. He moved with deliberate purpose, closed his hand around the naked blade and drew it downward, slicing his palm open. Blood dripped in rivulets from between the man's clenched fingers. The droplets splattered on Tyran's upturned face. The warrior tossed the now-bloody dagger aside, the thump of it hitting the grass was drowned out in the cacophony of battle. He opened his hand, revealing a gory slash, blood pouring from the wound.

With a mixture of horror and fascination, Tyran watched the rivulets coagulate into a long, thin, wickedly sharp dagger. A dagger of the man's blood. Its blade was red glass and its hilt glinted with rubies. It was semi-transparent, and when the warrior closed his hand around its hilt, the man's mangled palm remained visible through it.

Tyrannus exploded through Tyran's consciousness. The Shadow threw him to his hands and knees. Not in supplication or humility, but in an act of pure rage. "This one is mine! He sold his soul to me!" Tyrannus's voice roared from his throat.

"Be still." The man's voice was quiet but somehow filled his head and rang in his ears, drowning out all the screams and shouts of battle.

Tyrannus immediately froze.

The warrior pulled Tyran's head back by his raven-black hair. The man's all-knowing eyes met the sickly, yellow light of Tyran's. "You have already lost this fight."

"Why do you torment me? Don't send me into the abyss! You promised I wouldn't have to go until the end of time!" Tyrannus begged.

The cold creeping up Tyran's spine was terror, but not his own. What could possibly terrify an immortal, incorporeal spirit? Tyran screamed in his own head, a torrent of frustration building up within. He was desperate to yank free of the grip on his hair, but he couldn't lift a finger. He was paralyzed—both he and Tyrannus caged inside his body.

"My Word is my Word. Banishment, but not darkness, is yours." The man drew back his arm, and Tyran had barely a second to process before the man drove the blood blade up under his jaw and into his brain.

With the passage of the blade, Tyran felt Tyrannus's presence severed and separated from his mind. Sooty, black smoke poured out of his eyes and mouth. It tasted of dry ash and coal. Tyran gagged. He was losing himself—ripped in two—drowning and suffocating! *Make it stop!* he wanted to scream, but he had no voice.

After a long, agonizing moment, the last of the Shadow slithered out of him and coalesced into a perfect replica of himself. The creature had his face, hair, and height, but its eyes were dominated by an eerie yellow glow. Tyrannus vanished in a split second, fading into nothingness.

The man withdrew the dagger and Airith convulsed and vomited on the trampled earth. He'd regained the use of his limbs. He pushed himself to his knees, shuddering and gasping.

"By death you were bound, by my blood you are freed." The man grasped Airith's shoulder with one hand and drew back the dagger with the other.

"N-No!" Airith feebly raised a hand to ward off the attack.

The warrior ignored his plea and plunged the blood blade into Airith's chest.

Fire coursed through his veins, and he screamed. Of all the wounds he'd been inflicted with, this one eclipsed them all in sheer pain.

When Airith stopped to gasp for breath, the man leaned in and spoke softly into his ear, "Your soul was not yours to sell," and released the dagger's hilt.

As soon as the blood blade left his hand, it shattered. Airith screeched. A thousand tiny blade fragments exploded inside his chest cavity. The hilt shards tinkled against each other as they fell to the ground. Immediately, the silver in his blood closed the wound, leaving behind a small silver slice next to his heart.

"Gah!" Airith scraped at the newly formed scar, leaving scratch marks that healed as quickly as they were made.

He knew it was pointless—his body healed too quickly to allow the time he'd need to remove all the shrapnel inside his chest. He could feel the tiny stabs of pain with every breath—a cycle of slicing and healing. He wrapped his arms about himself and moaned, "What have you done to me?"

A hand rested on his head, like a father comforting his son. Or what he imagined it would be like. "I have given you back your name."

A sob too large to stay inside broke out, and he sagged against the man. Arms, strong, unyielding, encircled him.

"Airith, Airith, why do you fight me? Why do you make me strike you when I would rather embrace you? Every blow that falls on you strikes me harder."

Airith had no answer.

After a time, he took a trembling breath and attempted to support himself on his knees. He wiped at the tears that had streaked through the ash on his face. His hands were flecked with blood from the battle. He couldn't explain his sudden aversion at the sight of it. All he knew was the blood on his hands shouldn't be there, but it was. He was brought back to the moment his shaking hands had plunged into a cold creek, one drenched in Silver Blood which would never wash off. He clenched his fists.

"You should kill me," he stated plainly. "So many people would be better off if I were dead. I'm tired of life, tired of watching my hands carry out the evil in my heart and then regretting it every moment I live. Why haven't you killed me yet?" Airith looked up at the man, pleading. "It's either now or years from now after I've taken more people with me."

"Your soul was not yours to sell. It is mine. I formed you and named you. You are more my son than you are your father's. With my blood and blade, I have claimed your sins as my own."

"Why would you do that?" Airith asked in disbelief.

"You remember when you dreamed," the man stated.

In that moment, he did. How had Airith forgotten the many nights he'd been lost in his own dreams while Elyon stalked him? "Elyon," he gasped. "You're Elyon! The one the prince said he'd met."

"Yes. Remember the name I gave you."

And Airith did. "The redeemed," he sobbed. "But how can you redeem me? My conscience is stained with blood, and my heart is full of darkness and evil. Tyrannus didn't always have to make me do what I did. He liked to sit back and watch. He said we suited each other."

A patient smile played on the man's lips. "My blood is lodged in your chest. No Shadow can ever inhabit you again. You owe a debt of blood which I have paid."

"I can ... let go? I can forget their faces?"

"No, you will not forget, but I have forgiven." Elyon held out his hand.

Airith took it and once again found himself standing on the battlefield. The chaos seemed far away, as if he were watching it from a distance.

Elyon remained at his side. "A part of me is now in you. Go and do right."

Then he was gone, and the battle came back into focus.

Airith was in a daze. He blinked and stared at the shouting men on the ground and the roaring dragons in the sky. The battle swarmed around him, and he turned about in confusion. He caught sight of Kappin flying in circles, and slowly, Airith realized the dragon was calling frantically for him.

I'm here, Kappin, Airith told him calmly. He spotted Cala Man and picked it up.

Kappin landed in a crash next to him. *Where were you? I was searching and couldn't find you anywhere!*

I met Elyon.

Kappin narrowed his eyes and looked him up and down. *Has Tyrannus been feeding you hallucinations?*

No. Tyrannus is gone. My name is Airith. Tyran died today.

You must be hallucinating. Without Tyrannus, you and I are dead! You'd never get rid of him.

I didn't get rid of him, Elyon did.

Kappin took a step back and growled, *Do you know what he's done? If you no longer have the Shadow, you will die young! You have traded the past three years of our lives for nothing!*

I don't know what the point of my life has been, but I'd like to live what's left of it with a clean conscience. I was miserable, Kappin—you know that better than anyone.

Surely there was a better way to deal with that than throwing everything away for nothing!

It was not for nothing.

One of Sisinta's men stumbled into Airith, knocking him off his feet. The soldier spasmed and then lay still. Kappin watched with disgust as Airith pushed away the unfortunate man. An arrow protruded from the soldier's forehead.

Airith scrambled to his feet. *I'm leaving Sisinta, I'm leaving Aster, and I'm leaving Lower Quith! You can decide to come with me or stay.* Aloud, he yelled, "Retreat! Fall back to the city!" His voice barely carried over the roar of battle. *Kappin, mind-speak the order for me.*

You're dooming us! Sisinta will never forgive you! Kappin argued.

Are you with me or not, my friend? Airith stared into Kappin's large milk-white eyes.

"You give me no choice!" Kappin roared. "Without you, I have no master! And we made a vow. I curse you for putting this obligation on me!"

Airith grinned and quickly mounted Kappin. *Thank you. You're a loyal friend.*

Humph! Kappin allowed Airith to feel his annoyance and unhappiness.

Retreat! Lord Tyrannus has ordered a retreat! Kappin's mental voice echoed in all the minds he could reach.

The soldiers and silver dragons in the near vicinity paused their fighting, baffled. Victory seemed certain, why did they have to fall back? But Tyrannus was in command, so they retreated. The Sillians, men, Rackdarians and colored dragons did not pursue, but watched in astonishment.

Airith and Kappin joined the dragons taking to the skies and flew over the city walls into the back courtyard of the keep. The dragon and his newly-reborn master landed beside three colored dragons, chained and under the guard of Black Knights. Airith guessed why they were there—Dragonose's rescue mission. He jumped off Kappin's back and ran for the door. The Black Knights stared as he passed.

Airith paused at the door. "Come with me, the colored dragons don't need to be guarded."

"But my lord, Lord Sazecall—"

"Lord Sazecall is a traitor, follow me." Airith disappeared into the castle, and the Black Knights had no choice but to follow.

CHAPTER FORTY-EIGHT

DURREN

"Where's our father?" Kaydin demanded impatiently. The former prisoners crossed the main hall with Zray leading the way.

"Dragonose is in there." Zray pointed to the throne room doors. "Sisinta is in there with him."

Kaydin and Meredith stepped forward, but Falcon stopped them.

"What do we do?" Meredith asked.

"I think you three should wait with Scara and Bronze," Falcon said.

"Oh, I ... ah ... forgot to tell you something ..." Zray started.

"Oh no," Kaydin groaned.

"Sisinta knows I'm here, and she somehow knew we would be coming, so she surrounded the castle with Black Knights."

"How are we going to get out of here alive?" Meredith wondered.

"With my help." Across the hall, Airith emerged from the shadows with ten Black Knights at his back.

Meredith inhaled sharply. He watched an indecipherable war of emotions cross her face.

Zray remarked, "We're going to die!"

"Not if I can help it," Airith declared as he handed his helmet to a Black Knight. "Your dragons are waiting in the courtyard. Take them and leave quickly."

"We cannot let *him* tell us what to do!" Zray exclaimed.

Airith motioned for the Knights to stay in place. He dropped his tone so only the escaping prisoners could hear. "I'm sorry if it seems like I'm ordering you, but I'm only trying to help, and if you want Dragonose to live, I suggest you listen to me."

"How can we trust you?" Meredith demanded. "You killed Rand!"

Airith bowed his head. Guilt clawed at his insides, but a sharp pain in his chest reminded him the shards of the blood blade were there. Elyon had paid for his sins. He didn't understand how, but he had to accept what the High King had said or die in a world overcome with misery. "I guess you can't know for sure," he admitted.

Falcon put his hand on his brother's shoulder. They stared into each other's eyes for a long moment. "The yellow light is gone," Falcon murmured.

"Elyon took it," Airith whispered.

"We can trust him," Falcon declared to the others.

"Just like that. You're going to trust him because his eyes aren't changing colors?" Zray cried.

Falcon shushed him and said, "Yes." With tears in his eyes, he gripped Airith's arm and whispered, "Do you know how long I have waited for this? Do you know that no one but Elyon could separate you from the Shadow?"

"Yes," Airith answered quietly. "Thank you for not giving up on me."

A small smile played on Falcon's lips. "I had given you up for dead. Elyon was the one who refused to give up on you."

"You had better get going," Airith told him reluctantly.

Falcon nodded.

The puzzled Black Knights watched them file past. Airith waited until they were gone before taking a deep breath and pushing open the throne room doors. The Black Knights followed. Airith prayed their fear of him would keep them from questioning his actions.

Scorch marks on the floor and walls of the throne room testified to a battle, light against darkness. Sisinta looked up when the doors opened. Airith noted with satisfaction that his appearance had truly surprised her. Airith ignored Dragonose and approached Sisinta.

She stood at the base of the dais, one hand squeezing Dragonose's throat, the other gripping his wrist. In Dragonose's captured hand, a ball of fire blazed. Though her arms were deceptively thin, she easily held him in place.

In an even voice, he told her, "It was a terrible loss, my lady, but most of the army managed to flee into the city. We would have done better if all the Black Knights had been there with us." Airith glanced out of the corner of his eye at the captured man. He noted the similar features he shared with his children.

Airith admired him for his courage—he didn't seem at all anxious over his circumstances. He wanted to tell the man his children were safe but dared not acknowledge him.

"A failure? Impossible! We outnumbered them at least ten to one!" Sisinta released her grip on Dragonose's throat but still held his upturned hand of fire. Her face darkened in its cold beauty. "You will answer for this!" She glared at Airith. "Take this man away. He is Dragonose! He has the talent to manipulate fire. Put him in spelled chains and make sure there is no torch or light in his cell. Then return."

"Yes, my lady." Airith motioned to his men.

A Black Knight chained Dragonose's hands with blood iron. The metal contained drops of Sisinta's blood. He'd heard the chains worked on Paladalls, but wondered if they would truly constrict Dragonose's abilities. The ball of fire winked out with a wisp of smoke as soon as the metal cuffs locked in place. Sisinta released her hold, and the Knights rushed to remove Dragonose. Bowing to his once-queen, Airith took his leave.

Airith waited until they had descended a level toward the prison and there were torches burning brightly on the walls. He stopped the Black Knights and informed them that their services were no longer needed. The Knights glanced at each other uncertainly, and then pulled out their swords.

"I am afraid that you, General," one said, "are a traitor to your queen."

"I was afraid you would say that." Airith sighed.

The Knights watched apprehensively.

"I don't suppose any of you want to join me in my defiance?" he asked half-heartedly.

Their expressions were hard.

"No? Unfortunately for you, I have not put out any of the torches." Airith gestured to the walls. The torch flames shot up, roaring in intensity. The heat was almost unbearable, but Airith ignored it. Drawing his sword, he rushed his Knights.

They were in a bottleneck, crammed into the hallway with only one man at the front. The advantage was his. He cut down the first one easily. The remaining Knights burst into flames. Airith killed them quickly.

The flames extinguished as soon as he'd killed the last of them. The torch flames returned to their original sizes. Airith stood panting, looking down at the bodies crumpled before him. The sight brought sorrow. He was so used to feeling only guilt or hatred that simple sadness felt alien. Airith slowly turned around. Dragonose watched him with an unreadable expression.

"I don't believe we've met. My name is Airith, formerly known as Tyrannus, commander of Sisinta's army." He laughed at the self-mockery in his voice.

"Dragonose." The man nodded in greeting. "How did you—"

"I saw your chains were glowing while we walked." Airith shrugged. "I gambled on you breaking them." He frowned upon seeing Dragonose had not, in fact, broken the chains.

The man looked down at the shackles. The iron glowed bright red before melting from his wrists. "Blood metal has no effect on me," Dragonose explained. "I am not one of Sisinta's subjects, and her blood does not command me."

Airith nodded slowly in understanding. "She cannot command what is not hers." Airith filed away that information to process later. "Follow me." He retraced their steps, searching for minds to avoid any soldiers and knights. When they reached the corridor to the back courtyard, Airith halted. *Durren!* He couldn't let the baby fall into Sisinta's hands. He owed Rand, at least, that much.

"I know the way to the courtyard," Dragonose said.

Airith winced at his lack of control—he must have accidentally let Dragonose into his thoughts. "Do you think you can find your own way there? I have something to do first."

"Yes, I'm sure I can." Dragonose put his hand on Airith's shoulder. "Thank you."

Airith made his way through the halls until he reached the servants' living quarters. He cautiously opened the door of Durren's nursery.

With the windows covered and the fire low, the room was dim. He spotted the nurse sitting next to the fire, light snores emanating from her partly-open mouth. As silently as he could, Airith snuck to the foot of the cradle. The baby was asleep. Without waking him, Airith took a blanket and wrapped Durren. He'd almost reached the door when a loose floorboard creaked. He froze.

The nurse stirred, then opened her eyes. "What are you doing here?"

"I am taking him to Sisinta."

"Oh." The nurse's brow furrowed and her tone held a note of suspicion. "Why didn't you tell me to take him?"

"I didn't want to wake you."

"Well, I'm awake now." The nurse rose and reached for the baby.

"I already have him," Airith told her firmly, taking a step back.

"But I'm his nurse." The woman took another step forward.

"I am Sisinta's right-hand."

"You have no idea how to take care of a child, you might drop him."

"I will not," Airith denied hotly. "I think I can hold a baby." He glanced at the door. Sisinta was apt to hear the real news from the battlefield soon. "Sisinta called for him," Airith told the woman again in his most authoritative tone.

The nurse wavered and, at last, stepped back.

Airith strode out of the room confidently. As soon as he was around a bend, he broke into a run, trying his best not to jerk his precious burden.

The baby woke, and his piteous cries echoed down the hallways.

"Shh!" Airith tried to quiet the infant by talking to him in a low tone, but Durren cried all the louder. Thankfully, Airith had reached the back courtyard by then.

Kappin was waiting for him with Falcon on Scara.

"I thought you would have left by now," Airith said as he climbed onto Kappin's back with his free arm.

"I waited for you." Falcon eyed the crying child. "Rand's son?"

"Before he died, Rand asked me to make sure Durren did not fall into Sisinta's hands or his grandfather's."

Kappin pulled back his wings and launched himself into the air with Scara following.

Sisinta is not going to be happy, Kappin warned. *She will come after you.*

I know. In that moment, Airith was unconcerned. He pulled the baby to himself awkwardly with one arm, trying to protect him from the wind. Durren had quieted the moment they took flight and had settled back into sleep.

Airith watched the city disappear slowly into the distance. He hoped with all his being he would never set eyes on Malefic again.

CHAPTER FORTY-NINE

HOME

Airith and Falcon landed in the woods where Scara directed. From his seat atop Kappin, Airith spotted Dragonose and the twins standing next to Stavon a short distance away. He had so much he wanted to say to them but didn't know how he would say it. They would not forgive him, he knew, and he would not blame them. The one thing he did know was Elyon was the only firm unmoving point in his world.

He shifted the baby in his arms and sucked in a breath. The shards in his chest sliced him with tiny points of pain. A reminder. He had to ask for forgiveness but struggled to summon the courage to approach the twins. It was a curious feeling, fighting with himself rather than with Tyrannus. He felt a little odd when he did not hear the Shadow's voice in his head objecting, taunting, and patronizing. Airith kept automatically cringing, waiting for the mental punishment Tyrannus would inflict on him—usually calling up the nightmares he dreamed at night.

Airith realized Dragonose had the twins in his arms, and they were crying, whether in joy or grief he couldn't tell. He was embarrassed he had unintentionally intruded on the privacy of their emotional reunion. He looked away and found Falcon's eyes on him. Airith wondered what his brother was thinking and instinctively reached for his mind. When he read Falcon's thoughts, Airith dropped his gaze. Falcon was remembering their father before Rasfell's death. He used to greet Falcon, Cowin, Shar, and Rasfell as happily as Dragonose did his children.

I never witnessed our father that happy, Airith silently told his brother. *He was more apt to argue with Mother over me or ignore me altogether.*

He cares about you, Airith, whether either of you know it or not.

Airith wasn't going to argue with his brother. He dismounted and landed carefully beside Kappin with Durren still in his arms.

"Here, let me take him." Falcon reached out.

Airith hesitated before deciding to hand the bundle over to his brother. He watched in amazement as a big smile spread over Falcon's face when he fit his finger into Durren's tiny fist.

Airith's arms felt empty. He had fulfilled his promise to Rand—he had saved Durren, but he wished he could do more for the baby.

"Are you hungry?" Falcon asked Airith.

"I suppose I am." Airith was glad to focus on something else.

"We will have to leave this place soon. Sisinta will send men after us. But before Dragonose orders us to leave, we can eat something."

Airith nodded in agreement. Sisinta would send men after them, of that he was certain.

Falcon led him to a campfire where whiffs of pork, carrots, and potatoes came from a large pot. A young girl was laboring over it. Falcon tapped her shoulder. Her eyes widened when she saw Airith. Falcon asked her for food. She nodded, but eyed Airith suspiciously. As soon as she had served them, she disappeared into the crowd of soldiers. The brothers sat and ate by the fire.

"Maybe you should change into something else," Falcon suggested carefully.

Airith realized he still wore his Black Knight's armor—no wonder the girl had feared him.

"I can give you some of my clothes."

"Thanks," Airith murmured. After eating a few bites in silence, he asked, "What am I going to do now, Falcon?"

"I expect it might take you some time to get your footing. Maybe you should visit Mother." Airith started to object, but Falcon put up his hand. "I know you aren't on good terms with Father, and neither am I, but you must forgive him some day. If you don't, anger and hate will eat you up inside. Besides, I think you owe Mother an apology. She's been worried sick about you for years, and you left her without a word."

Airith sighed. He knew Falcon was right. But the problem was that he didn't *want* to forgive his father ... or the world. He had made the hate his reason for the way he was. If he admitted he was wrong to be angry, he would have to let go of it. He was ashamed to admit it, but he loved his anger. He nursed his hurt until he felt so sorry for himself, he was consoled. Maybe he could write his mother a letter and skip any emotional family reunions or rejection while mollifying his conscience.

I need you to help me forgive, Airith begged Elyon silently. *I cannot do it on my own, I have not the strength nor the will.* After a long moment, Airith asked Falcon, "Do you visit Mother often?"

"No," Falcon said sadly. "Father won't let me near Shaver Castle, but you might convince him to let you visit."

"Ha." Airith snorted. "You have more influence over him than I do. If you couldn't convince him to let you come, how can I?"

"You should at least try, Airith." Falcon shrugged.

"Maybe," Airith muttered. They ate the rest of their food in silence. When they had finished, Airith set his bowl aside and asked again, "What do I do with my life now, Falcon? I have a broken family, a tainted past, and I'm right back where I was three years ago—with a disease that's going to kill me." Privately, he wondered if the blood blade fragments would kill him first. What would happen if one migrated into his heart?

"You're not right back where you were, Airith. You have Elyon now and a chance to make a difference with the time you have left. You could join me in Athlon if you like," Falcon suggested. "The Sillians need help defending the borders and the Rackdarians have been plagued by raiders. Or you could marry and settle down with a family."

Airith glanced over his shoulder at a campfire where Meredith sat with Dragonose. Her arm was looped through her father's while he talked with Kaydin. She was watching Airith with an indecipherable expression, but all the same, he was sure he saw loathing there.

Airith turned back to Falcon. "I can never do that. I have only a few years left to live."

"You must ask yourself then, what does Elyon want you to do?" Falcon told him.

"I have to think about it," Airith murmured.

***

Meredith watched Falcon and Airith talk. They glanced in her direction. *Are they talking about me?* she wondered. Falcon was holding Durren, and she wanted to see Rand's son. She distracted herself by concentrating on her father's face. She loved the sound of his voice, smooth and deep, even more comforting than she had remembered. She clung to his arm, still having a hard time believing he was really there. She was so scared she'd wake up and find she was dreaming. He pulled her closer, pausing a moment in his conversation with Kaydin to smile at her. Meredith let Kaydin tell their father everything, she was just happy he was here.

"Meredith?" Falcon called. "I was wondering if you wanted to hold Durren."

Meredith couldn't speak. Somehow, without reading her mind, he just knew. She nodded. Falcon placed the baby in her arms. She could only stare and suppress the urge to cry. She wrapped her arms around the baby and whispered, "He looks like Rand."

Kaydin leaned over to look at the baby. "He looks very young. He cannot be more than a few weeks old."

"Isn't he adorable? I love his tiny nose and ears." Meredith smiled as she touched them.

"You're right, he's adorable." Dragonose laughed. "I remember when you two were that small. Seems like just yesterday."

"Sir," Airith spoke up.

Meredith startled violently.

Jade held out his hand, and Airith shook it firmly. "I'm indebted to you for my life and the lives of my children. I'm overjoyed that Elyon has freed you. Kaydin has been telling me about when you two were friends."

Airith ran his fingers through his hair and shifted his feet.

"Hello, Kaydin." Airith awkwardly nodded in his direction.

Kaydin gave him a close-lipped smile, closer to a grimace.

"I just wanted to say I'm sorry ... to all of you. I know it isn't enough, but I cannot go without saying it."

Kaydin looked at his feet, and Meredith kept her eyes on Durren.

Dragonose nodded but said nothing.

Falcon overcame the silence with talk of the battle. He and Dragonose compared their accounts while Kaydin eagerly listened.

Airith stayed next to Meredith and neither of them spoke.

She finally plucked up the courage to ask him, "What are you going to do—now that you're no longer Tyrannus's pawn and under Sisinta's command?" Airith winced, and Meredith realized she had allowed bitterness into her voice. "Why don't you come with us to Dolsulbane?" She asked in a softer tone.

Airith ran his fingers through his hair again. "I've actually decided to join Falcon in Athlon. He told me the Sillians need help. Sisinta has been trying to invade Higher Quith by sea."

"Oh." Meredith looked down at the sleeping Durren to hide her disappointment.

She hated that she didn't want him gone from her life again. She hated she still knew him well enough to read him, to know he was uncomfortable with their conversation. She hated that she wanted him to be happy. She hated that her eyes strayed to the sweep of his hair across his forehead and longed for his gaze to meet hers. She hated ... really, she couldn't hate him at all. But was it really the Airith she had known whom she wanted to hate? Wasn't it the Shadow who had corrupted him?

"I just want to tell you," she looked up at him again, "I don't hold you responsible for all those people you killed and the things you did and for Rand's death. I know it was the Shadow. It wasn't really you."

"Don't say that." Airith's voice was barely above a whisper.

"What do you mean?"

Airith raked his hair again. "They were just as much my deeds as his. I never thought I would say that, but I see now it's true. I knew what I was getting into, I knew I was treading on dangerous ground, but I was selfish and intentionally blind. Once I had started down that path, I couldn't turn back. I was too proud and overconfident. Falcon was right, pride was my downfall. It's true Tyrannus made me do things I wish I'd never done, but I went along with him. I listened to the lies he told me and the ones I told myself. I'm at fault even more than Tyrannus perhaps. Don't say I didn't do it, because I did." Airith was breathing heavily with the effort it took to state the truth.

Meredith wanted to use that information as an excuse to stop caring about him. But all she could think was, *I like this Airith better than the old one. The old Airith never admitted he was wrong.*

After a moment of awkward silence, Airith spoke up again, "I'm sorry about your book."

"What?" Meredith's gaze snapped up.

"Your drawing book. Sisinta still has it. I know you spent a lot of time sketching in it. I wish I could have retrieved it for you."

"You mean … you saw it?" Meredith felt a flush of embarrassment heat her face. Had he seen how many sketches of him were in it?

"Briefly."

A Rackdarian, presumably a chieftain, approached and addressed Dragonose, "Sorry to interrupt, but we need to get moving. Sisinta will be looking for our encampment, and one this large will not stay hidden for long."

"He's right," Airith said, "we should leave this place."

"Yes." Dragonose nodded gravely and stood. "Tell the army to prepare to move."

The Mountain Man hurried away, shouting out orders to the groups of soldiers and dragons.

"What about him?" Meredith indicated the baby in her arms. "He's important to many people—to Ironcall, because he's the new heir, and to us, because he's Rand's son."

Silence followed.

"Can we take him with us, Father?" Meredith asked. "I'll take care of him."

"That seems like the best option at the moment," Jade agreed. "Though he'll need to be given a prince's education. With my duties as Dragonose, I won't be able to provide him with one."

"I can teach him," Falcon offered. "I know politics, sword fighting, and the education a prince would need."

Dragonose nodded in agreement. "We can arrange to bring him to you when he's old enough to learn. In the meantime, we'll do our utmost to keep his whereabouts a secret."

Excitement surged through Meredith at the prospect of taking care of the baby, of loving him, and raising him. The momentous task wasn't going to be easy, she knew. She wished her friend had gotten the chance to be the father he had wanted to be.

★★★

Airith wasn't sure how he felt about Falcon having a hand in raising the son of the man he'd murdered. Thankfully, he didn't have long to think about it. Dragons and their riders were taking to the sky. The force of the downdrafts sent leaves and forest debris whipping through the air.

"This is goodbye, then!" Falcon shouted over the wind.

"Thank you for everything!" Kaydin called back.

Falcon smiled and, turning to go, called out, "Farewell, my friends. Elyon watch over you!"

"Mere," Dragonose called and waved her over where Stavon waited.

She gave her old friend a small smile. "Take care, Airith."

"Goodbye." Airith watched her go. Why was he sad? He had a new life ahead of him. It might not be a long one, but he had a future worth living, and beyond that—eternity. He wondered if he could feel the way he did now forever—spotless from the inside out.

Elyon loved him. Falcon loved him.

"Thank you," he whispered, and he knew Elyon heard him.

***

After Falcon and Airith had taken leave on their winged mounts, only Stavon, Scara, Bronze, and a few Rackdarians remained.

"We'll stay at my house in the Dragon Mountains." Dragonose told the twins. "I think this is as good a time as any to tell you both, I sold Stellmear Castle and all its lands."

"Oh." Meredith's eyes widened. She keenly felt Kaydin's own surprise and sadness.

"I'm sorry." Dragonose looked pained. "It was your birthright and inheritance, but after your mother's death,

I knew Sisinta would always be able to find us if I kept our lands and title. I've saved the money from the sale and will hold it in trust for you both when you come of age."

Meredith glanced over at Kaydin, and an understanding passed between them. It must have been an agonizing decision for their father to make—Stellmear had been in their family for hundreds of years. Meredith mourned a little. Never again would she and Kaydin run carefree through Stellmear's halls or visit the gardens their mother had loved so well. Then again, Stellmear had not been home for a long time now.

"We still have a home—Dragon's Rest, the house of Dragonose, in the mountains. Van'N is waiting for us there."

Home. The word sounded strange in Meredith's ears. But home was not Stellmear Castle, Quire Castle, or the Dragon Mountains. Home was where the High King ruled, where her father was at hand, where Kaydin faced the world with her, and where Durren lay safely in her arms.

"Home," Meredith said it aloud and again, "home." She laughed and grabbed her twin's hand. "We're going home!"

CHAPTER FIFTY

Runaway Home

Zray stood on a cobblestone street in the city of Tesson, his hat in his hands. Dragonose and the twins stood beside him. They had graciously offered to return him to his mother. Tesson was in Dolsulbane and close to a week's travel from the mountains, but they'd insisted.

Zray had agreed, reluctantly, since he was still fearful of flying. In the end, the desire to stay with his friends for as long as he possibly could outweighed his anxiety. But the week it had taken to get there had seemed far too short compared to the months they had been together. He'd already said goodbye to Stavon, Scara, and Bronze outside the city.

This was it, he had to say farewell. How could he say it when he didn't mean it? He twisted his well-worn hat in his hands and swallowed hard.

"I want to say thank you," Zray started. He took a deep breath and continued, "You stuck with me when most people would have left me behind, and I really wish I could have told Rand before he ... left ... that I appreciated what all of you did for me. I never thought I would say it, but I'm glad we went through the Dead City, got chased by vagwhar, and robbed by those bandits. I am glad we went through so many dangers together because ... you all taught me so much, and though I still do not understand why Rand did it just to meet Elyon, I have learned that we stand better together and not alone."

Zray was nearly knocked down with the force of Meredith's hug. At first, he was too startled to react, but eventually, he hugged her back, hesitantly.

Tearfully, she said, "You were, in a way, what kept us together. You made us laugh. When we would have lost heart, you lifted our spirits and kept us going. It is *we* who should be thanking *you*."

Kaydin approached, a grave look on his face. He held out his hand and the two boys shook hands sincerely. "I have to ask you to forgive me," Kaydin informed him. "I wasn't always patient with you and was less than what a good friend should have been, but I want you to know that is what I consider you, a friend."

"And I, you," Zray agreed.

"Don't forget us." Kaydin smiled.

"Never."

"Remember," Dragonose held out his hand also, and Zray firmly gripped it, matching Jade Stellmear's strength. "You will always be welcome in our home."

"I might take you up on that," Zray told him with a grin.

"Do you want us to go in with you?" Meredith asked.

Zray glanced at the house across the street. "No." He shook his head. "I think I would do better if I met my mother again alone."

"We understand." Dragonose nodded.

"So, this is goodbye, then." Kaydin sighed. "I will miss you, Zray, son of Urran."

"I will miss all of you." Zray declared with a smile. He watched them go, waiting until they had disappeared around a bend before turning his attention to his mother's house.

The porch veered at a wrong angle and a pane of broken glass had been boarded up. He felt guilty for leaving his mother to fend for herself and his sister alone. What was he going to say? He decided to start by knocking on the door.

Before letting himself change his mind, Zray walked across the street and firmly knocked on the old wooden door. Most of the paint had flaked off, leaving only a few flecks of blue still clinging to the wood. A well-worn broom leaned against the door frame—at least someone regularly swept the steps. Again, Zray felt a stab of guilt—he was the one not looking after those things for his mother. He knocked again.

Shuffling footsteps approached, then the bolt pulled back. The door opened to reveal a young girl about nine years old. Her hair was pulled back, and her dress was worn but clean. He recognized those big brown eyes, a glimpse of the little girl he'd once known. She was wiping flour off her hands on her white apron.

"What do you want?" she demanded while glancing over his strange attire.

Zray now wore the forest colors of the Rackdarians. "I'm looking for Welda."

"My mother is busy right now," the girl said.

"I'm sure she is, but do you think she could spare a moment to talk to me?"

She paused, still looking him over.

"Who's at the door, Lanya?" a voice called from inside.

"Some boy who wants to speak with you, Mother," Lanya answered without taking her eyes off Zray.

He heard footsteps, and then his mother was standing behind his sister in the doorway. Zray's voice caught in his throat. She was still beautiful, but the lines on her face testified to her hard work. Nevertheless, her dress was as clean as ever and her hair in the right place. Zray remembered what she had once told him, "Being poor does not give us an excuse to shirk from cleanliness."

"What is it you wanted to speak to me about?" she asked.

Zray felt his already unsteady confidence threaten to crumble. She did not recognize him after six years. "I wanted to ask you ... for your forgiveness." Zray's voice trembled.

"Forgiveness? Have you been stealing my chicken eggs?" His mother's brow darkened.

"No," Zray shook his head, "but I have stolen something else from you."

She drew back in surprise. "I'd not missed anything else."

"You probably don't even remember, I stole this some six years ago—I was eight years old."

Her brow furrowed. "No, I don't remember. What did you steal?"

"Your son," Zray stated breathlessly.

His mother's stunned expression froze. "Step into the light," she commanded.

Zray complied.

She gasped, and the next moment, he was in her arms. She was laughing and crying at the same time, hugging and kissing him, and running her hands over his face again and again.

"You are here, you really are! Are you real?"

There were tears in Zray's eyes now too.

"Where have you been all these years? Why did you never come home?"

"I was afraid you would be angry with me for leaving with Father," Zray told her as he cried into her shoulder.

"Shh, don't cry. I am not angry with you. I'm just so glad you have come home!" She patted his back, comforting him.

"I'm sorry for causing you so much grief," Zray said as he wiped away his tears. "If you will have me, I promise to make up for it."

"Come inside, my son. You can tell me everything that has happened." She placed another kiss on his cheek.

Lanya was still standing in the doorway, a look of uncertainty on her face.

"Do you remember your brother, Lanya?" his mother asked. "I suppose not, you were but a babe when he left, but now he has returned!" She laughed joyfully. "I have told her about you often."

"Hello, Lanya," Zray spoke softly.

"Hi." Lanya lifted her hand in a small wave, but hesitation remained in her eyes.

"I wish I could make up for all the years I was not with both of you," Zray mourned.

"By returning you already have." His mother pressed a kiss to the top of his head. "Come inside."

Before the door closed behind Zray, he saw three tiny dots of color—Stavon, Bronze, and Scara—high in the sky, disappearing on the horizon.

CHARACTER GUIDE

Elyon and His Allies

Elyon: [el-ee-on] The High King of Quith.

Falcon: Agent of Elyon.

Firefledge: [fie-er-fledge] Falcon's gryphon.

Gelsda: [gels-dah] A healer.

Basal Greed: [bay-sal] A Rackdarian living in the foothills of the Dragon Mountains.

Frana Greed: [fran-ah] Basal's wife.

Sisinta and Her Allies

Sisinta: [sis-in-ta] The Witch-Queen of Lower Quith.

Tyrannus "Tyran" Black: [tie-ran-us, tie-ran] Sisinta's second-in-command and general. Commander of the Black Knights.

Vobad: [voh-bad] Sisinta's personal servant and messenger.

X-Sayda Bloodgo: [ex-say-da blood-go] The only daughter of Chief Seldan [sell-dan] Bloodgo of the Outlands.

Lord Sazecall: [sayz-call] A northern nobleman in Sisinta's court.

Shaver Family and Household
Lord High Shaver: Lord of Shaver Castle and its surrounding lands.

Lady Emerald Shaver: Lady of Shaver Castle and Lord Shaver's wife.

Cowin: [cow-in] The second Shaver son.

Shar: The third Shaver son.

Rasfell: [rahz-fell]: The fourth Shaver son.

Airith: [air-ith] The fifth Shaver son.

Kenta: [ken-tah] The youngest Shaver child and only daughter.

Stellmear Family and Household
Lord Jade Stellmear: [stell-meer] Dragonose [dra-gon-ohs], Keeper of Dragons.

Lady Daelay Stellmear neé Amara: [day-lay ah-mar-ah] Lord Stellmear's wife and mother of the twins.

Kaydin: [kay-din] The elder twin son of Dragonose.

Meredith: The younger twin daughter of Dragonose.

Van'N: [van-en] An old family friend of the Stellmears, and the twins' tutor.

Quire Family and Household
Lady Seala Quire: [sea-lah kwhy-er] A distant relative of Daelay Stellmear.

Quaeor: [kway-or] Steward of Quire Castle.

Dallbim: [doll-bim] The elderly doorkeeper of Quire Castle.

Urran Family
Zray: A young minstrel from Tesson.

Urran: [ur-an] A well-traveled minstrel and thief.

Welda: [well-dah] Zray's mother.

Lanya: [lan-ya] Zray's younger sister.

Tieren Family and Household

Randarin "Rand" Tieren: [ran-dar-in ty-ren] Crown Prince of Ironcall.

Thia: [thee-ah] Rand's wife.

King Ralldole: [rall-dole] Current king of Ironcall.

Randurren "Durren": [ran-dur-en, dur-en] Randarin and Thia's son.

Other Notable Characters

Calldo Sambull: [call-doe sam-bull] A pacifist fisherman in Boldwind.

Baldgave: [bald-gave] Bandit leader.

Jad'N: [jah-den] Van'N's son, a wool merchant.

Zaylin: [zeh-lin] A young farmer in the rebellion of Ladle's Ridge.

King Daltaine: [doll-tayne] The elderly king of Tayose.

Dragons

Kappin: [cap-in] A silver wind and weather dragon bound to Tyran.

Captain of the Cala Drani [cal-ah dra-nee]—leader of Sisinta's silver dragons

Stavon: [stah-von] Dragonose's fire dragon. His name means *helper*.

Ignis: A volatile fire dragon and member of the Dragon Council.

Scara: A friend of Stavon. A young earth dragon.

Bronze: An earth dragon and member of the Dragon Council.

Cinereous: An anxious, elderly stone dragon.

Malachite: An outspoken poison dragon.

Permafrost: An ice dragon with a superiority complex.

Onyx: A nonconfrontational resonance dragon.

Cerulean: A long-winded water dragon.

Aurelian: A quiet prism dragon.

Horses
Pallindo: [pall-in-doe] Airith's old horse.

Vasgo: [vaz-go] Kaydin's stallion. His name means *wild one*.

Aldaydo: [all-day-doe] Rand's warhorse.

Moyna: [moi-nah] Meredith's white mare. Her name means *cloud*.

Lightning: Zray's stallion.

People Groups
Paladalls: [pal-ah-dahl] Magic users distantly related to the Sillian.

Sillians: [sill-ee-an] Tall, elegant, fair-skinned magic users.

Rackdarians: [rack-dahr-ee-an] Also known as Mountain Men. They reside in the foothills of the Dragon Mountains.

Humans: Make up the majority of Quith's population.

ABOUT THE AUTHOR

Grace R. Pringle has been telling stories since before she could read and writing since before she could spell. She attended the Institute of Children's Literature and heads the long-standing Signature Literary Society writer's club, composing flash fiction and turning writing into a game she plays with friends. Grace is also the author of *Soul Threads*, a comedy fantasy novella set in the same universe as *Silver Blood*.

Grace is married to fellow writer, Stuart Pringle, and together they have six children and two cats, all being homeschooled in a house overlooking the St. Lawrence River in Ontario, Canada.

Grace can be quoted as saying, "Doesn't God make amazing things?" to the kids in the backseat at least once every car ride.

If Grace isn't writing or reading, you'll find her listening to Breaking Benjamin, rearranging her house regularly, attending as many medieval fairs as possible, and drawing dragons.

To learn more and contact Grace, visit gracepringle.com.

www.ingramcontent.com/pod-product-compliance
Lightning Source LLC
Chambersburg PA
CBHW060808030726
47503CB00002B/387